THE GIRL
ACROSS THE
SEA

Noelle Harrison

THE GIRL ACROSS THE SEA

bookouture

Published by Bookouture in 2021

An imprint of Storyfire Ltd.
Carmelite House
50 Victoria Embankment
London EC4Y 0DZ

www.bookouture.com

ISBN: 978-1-80019-764-0
eBook ISBN: 978-1-80019-763-3

For Hailey for planting the seed.
And for my brother Fintan who was there right from the beginning.

'Who in the world am I? Ah, that's the great puzzle.'
Alice's Adventures in Wonderland, Lewis Carroll

I

ON THE ROAD

CHAPTER ONE

19 JUNE 1933

The last night they were together, Ellen left Brigid the necklace. Perhaps it was foolish to give a small child such a precious item, but it was the only legacy Ellen possessed. The necklace was a gold chain with a large pendant in the shape of a star embellished with sky-blue turquoise, pearls and rose-cut diamonds. The back of the pendant was fitted with a miniature picture frame. Ellen had inserted a small photograph of herself with Brigid as a baby in the frame.

Brigid had always loved the necklace. Her eyes would light up if Ellen put it on before she came into the nursery to kiss her goodnight.

'Where is Daddy taking you?' her daughter would whisper, her eyes gleaming as she reached out and touched the egg-shaped turquoise at the heart of the star pendant.

'Just another party, my darling,' Ellen said, bending down to kiss Brigid's soft cheek.

'When I'm big, can I come with you?' Brigid asked, her breath still sweet from her bedtime milk.

'If you wish, but they are terribly boring affairs,' Ellen said. How different she sounded from her old self, so proper, so *English*.

'How many pearls, Mammy?' Brigid's fingers moved to the ring of tiny diamonds sparkling around the turquoise stone.

'Five – the same age as you,' Ellen said, before kissing her daughter five times on her forehead and her cheeks until she was giggling beneath her.

That night had been last winter. Seven months ago. Ellen had had no inkling her world was going to be turned upside down. But she should have known. Her past was too weighted to shrug off forever. It had always been lurking in the background. A threat every time she had walked through the shopping district on Fifth Avenue, pushing Brigid's perambulator, and then holding her little hand when she could walk. Ellen had been living a life she didn't belong in, her day of reckoning in the shadows on every street corner on the Upper East Side. The possibility in the eyes of every stranger she met.

Now they were in their cabin on RMS *Britannic* on the eve of its departure to Liverpool via Galway and Cork. She had been dreading this day for weeks. Ellen could hear the clamour of the crew up above on deck. She knew it was a matter of a few hours before they would be leaving New York Port and setting off across the Atlantic Ocean. Giles was in the smoking lounge drinking brandy and playing cards. Their last words had been sharp. He had lost patience with her constant pleas to stay in America.

'The problem with you, Ellen, is you've been spoiled for too long,' he said in a low voice. 'You're an ungrateful wife. Look how much I am giving you!'

'I don't want to go! Please, Giles, please let us stay,' she had hissed, not wanting Brigid to overhear.

'For God's sake, enough!' he had snapped, causing Brigid to look up in surprise.

Tears bloomed in Ellen's eyes, and Giles immediately looked contrite.

'I am sorry, my dear,' he said, taking her into his arms. 'Trust me. You will be happy once we get settled.' He whispered into her ear: 'Another baby, perhaps?' He kissed her earlobe. She felt a wave of love and despair. If only she could stay forever in the protection of her husband's arms. He had reached out to Brigid behind her, and she felt their child join the embrace. The three of them entwined. She would have to rend them apart. How could she do it?

With Giles gone, Ellen prepared Brigid for bed. They were travelling with no servants, having decided to procure a new household once they arrived in Ireland. It was a relief to have no other witness to her despair. No judging eyes of a stern nanny upon her as she lavished her child with kisses.

Brigid was sitting up on the bed in her rosebud nightie. She didn't look in the least sleepy as she clutched her doll Annie to her chest.

'Mammy, I don't like it, everything is moving. I want to go home.'

Ellen barely noticed the gentle rock of the boat in the harbour. How would her little girl cope once they were in the middle of the vast ocean? What if there was a storm? She took a breath, brushed Brigid's soft curls with her fingertips.

'You're going on a big adventure,' Ellen had told her. 'Crossing the Atlantic Ocean! You might see whales.'

Ellen remembered the grief and panic of the journey over. How she had been saved by Giles. But the day that had stood out had been the one when she saw the big blue whale as it cut through the vast ocean right before her eyes.

Brigid was unimpressed. 'But why do we have to go?' she whined.

'Because Daddy is going to help make a national cathedral in

Ireland,' Ellen explained. 'Ireland is his home. And it's going to be yours.'

'And yours?'

Brigid had looked into her daughter's green eyes. Her chest tight, and her heart cracking. If only she could be sure her secret was safe. If only she could go back.

From the spring day when her husband had announced they were returning to Ireland, Ellen had been in a tumult. Every evening, circling the courtyard garden at their apartment building, the sweet-smelling scent of crab-apple blossoms on the trees closing in on her as she smoked cigarette after cigarette, trying to work out what to do.

It had not been long before Giles had noticed her lack of enthusiasm.

'Don't you want to go back home?' he asked one morning over breakfast. 'Every Irishman I know dreams of returning one day.'

He folded his paper next to his empty breakfast plate. Raised his eyebrows at her, his brown eyes questioning. She thought the words: *Every Irishman with your money, maybe.* But she didn't say them.

'Do you not realise how lucky we are,' he said, his cheeks flushed. 'I've been selected to work on the designs for the national cathedral in Dublin, and then after that the new airport in Collinstown. Everything is grinding to a halt here. The money's running out.'

'Yes, of course I know,' she said. Her husband had worked hard since they'd arrived in America. Steadily building up his reputation as an architect. Each building he'd worked on more impressive than the next. She had been so proud to look out of their top-floor apartment at Fifth Avenue and the skyline of Manhattan, which seemed to reach higher and higher with each passing year. Giles had worked on the Manhattan Trust Building and the Empire State Building, which was an amazing 102 floors. He had taken her up not long after it had opened. She had been terrified at first, but once he had convinced her to open her eyes, she had been thrilled with the view. Secretly, she admired the Chrysler Building the most. To her, it resembled a spectacular shiny tower from another world. But of course, she never told Giles that.

'Brigid will meet her grandparents, her aunts and uncles, and her cousins...' Giles continued to list the reasons for their return to Ireland. 'We'll be surrounded by family.'

Giles had always talked with affection of his family home in Blackrock, Dublin. The big white house with the ample lawn facing the sea. The past year she had noticed how much more he talked about it, how he ached for home.

'My new position is well paid. We will want for nothing, Ellen,' he had told her.

As she took her nightly walks around the courtyard garden, Ellen tried to imagine this new life back home in Ireland. Her and Giles with a litter of children. Family gatherings, safety and security. But it was a fantasy. Her husband's Ireland was a world away from her own. If she returned, she risked everything.

Giles wasn't stupid. He noticed her unease.

'What is it, Ellen?' he pushed. 'Why don't you want to go home?'

She shook her head, looking away.

'Is it because of your family?'

On the boat to America, not long after they had first met, Ellen had told him all her family were dead. Killed in a fire. He had never asked her any more details, discerning her distress at the time. Misreading its source. Giles had been wild with optimistic hope about his new life in New York. It was this quality which had drawn her to him. 'Go forward, and never look back.' That had been his motto. They had lived by it the entire eight years they'd been in New York, and he had never questioned her about her past in all that time.

'Why this sudden nostalgia for home?' she blurted out, pushing her plate of eggs away. 'We're happy here in New York. You always said we'd be here forever!'

Giles had got up from the table and strode over to her. Bent down and kissed her forehead, his face a picture of concern.

'My poor darling,' he had said tenderly, hands on her shoulders. 'Of course. So thoughtless of me not to think of your losses.' He knelt down and took her hands in his. 'But maybe it will help to go back? We could visit your parents' graves. I will bring you to the west and you can show me your old home—'

She snatched her hands away.

'No!'

Giles looked startled by her reaction. He stood up and pulled her up to him. She hid her burning face in his fresh clean shirt. She could still smell the soap.

'Then we will stay in Dublin and never set foot in County Mayo again, if that is what you wish, my dear,' he murmured above her head.

But Ellen's heart was thumping in her chest like a panicked bird. Ireland was a small country. There would be no hiding her past if they returned.

The gentle rocking of RMS *Britannic* loosened her resolve. Ellen stared down at the exquisite necklace in her palm. It had been the only thing she had brought from Ireland to America eight years ago. Now she was sending it back home with her daughter. Her heart lurched painfully when she thought how poor it would be as a replacement for her, despite its worth. She clutched the necklace in her hand, the sharp points of the diamonds digging into her flesh. Maybe she could run away with Brigid and sell the necklace? They would have money to live on. But it was an impossible dream. She couldn't stay in New York because Giles would find them.

Where to then? She had no one she could turn to for help. She knew he would find her wherever she went if she took Brigid. There was no doubt about his devotion to his daughter. But deep down there was more. Another reason she couldn't take Brigid. If they ran away together, the truth would come out about what she had done all those years ago. She would be on the run forever. How could she tarnish her daughter's future with her own past? How could she shame her husband?

'Do you want to go up onto the deck and look at the stars?' she asked Brigid, clutching on to as many moments as she could with her.

Brigid nodded, delight sparkling in her eyes.

She carried Brigid up on deck, tucked up in her shawl, and felt the rapid beating of her daughter's heart against her skin. It was a warm night, and the sky was a deep serene blue, littered with a thousand blinking lights. The skies were never this big in Ireland. New York City hummed like a leviathan, new skyscrapers soaring heavenward. Ellen pointed out the Big Dipper, the Little Dipper and the Northern Star. She wanted so much to say something meaningful. *Think of me when you look at the stars. For I will always be thinking of you.*

Her child had gazed at her with sleepy eyes, nestled closer. The scent of Brigid's skin against hers. She had breathed her in. Held her breath. She wanted to hold in this scent to her very last exhale. In that moment, she would have faced fire and brimstone if it meant she might stay with her child. But then she thought of how Brigid would react if she knew the truth. It was better to leave with her daughter still loving her than to stay and be repulsed.

Ellen ran away like a thief in the night. In darkness, one hour before dawn, just before the boat set sail, she placed the letter she'd written to Giles on the tiny locker by their bed, and laid the necklace upon it. The silver lamp was on in the cabin, casting a celestial light upon her husband and child as they slept, oblivious to her treachery.

She crept out. Although Ellen was running away, it felt as if this was the moment she had stopped running. She could never have gone back to Ireland. Because then she would have lost her daughter in an even more terrible way. She had done the best thing for her family, Ellen tried to tell herself. Brigid and Giles would now be free from her dark secret.

As the sun rose steadily above the city of New York, she walked the streets with no direction. The trapped heat from the day before began to rise from the brick and stone surrounding her. The skyscrapers gleamed bright and hard. Sweat slid down her trembling limbs. She stepped as if on hot coals. The joy of motherhood slipping from her as if life itself. She was a ghost walking block after block of the waking city. Deaf to the sounds of the streetcars, the hawking newspaper boys, and the clatter of the construction workers. Her heart was locked inside the necklace as her girl sailed across the sea. She had lost it forever and believed she would never get it back.

CHAPTER TWO

Mairead drove west in the lashing rain. It didn't stop the whole way from Oldcastle to Carrick-on-Shannon. The radio wasn't working any more in her old hatchback. The only sound was the swishing of the windscreen wipers and the relentless downpour beating on the roof as she splashed through small floods while the miles gathered behind her. She tried not to think of the same journey she had taken this time last year. Every Good Friday, she and her family made the trip west to visit her mam for the holidays. Niall next to her in the passenger seat, and Stella sitting behind. The three of them volleying trivia facts between them in preparation for the big game of Trivial Pursuit with her mam, which Niall always managed to win. Mairead gulped down the lump in her throat. She wasn't going to cry. Not in all this rain. She had to remain focused, get to her mam's place. Then... well, then what? Her mam wasn't the comforting type.

She didn't know who she was more hurt by in this moment. Her husband had done a terrible thing to her. She'd expected more support from her daughter, but Stella had rung her yesterday evening, at the last minute, to tell her she wasn't coming home for Easter.

'But I bought you a Mars bar Easter egg, like always,' Mairead had complained, the first stupid thing which had popped into her head.

'Ah sorry, Mammy, you have it,' Stella said. Her daughter sounded so distant, even though she was only across the Irish Sea in London. Mairead could hear a voice in the background. Was it male? She wanted to interrogate Stella but knew it would only make her hang up the phone.

'I haven't seen you since Christmas,' Mairead said, and she could hear the whine in her voice. Hated herself for it.

'I'll be back in the summer,' Stella said cheerfully.

'But what are you doing for Easter?' Mairead asked, immediately wishing she hadn't.

There was a pause.

'I'm going to Dad and Lesley's,' Stella said. 'They've moved into a new place in Islington. It's not far from Hackney.'

How could her daughter let Lesley's name fall so easily from her lips? It stung as if she'd pinched the soft skin on her throat.

'Mammy, are you still there?' Stella said.

'Yes,' she had croaked. She wanted to scream at her daughter how hurt she was that she'd taken things so well when she and Niall had broken up. But as a mother she should be glad Stella got on with Niall's new partner. It was as if her daughter had seen it coming way before Mairead ever had.

'It's been nearly a year,' Stella said. 'You have to move on.'

'I am,' Mairead snapped, sounding harsher than she meant. The beeps went then. She scrambled to change the mood before they were cut off.

'Have a lovely time,' she said. 'Love you.'

But she spoke to dead air. Why didn't Stella ever bring enough change when she called her?

. . .

As she passed through Carrick-on-Shannon the rain finally stopped, and the sun pushed out from behind the clouds. The road gleamed in front of her, and she was momentarily blinded by the light. She blinked her eyes and kept going. She had driven this road so many times she could do it in her sleep. She took the turn for home and bumped down the boreen, then up the drive. Since her father had died, over six years ago now, the house and gardens had deteriorated. Her mother never had the funds nor inclination to fix things up. But whenever Mairead broached the subject of downsizing, her mother got angry. Her workshop was here, and she would never give it up. Not until the day she died.

'But aren't you lonely, Mam, all the way out here?' Mairead had asked her mother last time she visited.

'Not at all,' her mother had said. 'Besides, I have Alfie,' she added, patting the head of her grey lurcher.

'Mam, he's a dog!'

'Yes, and better company than most people,' her mother said. 'You should get a dog now Niall has gone.'

Mairead found her mother's equation of a dog with a husband unanswerable. She shook her head.

'I like being on my own,' her mother continued. 'I can focus on my work.' She spread her arms wide, her fingers glittering with all the rings she'd set with precious stones. 'I don't need other people like you do, Mairead.'

Her mother had made it sound like a weakness, which was not true at all. Mairead thrived on being part of a team, which was why she loved her job so much. It was a calling as much as her mother's jewellery design. But her mother always made Mairead feel she was disappointed she was a schoolteacher. She had never been interested in Mairead's students' achievements or how she was respected by her peers. She had been far more taken with Mairead's brother Darragh's career as a musician turned barman. Darragh had just opened his own bar in New York even though he was a complete flake, and an illegal immigrant in America. Her mother had loved Darragh's Irish wife, Josie, an illegal too, and their two girls when she'd visited last year, but had been particularly unimpressed when Mairead had married an accountant despite the fact Niall had been able to provide so well for Mairead and Stella. He had also helped her mother out when Mairead's father died. But her mother had always complained that Niall had the shifty eyes of a liar and Mairead had settled too soon. Now, unbearably, her mother had been proved right.

She rounded the corner, and there it was, her family home: Ballinakill Lodge. The square grey stone house solid as a rock, the sash windows glanced by sunlight, and the green grass of the front lawn thick and wild, lush with fat raindrops. She had spent her whole childhood here. A rush of nostalgia swept through her as she parked the car beneath the big chestnut tree. How she wished her father were standing on the doorstep to greet her. His gentle understanding so different from her mother's. His invitation to take an evening stroll an opportunity to tell him all her troubles. His non-critical nods and encouraging words. So many times, she had wanted to ask her father how he had ended up with a woman like her mother. But of course, she couldn't ask him such a question. Her parents must have loved each other, for they had been together so many years. Her father ambling across their land with his small-holding projects. Sheep one year. Bees the next. Apple trees and homemade cider another year. While her mother remained hour after hour shut up in her workshop creating such exquisite works of jewellery she was listed as one of the top designers in the whole of Ireland. She made creations she could never afford to wear herself.

And then, so suddenly, her father was gone. Mairead would never forget the darkest day of her life so far. She had been in the middle of teaching her second-year history class about the Irish War of Independence when Sister Mary Stephen, their headmistress, had bustled into the classroom and asked her to step outside. There had been a phone call from her mother. Her father had fallen off a ladder cleaning the gutters and banged his head. He was in a critical condition in Sligo Hospital.

Mairead had called Niall in hysterics and, after organising childcare for Stella, he had driven them to Sligo like a maniac. She had arrived just in time to say goodbye. Her mother had stood stony-faced and white by the hospital bed, staring off into the distance. Mairead had tried to hug her, but she hadn't moved. When the doctor had explained that the only thing keeping her father alive was the ventilator, that he was already brain dead, her mother had instructed them to turn it off. 'He's gone already,' she had barked. 'Do it now.'

'No, Mammy, we need to call Darragh—' Mairead had cried out. She hadn't been ready.

But even more astonishing was the way her mother had marched out of the hospital room as soon as they turned off the machine keeping her husband alive. Niall had put his hands on her shoulders as Mairead held her father's hand while it slowly turned cold, and the room emptied of his life.

She had been so shocked and hurt by her mother's behaviour. Niall had assured her that her mother was grieving in her own way; she was emotionally repressed. But who was he to say such a thing? Mairead had buried her fury with her mother, her pain at the loss of her father deep down. But now, as she stared up at the roof of the house, she imagined the moment her father had fallen off the ladder, and the image in her mind was so vivid it was all she could do not to scream. Had he been afraid as he was falling? How long had it taken before he'd been knocked unconscious? He had been a relatively young man at the time. Not even sixty years old. It astonished Mairead that her mother could go on living under the roof of the house which had killed her husband.

What was she doing here? Mairead had automatically set off for her annual Easter visit, as was her daughterly duty, but now all she wanted to do was turn around and drive off again. Keep driving somewhere she had never been before, go sit on a beach and feel sorry for herself, wallow in the injustices of her life. But it was too late. And there was something else needling her deep down. Her life felt as if it had become a series of abandonments: Stella, Niall, her father dying... But it had all begun with her mother. Pushing her away for as long as she could remember. Mairead had always been aware of the fact her mother was special, and because of this she had to put up with her strange moods and detachment. And right now she needed her mam more than ever.

Mairead heard Alfie bark as the front door opened and he came running out to leap up at her car door. There on the threshold was her mother, squinting at her with the faraway look she always had when she'd been working for hours. She was wearing a long green shirt the same colour as her eyes. It hung off her, and she looked even thinner than last time Mairead had visited. But Mairead knew better than to question her mother about whether she had been eating or not. She thought of the box of mint cremes she had bought her mother for Easter, currently sitting in the bag of food on the back seat, and knew most likely she would be eating them all anyway. She got out of the car, softly nudging Alfie away while he licked her hands in greeting. At least he was pleased to see her.

'Hi, Mammy,' Mairead said brightly, pulling the bag of food out the back of the car, before walking towards her.

'I didn't think you were coming this year,' her mother said, her eyes dropping to Mairead's post-separation expanded waistline. Mairead could tell what she was thinking. She gave her mother two hours tops before she commented on her weight.

'Of course,' Mairead said. 'It's Easter—'

'I don't believe in God,' her mother said, turning on her heel, her clogs clopping on the flagstones as she went back into the shadows of the house.

'Well, it's the holidays,' Mairead said, following her mother inside and trying not to notice the layers of thick dust on everything.

'I didn't think you'd come without Stella. How's she getting on in London? She did so well to get into RADA, but I always said she had it in her,' her mother said, and there was a gleam in her eye.

She had always been more interested in her granddaughter's acting than her own daughter's life.

'She's loving it,' Mairead said, trying to ignore the prick of hurt as she followed her mother into the kitchen and hefted the heavy food bag onto the kitchen table.

'Jaysus, Mairead, what have you got in there? It's just us two.' Her mother dropped her eyes to her body again, and Mairead was suddenly aware how tight her jeans felt. And they were her big period jeans.

'I was going to cook for you,' Mairead said weakly.

Her mother shrugged.

'I'm very busy,' she said. 'I've a commission to finish.'

'Oh, what is it?'

Her mother frowned. 'I'll show you when it's done,' she said, turning away to stare out the window. A habit she'd always had when she was in the middle of creative production and didn't want to be disturbed.

Mairead stared at her mother's narrow back in the sea-green shirt, its soft silken contours cascading down her body. She was like a woman from another world, not her flesh-and-bone mother. Why did she feel so unwelcome in her own childhood home? She was hurt her mother didn't ask her how she was. Had never talked to her about what Niall had done to her, apart from shrugging and saying she wasn't surprised, which had made Mairead feel even worse.

'Maybe I should go,' she blurted out. 'You clearly want to be on your own.'

Her mother turned around and looked at Mairead wide-eyed.

'Don't be ridiculous,' she said. 'You're here now.'

They stood either side of the kitchen, silence pooling between them. Decades of unsaid things. It felt as if her mother could be the other side of the world, she was so far away from her. Why was she this way? What had happened to her to make her so unlike any other mother Mairead had ever known? Even Niall's mother, who had always disliked her daughter-in-law, still made a pretence at warmth.

She remembered a time when she was little, she had fallen over and cut her knee and was crying for her mother to pick her up and comfort her. Her mam had turned and walked away, leaving it to her father to comfort her.

'I want Mammy,' she had sobbed. 'Why doesn't she love me?'

'Of course she loves you, pet,' her father had said, dabbing her bloody knee with cotton wool. 'But she lost her mother when she was a little girl, so it's hard for her—'

'But she had Grandma,' she'd sniffed.

'Grandma is her stepmother,' her father explained. 'She had another mother before her. In America.'

Her father looked uncomfortable, entangled in too many revelations.

'Who is she? What's her name?' Mairead had whispered, tears forgotten in the wake of the surprising secret.

'She doesn't know.'

The ghost of her mother's birth mother had always been drifting around the edges of their family life. The reason her mother couldn't abide her daughter's tears, why she found it easier to kick a ball with her son than braid Mairead's hair. It was the excuse Mairead had allowed her mother all these years. Until her father had died. Then Mairead had lost patience. Her mother had insisted on a small funeral with just family. None of Mairead's friends could come. Mairead had lost her temper.

'I'm grieving too,' she'd lashed out. 'I need support from my friends because you've never given it to me.'

Her mother's green eyes had darkened.

'Now's not the time, Mairead,' she said in a cool voice.

'Why are you so cold? I haven't seen you cry once since Daddy died. What's wrong with you?' Mairead ranted. 'Why don't you talk about your mother? Like ever?'

Her mother spoke slowly as if each word was coated in ice:

'That is none of your business, Mairead, and has nothing to do with my husband's funeral.'

'He was *my* father too!' Mairead raged, but her mother had walked away yet again. Always walking away from her.

Mairead crossed the kitchen briskly, pushing away those painful memories of her father's funeral. She picked up the kettle and filled it at the tap.

'Let's have a cup of tea and a biscuit,' she said, infusing her voice with enthusiasm. 'It's been a long drive in the rain.'

'A quick one, but no biscuit for me,' her mother said. 'And you could do without it too.'

There it was: the little barbed comment about her weight. It hadn't even been fifteen minutes since she'd walked in the door. Mairead took a breath. Commission or no commission, she was going to make her mother listen to her this weekend. If her mam wasn't prepared to give her the support she needed, then Mairead was determined to find out why. Perhaps in the answer she would find the key to her own happiness.

CHAPTER THREE

Ellen stood outside 665 Fifth Avenue, the brick and limestone Georgian-style building where they had lived. She squinted up, hands shielding her eyes from the glare of sunlight, and wished she could go back in time. To the day of their marriage, when Giles had taken her by the hand and led her through the double doors held open by the doorman. It had all felt like a dream as they entered via a private landing, and her new husband had shown her around the spacious apartment on the top floor. She had fallen in love instantly. The living room and the adjacent east-facing dining room seemed as vast as the deck of the ship they'd arrived on. In the morning, the sun shone into the dining room and in the evening the living room caught the light from the west, with a view across the skyline of New York. In the evenings, they had the fire lit in the living room, and Ellen loved to walk across the polished herring-bone floors in her stockinged feet. So warm compared to the cold slate floors from home. That first day, Giles had stood at the window and pointed out all the construction sites along Fifth Avenue.

'We can watch the buildings grow,' he said, as if they were giant trees.

There were many rooms in her grand apartment, all of them modern and full of light. It could not have been more different from where she had grown up. Her favourite was the bathroom. The marble floors, the porcelain bath and the big white sink filled her with such calm. When she was pregnant, she'd spent hours lying in the bath, drifting off on a cloud.

They had moved in the fall of 1925, a month after their arrival in America. All she had possessed in the world was the dark green Louis Vuitton suitcase with its brass corners and locks, and a Louis Vuitton Steamer bag. Giles had been shocked she'd no more with her. He had expected her to have at least one big travel trunk. But she told him all her things had been lost in the fire that killed her parents. It was all she had left, and his face had filled with kind concern so genuine it had made her feel guilty.

It wasn't long before she possessed a whole new wardrobe, as befitted the wife of one of the most prestigious architects in New York City. Giles would give her a stack of dollars and off she would go to Saks on Fifth Avenue to try on the latest fashions. To her, these clothes with their dropped waistlines and raised hemlines felt light and free. She particularly loved buying silk stockings and had a collection in grey, white and beige. Her evening dresses were velvet and silk, adorned with feathers and sequins, and she accessorised with matching headbands. If anyone who had known her back home could have seen her all dolled up, they would have narrowed their eyes in disapproval. She dismissed the thought, just as she squashed the feeling she was an imposter in this sparkling world of dinners and country parties in mansions on Long Island. Prohibition laws appeared not to exist among the rich; plied with glasses of champagne and fancy cocktails, she inevitably drank too much. But it helped her to forget her life in Ireland. In New York she could abandon those heavy memories and let herself become weightless on bubbles. Dancing and dizzy in a gilded existence.

Giles made friends with ease. Most of them were heirs or heiresses to massive fortunes who seemed to spend their lives doing nothing. There were times when a little flame of rebellion flickered within her. On whose backs had this privileged few amassed fortunes to be frittered away on trivial pleasures? But for the most part she didn't think about hardship, averting her gaze from the poverty she saw on the streets of New York because it brought back memories of Ireland. She was determined to have fun. If she was going to be damned for her sins, she may as well live it up in the most exciting city in the world.

Even when she became pregnant, Ellen didn't stop her socialising. She suppressed her nausea with clandestine cocktails – gin with honey syrup and lemon or, after dinner, a cocktail introduced to them by a friend from New Orleans called Grasshopper: crème de menthe with cream and crème de cacao.

In her low-waisted and flowing frocks, Ellen was able to hide her condition for weeks. But one Saturday night in February, when she must have been almost five months pregnant, Giles finally noticed. He had entered her bedroom just as she was slipping out of her dress for his weekly visit under the covers.

'My dear!' Giles exclaimed in astonishment, staring at her stomach pressed against the silk of her undergarments. 'Are you with child?'

She nodded as her throat tightened. She had been hiding from the truth of it for months. It wasn't that she didn't want a child. It was just she had never really thought about it. She was still so young. She had had dreams which didn't include being a mother.

But Giles had been overjoyed. She had never seen him so happy. He had swept her up into his arms and showered her with kisses.

'My darling girl, I adore you,' he had whispered. His words had felt unearned. She was not who he thought she was. She didn't deserve his affection.

After a visit to the doctor, and confirmation their baby was due the beginning of June, Giles insisted that Ellen live a quieter life. He was worried too much dancing might harm mother and baby.

Her husband was over-protective, but as Ellen began to show she was glad not to be looked at by their friends. She was the first of all the wives to be pregnant and the constant questions of the others – *What does it feel like? Aren't you frightened?* – began to fill her with anxiety. She knew only too well that having a baby was dangerous and she could die.

As she got bigger, the only time she went out was to the movies. She liked to go to the new Paramount Theatre on Times Square on her own every Tuesday afternoon. As soon as Ellen entered the shadows of the movie theatre, she could have been stepping back inside the Picture House on Thomas Street in Sligo with her best friend. Of course, the New York Paramount Theatre was so much bigger and fancier, and she didn't have to sit through newsreels on the War of Independence to get to the main picture. The orchestra was far grander than the one tinny piano played by Paddy Flannagan at the back of the Sligo Picture House, but the moment she sat down in the plush seats at the Paramount Theatre and became enthralled with the silent movie playing on the big screen, she could be back home. Except someone was missing. Her fellow dreamer. The two of them used to imagine themselves as Lillian and Dorothy Gish – two movie-star sisters conjuring up imagined worlds far away from the bleak reality of conflict-torn Ireland. It was in the dim smoky interior of the Picture House in Sligo that Ellen's dream of going to Hollywood had been born. She wanted to do what Lillian Gish had done in *Broken Blossoms*: reach out from the screen and twist everyone's heart. She had never forgotten when they had seen the movie, how real it had felt to watch Lillian Gish's terror as she hid in the closet from her drunk and brutal father. They had clutched hands in the dark as tears trailed their cheeks. Their heroine was so sweet she had smiled even in death. But that was a fantasy. Not even the best of people smiled when they died. Ellen knew this now.

In the Paramount Theatre in Times Square, Ellen leaned back in the velvet seats surrounded by the Paramount's elaborate murals. She remembered all those times past and then she let them go, drifting away like the smoke from her cigarette. As soon as the lights dimmed and the film began, she was lost in make-believe. She imagined herself in the films. It was her, not Mary Pickford, as Little Annie Rooney, and her, not Greta Garbo, in *The Street of Sorrow*. She imagined her own life as a strip of celluloid with her as the main star. After all, wasn't she acting every single day?

As she watched her idols – Mary Pickford, Alla Nazimova, Lillian and Dorothy Gish, Asta Nielsen, Greta Garbo and Esther Ralston – Ellen rested her hands on her growing belly and sobbed in the dark. Despite having made it to America, her dream of acting felt even further away than it had on those rainy afternoons in the Picture House in Sligo. She was to be a wife and a mother. Her duty to be good and kind. But in her heart, Ellen knew she was none of those things. She was as dark and mysterious as Alla Nazimova in *Salome*, and as mercurial as Louise Brooks. Ellen longed for the young actress's liberation, symbolised by her short black crow hair, smooth and gleaming as it framed her perfect heart-shaped face. Her own hair was an unruly mass of red curls. One day, after seeing Louise Brooks in *The American Venus* for the fifth time, Ellen had got her hair cut into a bob. She had been giddy with the new freedom of her cool nape and framed face. Had almost forgotten she was so big with the weight of her baby. Giles had been furious when he'd seen her new hairstyle.

'It's unfeminine,' he had complained, though he stopped complaining when she revealed how liberated it made her feel beneath the bed sheets.

Ellen felt a sudden intense longing for the old days before she got pregnant. Those few whirling weeks of parties, dancing with her New York and Long Island friends, their names already forgotten.

Where were all those friends of theirs now? They had vanished overnight, not long after the Crash in 1929. All the bright young things, the children of tycoons gone bust, had been forced to give up their Fifth Avenue mansions and return home – wherever that might have been. Everything had changed so dramatically in a matter of weeks. She and Giles had been lucky because he still had his tenure as an architect. But his mood had been dark. He returned in the evenings grim-faced from having to turn away so many men willing to risk their lives on skyscraper scaffolds for a few dollars. As the city around her became more desperate and the Depression deepened, Ellen turned all her attention to her three-year-old daughter, Brigid. She rarely left the apartment. Brigid had become her world. She had chased her dreams of acting away because, once her baby girl had been placed in her arms, nothing else mattered. Motherhood hadn't been easy because she had never known her own mother, but it was a powerful force she couldn't deny.

Giles employed an Irish nanny, Maureen Fitzgerald. Ellen had been nervous to have another Irishwoman in the house, but Maureen had left County Cork as a little girl, in the 1870s, two decades after the devastation of the Famine. Her memories of Ireland were different from Ellen's. Both chose never to share them. Maureen showed Ellen what to do with Brigid. She was efficient but kind. Sometimes she would look at Ellen quizzically, cocking her head to one side.

'Just how old are you, girl?' she'd ask.

'Eighteen,' Ellen would reply, blushing at the lie.

She knew what Maureen was thinking. Giles was old enough to be her father. But her husband was nothing like her father.

What was she doing, standing outside their empty home? Everything had been boxed up and shipped back to Ireland or given away. A new family were moving in. She no longer belonged on Fifth Avenue. The late-morning sun beat down upon her, making her scalp feel hot beneath the straw-and-ribbon picture hat.

Ellen blinked and looked up one last time at their old apartment framed against the searing blue sky. She picked up the green Louis Vuitton suitcase, the one she had arrived with all those years ago. It was all she had taken with her when she'd got off the RMS *Britannic*. Ellen gave a little sob of distress. What had she done? The boat had departed and would be pushing its way out to sea. She could almost hear Brigid's cries for her, and Giles's confusion and hurt. His rage once he realised she had abandoned them. The case felt like it was filled with bricks as she stumbled back down the street. She had to get out of this city because every corner, every building held a memory of the dream she had allowed herself to believe in for the past eight years.

Light flooded in from the high arched windows in Grand Central Station. Ellen walked through the shafts of bright sunlight, in and out of the shadows. According to the brass-sided clock atop the information booth it was fifteen minutes past midday. She had no idea where to go. The concourse was busy with people who knew exactly where they were headed. The bustle of the train station was making her feel sick and dizzy. She should have stayed on board the ship with her family; she should have confessed all to Giles. Instead she had run away, not because she was a coward but because it was the only way to protect them. All the same, she felt like a stinking rat of a mother as she wandered over to the information booth.

'How can I help you, ma'am?' a young man with small round spectacles asked.

She pulled the purse out of her coat pocket. It was heavy with quarters she had managed to filch from Giles's waistcoat pockets, and dollar notes she'd slipped out of his wallet. But the total didn't amount to much. Since the Crash, Giles kept a close eye on his money and never gave her stacks of dollars like he'd done in the early years.

'Where are you travelling to this afternoon?' the man in the information booth asked her, a note of impatience in his voice as a queue formed behind her.

She stared back at him, her mind a blank.

'Ma'am?' he asked her again, his tone sharp, while the queue behind her muttered their annoyance.

'How do I get to Hollywood?' she whispered, grasping at her age-old dream.

'Don't you know what city it's in?' the clerk asked her in mocking tones. Ellen's cheeks were smarting with embarrassment. She shook her head.

'Los Angeles, which is right the other side of America, miss,' he said. 'You're going to have to change trains in Chicago. Do you know just how long that's going to take you?'

She shook her head again.

He sighed, clearly thinking her another hopeless dreamer.

'Three or four days,' he said. 'If you want to leave right now, you could take the Twentieth Century Limited to Chicago, departing at five o'clock this afternoon. If you go over to the ticket office, you can purchase a sleeper ticket. The train arrives in Chicago at ten o'clock in the morning.'

Like a fool, Ellen handed over fifty-one dollars for a single ticket. She had thirty-nine dollars left. It was not going to be enough to cover the onward journey to Los Angeles. She would have to find a way of making some money once she got to Chicago. There was a part of her that didn't care where she ended up or how she was going to survive. She had lost her little girl, and she might as well be curled up in a gutter down a New York back alley for all she cared. Then again, there was another part of her, the part that had existed before her daughter was born, the part that flickered to life every time she watched a movie. Eight years ago, when she left Ireland for New York, she had become a new person. Perhaps if she went to Hollywood, Ellen could transform herself again. She could make her mark on the silver screen, a mark that her little girl might one day find.

The train was half empty. Ellen drew the curtains on her sleeper, not wanting to see or talk to anyone. She sat in the corner, nibbling on the bun she had bought in Dean's Bakery on Fifth Avenue on the way to the station. It was hard to swallow the sweet dough, her throat was so tight with nerves. Once she arrived in Chicago, she would be on her own. Somehow she had to find a way to pay for a ticket to Los Angeles. With a jolt, she remembered an address. She had read it so many times and yet she had completely forgotten until this very moment that she did know one person who lived in Chicago.

She put down her bun on its paper bag and pulled the old boat ticket out of her purse, glad now that she had kept it all these years. She turned the ticket over and on the back was scrawled:

Alec Lavelle, 537 Lakeside Drive, Chicago, Illinois.

Her hand shook as she put the ticket back into her purse. Her old guilt tugged at her. Chicago was a big city; there was no reason to suppose she would ever bump into him. But should she seek him out?

The conductor blew his whistle and the train gave a lurch as it slowly chugged out of the station. Ellen put both her hands on the window and bowed her head. It was unbearable to look at New York City, brimming with memories of her daughter and her husband, and yet she must. She raised her face and stared at the receding streets. The hypnotic skyline of her husband's beloved skyscrapers shrinking in the distance. Tears trailed down her cheeks, pooling on her lap, and dampening her skirt.

'Brigid,' she whispered in agony. 'Oh, Brigid.'

But her little girl was such a great distance from her now, out at sea. She shuddered as grief swept through her, certain she would never see her again.

CHAPTER FOUR

Mairead was left on her own in the kitchen after her mother disappeared into her workshop with her mug of tea.

'Will you not sit down for a few minutes with me?' she'd asked.

'I told you, I've this commission to finish by Tuesday,' her mother explained as she edged out the door.

'But it's Easter weekend, you should take some time off,' Mairead complained.

'Unlike you, Mairead, I don't get paid holidays,' her mother said tartly on her way out. 'Artists have to work all the time.'

Why was her mother so defensive? Making her feel needy and boring because she did an ordinary job – unlike her mother, the great talent. It had always been this way. Her mother burrowed away in her workshop while her father was left to deal with most of the childcare and housekeeping. Had her father been happy to play second fiddle to his wife? Mairead had never heard him complain. He had seemed genuinely proud of her.

Mairead sighed, sitting down heavily on a chair at the kitchen table. Her tummy groaned. She pulled the shopping bag towards her and rummaged inside for the Kimberley biscuits. She had bought them for her mam. They were the only biscuits she professed to like, but Mairead knew she'd be the one who ate them all. She bit into the soft ginger sponge and the squidgy marshmallow filling, taking in the state of the kitchen. It was a mess. The big table was littered with papers and books, some of which were thick with dust. Thank goodness the slate floor was grey because she could feel it sticky under the soles of her shoes. As for the sink, it was frankly disgusting. Piles of dirty plates stacked next to it. How could her mother live like this?

She gave another big sigh and helped herself to a second biscuit. It would seem that, having just spent two days cleaning her own house, she was now going to have to clean her mother's.

It took three hours to get the place cleaned to Mairead's satisfaction. Of course, her mother didn't possess a pair of rubber gloves and had very few cleaning products. Mairead's hands were red and stinging from all the scrubbing. She hadn't stopped at the kitchen but had gone on to clean the bathroom and the rest of the downstairs. She drew the line at tackling her mother's bedroom, and her old bedroom, though dusty, was as she had left it last time.

Her mother hadn't emerged once while she was cleaning, not for a cup of tea or a chat. Mairead pushed down the hurt. Her mother was on a deadline, she had to remember that. It was the way things always had been.

Mairead glanced up at the clock on the kitchen wall. It was nearly seven already and she hadn't got anything ready for dinner. Washing a couple of potatoes, she pricked them with a fork and flung them into the Aga. Baked potatoes then, with butter and cheese. She was too tired to think of anything else. She opened the fridge and took out the bottle of white wine she'd been cooling since she arrived and poured two big glasses. Surely her mother wouldn't mind a little interruption now? She had to take a break sometime.

On her way to the studio she paused by the porch doors, which looked out across the back garden to the Atlantic. Today the sea was dark and churning, and grey rain clouds scudded across the sky. Even so, the sight of the sea lifted Mairead's spirits. It was different here in County Mayo from where she and Niall had settled. Sometimes her own home in County Meath felt enclosed with leaden skies, land-locked with bogs and fields. Being in Mayo always made her feel lighter.

Since both her hands were full with the glasses of wine, she gave a desultory knock with her head on the studio door, and pushed it open. It was an airy space, with giant skylights. Originally an outbuilding, her father had converted it for her mother when they'd first moved in. The walls were the old grey drystone, laced with spider webs, and there was a stable door. The studio was neat and tidy, in complete contrast to the rest of the house. Mairead was surprised to see her mother wasn't at her workbench and the door was open. She walked outside and saw her sitting under the big chestnut tree in the front garden, leaning back against its broad trunk and staring up at the festoons of white blossoms. She looked so at peace in her long flowing green shirt the same colour as the spring grass. The rainclouds had moved on, and the wind had dropped, as sunlight shafted through the boughs of the tree. Mairead felt a wave of irritation at her mother. This hardly looked like she was working. Had she forgotten all about Mairead slaving away inside her house? She swallowed down her annoyance as she walked over towards her.

'I brought you some wine,' she said, standing over her mother, who opened her eyes as Mairead's shadow fell across her.

'How long have you been out here?' she asked, handing her mother the glass of wine.

Her mother shrugged. 'A little while,' she said, sipping the wine.

'Why didn't you come and get me?' Mairead said, sitting down clumsily on the grass by the tree.

'Because I wanted to be on my own,' her mother whispered.

The words felt like a soft punch in Mairead's belly.

'Well, I've put baked potatoes on,' she said. 'I didn't know what else to cook.'

'Thanks, let me know when they're ready,' her mam said, putting her glass of wine down on the grass, then standing up and retrieving it.

'Where are you going?' Mairead blustered. 'I've just sat down—'

'I need to get more done tonight,' her mother explained, no apology.

'What's wrong with you?' Mairead couldn't stop herself from reacting. 'I've come all the way to see you, and you just keep walking away from me—'

'I told you, Mairead, I've a deadline.'

'It can't be that pressing if you've time to sit out here on your own. Why didn't you come and find me?' Mairead said, emotion rising in her voice.

'Because I needed a bit of peace.'

'Well, I need to talk to you,' Mairead flung back. 'My marriage has fallen apart, and since it happened you've said nothing to me. Nothing. What kind of mother are you?'

'I've always said there's more to life than being a wife,' her mother responded.

'I was trying to make my marriage work.'

'Oh, Mairead,' her mother sighed. 'Your husband is gay, and we've all known it since forever. I'm surprised it lasted as long as it did.'

Mairead gave a gasp. Her mother had known about Niall! Why had she never spoken to her before? Warned her?

'You never said!'

'I didn't want to interfere,' her mother said uncomfortably. 'And there was Stella to consider.'

'But you're supposed to interfere, you're my mother. Didn't you want me to be happy?'

'I doubt you would have listened to me at the time, Mairead.'

Mairead knew her mother was right. She had been so determined to be the perfect wife and mother. Couples didn't break up in Ireland. Divorce was illegal and people stayed together for life. That's just how it was. But Niall had bailed on them. Run away to London with his lover. Told their daughter he was gay before he had told her, his own wife! Niall and Stella, and now it seemed her own mother, had expected Mairead to have known, but she hadn't. It had been such a huge shock. She had thought her husband no longer wanted to have sex with her because she had put on weight after she'd had the baby.

When Stella was five, Mairead had suggested she try to get pregnant again, but Niall had revealed he didn't want to have any more children. Stella had been an accident. He was glad to be her father, but he had never planned for more than one. Mairead had been so shocked. Niall had never admitted this to her before they had got married. She should have left him then. But she didn't. Instead, she had begged him, and he had said he'd think about it. The subject was never raised again. Her husband stopped touching her. As the years passed, she thought this was what happened. Only young couples had sex. She had been scandalised to catch her mother and father in a passionate embrace one day when she'd arrived unexpected the year before he died. They had been in their fifties!

Niall wasn't a bad man. In her heart, she knew this. He was a good father and had provided for her and Stella for years. It must have been hard for him too. But she couldn't help being angry with him. His lie had robbed her of so much. She could have had more children if she had been married to someone else. How had she not noticed her husband was gay when her own mother had worked it out?

She had been Niall's first, there had been no girlfriends before her, but they had both been so young she hadn't suspected anything. Besides, being gay was officially illegal in Ireland, so of course Niall had tried to hide who he was to the whole world for all those years of their marriage. It wasn't until March 1983, when they had heard on the radio about the outcome of the trial of five men who beat a gay man to death in Fairview Park, that Mairead noticed changes in her husband. He had been so angry as he'd driven her to work that morning.

'Suspended sentences!' he spat. 'They killed him!'

'It's terrible,' Mairead had agreed.

'It's like they're condoning gay-bashing!' he said, furious.

Mairead had looked at Niall in alarm.

It was a terrible incident, but why was he so worked up?

Six months later, she had returned home from work to find a letter on the hall table. He was sorry, but now Stella had left home, he couldn't hide who he was any longer. She must have worked it out after all these years. He had fallen in love and had left for London with his new partner, Lesley Burrows, an Irish musician whom he'd met at Dublin's first Pride march. In the letter, Niall wrote that he'd already told Stella. Mairead had been completely astounded. She had collapsed on the hall rug, hand to heart.

'No, Niall,' she had whispered. 'No, I never worked it out.' She hadn't even known he had gone to the Pride march.

Waves of fury, heartache and, strangely, jealousy at his new life in London, had assaulted her for months afterwards. Now she redirected her anguish at her husband towards her mother.

'Why didn't you tell me Niall was gay?' Mairead wailed.

Her mother couldn't meet her gaze.

'I'm sorry, Mairead,' she said. 'But at least it's out now. And it's for the best.'

Her mother's voice warmed, and her green eyes lit up as she went on: 'You're free at last, with your whole life ahead of you!'

'It's too late, Mam. I'm thirty-seven this year.'

Her mother gave a hoot of laughter. 'That's not old. You got married too young. Now's your chance to see the world, Mairead. Have some fun. Leave that wretched job in the convent school.'

'I like my job,' Mairead countered.

Her mother raised an eyebrow disbelievingly.

'You've been there years with those nuns breathing down your neck,' she said. 'Look, all I'm saying is see this as an opportunity. The nest is empty. You can please yourself.'

'I'm not like you,' Mairead lashed out, angry at her mother's flippancy. 'I don't want to be on my own.'

'I didn't choose to be alone, Mairead,' her mother said icily.

Mairead felt instantly guilty. Of course her mother didn't want to be a widow. It had been mean to say she wanted to be on her own. But a voice in her head was needling her: *You're jealous of your mother because she's strong and you're weak.*

'But you've never wanted to spend time with me,' Mairead pushed. 'Why did you have me if you didn't want me?'

Her mother looked at her, astonished.

'What a stupid question,' she responded, edging her way back to her studio.

She doesn't care if I'm upset, Mairead thought. *All she wants is to get back to her precious jewellery commission.*

The sight of her mother sidling away from her made her furious.

'But you've never been like other mothers,' Mairead kept going, feeling the heat rising in her. 'You're not normal. I should know, because if Stella came to see me, I'd drop everything just to be with her. But you're so selfish—'

'You're acting like a spoilt child, not a grown woman,' her mother interrupted. 'And you're the one being selfish, pulling me into this dramatic outburst when I need to get back to work.'

'Work, work, work, that's all you do!' Mairead raised her arms to heaven. 'Why don't you want to be with me?'

'Stop this nonsense now,' her mother said crossly. 'I've had enough of your hysterics.'

Before Mairead had a chance to say more, her mother stalked back to her workshop and slammed the stable door closed.

'What's wrong with you?' Mairead called after her.

Anger beat like a furious bird inside her chest. She wanted so badly to scream at her mother and get a reaction. She would have preferred her mother to shout back at her, but this cool indifference drove her wild.

There had always been this distance between them. It hurt so much to think her mother had worked out Niall was gay years before he'd left that terrible letter for her. She had never tried to tell her or support her in any way.

Mairead had worked hard at her relationship with Stella. Had wanted them to be close like best friends. Warm and intimate and so different from what she had with her own mother. To a certain extent, she and Stella were close, but her daughter was a daddy's girl too. Since Niall had left, she had felt wounded by Stella not taking her side. Mairead felt the tears welling up. How she wished her own father were here to give her one of his magnificent hugs. She stomped back into the house, trying not to hold on to her anger at her mother for his sake. Her father had always managed to warm her mother up. Soften her angular edges. Of course he loved her, but sometimes Mairead heard his gentle admonishments when her mother was too brittle or cold towards her family.

For her father, she'd light the fire and heat up the cold dining room. For him, she'd lay the table and call her mother in for her baked potato. And for him, she'd not complain when her mam slunk off back to her workshop. She would sit in his old armchair and gaze into the ebbing flames of the fire while Alfie lounged in front of her, dreaming of chasing rabbits. She would try to get used to her new life of solitude.

Mairead made a promise to herself. If her mother wanted to be left alone, fine. This would be her last trip to see her until Stella came back in the summer. Her mother didn't need her. Mairead had to let go of this yearning for her mother's full attention. To finally accept that she was never going to get it.

As Mairead sat on the grass, her back against the big chestnut tree, sipping on her glass of white wine, she looked across the wild garden at the distant blue sea. She knew the answer to her mother's cold ways lay across the ocean. The past she never spoke of, and the mother who had let her go. She had always longed to know the story of her lost grandmother, but it was a secret her mother had refused to reveal. Mairead doubted she ever would.

CHAPTER FIVE

The fierce midsummer heat was like a hot brick against her skin as Ellen stepped out of La Salle Street train station onto the busy streets of Chicago. She felt exposed and vulnerable as she set off along the sidewalk, clutching her green suitcase. She had no idea what direction she should go in or where would be the best place to find work and lodgings. Her eyes were drawn to the silhouettes of tall buildings against the bright blue summer sky, and she moved towards them, entering a canyon of shadows, letting the coolness of shade relieve the heat building up in her body. Giles had told her about the Chicago Loop, and she believed this must be the district she was walking through. He had told her the city was situated on Lake Michigan, which was so vast it was like the sea. Ellen didn't believe any lake could be like the sea. She remembered the lake at the big house back home. Fringed by dripping green trees, still and sometimes stagnant. In summer, little flies hovered above its surface. It had felt stuck in time. But the sea was always moving, forwards and backwards. It never stayed the same.

Ellen found herself at the foot of a staircase to an elevated streetcar station. With no better idea, she clambered up the steps and bought a transit ticket to Lincoln Park because she reckoned it might be cooler there than anywhere else in the city. The heat was oppressive, and her pale Irish skin was prickling in protest. As the streetcar trundled through the city it felt at times as if she were back in New York. There was that same atmosphere of relentless poverty, yet in Chicago it seemed even worse. They passed a long line of men standing outside a soup kitchen offering free soup, coffee and a doughnut. Giles had been right. She was spoiled and ungrateful to choose to walk away from all she had once possessed. But if she had returned to Ireland, it would all have been taken from her anyway. She swallowed again, her mouth dry. She was desperate for a cold glass of water, or a soda. How was she going to find work in a city heaving with unemployment? Her few dollars weren't going to last long.

At the sight of the park, Ellen got off the streetcar and walked towards its green expanse. By now it was lunchtime and her stomach was rattling with hunger, but she kept on walking. As she walked, there was a shift in the thick city air. A soft hush of breeze. There on the horizon was a tip of blue. She took a breath. Lake Michigan. Giles had been right. It really did look like the sea. As she got closer, she could see a shoreline, just like the one at Long Island. On this side of the park, life was clearly better. Ellen took in the view of Lake Michigan. She could see no end to it. Along the shoreline promenade couples walked arm in arm, and she saw three nannies pushing perambulators. As a mother, caring for children was a job she was an expert at. She could try and find an agency like the one she had used in New York to find a nanny for Brigid. She felt a stab of pain in her heart at the thought of her daughter.

Ellen stopped walking and put down the green suitcase. Her shoulder was aching from carrying it. She watched a nanny lifting a crying baby out of its pram and comforting the child. The sight brought tears to her eyes. How could she consider looking after someone else's child after abandoning her own? The idea of living in a big house like she had in Ireland with the hierarchy of servants and mistresses made her feel queasy. She wanted none of the old world.

Ellen picked up her case again and made her way back across the park and northwards. She walked until her feet were swollen and sore in her shoes, and her stomach was aching with hunger. As she stepped out of the park, back onto the sidewalk, she saw a restaurant across the street, its flat brick exterior adorned with a neon sign: *The Green Leaf*. It felt like an omen. Green had been the colour of her childhood. The deep verdant green of Ireland's wet grass and thick woods. She crossed the street and pushed the door open.

The waitress looked young, although she wore bright red lipstick, had peroxide blond hair, and possessed a confident air as she took Ellen's order of a chicken salad homestyle. The price of 90c included a beverage, so Ellen asked for a glass of soda. The waitress, whose name was Gladys according to her name pin, brought her back a tall glass with a red-and-white striped straw. She couldn't help recalling the last time she had taken Brigid for a soda at Mary Elizabeth's Tea Rooms on Fifth Avenue. They had both drunk through red-and-white straws, giggling as they made unladylike noises while hoovering up every last drop of liquid at the bottom of the glass.

'Say, are you OK?' Gladys was peering down at her.

Ellen wiped her eyes with the back of her hands.

'Yes.' She sniffed.

'Well, you sure don't look it,' Gladys said. 'Use your napkin. I'll get you a clean one.'

Ellen dabbed her eyes with the napkin and pushed back into her window seat. The restaurant was quiet enough. Just one group of male customers at a table over the other side. Ellen noticed Gladys hitching up her skirt a little to show off her legs before flirting with the men as she wrote out their bill. It clearly worked as one of them handed her a big wad of dollars as a tip, then they all got up and left.

After delivering her chicken salad, and a fresh napkin, Gladys returned with a small glass of clear liquid.

'This will make you feel better, honey,' she said, giving her a wink.

Ellen lifted the glass to her nose and sniffed. It was gin. She took a sip of the liquor. It was smoother than she expected and she felt its burn in her belly immediately. Taking another sip of the gin to give herself courage, she thanked Gladys then asked tentatively, 'I'm looking for work.'

'Oh honey, you and every other lost dame in Chicago.' Gladys laughed.

Ellen felt her body sag.

'But that don't mean I can't help you,' Gladys said. 'You're Irish, right?'

Ellen nodded.

'That's a good thing, because the fellas who own this joint are Irish,' she said. 'I know they're looking for an Irish girl.'

'To waitress?'

'Nope,' Gladys said. 'Not in the restaurant. They're looking for a girl with your look: red hair and pale skin.'

'Oh, I don't want to do anything...' Ellen didn't quite know how to put it, but she was not desperate enough to sell her body, not yet.

'No, no,' Gladys reassured her. 'The Irish are totally against any of that sort of thing. Not like the Italians over in the South Side – that side of town is steeped in brothels. Honey, they want an Irish girl to perform. Can you sing?'

Without waiting for an answer, Gladys went on: 'Dumb question, huh – of course you can sing, every Irish girl can! They're looking for a red-haired, pale Irish girl to sing some of the Irish songs, as well as with the jazz band. Angie's our main singer. She's from down south. Boy, does she have a voice!'

Ellen was confused. She could see no sign of a jazz band in the quiet and dimly lit restaurant.

'They want a singer for here in the restaurant?'

'Oh no, this place is just a front, honey. You eat your chicken salad, and then I'll show you.'

After Ellen had finished her food and paid her 90c plus 30c tip, Gladys turned the sign to *Closed* on the door of the restaurant and waved for her to follow.

'You can leave your case right there,' she said, then led the way to the back of the restaurant, through the kitchen and into a long corridor with a green velvet curtain at the end. Gladys pulled it back to reveal a door with a hatch in it. She knocked three times on the door, and the hatch slid back.

'Hey, Tommy, think I've found your Irish girl,' Gladys said. 'Say, what's your name?' She turned to Ellen.

'Ellie,' Ellen said, not wanting to share her full name, just in case.

The door opened and, to her astonishment, Ellen found herself entering the noisy, smoky interior of a speakeasy. A band was playing the new jazz music she had so loved in her early days in New York when they used to go to the Cotton Club in Harlem. There was a tall black woman singing one of Ellen's old favourites, 'Bye Bye Blackbird', while waitresses bustled among the thronged tables. Gladys introduced her to Tommy, the owner of the restaurant. He looked Irish with his broad grin and the jut of his jaw, but when he spoke, he sounded American.

'What songs you got?' he asked, gesturing for her to take a seat at his table.

A part of her wanted to run away. She had never performed in front of people before, and besides, speakeasys were illegal. Though, considering the fact she could see two cops sitting at the next table and drinking whisky, it clearly wasn't a law which was being enforced in Chicago. But then there was the other part of her. If she could become someone else, even for a few hours, she could find a way to live. It was what was driving her to go to Hollywood and make a career acting in films. She had to start somewhere.

'What kind of songs do you want me to sing?' she asked.

'We want a bit of everything,' he said. 'Jazz is great, but we also like the blues, and sometimes we want to hear songs from the old country. What you got?'

'I can sing "The Rising of the Moon", "The Wind That Shakes the Barley"...' She paused, remembering the rebel songs she'd sung in the woods with her best friend. The thrill of their fury letting rip.

'That it?' Tommy asked, looking unimpressed.

'I can sing "Bye Bye Blackbird" too.' She glanced at the woman singing, who she guessed must be Angie. 'The song I know best is "The Last Rose of Summer".'

She immediately wished she hadn't told him this. More memories surfaced of summer days back at the big house in the west of Ireland. Smelling fragrant roses thick with the scent of late summer. Hearing the drone of bumblebees. Those rare lazy and free days of her childhood.

'That'll do for now,' Tommy said. 'When Angie finishes up, you can sing us a few songs. Then we'll see if you got the job.'

All the old words came flooding back. She had always loved singing. After her first few tremulous notes, and the mocking eyes of Tommy, she had taken a deep breath, and let her voice fly. There was no effort required. She launched into 'The Rising of the Moon', and the jazz band, unsure how to accompany the Irish tune, left her to it. When she'd finished, there was silence. She licked her dry lips and turned to the violinist.

'Do you know "The Last Rose of Summer"?'

'Sure do,' the man replied. 'The tune is 'The Young Man's Dream', right?'

Aisling an Óigfhear. Its Irish name echoed in her head. The melody she knew so well. And the words from an old poem by the poet Thomas Moore, she knew as well as her prayers. As a child, it had been her party piece.

> 'Tis the last rose of summer
> Left blooming alone;
> All her lovely companions are faded and gone.
> No flower of her kindred,
> No rose-bud is nigh
> To reflect back her blushes
> Or give sigh for sigh
> I'll not leave thee, thou lone one.
> To pine on the stem...

Her voice trembled with emotion. She had fled Ireland under such terrible circumstances, and rather than go back she had fled a second time, abandoning her little girl to go back without her.

> So soon may I follow
> When friendships decay
> And from love's shining circle
> The gems drop away!

It hurt so much to sing the final words because it felt as though she was singing about Brigid:

> When true hearts lie withered,
> And fond ones are flown,
> Oh! who would inhabit
> This bleak world alone?

No, she told herself, Brigid was not alone. She had her daddy and all his family around her. It was she, Ellen, who was in the bleak world alone. She felt a tear rolling down her cheek as she finished the song.

The atmosphere in the speakeasy had changed. The first face

she saw clearly was Angie's, her dark eyes soft with sympathy. Ellen looked down at the misty eyes of some of the men in the audience. She realised she was among her countrymen here, some of them second generation, but none had forgotten their heritage.

The old Irish songs bloomed within her and a yearning for the home she could never return to became entwined with her heartache as a mother. She sang 'The Wind That Shakes the Barley' and finished to resounding applause. When she looked over at Tommy, he gave her a smile and a nod. She guessed she had the job, although she had no idea what the pay was.

'You got a place to stay?' Gladys asked her as she brought her back out into the restaurant to collect her bag.

'No, can you recommend anywhere?' Ellen asked her.

'You know Chicago?'

'No, I just arrived this morning from New York.'

Gladys tossed her blond hair. 'Well, I like you, Ellie Irish, so you can stay in my lodgings and share the rent – how does that sound?'

Ellen's spirits lifted. She had been dreading looking for a place to stay. She'd already seen several dour flophouses on her walk through Chicago that morning, and the thought of sleeping in the same room as a dozen strangers had made her stomach swirl with nausea.

'That sounds grand!' She accepted Gladys's invitation without hesitation.

Ellen moved in with Gladys that night. Her new friend lived four blocks away from the Green Leaf Restaurant on the top floor of a four-storey brick building. Gladys unlocked the door to a one-room apartment. It felt like stepping into an oven, so much heat had built up during the day. On the far side of the room, in front of the grimed window, was a big bedstead piled with clothes, which

Gladys scooped onto a chair. There was a wonky wardrobe stuffed with clothes too. Ellen spied at least one fur, which surprised her. She doubted Gladys could afford such luxuries on her waitressing salary.

'Gifts,' Gladys told her, when she saw her looking. 'What side of the bed you want to sleep on?'

'I don't mind,' said Ellen.

'OK, I'll take window side, catch what breeze can get through. The darn thing's jammed so I can't open it wide in summer or seal it shut in winter. And oh boy, does it get cold in winter.'

For now, it was Midsummer's Eve and the heat was stifling.

Gladys pulled a bottle of gin out of the cupboard. 'Let's celebrate your new employment.'

They sat on the bed, as there was nowhere else to sit apart from one lone chair at a table between the bed and the kitchenette.

'Washroom's down the hall,' Gladys told her as she poured Ellen a glass of gin.

That night Ellen discovered she had stumbled into the North Side of Chicago, which was firmly Irish.

'Lucky you didn't go to the South Side,' Gladys had teased her. 'The Italians might not be so kindly to a lost Irish girl. You could have ended up working in one of their filthy brothels!'

'So is the Green Leaf owned by the Irish gangsters?' Ellen ventured, worried that her new employers might be mobsters.

'Sure, they can be tough, these guys, so don't ever cross them,' Gladys said. 'But they look after their own.'

Ellen remembered watching the movie *The Public Enemy* with James Cagney and Jean Harlow in the Paramount Theatre. Despite the fact he was a criminal, she had found herself willing Cagney's character to come out on top.

Gladys told Ellen a little of her story. She had grown up in Kansas, where her family had been farmers. Her grandparents were Irish and had come over from Waterford. By the time her father was born, her grandpa had acquired a good bit of land. Their lives had been good until the crops started to fail.

'I remember running through fields of golden wheat when I was a girl,' she said, her eyes shining. 'Oh boy, life was a dream.

'But then it just stopped raining – not just for a month or two but year after year. And storms blew up. Ripping up the earth and any darn thing we were trying to grow. You don't know what dry is until you've been in one of them dust storms. It gets in all your cracks and crannies. Like right between your teeth.'

Gladys took another swig of her gin.

'Pa lost it all – the whole damn farm and all his livestock.'

'That's terrible,' Ellen said.

'My family packed everything they could into the truck and set off in the hope of finding work picking fruit in California. Got no idea where they're at now,' she finished sorrowfully.

'Why didn't you go with your family?' Ellen asked, curious.

'I didn't want to be a burden on them,' she said. 'I'm the eldest of six. Reckoned I could take care of myself. And I sure have,' she added proudly.

Ellen skirted around Gladys's questions about her own background. It was easier not to admit she had been married, and a mother. She had left her wedding and engagement rings next to the necklace on the locker in the cabin by her sleeping husband two days ago, so there was nothing to give her away. Instead, she told Gladys her big dream.

'I'm aiming to get to Hollywood.'

'You want to be in the movies?' Gladys didn't laugh, and Ellen was grateful for that. 'Well good for you,' Gladys said. 'I got big plans too.'

Ellen waited for Gladys to expand, but instead she gave a yawn, stretching like a cat on the lumpy bed.

'It's late,' she said. 'Time for bed!'

. . .

In those first weeks Ellen kept as busy as she could. She tried to forget who she had been. Told herself every morning she was Ellie from County Galway. Eighteen years old and innocent as a lamb. It worked for a while. But sometimes she'd feel a terrible pain in her heart, and an image of Brigid would rise within her. She'd push it down, keep on singing, her voice turning shrill for a few notes. Sometimes, when she was alone in their lodgings, she took the old boat ticket out of her purse and reread the address on the back: *Alec Lavelle, 537 Lakeside Drive, Chicago, Illinois*. She knew it by heart now.

She imagined knocking on the door and introducing herself. *Ellen Lavelle*, she'd say, and then add: *I'm your daughter*. Would he believe her? Or would he deny her? There was too much at risk to ever chance it. And yet a part of her craved to see his house. To go and speak the truth, no matter the consequences.

On her third Sunday off, the need to see where she could have ended up became too much. Ellen got up early and headed off while Gladys was still softly snoring in the bed. She passed the lines of unemployed outside the soup kitchens and walked across the North Side of the city to where the Gold Coast neighbourhood nestled by Lake Michigan. She followed the shoreline, in awe of the huge mansions with their turrets and towers. Families were setting off for church dressed in their Sunday best. Ellen slipped behind one of the trees and watched from across Lakeside Drive as the door opened on number 537. She watched the familiar yet unfamiliar figure of Mr Alec Lavelle and his wife, and a boy too, as they made their way down the steps. Despite the early hour, it was oppressively hot, and Mrs Lavelle was fanning herself with her Bible, her face hidden by a broad-brimmed picture hat decorated with a green ribbon. The boy looked to be about fourteen; judging by the scowl on his face, he was uncomfortable in his Sunday suit. His father opened the doors to the garage and reversed out a gleaming car in green and cream. She thought it might be a Packard. Tommy had one just like it. Father, mother and son got into the car and drove off towards the city. She could have set off after them and looked for the church they were going to. Or she could have stayed to greet them on their return. But she didn't. She stood quite still, staring at the magnificent house on Lakeside Drive and thinking about the lives lost, the ones left behind in Ireland.

Then she turned on her heel and walked back into the hot heaving city full of desperate folk. She got back to the lodging house to find Gladys gone. Relieved there was no one to see her tears, Ellen took the boat ticket out of her purse and ripped it up into little pieces. She had to forget about her past if she was to have any kind of future.

CHAPTER SIX

It was exam time at St. Bernard's Convent. The air was thick with
stress and anticipation as Mairead clacked down the school corri-
dors in her work shoes, heavy-soled loafers. Her daughter Stella
hated them. Said they were too old for her mam. But Mairead was
nearly forty. She *was* old; well, at least she felt it. They were
comfortable and that was what mattered when you were on your
feet most of the day.

She gave each white-faced girl she passed a kind smile. Let
them away with any school uniform infringements such as
untucked shirts or nail varnish. She'd never been one for those kind
of school rules anyway.

The truth was Mairead thrived during the intense examination
period. There was a special quality to being in school at this time of
year. All the students in non-examination classes were already off
on their summer break. There was a hushed silence blanketing the
school buildings. These were the special few girls. Mairead was the
teacher always willing to stay late or give extra guidance and
advice.

The weather was hot this year. If she wasn't invigilating, she sat outside by the sycamore tree at the edge of the playing fields eating cherries and reading the green hardbacked biography of Frida Kahlo her brother had sent her for Christmas last year. Frida Kahlo's life had been tough, and her marriage disastrous, yet she had created so much art out of her suffering. Mairead was bewitched by the Mexican artist's haunting self-portraits. Staring at the colour illustrations, Mairead imagined she was in Frida Kahlo's Mexico, living a life full of passion rather than that of a schoolteacher in midlands Ireland. But she did love her job. This year she was particularly proud of her girls taking Honours History for the Leaving Certificate. They were a hardworking and clever group. They all had offers from universities in Ireland, as well as England and Scotland. Of course, she would never swap any of these A-list girls for her own daughter, but there were times she'd wished Stella had been more academic. She had just scraped through the Leaving and was completely disinterested in university.

Ever since she was eight years old, after her first performance as Mary in the Christmas nativity play, Stella had wanted to be an actress. All her spare time had been poured into dance classes, singing lessons and drama groups, encouraged by Niall – living out his own thespian dreams through his daughter. Mairead had hoped Stella would grow out of her desire to be in the Royal Shakespeare Company but, if anything, she became even more determined. In her final year at school, she had poured all her time and energy into her drama class production of *The Tempest* rather than the Leaving Cert. Mairead and Niall had fought over it; surely, as an accountant, he understood the importance of a proper job? Of course, her mother was cheering on Stella. Any opportunity to undermine Mairead. Though she had been happy to hear her mother's praise for Stella's unorthodox interpretation of Caliban.

'Quite magnificent,' she'd said, hugging her elated grand-daughter.

Mairead had swelled with pride. Yes, Stella's had been the

stand-out performance. But that just fuelled Stella's unrealistic dreams to be an actor.

'Don't you want Stella to be happy?' Niall had sniped after she had given Stella yet another serious talking-to about going to university.

'Of course I do,' she said. 'She doesn't have to give up acting. Lots of universities have brilliant drama societies. It can be a hobby—'

'You've got to stop trying to control everyone, Mairead,' Niall interrupted. 'Stella doesn't want to go to university. It's not for her.'

She had been furious. How dare he call her controlling. All she had wanted was what was best for their child.

Well, in any case, she had given in. Especially when Niall had helped Stella apply for drama college and drove her to London for her audition. They had taken the ferry together. The two of them thick as thieves. No wonder he had been so keen to get away from the prying eyes of his wife. Thinking about it now, he had probably met up with Lesley when he was over in London.

When she'd seen Stella's joy, the day she received the acceptance letter into RADA, Mairead *had* been happy for her. After all, it was good that Stella had got out of Ireland and was forging ahead in her new life in London. All the young people were leaving because there was little for them here. *Be grateful she's not gone to America*, Mairead told herself as she drew up into her spot in the convent school car park. That's where all the young were off to now. Everyone under the age of thirty was in the lottery for a green card or, like her brother, had gone there as an illegal, and now they couldn't leave. Even though his daughters were born in America, and he ran his own bar, Darragh was still an illegal alien because he'd outstayed his initial visa. He risked losing it all if he ever came back to Ireland. Thankfully, Stella was just across the Irish sea. Not so far away.

· · ·

On the way into the main school building, Mairead had caught sight of Eoin, the computer teacher, getting out of his car.

'Hiya, Mairead,' he'd called, taking long strides towards her.

He was about the same age as her, but his boyish smile made her feel so much older. With grave misgivings, Sister Mary Stephen had employed Eoin last year to teach a weekly computer skills class. Of course, the headmistress knew it was important for her students to learn how to negotiate computers – 'It is the future!' she had declared, announcing his appointment last year. To her regret, she had been unable to find a Catholic female qualified to come in and teach a class at the convent one day a week. Eoin Montgomery, who ran his own business selling and servicing computers, had been the only applicant. He was at least Catholic, but it did not please Sister Mary Stephen that he was male, youngish, single, and not unattractive with his thick brown curly hair and hazel eyes. Nearly every girl at the convent had a crush on him. His classes were the best attended.

'Hi, Eoin,' she had said as he waited for her to join him. Feeling a blush creeping across her cheeks as he gave her a warm smile, she'd scolded herself for being no better than the smitten schoolgirls.

'What are you doing here today?' she'd said. 'I thought all your classes were done for the year.'

'Sister Mary Stephen asked me to call in. The computer won't work.'

'You'd think she'd get another. Just one computer in the whole school!'

'You should suggest it, being one of her favourites,' Eoin said.

Mairead blushed even deeper. 'Oh, I'm not—'

'Sure, you are!' Eoin had said, opening the door for her.

They parted ways in the entrance, Eoin heading down to Sister Mary Stephen's office, while Mairead made her way to her classroom in her clacking shoes, suddenly aware that Stella was right; they were very dowdy.

Her students would be taking their final paper in Irish History that afternoon and they had begged her to go over old papers with them this morning. Of course she had agreed, glad not to have to spend the morning at home on her own. Trying not to think how she was going to spend the vast empty summer without her daughter, whose drama school term went on until August.

As for Niall, she hadn't seen him since the day before he had left her the horrendous letter. What a coward he had been. All he had given her were a few words in biro written on the back of an old shopping list and folded up on the hall table.

Dear Mairead,

I am sorry but I can't live this lie any longer. Now Stella has left home, I can't stay with you in Ireland. You must have guessed this day would come. We've been pretending to be a couple for too long. But when I went to the Pride march to protest the outcome of the Declan Flynn case, I met someone. His name is Lesley, he's a musician and I love him. I've moved to London to be with him. Don't worry, Stella knows already. She guessed a long time ago – she's such a great girl, so supportive. I hope you can understand. I am sorry if you feel betrayed, but you must have known.

I hope you find love too because you deserve to be happy.

Niall x

Every single word of his letter had burned in her heart. It had felt so inadequate. How dare he suggest she must have known! How dare he expect her to accept his huge deceit! The worst part was the way he had used Stella to validate what he had done. He had got their daughter on his side before she had had a chance to respond. The letter had been waiting for Mairead on a Friday after school. Stella had left a week earlier to start college in London. She had thought it was going to be her and Niall's first empty nest weekend, but it had turned into a big black hole. She had closed all the curtains and sobbed in bed for the whole weekend. Somehow, she had managed to drag herself up on the Monday morning and go into school. When Diana, the physics teacher and her closest colleague, noticed her red eyes, she'd told her she had a cold. She hadn't been able to admit what had happened. She had felt so ashamed of her failure as a wife.

Mairead had stumbled through the autumn spending most nights eating too much chocolate and watching the new Irish soap opera *Glenroe*. Trying to blot out the hurt. Christmas had been hard, but at least Stella had been home. The house had felt strange without Niall, though. When he'd phoned on Christmas Day, Mairead had refused to speak to him.

'Come on, Mam,' Stella had coaxed, holding out the receiver, but Mairead had backed away.

'I don't know what to say to him,' she'd said.

It was true to a certain extent. She didn't know what to say to Niall, but at the same time she had *so* much she wanted to say. How she had given him the best years of her life, and in return he had discarded her. Not to sit down and talk to her before he left was almost worse than leaving her. So why should she forgive him? She wasn't ready for that yet.

In the end, Niall had sent her another letter. She had received it on Valentine's Day, which had felt like a sick joke.

Dear Mairead,

I understand from Stella you are still very upset about what has happened. Please believe me that I never intended to hurt you. Maybe one day, you'll understand that when you fall in love things can get messy. The fact is we are still Stella's mother and father and I believe your refusal to communicate with me is distressing our daughter. I know it must be hard, but please, can you try for her sake?

There is also the issue of our house. Lesley and I are looking at property in London. For me to afford to buy in London we would need to sell the house in Kells. I've talked to Stella about it and she's fine about the change. She doesn't envisage herself moving back home after drama school anyway, and I am sure you would prefer to live somewhere more manageable. I know you always loved the house, so I feel bad writing to you about this. I would prefer to talk on the phone about it, if you would only take my calls. Obviously, I don't want you to feel pushed around, but would you consider selling so I might be able to get a property to start over in London?

Love Niall x

He had actually given her an 'x'! The letter had ignited her anger. Every single part of it felt patronising. How dare he insinuate that neither of them had ever been in love before! They *had* been in love. She remembered how romantic Niall had been when they first met. The letter felt like poison in her veins. She loathed the way he'd manipulated Stella into going along with it, making her feel it would be unreasonable of her to refuse. It was all too much. When she didn't reply to the letter, he kept trying to ring her. For the whole of March, every day after school, there had been a message from Niall on her answerphone. In the end, she had written telling him she needed more time. *Once the academic year is over, I'll get back to you*, she had promised. Well, the year was nearly done, and she still didn't know what to do.

She hadn't talked to anyone at school about her marriage break-up, although she had stopped wearing her wedding ring. Professionally, she was still Mrs Tully. She had to be, because she worked in a Catholic school and divorce was illegal. She was expected to consider herself a wife despite her husband's desertion.

Mairead let out a sigh and picked up one of the past History Leaving Cert papers. She sat on her table and let her loafers fall off her hot feet. It was sandal weather, but she didn't own a pair; it was so rarely hot in Ireland. Her girls mirrored her, sitting on their desks, some of them cross-legged as she went through the paper and they discussed potential answers. They were interrupted by a knock on the door, followed by Sister Mary Stephen sweeping into the classroom. The girls quickly hopped off their desks as Mairead slid off her own table, but the headmistress didn't even seem to notice.

'Mrs Tully, can you come to my office now?' she asked, a grim expression on her face.

For a minute, Mairead thought the nun had found out about her marital situation and was about to sack her. But Diana, her friend and colleague, was separated too, and though everyone knew, no one had made an issue of it. Mairead had assumed that would be the case for her too. Could it be that one of Stella's friends had told their mother, who had then complained to the school board?

Mairead slipped on her loafers and followed Sister Mary Stephen to her office. As soon as the door was shut, she indicated the telephone receiver on the desk and gravely informed her that a call had come through for her. Nausea swept through her; the last time this had happened was seven years ago, when her father suffered his fatal fall. Was history repeating itself?

She picked it up, her heart thumping with dread. Please, not Stella... Niall...

'Hello,' said the voice. 'Am I speaking to Mairead Tully?'

'Yes,' she whispered.

'It's about your mother...'

Mairead dashed down to the classroom to tell her girls there was a family emergency and she had to leave immediately.

In the car park, she dropped her keys and accidentally kicked them under the car. What an idiot she was! She got down on her knees, vainly trying to reach them.

'Are you OK?' It was Eoin again, his voice cheerful.

She straightened up and his expression changed when he saw the look on her face.

'What's happened?'

'It's my mother,' she said. 'She's in Sligo Hospital. I have to get to her—' She took a breath, guilt sweeping through her. She hadn't seen her mother since April when she'd been home for Easter. After their argument on the first evening, she had left early on the Saturday morning. She had lied to her mother, telling her an old friend from Dublin was coming for a visit.

'But I thought you were here for the weekend.' Her mother had frowned as she drank her morning tea, shirtsleeves already pushed up past her elbows and ready for work.

'You're busy anyway with your commission, Mam,' Mairead had said. 'I'm only in the way.'

Her mother hadn't contradicted her.

'Well, you may as well take all this food back with you.' She sniffed. 'I will never get through it, and it'll go off.'

Mairead had noticed how thin her mother's arms had become as she opened the kitchen cupboard and waved her hands at all the food Mairead had bought.

'Mam, are you eating?' she asked.

'Stop now, Mairead, I'm not your child,' her mother said curtly. 'Safe journey home,' she had added, waving goodbye over her shoulder.

Her indifference had hurt. So much so that Mairead hadn't been back. Why put herself through a weekend when it left her feeling small and unloved? But now she felt terrible that things had been left so awkwardly between them. She knew in her heart that her father would be disappointed in them both for not trying harder.

'Are you OK?' Eoin asked as she bent down and desperately tried to reach her car keys.

'My keys are stuck under the car.'

Eoin crouched next to her, and then lay on his stomach, stretching his arm under the car.

'Got them,' he declared, dragging the keys out. 'Is your husband at home?' he asked, handing the keys to her. 'You should get him to drive you.'

She shook her head, biting her lip. 'No,' she whispered. 'He's in London.'

'Look, let me take you,' he offered, concern etched on his face. 'You're in no state to drive. You're shaking all over.'

'You can't do that, Eoin – Mam's in Sligo, that's a two-and-a-half-hour drive.'

'It's fine. That's the advantage of running your own company. I don't have a boss to ask,' Eoin said. 'I'm also insured to drive any car.'

'But how will you get back?'

'Don't you worry about that. I can take the train.'

She pressed her hand to her forehead, a wave of nausea sweeping over her.

'It's too much to ask—'

'You shouldn't be on your own,' he insisted. 'And we're friends, right?'

Eoin was a fast driver, but she felt safe with him as they sped along the twisting road to Mullingar. She had been unable to get much information out of the nurse on the other end of the phone. All Mairead knew was that her mother was in the hospital and asking for her. Worst-case scenarios flashed through her head as she relived the day her father fell off the ladder while cleaning the gutters. What foolish thing had her mother done to end up in a hospital bed?

As if he knew she couldn't face talking, Eoin asked whether she wanted to listen to the radio.

'It doesn't work,' she muttered. 'I've a tape deck, but I keep forgetting to put tapes in the car,' she added, feeling like a failure.

'No worries.' Eoin wriggled around in his seat and pulled a

tape out of his back pocket. 'I've a mixtape I was going to drop in to my sister.'

The music was a welcome distraction. She looked out the window at the racing green fields as she listened to U2's 'New Year's Day'.

'You like U2?' she asked him.

'Yeah,' he said. 'Doesn't everyone?'

She shrugged. 'I prefer Led Zeppelin, Deep Purple, Iron Maiden...'

Eoin glanced at her, surprised.

'You do?' he said. 'Never took you for heavy metaller, Mrs Tully.'

'Call me Mairead. Please,' she said.

Joni Mitchell's 'A Case of You' came on next. Her mother liked Joni Mitchell. She was always playing her album *Blue*.

Guilt swept through Mairead again. She should never have ignored her mother the last few months. Come to think of it, her mother had phoned last night. The message on her answer machine hadn't said what it was about, only that it was her. Mairead hadn't rung back, determined to let her stew for a change. She had lost count of the number times she'd left messages for her mother, who never called back. But she should have known. Her mother would never have called unless it had been important. So not an accident then.

As Eoin parked the car in the hospital car park, Mairead ran through every possible scenario that might await her inside. She had no idea what was wrong with her mother, but it had to be serious if she'd got them to call her at work.

'Do you want me to come in with you?' Eoin asked as he switched off the engine.

'No,' Mairead said. 'I'm sorry I dragged you all the way over here.'

'It's fine, Mairead. I wanted to help.' He paused. 'I'll wait here for you. Just in case you need me.'

She felt quite overwhelmed by his kindness and could feel tears threatening.

'Thank you,' she whispered, scuttling off across the car park before she started to cry.

She wasn't sure what she had been imagining. Her mother hooked up to life support? At the very least, tucked up in a hospital bed. But when she walked into reception, there was her mother sitting in a wheelchair. She almost jumped in fright when she saw her.

'There you are,' her mother said. 'I've been waiting hours.'

'Mammy, what's going on?' She knelt down by her mother's wheelchair and looked into those glinting green eyes. There was something there. She could see the fear.

'I'll tell you when we get home,' she said.

'But I want to talk to a doctor,' Mairead protested.

'I've already been discharged,' she said.

'Tell me what happened.'

'When we get home,' her mother insisted.

'But, Mam, what's going on? You look terrible.'

Her mother appeared tiny in the wheelchair. A lot older than her fifty-seven years. Her face was wan and pale. She had got so thin.

'Please, Mairead,' her mother begged, sounding more vulnerable than Mairead had ever known. 'Just take me home. Alfie's been shut up in the house overnight.'

'What! When were you admitted?'

'Yesterday, I did try to call—'

Mairead felt another wave of guilt.

'You should have left a message,' she said in a small voice.

'I prefer talking in person,' her mother scolded. 'I was going to get myself home, but they insisted I call family. Have someone with me.' She pressed her hands down on the wheelchair arms and raised herself up slowly.

Mairead was forced to reach out and take her hand.

What was going on? Mairead had never seen her mother sick in her entire life. It felt so strange to be helping her out to the car park.

'Mam, a friend drove me and he's waiting in the car.'

'What?' Her mam looked at her wide-eyed. 'Why would you bring someone with you, Mairead?'

'I thought— I got a fright—'

'You thought I was on my deathbed,' her mother interrupted, giving a croaky laugh. 'Not quite yet.'

'Mammy! Stop!'

As they approached the car, Eoin got out and stood waiting, a smile plastered on his face, although Mairead could see he was embarrassed. She felt mortified to have made such a drama. Now he was going to see right inside her life.

Her mother paused and whispered in her ear. 'Well done, Mairead, good for you.'

'No, Mam,' she hissed. 'He's just a friend, another teacher—'

How could her mother be thinking like this? It had been less than a year since Niall had left.

After introductions were made, Eoin drove them back to her mother's house.

'Would you like to come in, and have a cup of tea, a sandwich?' she asked. She could hardly expect him to go straight to the train station. 'There's a late train at 5 p.m., I can drop you off in time to catch it.'

'Sure,' he said. 'I'm in no rush.'

It was strange to see Eoin from her school life offering his arm to her mother as they went into her childhood home. Mairead showed him the way to the kitchen as Alfie bounded around them.

'He's mad for his walk,' her mother said.

'I can take him for a quick run,' Eoin offered. 'I could do with stretching my legs.'

'I like him,' her mother said once Eoin had left with Alfie. 'He's perfect for you.'

'Don't be daft, Mammy,' Mairead said. 'I'm still married.'

'Now you're the daft one, Mairead,' her mother said sharply. 'Your husband is never coming back. You know that, right?'

'Let's not talk about me,' Mairead said, ignoring the sting of her mother's words. She sat down and spread her hands on the table. 'What's going on? Why were you in hospital?'

Her mother looked down at the table and traced the whorls of the old wood.

'I can't tell you when you're looking at me like that,' she said, her voice very quiet. 'Make the sandwiches, do something so you're not staring at me.'

Mairead felt a creeping dread in the pit of her stomach. Now she wanted to put off whatever her mother had to tell her.

'Maybe we should wait to talk until after Eoin's gone?' she asked her mother softly.

'I think that might be best, Mairead,' her mother said, blinking back at her.

After the sandwiches and tea, her mother went to lie down on her bed with Alfie. Mairead had long since stopped trying to convince her mother not to let her dog on the bed. She drove along the coast road with Eoin to bring him to the station. It was a glorious day. The sea glittering azure in the distance, and the hedgerows bursting with wildflowers.

'Ah, I love the west,' Eoin sighed. 'I used to come here on holidays as a child with my family. We went further north, to Donegal.'

As if sensing her stress, he chatted away about his childhood summers in a holiday home in Bundoran. Mairead couldn't focus on what he was saying; a voice in her head kept speculating about what her mother was going to tell her. Trying to ignore her fears, she kept her eyes on the road as the green fields flicked by and the blue sea danced in the distance.

'Thanks so much, Eoin, you've been an absolute star,' Mairead said as she pulled up outside Sligo train station.

'No worries,' he replied. 'Let me know how you get on.'

'Yeah, I've no idea what's wrong.' She switched off the engine and turned to face him.

Eoin gave her a long look, and she could see the sympathy in his eyes. She looked down at her lap. Hastily changed the subject.

'Let me buy your train ticket, it's the least I can do.'

'Not at all.'

Mairead looked up again into his hazel eyes. He held her gaze, and she found herself blushing as she remembered her mother's words: *He's perfect for you.* How would she know? Mairead didn't think she'd ever be able to trust another man after what had happened. And yet, did she really want to spend the rest of her life alone?

'So, are you finished teaching classes for the summer now?' she said, desperate to change the subject, realising too late that he was aware she already knew the answer.

'Yes, that's me done until the autumn,' he said. 'How about you?'

'Just been helping some of the girls prepare for their exams. Today was my last session.'

'So free as a bird for the summer?' he asked, and his question felt a little loaded.

She was aware of the absence of her wedding ring. He must have heard the whispers in the staff room. Known she was separated. She wondered what his story was. She could see there was no ring on his finger. He was so lovely; surely, he had a girlfriend? But she didn't dare ask.

'You're going to miss the train,' Mairead said, feeling impelled to break the sense of something building between them. She opened the car door and got out. He got out the other side.

'It's great we got a chance to get to know each other better,' he said softly. 'I hope everything's OK with your mam.'

'Thanks.'

He gave her a hug. Having his arms around her felt wonderful. As he stepped back, she realised no one had hugged her since Niall had left, apart from Stella. Eoin turned on his heel and strode into the station. Mairead clasped her hands in astonishment. Had he been flirting with her? In fact, had they been flirting since the day they first met, and she just hadn't realised they'd been doing it?

The train chugged out of the station as Mairead got back into her car. She had nothing with her to stay overnight, but she wasn't leaving her mother alone. The last of the exams had taken place today, so she was officially on her holidays. She took a deep breath and headed back to her mother's house, her stomach tight with dread.

Mairead pushed open the door to her mother's bedroom. Her mam was lying on her side, wrapped around Alfie, staring out of the window. The big chestnut tree swayed in the summer breeze. She carried in a cup of tea and placed it on the bedside locker and began to tiptoe out of the room.

'I had a biopsy.'

She turned around. Her mother was sitting up in bed, hugging the dog. She was stroking his ears and staring into his face as he licked her hands in adoration.

'I have cancer,' her mother told Alfie the dog.

Horror swept through Mairead. Cancer. But lots of people survived cancer. Her mind raced. She'd have to move in with Mam and help her get through the chemotherapy and the radiation treatment. But she was tough. She'd get better.

'It's terminal,' her mother said in a flat voice to Alfie as he wound around her, licking her face.

'No!' Mairead let out a screech. 'No, Mam, we can get you treatment—'

Her mother sighed. It was long and heavy.

'I am sorry, Mairead, but it's pancreatic cancer. There's no cure.'

'You can't think like that, Mam,' she said. 'I want to talk to your doctors. We'll go back to the hospital tomorrow, and I'll make them talk to me. Surely you can go on chemotherapy—'

'I don't want it, Mairead,' her mother said, her voice suddenly firm. 'The prognosis is the same whether I have chemo or not. It's terminal,' she said again.

'That's an awful word,' Mairead said, tears filling her eyes. 'You're only fifty-seven!'

At last, her mother looked up at her. Her green eyes had never looked so brilliant.

'I don't want to die in a hospital, Mairead,' she said. 'I want to be here, with Alfie, looking out the window at the sea.'

Mairead nodded. Her whole body felt numb with shock.

'Will you come live with me? Can you do that?'

'Of course, Mam,' Mairead said, stumbling over to the bed and falling on her knees by it. Alfie pushed his muzzle into her face, licking her in frenzy. *He just wants to fix it all*, she thought.

Her mam placed her hand on Mairead's head.

'Thank you,' she said softly. 'You're a good daughter.'

Her mother had never said such words before. They lanced her heart, made the lump in her throat swell. Her mam stroked her head, and each touch made Mairead ache. She wasn't a good daughter at all. She had resented her mother for years. But she'd always thought they'd have time to heal the rift between them.

'Will you call your brother and tell him?' she said. 'I can't face it. And Stella?'

'Yes, of course, Mam,' Mairead said, feeling the weight of the tasks heavy on her.

'There's something else,' her mother said in a low voice.

Mairead looked up at her mother. She had never seen such an

expression on her face. As if she was about to cry, but squeezing her eyes so she didn't.

'I want you to find my mother.'

Mairead frowned, confused. 'But Grandma died when I was eight.'

Mairead's memories of her grandmother were hazy. Her only memory was of a tall woman with white hair telling her off for sucking her thumb. She had been a little frightened of her. She didn't remember her grandfather at all because he had died when she was still a baby.

Her mother bit her lip, her face squeezed tight now.

'I want you to find my birth mother; she might be dead, but then, maybe not,' she said in a voice barely above a whisper.

'Oh, her,' Mairead whispered.

Her mother's request stunned her. For most of her life she had been asking her mother about her birth mother, only to be told it was none of her business. The woman had abandoned her mam when she was a little girl; she'd always said she wanted nothing to do with her.

'But why, Mam? I thought you didn't want to know her—'

Her mother sighed. 'Since I found out I'm sick, I can't stop thinking about her,' she said. 'I need to know why she ran away. It's like this big chain I've been dragging around my whole life.'

'Are you sure you want to know the truth?' Mairead said, thinking about her own ruined marriage. How it had felt as if the truth had destroyed her.

'Yes. Because I've never stopped missing her, Mairead,' her mother said. 'I dream of a reunion, or at the very least some kind of closure. I need to know why she left me.'

Her candour was uncharacteristic. It made Mairead's heart ache for her mother in a way it had never done before.

'I need you to find her,' her mother insisted. 'Her name was Ellen.'

CHAPTER SEVEN

20 OCTOBER 1933

Ellen heaved on the window yet again and tried to push it up, but it was jammed tight. She gave up, wrapping her shawl tighter around her shoulders as her teeth chattered. It was hard to believe just a few weeks ago she and Gladys had been sweltering in their little room. Now an icy wind whistled across Lake Michigan. She had experienced cold winters in New York but always in the comfort of their apartment on Fifth Avenue. Her lodgings in Chicago were another matter altogether. She felt as if the cold penetrated every nook and cranny of the dingy room with holes in the floorboards and peeling paintwork. Their little stove sputtering uselessly. Gladys had warned her from now on it was only going to get colder. Ellen had months of freezing weather to look forward to. Snow, ice, and fearsome winds.

When Gladys was there, it wasn't so bad. They'd get into the lumpy bed together, all their clothes piled on top. Wrapping Gladys's fur about their bodies, they'd sip contraband gin under the covers. Hugging each other like a pair of drowning sailors. But Gladys had been away for two nights now, as was her wont from time to time.

Ellen didn't like being left alone at night because then all her memories would come crowding in on her. Sometimes it felt like she couldn't breathe from the weight of them. Some mornings she might wake up to see her daughter staring down at her with those green eyes accusing. It was hard to do anything then. Sleep. Eat. Get dressed and go into work at the Green Leaf. The only relief was singing. Then she forgot about who she was and became another girl. A conduit for the thoughts and feelings of the punters as she pulled on their heartstrings with her voice, her eyes and the sway of her hips. It seemed she was a natural performer.

When Gladys showed up again, she would be laden with food and booze. They would make jelly and cream cheese sandwiches on thick crusty bread and drink whisky out of teacups while Gladys regaled Ellen with the story of her latest adventure with Tommy Murphy, owner of the Green Leaf and a major player in the North Side gang. Ellen had given up bothering to warn Gladys because she could see her friend was hell-bent on living on the edge. Her self-belief and confidence reminded Ellen of herself before she had run away from Ireland. Gladys was now working with Tommy, who, apart from the speakeasy, doubled as a shady bookkeeper for the Irish mob.

'It's such an easy scam,' Gladys had confided in Ellen. 'Tommy brings me down the dog track and we pick out a few dumb guys. I flutter my eyelashes at them and, after a few drinks, I persuade them to place bets on no-hopers. Tommy puts a big wad on the winning dog and voila!'

Gladys pulled some dollars out of her brassiere and fluttered them upon the bedcovers.

To Ellen, it sounded a risky game. What if one of Gladys's dupes worked out she had tricked them? When Gladys suggested Ellen come in on the con, she had turned her down.

'Say, are you judging me?' Gladys got all prickly.

'No, I just don't have your charm to persuade those guys to bet on losers,' Ellen had explained.

'That ain't true,' Gladys said. 'I see the way the fellas look at you when you're belting out a tune.'

'That's only because I'm acting when I sing.'

'Well, I'm pure actress at the dog track too!' Gladys exclaimed.

'Why don't you come to Hollywood with me then?' Ellen urged. She was worried by the life Gladys was living, hanging out with Tommy and his kind. She'd heard enough to know it wouldn't end well.

'Aw, what would I be doing over in California?' Gladys said. 'Chicago's where I'm at!'

'Every day someone's getting shot, North Side or South Side,' Ellen said, shivering as she said the words.

'They don't shoot girls!' Gladys said confidently, counting up her dollars. 'Say, how much you got saved now?'

Each week since she had begun work at the Green Leaf, Ellen had been amassing her stash for the train fare to Los Angeles. Once she added her tips from the night before, Ellen reckoned she had enough for the train fare and rent for a couple of months before she had to find work in Hollywood. She was waiting until Gladys showed up to try one more time to persuade her to come with her. Ellen's livelihood in the speakeasy was a double-edged sword. It meant she'd been able to get the money together to move on quickly, but she had been thrust into a world that made her very uneasy. This was violence without any purpose. It made no sense to her. One day an Italian was shot, the next an Irishman, seemingly without any reason other than to get back at each other. In Ireland violence had been a different matter. A fight for survival.

Ellen had never walked the streets of South Side Chicago, having been warned by Gladys not to risk it because she was known as one of the Irish girls. Ellen wanted to get the hell out before she got caught up in the warring gangs. But she owed Gladys. If it wasn't for her Kansas friend, she might have starved on the streets when she first showed up in Chicago. Her first week singing, her purse with all her dollars had been stolen in the speakeasy. Ellen hadn't had the rent and Gladys had covered her.

'Just write me an IOU,' she had said, winking at her.

The light was beginning to fade, and it was time to get ready. She shrugged off her shawl and peeled off her layers of clothing, thinking of the warmth of the speakeasy once she got inside. She put on a sparkly emerald-green dress that belonged to Gladys but which her friend said suited her more.

'Makes your red hair look on fire!'

It was way too cold to go down the freezing corridor to the washroom, so she dabbed her wrists, behind her ears, and under her arms with some of the fancy eau de toilette Tommy Murphy had bought Gladys. Her Kansas friend called Tommy her fella, despite the fact he was married with three children. Ellen had had plenty of offers from would-be beaus, but she had turned them all down. She had learned her lesson. Men held you back.

She painted her lips scarlet before plucking one of Gladys's heavy coats from the wardrobe and wrapping it around her. She could have taken the fur, but the truth was she never liked the feel of animal skin upon her own. Besides, she felt less conspicuous in the dark woollen coat.

Outside on the street, the wind cut into her face. She lowered her head, her hat pulled down tight, and her collar up to protect the bare nape of her neck. It was four blocks north to the Green Leaf. Not worth the streetcar ride or a cab. Though Tommy always got her one when she had to go home. He was decent like that. She glanced at the slender gold watch on her wrist. It was the only item of jewellery given to her by Giles that she had kept. The thought of her husband seemed so strange to her now. What would he make of her new life as a nightclub singer in the speakeasies of Chicago?

'He just wouldn't believe you had it in you, Ellie,' she whispered to herself. He didn't even know she could sing. Her husband had never known who she really was.

She pushed thoughts of Giles away, because always on their tail would be memories of Brigid. Those men thought she was singing to them every night in the speakeasy, but the reason she pulled on their heartstrings was because she was always singing to her daughter, no matter what the song.

Ellen hadn't even turned the corner onto the last block before she knew something was up. The street seemed strangely empty. It was eight o'clock on a Friday night and usually the sidewalks were heaving with revellers. But it felt like she was the only one walking apart from the odd hobo or drunk shrinking into an empty doorway. She crossed the street and turned to walk down to the Green Leaf. Ahead of her were four cop cars mounted on the sidewalk outside the restaurant. People were being herded into the back of a police van. She stood frozen in shock as she saw Gerald the violinist and Pete the saxophonist being manhandled by the cops. The scene didn't seem real at all. She had seen cops every single night she'd sung at the speakeasy. Sitting drinking whisky out of teacups, just like everyone else. Now they were rounding their fellow drinkers up, waving batons at them and barking orders.

Before she knew what to do, she felt someone grab her arm and hoist her back into a side alley.

'Don't let them see you, for Christsakes!' It was Angie, all muffled up in her fur. The whites of her eyes glinting in the dark alley.

'What happened?'

'The Italians, that's what happened. Guess their police bribes are bigger than the Irish mob's,' she said. 'And then there's those new men from Hoover's Bureau of Investigation. They ain't taking any bribes.'

'Where's Tommy?' Ellen's throat went dry. She wanted to say Gladys's name but she couldn't get it out.

Angie gave a long low whistle.

'Oh boy, he has sure done it,' she said. 'Word is he conned the wrong guy at the dog track. One of Capone's fellas who didn't get banged up with his boss.' She shook her head. 'I don't reckon he'll be safe any place in Chicago now.'

'Gladys?' Ellen whispered.

Angie gave her a hawkish look. 'You need to stay away from her, Ellie, that girl is dangerous.'

'But we share a room—'

'Look, my betting is she and Tommy have hightailed it out of here for a while,' she said. 'I've got a new gig at one of the South Side speakeasies. I can put a word in for you, but I don't think they take on white girl singers.'

'It's OK,' Ellen said. 'I was leaving anyway. I'm going west.'

Angie nodded.

'I reckon that's the right choice, Ellie. You get going. Tonight now. Don't go back to your place. Just keep on walking to the train station, you hear me?'

To her surprise, Angie hugged her. They had never had such a long conversation before.

'You take care now, Ellie Irish,' she said.

'You too, Angie.'

Ellen had to go back to her lodgings because that was where her money was stashed. She scurried down the dark streets, this time the wind behind her pushing her onward. She knew there was a train leaving that night for Los Angeles because she had gone down to the station weeks ago to find out all the train schedules and ticket prices.

Round the last corner, she looked over her shoulder. There was a couple walking in the other direction on the opposite sidewalk, and a hobo shuffled past her. She pushed through the outside door and ran up the staircase, almost tripping on her green dress. As she unlocked her door, she prayed Gladys would be on the other side, sitting up in their bed with a bottle of gin for them to share. Complaining about the cold. But the room was as she had left it. Her instincts were screaming at her to move fast. She pulled the green Louis Vuitton case out from under the bed and the sight of it brought a jolt to her heart. It had come with her from Ireland all the way to New York, and then on to Chicago. It was battered now, and worn from the years. But she remembered it as it once was. The brass corners shiny, the green exterior unscratched. Full of promise as it caught the light in the hallway of the big house back home in Ireland. She swallowed down the memory. Pushed it to the back of her mind as she went into the little kitchenette, opened the cupboard and took out the coffee tin. She pushed her hands into the coffee grounds and pulled out her dollars. But it wasn't enough. She thrust her hand back in; just a couple more dollars came up. She poured the coffee grounds out onto the counter. A small square of paper fell out. She unfolded it.

IOU 40 DOLLARS LOVE GLADYS

She gasped in horror.

'No! no!' she sobbed. A part of her was furious with Gladys. How could she rob her of her hard-earned cash? But then in her heart she knew Gladys probably had intended to pay her back from her winnings at the dog track. She couldn't believe her own friend would steal from her.

Ellen counted what was left: forty-eight dollars. It wasn't enough to get all the way to Los Angeles, but she had to give it her best shot. She couldn't stay in Chicago. Not after what Angie had told her. She knew enough to know that the men looking for Tommy would turn up at her lodgings soon and she didn't want to be there when they did. She tore off the sparkly green dress and pulled on one of her old New York dresses. Blue silk and classy. She pulled out the only fur Gladys had left in the wardrobe and stuffed it in the case. She would sell her watch and the fur once she got as far away as she could. Surely that would be enough to set her up in Hollywood? She had no plan. Just the hunger to act and the hope that she would be lucky.

She locked the door behind her. No point leaving it open in case Gladys turned up. As she was hurrying down the stairs, she realised she hadn't left her friend a note of farewell. But the skip in her heart told her she didn't need to. She had a feeling Gladys would never be coming back. She gave a little hiccup of grief as she came to the last step. How many times was she going to have to run away?

Just as she was about to take hold of the door handle to the street, it was jerked out of her grasp. She came face to face with a dark-haired man, his face full of fury. He had a scar on his forehead and was broad and stocky.

'Hey, slow down, Charlie,' a voice came from behind him. 'You're going to knock the dame down.'

Charlie pushed past her as a tall thin man emerged into the dim hallway. He was wearing a trilby and a big overcoat.

'Hey, doll, where you running to this late at night?' he said, looking at her suitcase.

'My mother's sick, I'm taking a bus home,' she squeaked, not daring to look in his eyes.

'Where to?' His eyes narrowed.

'Kansas.' She said the first place which came into her head.

'Thought there was no one left in Kansas City!' the man said sarcastically. 'All blown out by those big dust storms.'

'Come on, Rick.' Charlie was at the foot of the staircase. 'Stop flirting with the dame.'

She could feel Rick's gaze upon her as she squirmed under his scrutiny.

'OK, doll, you go on,' he whispered. 'I seen you sing. Be a real shame to break your wings.'

She raised her eyes and he was smiling at her, his teeth bared like a dog.

'Scram,' he hissed. 'Before my pal Charlie works out who you are.'

She bolted out the door and legged it down the street, barrelling into the icy wind. She ran down the sidewalk, not even stopping to see if there was a streetcar. Her fragile Chicago life had fallen apart, and she was on the move again.

The green case banged into her leg as she pushed against the icy air and the last leaves from the trees whirled around her. Her hat nearly blew off and she held it down with her free hand. Only a few more blocks and she was at the train station. As she ran, she thought of Brigid again. Her daughter was in Dublin now with her father in the big white house by the sea. She had thought nothing could be worse than going back home to Ireland. But this was worse. Her ending in Ireland would have been short and decisive rather than this terrifying sprint to the train station. Her dreams of being an actress were futile. Who was she kidding? Her life now was untethered. No one to love and none who needed her. She had even lost Gladys.

She made it to the train station, not daring to look behind her; terrified any minute she'd feel Charlie's heavy hand on her shoulder. The Santa Fe to Los Angeles was leaving in twenty minutes, but her money was only enough for an upper berth to a place called Flagstaff in Arizona. She would just have to stay on the train as long as possible. Try to dodge the conductor. Anything would be better than spending one more minute in Chicago.

As the train pulled out of Union Station, too late, it hit her. She was putting even more distance between herself and Brigid. More than the sea, a whole vast landscape of great plains and mountain ranges. She pressed her trembling fingers to her face. Her grief as raw as the day she had abandoned her daughter. She was bad through and through. She had recognised the fury of violence in the thug Charlie's eyes because she had felt that same fury once herself. She knew how anger could make you do terrible things. For an instant the lights flickered in the train carriage, and she saw the hallway again in the big house and a pool of crimson blood. The death and destruction of her own making. She deserved to suffer for the rest of her life.

The train began to pick up speed, and Ellen thought about getting up. Walking down its length and opening the door in the very last carriage. She pictured herself taking flight and throwing her body onto the tracks, or off into a ravine, or over a bridge into the sky to fall and fall and fall and never get up again. All that would be left of her would be the green suitcase with the brass corners, a bunch of clothes, and a crushed fur. But as she squeezed her eyes shut, she saw her life as if it were on a movie screen flickering in black and white. She dressed it up with fiction. The mobster's moll, the speakeasy songstress, running away in the middle of the night. The gangsters hot on her heels. But she had endured. Ellie was a fighter. She had to survive so that some day Brigid could find her. She believed in the bond between them. The world was not so cruel as to break it forever. There must be a way they could see each other again.

Ellen opened the green case and pulled out the small bottle of gin she'd thrown inside. She took a swig to calm her nerves. She had to keep going for Brigid's sake.

CHAPTER EIGHT

Mairead's mother gave her the turquoise necklace the night after she told her she had cancer.

'This is yours now,' her mother said, opening a drawer in her dressing table and extracting the necklace.

Mairead gawped at the sight of it. She had never seen the necklace before and couldn't believe her mother owned such an ornate item. Her mother always wore her own silver jewellery designs, which, though precious, were minimalist.

Her mother dangled the necklace out to Mairead. It was gold with a huge star-shaped pendant inlaid with sky-blue turquoise, pearls and rose-cut diamonds.

'Where did you get it from?' Mairead asked, ogling the necklace.

'Take it, please,' her mother said, grabbing hold of Mairead's hand and forcing it into it. Mairead looked down at the beautiful turquoise stone. The blue of it was so intense it made her think of swimming in the sea.

'It's stunning, Mammy,' she said. 'And must be worth a lot, I can't—'

'It belonged to my mother,' her mam said, stepping back to her bed, and sitting on top of it. 'Not my stepmother. My birth mother. Ellen.'

Mairead had known nothing about her mother's birth mother apart from the stark fact she had abandoned her daughter and husband the night before they were due to sail from New York to Galway in 1933.

'My father gave me the necklace just before he died,' she said. 'He said my mother had left it for me the night she disappeared.'

Her mother wrapped her arms around her thin frame and sighed.

'I had been angry he had hidden it from me my whole life, but he was so sick by then there was no point in telling him so.'

Mairead placed her finger on the giant turquoise. Its opaque blueness was hypnotic.

'I began to wonder what else he hadn't told me, but it was too late to ask him. After he died, I was so busy with you and Darragh, your daddy and my career. Every time I took the necklace out to put it on, I took it off because it felt wrong.'

Her mother began to pleat her bedcover between her hands.

'I decided the best thing was just to let it be. I had my stepmother. I had all of you. My birth mother had played no role in my life.'

Mairead remembered she had tried to ask her mam about her past, but she'd always been cut short.

'It's not important,' she had been told. 'She left us. And my father remarried. Grandma Olivia was my real mother. She raised me.'

But now at last her mother was opening up to Mairead. It felt like such a delicate thing. Like a small flower. She spoke carefully. Inching her way to more information.

'Why are you telling me this now, Mam?' Mairead asked. 'You always said she wasn't important.'

Her mother shook her head.

'I was lying, of course. I just didn't want to deal with my feelings. Bottled them all up.'

Mairead found herself feeling sorry for her mother. This terrible thing had happened to her as a little girl. No wonder she found it hard to relate to her own daughter.

'But now, Mairead, I need to know what happened to my mother. I just can't rest until I do. I need closure.'

Mairead held the necklace up to the light. The diamonds sparkled, bouncing tiny rainbows off the bedroom wall.

'Did you ever wear the necklace?' she asked her mother.

'No, never, but I took it out sometimes to look at it,' her mother confided.

'It's so beautiful,' Mairead said.

'Yes, it is,' her mother said. 'But it never made me feel good. When I would take it out and look at its opulence, it would make me very sad. But somehow I couldn't bring myself to part with it; I needed to know it was there in my dressing table drawer, even though it brought back painful memories.'

'Like what?' Mairead pushed gently. Years of suppressed curiosity bubbling within her.

'I remembered my mother kissing me goodnight, and she would be wearing the necklace,' her mam said. 'The scent of her perfume sweet as roses, and the sensation of her skin against mine. So soft.'

'Do you remember what she looked like?'

'Yes.' Her mother paused and licked her lips. 'She had red hair. Like you.'

Her mother's words gave her a start. Mairead was the only one in their family with red hair. She had hated its brilliance, because people always touched it and commented on how bright it was. She had often wondered why she was the only redhead in their family. Now she knew: she had inherited it from her grandmother.

Mairead weighed the heavy pendant in her cupped palms. She knew nothing about jewellery, but even she could tell it was valuable. Her grandparents must have been wealthy when they lived in New York. She had been told enough times her grandfather had been one of the architects working on the new skyscrapers in Manhattan, but there had been a big gap in the stories when it came to his first wife, Ellen.

'I remember she took me to the theatre to see *Alice's Adventures in Wonderland*,' her mother said in a quiet voice. 'She was so excited. More than me, I think!'

Mairead looked at her mother with new eyes. She had always seen her as an Irishwoman through and through. Belonging to the rugged Atlantic coast. But she had been a little girl in the big city of New York once. She had been born in America.

'Mammy, you're American!' she exclaimed.

Her mother shook her head.

'Not any more, I was registered as an Irish citizen by my father when we returned to Ireland,' she said. 'I have actually looked into it because I thought it might help Darragh get his US citizenship.'

Mairead's thoughts turned to her brother, who had been distraught when she had rung him with the news of their mother's cancer that afternoon.

'Darragh wants to come home, Mam.'

'He can't.' Her mother shook her head emphatically. 'He'll lose everything. I won't let him do it.'

'But, Mammy, he just wants to be with you,' Mairead protested.

'Tell him I'll come see him before I get too sick—'

Mairead looked at her mother's wan face. She could see in her eyes she was lying, but she didn't know what to do about her brother either. As an illegal immigrant in America, he was left with a terrible choice. Either give up his whole life in New York and come home to see his mother die, or preserve his life, his family, his bar and miss their last goodbye.

'I could go with you, and Darragh could help us find your mother,' Mairead suggested.

Her mother's eyes flickered. 'I just want this to be between us for now, Mairead,' she said.

'But why? Wouldn't it be easier for Darragh to find out things, seeing as he lives in New York?'

'He'll tell Josie,' her mam said, referring to her daughter-in-law. 'Then she'll tell her family in Wexford, and I just want to keep this business private for now. Between you and me. Not even Stella must know.'

Mairead understood how Darragh could be. She loved her brother, and he was a big-hearted soul, but he had no tact, no ability to keep secrets. He had a tendency to bulldoze his way forward without considering other people.

On the phone this afternoon, he had pushed for her to persuade their mother to have chemotherapy.

'She says she won't,' Mairead told him. 'She says there's no point.'

'She needs to fight it.'

'I'll try, but I can't force her.'

Her brother was in shock and denial. She could tell by his tone that he thought there was hope, but he hadn't seen their mam since she'd last visited him. Mairead had noticed a big change in her since Easter. Her mother's movements were so much slower, heavier with pain, and her appetite was minuscule. She told Mairead that it hurt to eat; it was all she could do to eat light food such as slices of pear or braised tofu.

'Turn the necklace over,' her mother said. In the back of the pendant was a small black-and-white photograph of a woman with a baby.

'Oh my God, Mam! Is that you as a baby?' she asked, astonished her mother had never shared this image with her before.

'Yes, with my mother, Ellen,' she said. 'You look like her.'

Mairead stared at the image of the young woman and baby. She was so young, like a child herself. Staring intensely at the camera and clasping the baby tightly. There was a look of her own daughter Stella in her mother as a baby. The generations of women in her family woven into each other.

'There are other pictures,' her mother revealed.

Mairead looked up at her with a start.

'I've never seen them,' she said.

There were spots of pink on her mother's cheeks.

'I stole them from my father's house,' she said, her voice almost a whisper. 'He had hidden them under a loose floorboard in his study. I found them quite by accident because I tripped on the floorboard. It was when you were a baby, and we were visiting him and your grandma Olivia...'

Her mother paused, and spread her hands on her bedcovers.

'I had gone inside to get a glass of water and was walking into the house through the porch windows, which led through the study. Do you remember the house in Dublin where your grandfather lived?'

'Vaguely,' Mairead said. 'I remember seeing Grandma Olivia there. It was white and there was a big garden right by the sea.'

'That's right,' her mother said. 'I spent most of my childhood in the garden playing on my own. It was left to my half-brother, Leonard. He sold it.'

Uncle Leonard. He hadn't been mentioned for years either. She had heard the bitter tale so many times. How he had been left everything – all the money and the big house in Blackrock when Grandma Olivia passed away. Her mother, despite being the eldest child, had been left with nothing because she was a girl. Leonard had sold up and emigrated to Australia, barely a year after Grandma Olivia had died.

'Mammy, should I tell Uncle Leonard you're sick?'

Her mother shrugged. 'We lost contact years ago; I've no idea where he is now.'

The idea of cutting her own brother out of her life seemed impossible, but Mairead left it. Her mother was different from her. Besides, she wanted to know more about the photographs.

'So when I got up after tripping, I could see there was something under the floorboard. I prised it away and the plank came free. Behind it was a dusty old album. Without thinking, I put it in my bag, which I'd left in the hall.'

'Where is it now?' Mairead asked.

Her mother pointed at the wardrobe.

'In the top,' she said. 'Under a pile of jumpers.'

Mairead stood on a chair and hunted around in the top of the wardrobe. Her hand landed on the soft leather of an album cover. She dragged it out and stepped off the chair. Sat down on her mother's bed and placed it before her. Without saying anything, her mother opened the first page.

It was a photograph of a young couple standing in front of a picture palace in New York City. The man was a younger version of Grandfather Giles and the woman was not the grandmother Mairead had known. It was the same woman as in the back of the necklace.

Underneath were the words *With Ellen.*

'My goodness, it's a while since I've looked at these pictures, but she really does look like you, Mairead.'

Ellen was small, with curly hair. In the picture, it was cut short in a bob, and she wore a cloche hat. She had big round eyes like Mairead's. Her lips were pressed together and quite narrow, but she had a slight protrusion of her front teeth just like Mairead had.

Ellen looked like her! No wonder her mother had resented her all these years.

Her mother turned the page. The same couple, this time proudly holding a baby. Pictures of a little girl with dark curls and a small dog. The woman holding the child and beaming with joy. The child was her mother.

It was a whole other life. Mairead felt like she was looking at one of her school history books and yet this was the real story of her mother's childhood before she had come to Ireland. She had lived through the Roaring Twenties in New York. Been there during the Wall Street Crash. Of course Mairead had always known this, but to see it in front of her in black-and-white photographs made it real.

'That's a picture of us in front of our apartment building on Park Avenue,' her mam said.

'You lived on Park Avenue?' Mairead asked, incredulous.

'It wasn't as expensive or exclusive to live there then, although I do remember our apartment seemed huge,' her mother said, staring down at the photograph. 'There was a wooden parquet floor in the dining room which the maid polished every week. Afterwards, I used to skate on it in my stockings.'

'Do you remember the dog?'

Her mother frowned. 'Yes... he was called Buttons,' she said. 'I think my parents gave him to my nanny when we left New York. I missed him a lot.'

Mairead wanted to ask so many questions about her mother's life in New York. Clues as to how she might find Ellen now, what had happened to her. But her mother suddenly pushed the photograph album away.

'I need to sleep,' she said, sinking down onto her pillows.

'Can I get you anything?'

'No, just leave me alone.' Her mother's voice had reverted to its usual coolness. Mairead forced herself not to take offence. Her mother was sick and suffering. No wonder she was short with her.

She picked the album up off the bed and carried it into her old bedroom. Looked at the photographs again and again. Always she was drawn to her grandmother Ellen's face. She stared at it as if trying to solve the mystery of her disappearance. She looked like an ordinary girl. She was clearly a doting mother. What could have made her abandon her child in the way she did?

Mairead closed the album and took up the necklace again. It twisted in her hands in the shafts of moonlight falling through her open curtains. Mairead could never have imagined owning such a thing herself. It was breathtaking, as rare and extravagant as Ellen in her silk dresses and furs in the photograph album.

. . .

Mairead tossed and turned, restless in the bed. She had brought no night things with her. It was the second night she was sleeping in an old T-shirt of her mother's, which added to her overall sense of confusion, guilt and shock. Her mother had terminal cancer. No, she wasn't going to believe it. Miracles happened all the time. She'd heard the stories of people healing themselves from cancer with alternative therapies. If her mother refused to have chemotherapy, then she would find out what else they could try. She lay in bed, her eyes pinned wide open, looking at the necklace catching the moonlight where she had hung it on the mirror on her childhood dressing table. Her mother was not going to die. She was too young. Mairead wasn't going to let it happen.

She must have dropped off eventually because she woke with a start to hear rain falling outside. Behind the sound of the rain, she heard her mother calling out.

'*Mammy!*'

Mairead sat bolt upright in bed. Was that really her mother's voice? She sounded quite unlike her usual husky, scathing self.

'*Mammy! Where are you?*'

The wail rose again, and the sound of it made Mairead shiver. Reluctantly she got out of bed and pulled on one of her mother's old baggy sweaters.

Her mother was curled up on her bed in the place between dreams and lucidity. Her head was in her hands, and Alfie was nosing his muzzle through the gaps in her fingers.

Mairead put her arms around her mother's shoulders as the older woman dropped her hands, heavy upon the sheets.

'I was dreaming about my mammy,' she whispered. 'I had forgotten...' She sighed, turned to look at Mairead. She was startled to see tears in her mother's eyes. She had never seen her cry before.

'I remember waking up in the morning and she wasn't there,' she said, her voice trembling with emotion. 'My father... oh, he was so angry...'

'Was this on the boat, Mammy?'

'Yes, the first day of our journey,' she said. 'When I fell asleep, she was sitting on the end of my bed, but when I woke the next morning, she was gone off the ship. We were in the middle of the sea.'

Her mother gave a shaky sigh.

'I was scared she had fallen overboard, but my father told me she had left him a letter.'

'What did it say?'

'He wouldn't tell me. I watched him rip it up. He refused to discuss it and said I was never to talk of her ever again.'

'He never told you what happened to her?'

'Never. On the boat I cried and cried. Told him I wanted my mammy every day. In the end he had to spank me. I remember his exact words: "Brigid, your mother is dead to us."'

'He never told you where she went?'

'No.' Her mother looked up at her, wiping her wet eyes with the sleeve of her pyjama top as Alfie licked her cheeks. 'I was banned from talking about her. We had to tell everyone she died so he could marry Grandma Olivia.'

'So, my grandfather was a bigamist?' Mairead asked, feeling shocked.

Her mother shrugged. 'I never thought of it like that.' She gave a short laugh. 'No wonder I was banned from mentioning it!'

Mairead sat down heavily on the end of her mother's bed.

'Please find her for me, Mairead,' her mother said after a while. 'I tried to cut her out of my heart. But she was so loving. Always tucking me into bed, reading to me. We loved *Alice's Adventures in Wonderland* and *Alice Through the Looking Glass*. Once, we had a Mad Hatter's tea party! Imagine! I dressed up as Alice, my mother was the rabbit and my father the Mad Hatter. Nanny was the March Hare and the maid the dormouse.' She gave a sniff, smiling at the memory. 'Oh, those first years in Ireland I missed her so much. I prayed and prayed for her to come find me. I imagined she had got lost like Alice. Fallen down a rabbit hole or stepped through a looking glass. But she never came back.'

Mairead felt a little stab in her heart because her own mother had never been as loving towards her. She had never read her stories. That had been her father's domain. And there had certainly never been any fancy-dress parties.

'But when my father met Grandma Olivia and married her, I gave up.' She gave a hard bark of a laugh. 'I thought I could turn all that love off. Be indifferent. The truth is, my heart is still broken. She did a dreadful thing. What kind of woman abandons her daughter?'

Mairead bit her lip. She had always felt a sea between herself and mother. Shifting waters and uneven ground. As if her mother had been a stranger to her, the whole of her life. She too had felt abandoned by her mother, but in a different way.

'It's why I was always careful with you,' her mother said, as if reading Mairead's thoughts.

'What do you mean?'

'I tried not to let you get too attached to me.' Her mother faltered. 'Because I was too close to my mother and when she was gone—'

Her mother broke off and looked away. Mairead felt as if she'd been punched in the stomach. Her mother had *intentionally* pushed her away all these years.

'So, when I'm gone, I hope it won't hurt as much as when your daddy died,' her mam said, in barely above a whisper.

'Stop it, will you?' Mairead stood up. Anger arching through her body. 'How can you say such a thing?'

They stared at each other. Mairead's face was tight with emotion, her eyes swelling with tears.

'Oh...' her mother said weakly.

'Of course, I love you, Mam,' Mairead said. 'I'm going to do everything I can to help you get better.'

'Oh, Mairead,' her mother said, her eyes full of sorrow. 'I'm sorry.'

The words fell like stones at her feet. Mairead was frozen in surprise. Her mother had never said sorry to her before.

'Will you help me find my mother, Mairead?' she asked in a weak voice.

'She could be dead.'

'Maybe,' her mother said. 'But I want to know what happened to her. I've been carrying this rejection around my whole life. The only way I can let it go is to know the truth.'

CHAPTER NINE

Ellen walked down what looked like the main street in Flagstaff, Arizona. She passed a hotel and a grocery store. The conductor had kicked her off the train late last night despite her pleas to let her stay on until Los Angeles. People had turned away with embarrassment at the spectacle as she had been ordered off at the next station.

'Consider yourself lucky I don't get the cops involved,' the conductor had admonished her.

She spent the hours before dawn curled up in a corner of the waiting room at Flagstaff station. She was still stiff from being confined in her berth, let alone sleeping on the hard bench in the station. While she had slept that first night, the train had cut across the centre of the country. She had woken the next morning to a different America to either New York or Chicago. Staring out the window as the hours passed, looking at the vast dusty plains Gladys had told her about. When they'd made a stop in Kansas, she imagined her old roommate jumping on. Ellen missed her. Gladys's company had provided a buffer against the reality of being without Brigid. She prayed Gladys had got away from the

Italians and the cops. That her new friend was OK wherever she was. She would never know. She doubted their paths would cross again. On her own, Ellen felt exposed and broken. At this time of year, back in the garden of their apartment building in New York, the leaves on the trees would be turning gold, red and brown. Brigid would be kicking through piles of them in her green coat and new winter boots, her dark brown hair the same colour as the burnished horse chestnuts. With her daughter by her side, Ellen had felt she had purpose. Being a mother had made up for everything she had left behind in Ireland. When she closed her eyes, she could smell the scent of the crisp fall day in New York. The earthiness of their garden, the fragrance of apples as she and Brigid crunched into them, grinning at each other. She could still smell her daughter. The soft sweetness of her pure skin. It made her ache in the pit of her belly. When she had opened her eyes again, Brigid was gone, the trees were gone and she was staring out at boundless prairie, barren and desolate.

Despite it being fall, and morning still, in Flagstaff, Arizona the sun blazed down upon her, and the sky was seamless blue. She could feel it pinking her pale skin even though she wore her hat. She crossed to the shadier side of the street. Her stomach was rattling with hunger, but she only had twenty cents left in her purse. She still had Gladys's fur and her wristwatch, but there was no sign for a pawn shop in Flagstaff where she could exchange them for money. She walked past the door of a diner and the scent of fried potatoes made her mouth water. She stopped to look inside. The place was half empty. Maybe they'd let her wash some dishes in exchange for a meal?

She approached the counter, her eyes drawn to a cherry pie oozing with red filling under a glass dome. She licked her lips, imagining its sweet tartness in her mouth. The diner was empty apart from two men sitting in a booth at the back. Ellen slipped onto one of the stools at the counter and waited.

The waitress took her time serving the men, before ambling over to Ellen.

'What ya want, lady?' she asked, looking her up and down. 'We got corn cakes and bacon strips, eggs and French-fried potatoes, or eggs and hot cakes, all with coffee.'

Ellen pushed her hair under her hat, and smoothed down her dress, grubby from her journey. She so badly wanted a piece of the pie, but she should be sensible and get the breakfast meal.

'How much?'

The waitress frowned at her. She had a sharp face, with beady eyes. 'Thirty-five cents for the first two, thirty cents for the eggs and hot cakes. Free coffee refill.'

Ellen opened up her purse and counted out her twenty cents.

'Can I have a slice of cherry pie instead?' she asked.

'That'll be thirty-five cents,' the waitress told her. 'We got toast and coffee too for twenty-five cents.'

'Oh,' Ellen said bleakly. 'I guess I'll just have a cup of coffee then.'

She tried to build up the courage to ask if she could wash dishes for her dinner, or a piece of pie, but the waitress was so unfriendly it was off-putting. Where had her pluck gone? The audacity which had got her to America in the first place? It was as if the eight years of her marriage had softened her. And the loss of Brigid had knocked all the bravado out of her.

The waitress poured her a cup of black coffee.

'It's extra for cream,' she said.

'I wonder—' Ellen began to say.

'Yeah?' the waitress said, hands on hips.

'Can I wash the dishes in exchange for dinner?'

'We got a pot-washer. Ain't no jobs here, lady.' The waitress looked her up and down. 'Ain't you got a fella to buy you your breakfast?' Her tone was sarcastic.

Ellen's cheeks bloomed red.

'No, I'm on my own,' she began.

'You don't look like a hard luck story in your Sunday best.'

'Aw, Cherie, leave her alone,' a voice said from behind Ellen. 'The girl's hungry. Have you no heart?'

'I can't be giving out free food, Frank,' Cherie said crossly.

'Looky here,' Frank said. 'I'll buy the little lady her breakfast.'

Ellen wanted to refuse the stranger's offer, but she was so hungry. He was a big friendly-looking man, with a trilby hat on his head and rolled up shirtsleeves exposing meaty arms.

'Well, all right then,' said Cherie. 'What you want?'

'Eggs and hot cakes,' Ellen said, feeling humiliated, but so hungry she couldn't refuse the offer.

Cherie poured her a cup of coffee and went off to get her food.

'Thank you,' Ellen said, as Frank sat down next to her at the counter.

'You're welcome,' he said. 'You're new to town, right?'

She nodded.

'You staying put, or heading elsewhere?'

Ellen took a gulp of the black scalding coffee.

'I was thinking...' She faltered. 'I want to get to California.'

Frank barked a laugh.

'You've a ways to go, little lady. You got transportation?'

She shook her head, just as Cherie returned and placed the plate of eggs and hot cakes on the counter in front of her. She dived in, unable to stop herself.

'Well, this is your lucky day. Me and my colleague Vernon here are driving down to Phoenix today. We can take you there. You'd be best placed to get work in Phoenix. It's a city. Lots of visitors.'

At home, in Ireland, she would have taken a lift from a friendly stranger without a worry, but here in a place she'd never been before she wasn't so sure. She scooped more food into her mouth and her mind began to clear from the fog of hunger.

'Thanks,' she said. 'But I reckon I should stay put and look for work in Flagstaff so I can save up the train fare to California.'

Frank raised his eyebrows. 'You heard Cherie: there isn't any work for no one on Route 66. Everyone is on the move. Your best bet is to keep on going south-west or stop in Phoenix, otherwise known as the Valley of the Sun to earn your train fare.'

She cut into one of her eggs, the yolk spreading like a gold lake on her plate.

'There's casinos, and clubs there where you could do well. Pretty girl like you,' Frank continued. She stopped eating, considered what he was saying. She was used to men telling her she was pretty. She knew it was just talk.

'Look, if you're worried about your safety, let me put your mind at rest.' Frank pulled a badge out of his inside jacket pocket. 'I work for the Bureau of Investigation, as does Vernon.'

Ellen immediately tensed. If Frank was trying to allay her fears, his revelation had the exact opposite effect. Her weeks in Chicago had trained her to be wary of cops, in particular the new Bureau of Investigation agents.

'What are you doing here?' She braved the question.

'This is one of our pit-stops, we always come here for breakfast,' he said. 'We've been on the road for days. Heading down to Phoenix.' He didn't tell her why.

Ellen took a sip of her coffee and considered her options. If there was no work in Flagstaff, she didn't have much choice. She'd no money and would have to hitch a ride anyway. She didn't like cops but at least Frank had been upfront with her. It sounded like they had nothing to do with her world in Chicago.

'OK, thanks,' she said.

'No problem,' Frank said. 'Where you from anyway?'

'Chicago...' She paused. 'New York.'

'No, where you came from, darling? That ain't no New York accent.'

'Ireland,' she said, head down into her food.

'The old country! Should have guessed with your red hair and lily-white skin.'

She squirmed under his gaze, regretting her decision to take a ride, but he was from the Bureau of Investigation and the waitress knew him. He wasn't a total random guy. She needed to keep moving towards California. Everything was pinned on her fragile dream. As long as she kept going, she wouldn't have to face all that she had lost.

As she finished off her coffee, Frank's fellow agent joined them.

'This here is Mr Vernon Willis,' Frank told her. 'Originally from Iowa.'

Vernon tipped his hat at her. Like Frank, he wore a heavy overcoat more suited to back east than the Midwest. He was taller and bigger than Frank, close-shaven and with eyes the colour of the Arizona skies.

'What's your name, ma'am?' Vernon asked, his tone far more formal than Frank's.

'Ellen,' she said.

'Mrs or Miss?' Frank intervened, his gaze piercing.

'Miss Ellen Lavelle,' she said, steering clear of both her married name and her stage name in Chicago.

Frank slapped the money for the food on the counter, as she slipped off her stool and picked up her case.

'We'll be seeing you, Cherie!' He waved goodbye.

The waitress had crossed her arms and was shaking her head at them. Ellen wasn't too sure who she was disapproving of but felt her glare as she followed the men to the black Ford parked outside the diner.

Frank opened the back door for her. She pushed her case in before her and then settled into the back.

'It's going to take us all day to get to Phoenix, so you make yourself comfortable now, Miss Ellen Lavelle,' Frank said as Vernon took off his heavy overcoat and put it in the back with her. Frank settled into the driver's seat, while Vernon got in beside him, his gun on display in its holster.

They took off along the dusty road out of downtown Flagstaff. As they headed west and south they overtook a whole line of trucks, pickups, and cars overflowing with families and belongings.

Before long though they turned off onto another road passing through sparse parched forest and hilly territory. The earth seemed to redden and she gazed in wonder at the strange mountains. Giant boulders in huge formations. The sky was clear blue, and she saw a huge bird circling above.

'It's an eagle,' Vernon told her, turning round in his seat to offer her a cigarette.

She gazed in wonder at the beautiful sweep of the bird. How powerful it looked, gliding above them. The landscape was hypnotic. She wished they could stop the car and she could walk in her bare feet on the hot red earth. Examine the strange bulbous plants called cacti, covered in spikes. There was an energy in this place which felt otherworldly. She had got this feeling in church sometimes. She would be praying on her knees and next thing she would be floating above herself looking down. This was how it felt in this valley of rocks which looked like cathedrals, scorching blue sky, and swooping predatory birds. The air was still, and yet it felt within her that a storm was raging. There was a ringing in her ears. A voice whispering to her. *Get out of the car. Get out.*

But they didn't stop, and of course she didn't ask them to. Where would she have gone? Disappeared into the ancient rocks?

Eventually they left this strange place and began to wend uphill. The floating sensation left her. Up and up the Ford struggled. Ellen didn't want to think how far they would plunge if the car went off the edge of the narrow winding mountain road. At last, they began heading downhill again and the land softened around them. Trees, their piney scent wafting into the car's open windows. Pleasantly refreshing and lifting the stench of body sweat from both men.

Ellen thought about what she would do when they arrived in Phoenix. Frank referred to its vicinity as the Valley of the Sun. A place wealthy tourists came. Surely, she could get work in a hotel or restaurant to tide her over until she could get to California?

The Ford scaled another high mountain, at the top of which was the mining town of Jerome. The whole place was stark and barren, with not one tree for shade.

'Used to be booming,' Fred shouted over his shoulder at her. 'But the Depression has hit it hard.'

They kept on down the other side of the mountain and into the town of Prescott. Frank pulled up at a gas station to fill up the car.

'You hungry?' Vernon asked her while Frank was paying for the gas.

'I'm fine,' she said. The sun was beginning to sink in the sky, and she was anxious to get to Phoenix before nightfall. But when Frank came back to the car, Vernon suggested they get a meal in the hotel diner.

Her appetite was gone, but Frank insisted on buying her the same dinner as them: chops, French-fried potatoes, biscuits and coffee for 75c.

'Have you heard of Mr Clyde Barrow and Miss Bonnie Parker?' Frank asked her as he tucked into his chops.

'Yes, they're on the run, aren't they?' Ellen answered, confused by how random his question had been.

Everybody she knew in Chicago had talked about the shoot-out with the Barrow Gang in Iowa. Of course, the people Ellen had known in the North Side gang had wanted the outlaws to get away despite their violent crimes. She couldn't help but be fascinated by the idea of a woman with a gun as tough as her fella.

'Well, Vernon here was at the big shoot-out in Iowa,' Frank told Ellen.

Vernon shrugged, pushing his plate of food away. 'They're nasty dangerous folk,' he said. 'We arrested Blanche Barrow, and she was pure hellcat.'

'We'll get them,' Frank said. 'It'll come down to a small mistake. Or a snitch. That's what it always comes down to in the end.'

'So why are you going to Phoenix?' Ellen ventured to ask. She had read in the papers that Bonnie and Clyde hung out in Iowa, Texas and Louisiana. This was nowhere near where they were now.

'We're following the trail of a stolen car,' Vernon said. 'That's all we can say right now.'

It sounded like menial work. She didn't see how it would help them catch Bonnie and Clyde, but she said nothing else. She quickly ate her food. The diner was empty apart from them and the lone waitress. The whole town felt deserted.

'What do you think of Bonnie and Clyde? You think they deserve the electric chair?' Frank asked her.

'I don't think anyone deserves the electric chair,' Ellen said, in a low voice.

'You're only saying that because you haven't lost someone you love to violence,' Vernon said to her. 'You'd feel different if you had.'

All of her wanted to contradict him, but she held back. The last thing she wanted to do was share anything about her past with these two lawmen.

'I don't think it'll come to that anyway,' Ellen said. 'They've gone too far now. I don't think they'll stop until they get shot down. They won't surrender.'

'You're talking as if you have some authority on such things,' Vernon said, looking at her with interest.

'I grew up during the Civil War in Ireland,' she said in a stiff voice.

'Oh yeah, you heard of it, Vernon?' Frank said turning to her. 'Half of your people sold out on the other half, right? Anti-treaty and pro-treaty with the English.'

Ellen shook her head, regretting mentioning the Civil War. It had no comparison to the senseless rampage of violence Bonnie Parker and Clyde Barrow were involved in.

At last, they paid up and got back into the Ford.

'Not long now,' Frank said cheerfully, as Vernon took over in the driver's seat.

The sun was close to the horizon as they headed south from Prescott. Ellen had never seen such a setting sun before. A giant orb of scorching orange slashing the sky with simmering red and brilliant pinks. The landscape was foreign to her. The red earth, and the strange cacti plants. It was wide and flat, with the long straight road. No lush green fields of Ireland, no crashing ocean waves. No city skyscrapers of New York, no ruffled Lake Michigan from Chicago. They were far, far away from any sea. Here in this desert landscape, Ellen had no reference points to remind her of any of her previous lives. She was the same age as the outlaw Bonnie Parker. She wondered what it was like to be her. Had she transformed who she was just like Ellen had? Her heart felt heavy and old. Weighted with guilt.

She stared out the front of the Ford as the two men smoked and talked in low voices. It was impossible to hear what they were saying from the back of the car. Her eyes drifted up to the star-littered sky. She searched for the Big Dipper. It made her think of her daughter. The last night she had held her up to the stars on the deck of the boat in New York harbour. It had only been four months ago and yet it felt the longest time of her whole life. Brigid might be looking out of her bedroom window in Ireland and gazing at the same constellation. Which of course wasn't possible because in Ireland it would be a different time of day.

As the car sped along, Ellen's eyes began to close. She was bone-tired. The hum of the men's chat lulled her. She found herself lolling against the side of her window and sinking into the back seat of the car.

When Ellen awoke, she didn't know where she was. But something was happening to her. There was a weight upon her body, and she could hardly breathe. As she came back into awareness, she remembered she'd fallen asleep in the back of the Ford. But they were no longer moving. She was outside on her back in the earth. She was being crushed, and she could feel hands prising apart her legs. She gave a scream and raised her arms, trying to push the man off her.

'She's awake.' She heard his voice. It was harsh, a growl. But it was Frank all the same. 'Hold her down, Vernon.'

Her arms were pinned to her sides, and a hand stinking of tobacco was placed over her mouth. She tried her best to kick but it was no use. Frank grunted as he thrust up inside of her. It felt as if he was ripping her apart. Tears leaked out of her eyes as she struggled beneath him.

'Stop fighting, girl, and it'll be over quicker.'

But she couldn't stop. She bucked like a wild horse as Frank ground into her. At last, he gave a deep grunt and collapsed upon her. She felt him wilt inside her. *Get out of me*, she wanted to scream. But he took his time, slowly lifting himself off her body. She felt her thighs wet and wanted to vomit at the thought of what he had left inside of her.

At last Vernon removed his hand and she howled at the men.

'Get off me,' she screamed. But he held down her arms still.

'What a princess,' Vernon commented in a cold voice 'For a whore.'

'I'm not—'

'Who are you kidding? Nothing's for nothing,' Frank said harshly. 'We bought your breakfast and your dinner, been driving you all day.'

'What did you expect?' Vernon chimed in. 'Dressed like that and wandering around on your own?'

She was sobbing now. Not just from the shock of what had happened to her body, but at the transformation of her two travelling companions. What had happened to the friendly banter? She had thought they respected her.

'Oh, stop your yawling,' Frank said, exasperated. 'We've got liquor in the trunk. We'll give you a bottle of whisky after to make you feel better. Come on, Vernon.'

To her horror, Ellen made out the figure of Vernon in the dark, throwing off his big black coat, like a dark cape, and undoing his belt.

'No, no,' she begged. 'Please, no—'

But her voice was cut off as Frank's hand clamped over her mouth, and then Vernon was on top of her. He stank of whisky and tobacco, and bile rose in her mouth as he assaulted her just as Frank had. Outrage seeped out of her into despair. He was too heavy and too big for her to budge. She stopped fighting and lay limp underneath the heaving man. Now her thoughts were spinning out of control. What would happen to her once he'd finished? These men worked for the law. They could do whatever they wanted to her. She imagined her dead body left to rot in the desert, picked at by ravens.

'There's a good girl,' Frank said, noticing she'd stopped struggling while his friend kept on huffing over her.

Cold loathing filled her. She wanted to kill him. She had felt this way once before. Far away from the desert of Arizona. Back home in Ireland. If she closed her eyes, there was the entrance hall at Merview House. The chandelier glittering with bright menace, the white marble floor and the pool of deep red crimson blood. In her mouth she could taste the violence she had let rip, metallic and fierce.

At last Vernon was finished, and the two men freed her. She struggled to her feet and backed away from them. She had no idea where they were. It was completely dark apart from the stars and a campfire. All she knew was she had to get away. She began stumbling off across the dirt ground.

'Where you going, little lady?' Frank jeered. 'Don't you want a ride to Phoenix? You ain't gonna get there on foot. But we'll look after you – right, Vernon?'

'We sure will,' said Vernon, lighting a cigarette. 'Come on, we'll crack open a bottle of whisky.'

She would rather die than stay with the two lawmen. Ellen ran away into the pitch-black. Behind her she heard Frank's distant call:

'Come back, you fool woman.'

. . .

She ran on into the dark. She didn't care about snakes, or cacti or anything else. And when she could run no further, she fell down, shivering. The desert night was freezing, and she only had her blue silk dress on. Everything she owned – her green case with Gladys's fur, her purse, her coat and hat were all in the back of the Ford. But she wasn't going back. She lay down on the hard earth, and she thought, *This is it. This is the night I die.* How strange, that it would be in a place so dry and barren, rather than back home in the lush fields of Ireland, next to all her kin who had gone before her. And all of hers who would go after.

CHAPTER TEN

There was no convincing her mother. Mairead had thought the request to find Ellen had been a one-off outburst, but every day as her mother got sicker, her demands intensified.

Mairead had so much to deal with. Instead of settling into the long summer break and resting, she was thrust into the intensity of her mother's cancer, trying to get her to take natural therapies and sorting out care for her. Her mother absolutely refused to consider the possibility of a hospice if she deteriorated. She had agreed to drinking raw juices, which took ages for Mairead to prepare, but it hadn't made a bit of difference. Mairead was with her mother all day long until a kind neighbour, Janice, offered to help. As far as Mairead could tell, Janice was her mother's only friend. They had bonded after Janice was widowed the same year as her mother. Janice was practical and had a nurturing air about her which made Mairead feel better instantly. She was a gardener and encouraged Mairead's mother to come out of her workshop and sit under the big chestnut tree while she pruned and attended to their wild flowerbeds. Mairead was so grateful for her support and help. When Janice arrived, Mairead took Alfie for long walks by the sea on her own. She would gulp in big lungfuls of sea air and try to slow down her racing heart. Everything was happening too fast. She felt like she still hadn't taken in the news of her mother's cancer properly.

As the weeks went by her mother stopped going into her work-shop. She said she was too tired to make jewellery. This worried Mairead even more. Her mother had never stopped creating her whole life. Instead, she wanted to sit by the fire and reread old classics: *Wuthering Heights* and *The Moonstone*, along with poetry by Yeats. Each day her energy lessened as she ate less and less. Yet no matter how weak or sick her mother was, she kept asking how she was getting on with the search for Ellen. Mairead felt as if she was sinking under the pressure. She kept insisting her brother Darragh was better placed to find things out as he lived in New York, but her mother absolutely refused to tell him.

'All he does is try to bully me into having chemotherapy, Mairead,' her mother confided. 'I find his conversations stressful. It's my body and I will do what I want with it.'

It was strange to find the tables had turned. Darragh had always been their mother's favourite, but now it was Mairead she looked to for everything. Maybe this was just the way it was supposed to be? In these weeks of the last summer of her mother's life, they finally had a chance to bond as mother and daughter, the way Mairead had always longed to. Close, trusting, sharing secrets.

Mairead tried her best to fulfil her mother's hope to find Ellen, but it was an overwhelming task. In her mother's house there were plenty of books that dealt with her grandfather's achievements, the buildings he had designed in America and Ireland, but his first wife had left no such legacy.

Every day her mother told her the stories she could remember of her childhood in New York. Walks in Central Park. Trips to big stores with beautiful dolls bought for her. Going to the picture theatres. Through these snippets of memory, Mairead was able to slowly build up a picture of Ellen. She had been a loving mother. Knew a lot about movies and sang songs to her daughter when her husband wasn't around. Her mother tried to remember them, but there was only one which had stuck: 'The Last Rose of Summer'. Mairead had hunted in the stack of records downstairs and had found a Nina Simone cover version of it. She brought the record player up to her mother's bedroom and played it for her.

'It's different from how my mother used to sing it,' her mother said. 'But I'll never forget the words – *When true hearts lie withered, And fond ones are flown, Oh! who would inhabit, This bleak world alone?*

'For years it felt like that was what my mother had done to me,' her mother said. 'Left me all alone. Took the sunshine out of my life. So that my heart withered.'

One morning as Mairead brought in her morning cup of herbal tea, her mother sat bolt upright in her bed, her eyes wide open.

'I just remembered something,' she said. 'My mother kept asking my father if we could stay in America. She really didn't want to go home to Ireland. I think she was frightened—'

'We need to find out where she came from in Ireland,' Mairead had said. 'That will tell us why.'

'She asked him if we could go to California,' her mother added. Her eyes shining. 'Maybe that's where she ended up!'

Mairead didn't want to dampen her mother's memories and the hope they brought her, but trying to find out whether Ellen had ended up in California would be like searching for a needle in a haystack. She reckoned the best approach would be to focus on where she had come from in Ireland.

It was Eoin who gave her the idea of looking at the passenger lists of the boat her grandfather had been on to see if anyone with the first name of Ellen might have emigrated on the same route in 1925. If there was more than one Ellen, then they had no way of knowing if it was her grandmother. But if they were lucky there might just be one Ellen on the same passenger list as her grandfather.

'Didn't your mother say they met on the journey to New York?' he'd suggested.

'Yes!' She'd been excited by his idea. 'She said he'd saved her.'

'I've a friend doing a PhD on immigration stories from Ireland to New York in the twenties and thirties,' Eoin said. 'I'll ask his advice on how to get hold of the passenger lists.'

'Are you sure you don't mind?'

'Of course not, this is all so fascinating,' Eoin had assured her.

Eoin had been intrigued by the mystery of Mairead's lost grandmother. She had felt guilty revealing her mother's secret to him, but it had just slipped out. Since the day he had driven her to Sligo, he had been telephoning her every evening to see if she was OK. She had never expected to hear from him again, but she had misjudged him. He had called her up the very next day and she had tearfully told him her mother's diagnosis.

'I'm so very sorry, Mairead. Promise you'll let me know if there's anything I can do. Is there anything you need from school, for instance?'

'Well, I did leave some of my books in the staff room,' she'd said. 'Would you be able to mind them for the summer? I don't like to leave them there.'

'Of course. If you need them, I can bring them to you.'

'No, it's fine, just look after them,' she said. But ever since that first day, they had talked nearly every evening, sometimes for hours. His conversations had helped her feel normal in such a strange situation. One day they might talk about politics and what was going on in the world, and other times they'd discuss films they'd seen, bands they liked and books they were reading.

'Didn't know you were into true crime stories, Mairead,' Eoin had teased her after he'd collected her books from the staff room.

'It's my guilty pleasure,' she had said, smiling as she pressed the receiver to her ear.

Other times, Eoin would tell her a little more about himself. He'd grown up in Dublin in the Northside of the city. His parents had both been civil servants and he had four older sisters. Maybe that was why he was so understanding: because he had been raised by women. It was a relief to have someone to talk to about something other than her mother's cancer.

Somehow it was easier to talk to Eoin than her own daughter. It was always so hard to get hold of Stella. She didn't have a telephone in her flat. No one ever seemed to answer the shared telephone in the hall of the building she lived in. This meant Mairead had to wait for Stella to ring her. When she had finally told her daughter about her mother's cancer, Stella had been so upset, she couldn't bring herself to tell her it was terminal.

'Oh Mammy, I'd better come home and help you,' Stella said after she had managed to stop crying.

'Don't you have your end of year show? Aren't agents coming to see you?'

'Yes, but this is more important,' Stella had said. 'I want to be with you and Granny. Is she getting treatment?'

Mairead had avoided her daughter's last question.

'Your granny wouldn't want you to abandon your show. It's everything you've worked towards all year,' Mairead said, knowing for certain this was true. Her mother would never want Stella to walk out on such an opportunity. 'Come as soon as it's over.'

'Can I talk to Granny? Ask her myself?'

'She's sleeping right now, I don't want to get her out of bed,' she said. 'But call tomorrow night and you can talk to her.'

'OK,' Stella had said. 'Mammy, have you told Daddy?'

Mairead had stiffened. 'No, why would I?'

'Come on, Mammy, you can't cut him out—'

'He was the one who left, Stella,' Mairead said, shocked by how cold her own voice was. 'Look, tell him if you want. But I've enough to cope with. I don't want to talk to him.'

Stella had sighed, and Mairead had felt guilty. It wasn't pleasant for their daughter to be caught between them. But she couldn't help how she felt. She missed her terribly. Every time Stella rang, she was tempted to tell her to come immediately, but when Mairead suggested it to her mother she reacted as expected.

'She must take part in her end of term show. An agent might

pick her up,' her mother had insisted. 'She's very talented, Mairead.'

Her mother's praise of her daughter made Mairead proud. Although, she wished just once her mother had said something similar about her. But her mother had never once called her talented at anything.

Eoin had filled the space Stella left. A few days before the August bank holiday weekend, he called her up in excitement.

'My friend found out your grandfather – Giles Rose – was on the first-class passenger list of the RMS *Athena*, which sailed from Galway to New York in 1925.'

'Yes?' Mairead asked, sensing there was more to tell her.

'I looked through the lists of all the first-class passengers and there is a woman aged seventeen by the name of Ellen Lavelle.' He paused. 'Of course, if she wasn't her and your grandmother was in steerage there's no way we can find out. Although I think if he was in first class it's likely she was too.'

'She possessed a valuable necklace, which my mother gave me,' Mairead said. 'So, I imagine she was from a wealthy family in Ireland.'

'Right, well then I expect they boarded separately and met on the crossing over.'

'What was her name again?'

'Ellen Lavelle.'

Mairead whispered the name under her breath, pressing her hand to her chest.

'So, I did a bit of research into the Lavelle family in Ireland,' Eoin said, rushing through the information in his enthusiasm. 'They owned a big house called Merview with land near Ballycastle in County Mayo. At the turn of the century two brothers lived there. Alec and Rafe Lavelle. Alec was married to an Englishwoman, Dorothy Lifford, and they had a daughter called Ellen, born in 1908.'

'Eoin, this is incredible! How did you find all this out?'

'It was my friend Sean, not me,' Eoin admitted. 'He's obsessed with history like you.'

'Tell him thank you so much,' Mairead enthused. 'I can't wait to tell my mother.'

'I think it's likely to be this Ellen Lavelle,' Eoin said. 'Because if she was born in 1908, then she would be seventeen in 1925 when she took the boat.'

'It fits,' Mairead said.

'Sean found out a little more about her family too,' Eoin continued. 'Her mother died in 1910, and her father, Alec Lavelle, moved to America in 1919. Rafe Lavelle fought in the Irish War of Independence with Michael Collins.'

'I wonder why Alec didn't take his daughter, Ellen, with him to America in 1919.'

'Maybe he thought she was too young? She must have been moving out to be with him in 1925.'

'It's all a bit strange,' Mairead commented. 'My mother has no memories of a grandfather in America.'

'Yes, and what's even odder is he settled in Chicago not New York.'

'I wonder why Ellen didn't go to her father in Chicago?'

'Maybe she fell madly in love with your grandfather, Giles Rose, and her own father didn't approve? They could have been estranged.'

'I'm going to ask my mam. There could be something she's forgotten.'

There was a slight pause in the conversation and Mairead had the feeling Eoin was building up to something.

'So how is your mother doing?'

'She's OK,' Mairead said. 'She's in a bit of pain, and she's got very thin but she's still walking around. Sometimes we go down to Strandhill with Alfie for a little stroll by the sea. The doctors said things can be like this for a while and then suddenly she might go downhill.'

Mairead and her mother walked along the long stretch of beach at Strandhill whenever her mother felt strong enough.

Framed by the blue silhouette of Ben Bulben mountain, they'd potter along in silence watching Alfie, his ears flapping in the sea breeze as he ran ahead. If the tide was in, the sea roared wild and untamed. Or if it was out, it became a mirage of sparkling blue on the horizon. These moments in silence were the closest Mairead had ever felt with her mother. She tried to appreciate each precious minute, but it was hard to stop her mind from skating forward to when their walks would be over forever.

'Would you like to go and find this ancestral home together?' Eoin broke through her thoughts. 'Merview House in Ballycastle. It's not that far from you, is it? About an hour or so's drive? Do you think your mother would like to come with us?'

'But you're in Dublin!' Mairead said. 'It's a long way for you to come.'

'I'd like to see you,' Eoin said. 'Don't you think it might help your mother too?'

A sleepy mist rose off the fields as Mairead looked out of her bedroom window. It was the first Saturday in August. Today Eoin was going to drive down from Dublin and bring her and her mother out to look at Merview House in Ballycastle. She had relayed all that Eoin had found out to her mother the same night he'd told her.

'He's clever, this man of yours,' her mother had commented, giving her a sly smile.

'He's not my man, he's just a friend,' Mairead had admonished her.

'Well, he must like you a lot, if he's coming all the way down to spend the day with you and your dying mother.'

Mairead had winced. 'Stop, Mam!'

She had asked her mother if she remembered any mention of a grandfather in Chicago called Alec Lavelle when she was a little girl.

'No, not at all,' her mother said. 'I don't remember my mother talking about any of her family in Ireland. But I was only little—'

'Do you think it could be her? Ellen Lavelle?' Mairead asked her mother.

Her mother looked back at her with unblinking green eyes.

'Yes,' she said. 'I just feel it is.'

Mairead was nervous to see Eoin again. She changed three times from jeans into a dress and back into jeans again. By the time he pulled up outside her mother's house, the mist had completely burned off. The blue sky was patched with tiny fluffs of white clouds, and the green fields simmered lush with grass. Having chatted away every night with such ease, now they were in each other's presence, Mairead felt awkward and nervous. But she kept her focus on helping her mother settle into the back of the car. Despite the warmth of the day, her mam was shivering.

'Are you sure you're well enough to come with us, Mam?' she asked her. 'I can call Janice. See if she can come over.'

'There's no way you're leaving me behind,' her mother said in a determined voice as Alfie jumped into the back seat next to her. 'I have to see this house.'

Mairead tucked a blanket around her mother, loading Eoin's boot with a picnic she'd made and a thermos of herbal tea for her mother, as well as more blankets.

'OK then,' Eoin said in a cheerful voice. 'Off we go.'

With her mother in the back of the car, Mairead felt self-conscious and her conversation with Eoin was more formal than it usually was on the phone. She asked him about his business, and he told her the demand for computers was growing.

'I wouldn't be surprised if in less than ten years' time everyone has their own personal computer,' he observed.

'I don't see how ordinary people could ever afford it,' Mairead said, remembering the fuss Sister Mary Stephen had made over the cost of the one school computer.

'They'll become more affordable,' he said. 'It's exciting to see all the developments in technology.'

Mairead couldn't help thinking how they were opposites in their professional lives. Eoin's work was all about the future, and hers was about delving into the past.

They stopped in the village of Ballycastle to use the toilets in the pub.

'Do you know how to get to Merview House?' Eoin asked the publican.

'That's the big house for sale,' the man told them before giving them detailed instructions of how to find it. 'It's a bit hidden away,' he warned.

They were directed inland away from the sea. The roads narrowed to lanes. The hedgerows grew thicker on either side of the road. They were steadily driving uphill. At the top, where the road appeared to end, was a big oak tree. They kept going past the tree, and over the other side of the hill, around a sharp bend. As she looked out the window, Mairead could see a tiny estuary snaking alongside the road beneath the bushy hedgerows. Ahead a stone wall emerged from the undergrowth. Eoin took a sharp right and then drove through an opening in the wall down a bumpy boreen. The trees closed in around them, heavy with foliage so it felt like they were driving down a long green tunnel. They reached a gate, a little fallen off its hinges, with two stone pillars on either side. On the wall, in faded script, was the name MERVIEW HOUSE. Eoin pulled the car up alongside it.

'Well, there's no sight of the sea from here,' he said. 'Wonder why it's called Merview House?'

'Maybe on the other side,' she said, getting out of the car and turning to open the back door for her mother.

Eoin walked ahead, Alfie at his heels, as Mairead helped her mother approach the broken gates, which were padlocked. The lock was so rusted it appeared no one had opened it in a long time.

They walked along the boundary wall, and after a while came upon a part where it had cracked and some of the stone had collapsed.

'Let's squeeze through the gap in the wall,' her mam said.

'Are you sure you can manage, Mam? Surely, we shouldn't trespass anyway?' Mairead said.

'Oh. I don't think there's anyone around,' Eoin said, encouraging her mother, who had already broken free from her and was sliding through the gap in the wall.

Mairead looked at Eoin and he shrugged, a smile on his face. They followed after her mother as Alfie trotted ahead of them, excited to sniff all the new scents. Suddenly, he went quite still as a small rabbit hopped into sight.

'Oh no, Alfie, don't.'

But of course, Alfie tore off, though the rabbit disappeared into the trees.

'He'll be back,' her mam said. 'There's no controlling his instincts.'

They followed the way the dog had gone, walking through the trees. Some had fallen over, and the woods felt thick with the scent of undergrowth. She took her mother's elbow, but she shook her off.

'I'm fine, Mairead,' she said. 'Not dead yet.'

Mairead bit her lip at the rebuke and stumbled on a root. As she slipped Eoin took her hand to stop her from falling. She felt his fingers clasp hers in a comforting squeeze before letting go.

Alfie returned to them as her mother said he would. The little stream which Mairead had seen alongside the road meandered through the woods, bubbling and burbling over stones as it wended its way. A wood pigeon cooed, and the trees rustled. It felt as if they were stepping back in time. Her mother stopped walking for a second and stood very still.

'These woods,' she whispered. 'My mother used to tell me she played with the flower fairies in the woods when she was my age. She had a friend and they played together.'

'Do you think it was these woods?'

'She never described them in detail. Or I don't remember. What does come back to me is she told me they called themselves the names of flowers. Forget-me-not and Bluebell! Two blue flowers but different shades of blue.'

'That's so beautiful, Mam,' Mairead said.

'I had never been in any woods in New York,' her mother said. 'There were no flower fairies in our garden on Park Avenue, that was for sure. But sometimes I used to imagine I saw fairies in Central Park. Mammy would take me there to walk among the trees.'

Out the other side of the woods, they entered a wild garden. In front of them stood Merview House. It was a big Georgian stone edifice, with a grand portico with pillars.

'Looks like it was built at the end of the eighteenth century,' her mother said; thanks to her own father, she had an appreciation for architecture.

'So sad it's been allowed to decay,' Eoin commented.

'It would be too expensive to keep it running,' her mother said, approaching the old building.

The windows were boarded up and the front door was padlocked. They wandered around the side of the house.

To their surprise, the back door opened on first try.

'Do you think it's OK to go inside?' Mairead asked.

'I'm past asking anyone's permission,' her mother said defiantly, pushing the door open and stepping over the threshold.

Eoin and Mairead had no choice but to follow her. They entered an old kitchen. Thick cobwebs hung from the ceiling and there was a coat of dust on everything. It was as if the kitchen was frozen in time. They had expected to find it stripped of its contents, but everything was still in place: pots hanging from the ceiling, covered in cobwebs; plates on a dresser; even cutlery in the drawers.

'It's like a living museum,' Mairead said.

They left the kitchen and followed a corridor that led into the entrance hall. The remnants of an old chandelier still hung above them and there was a sweeping staircase. Most of the stairs were missing.

'No, Mam, it's too dangerous!' Mairead protested as her mother put her foot on the bottom step.

'I think Mairead's right, Mrs Brady, we shouldn't risk climbing it,' Eoin said. 'Could be dangerous. The floors might be rotten upstairs.'

For a moment, Mairead thought her mother was going to ignore them. Her hand gripped the balustrade and she looked up to the top of the staircase with such an expression of longing on her face. As if she might find her mother upstairs after all these years. In the end, though, she dropped her hand off the balustrade and scuffed the floor with her shoe. Kicking aside thick dust and muck to reveal a dirty marble floor.

'Looks like it was once white,' she said to them.

'It was clearly a very grand house in its time,' Eoin said.

'I'm surprised it wasn't burnt down by the anti-treatyists during the Civil War,' Mairead commented.

'Did they do that?' Eoin asked her.

'Yes, they destroyed several of the Big Houses as a protest against the treaty with the British,' Mairead told him. 'These houses symbolised the British landlords and all the suffering that had been imposed on generations of Irish people—'

'Yes, but Merview House didn't belong to a British family,' her mother interrupted. 'The Lavelles were Irish. My mother was Irish.'

'That must be why they were left alone,' Mairead continued. 'Remember you said one of the brothers fought in the War of Independence with Michael Collins?' She turned to Eoin.

'Yes, Rafe Lavelle.'

On the far side of the entrance hall was a dining room. Most of the wallpaper was gone, but she saw patches of the old flock pattern in deep crimson. Her mother tore a little of it off. Put it in her pocket.

'I wonder who owns the house now?' Mairead said. 'Why they've let it fall into ruin.'

'We can call into the estate agent's in Ballycastle, and find out,' Eoin said. 'Remember the publican said it was for sale?'

They walked through all the rooms downstairs. The house had been cleared of valuables such as the original fireplaces, but everything else remained. As if one day everything had just stopped dead like in the story of Sleeping Beauty.

They walked a full circle. The main living room was at the back of the house next to the kitchen and overlooked a jungle of a garden.

'I still can't see the sea,' Mairead said.

'Maybe if you were upstairs, you could see it in the distance,' Eoin said.

They went back outside into the jungle garden. She took her mother's arm and this time she didn't resist as they walked behind Eoin while he made a path for them through the tangled grasses, avoiding clumps of stinging nettles.

'Oh, look at this,' he declared.

At the end of the garden was a small lake. The tiny babbling brook in the woods must have fed into it. It was thick with weeds, and almost looked like flat green grass.

Her mother gave a little gasp.

'The lake! I had forgotten,' she said. 'My mam talked about the lake. Said it was a sad place.'

Mairead picked up a stick and stirred the sludgy green water as if it were soup. It shifted, as little flies hummed above it. A small blue damselfly darted across the still water towards clumps of bright blue forget-me-not flowers on the other side.

'Look, Mam, forget-me-nots, like you said.'

Her mother nodded but said nothing. She began to wander on her own towards the flowers.

'Do you see the water lilies?' Eoin turned to Mairead. 'They're so big!'

Huge white flowers floated on flat green hearts upon the tranquil lake. It was as if there was a haze above the water.

'It should feel peaceful here,' Mairead commented. 'But it

doesn't.'

The air was as thick and soupy as the green lake. The buzzing of insects seemed to vibrate around her. She imagined she could hear a humming of some unspoken darkness. She shivered.

'Are you OK?' Eoin asked her.

'Is it me or is it a bit spooky?'

He smiled at her. Amid all the greenery, his hazel eyes had turned a deep woody green.

'It does feel haunted, for sure,' he said.

They stood in silence for a while as the green lake popped with bubbles from fish beneath its surface.

'How are you getting along with your mother?' Eoin said to her, now that her mam was out of earshot. 'Are you OK?'

She nodded. 'I guess. Mam's cancer doesn't feel real, especially on days like today.'

'She seems to be doing well.'

'I think she's hiding a lot of the pain she's in.'

'She's an amazing woman.'

In the past, Mairead might have been annoyed by Eoin's admiration of her mother. But not now.

'Yes, she is,' she said softly.

She looked across the lake to the patch of forget-me-nots where her mother had wandered but to her alarm, she was no longer visible.

'Eoin, do you see where my mam went?'

'She was just across the lake,' he said. 'I'm sure she's fine. Alfie's gone too. He's probably with her.'

Mairead walked briskly around the side of the lake. She wasn't sure why she felt so worried but she didn't like this place. The skeletal house loomed behind them with its caved-in roof and boarded windows, while the land around the lake was wet and boggy. One of her legs plunged into a hidden pool of sludge and she nearly fell over.

'Oh help!' she yelped.

Eoin grabbed hold of her arm and yanked her out. Her left leg below the knee was covered in mud.

'What if my mam has fallen into a bog?' she said, feeling a flutter of panic.

They moved faster now through the long rushes to the clumps of forget-me-nots but there was no sign of her mother. On the other side of the lake was a sweeping overgrown drive which snaked through the trees.

They began to jog down the drive together. Mairead trying to suppress the panic. How could their mother have got so far in so little time? At the end of the drive, next to the padlocked gates, was a small lodge. They looked inside, but it was empty. Its roof had fallen in and it looked as if it had been used as a cattle shed, judging by the straw covering the floor and a broken water trough in one corner.

'Mam!' Mairead called but she couldn't see her anywhere. 'Alfie! Here, boy!' She whistled but the dog didn't appear.

'Maybe she's back at the lake and we missed her,' Eoin suggested.

They ran back down to the garden and the lake but there was no sight of her mother.

'What could have happened to her?' Mairead said, close to tears.

'We'll find her,' Eoin reassured her.

They ran back up the drive again and there all of sudden Mairead saw her mother. She was standing outside the lodge, Alfie at her side. It made no sense that she hadn't seen her or passed her either time they had come this way.

'There she is!' Eoin declared.

Her mother was staring intently at the lodge. In one of her hands she clasped a bunch of the forget-me-not flowers. As she got closer, Mairead realised it wasn't the lodge her mother was looking at but tangled rose bushes so in badly need of a prune that the thorns were huge and spiky. The roses were almost dead, their yellowing white petals full-blown and withering.

'So soon may I follow,' her mother whispered as Mairead

approached. Something told her not to ask her where she'd been. To Mairead it felt as if for those few moments her mother had slipped behind a veil in the fairy woods. Maybe it had been a preparation for when her mother would be gone for good?

They drove back into Ballycastle. The day had clouded over and become a little chilly. Although she'd packed a picnic, they decided to get toasted sandwiches in the pub. She didn't want her mother to catch a chill. They went back into the same pub as before.

'Did you find Merview House?' the publican asked as he poured them three glasses of Guinness.

'Yes, we did,' Eoin said. 'It's in a pretty bad state.'

'Terrible shame.' The landlord shook his head sorrowfully. 'It's been empty for as long as I can remember.'

'Do you know who owns the house now?' Eoin asked him.

'I think it's some family in America,' he said. 'You'd be best to check with Johnny Gallagher, the estate agent.'

'How long has it been for sale?' Mairead asked.

'Not that long. Just went up this summer. Not sure why they hung on to it for so long. Might have been caught up in legalities.'

They settled into the corner of the pub, sipping on their Guinness.

'Are you sure it's a good idea for you to be drinking Guinness, Mam?'

'Stop fussing, Mairead,' her mother said. 'You're ruining what little fun I can have.'

Mairead blushed, feeling embarrassed in front of Eoin.

When the publican came back with their sandwiches, Eoin asked if he could tell them anything about the family who'd lived at Merview House.

''Twas the Lavelles, right enough,' he said. 'I don't know what happened to them. Although it was said the place was haunted. We were warned away from going up there when I was a boy.'

'Did you ever hear of a girl or a woman called Ellen Lavelle?'

her mother asked.

The publican shook his head. 'No, but ask Johnny. What I do know is there's a story the house was built on a fairy fort. And there's no good fortune to come of that.'

'Oh, that's why it seemed like such a dark place,' her mother said quietly. 'No wonder Ellen left.'

Living in the west of Ireland, Mairead had grown up with a keen awareness of fairy lore. She had been warned by her mother and father of the importance of not damaging hawthorn trees as they belonged to the fairies. In particular it was bad luck to enter a fairy fort, let alone build on it. She could see by the expression on Eoin's face that his Dublin childhood had not included such wisdom, but he didn't say anything because her mother was clearly so taken with the idea.

After their late lunch, they walked down the main street in Ballycastle to the estate agent's.

'Look!' said her mother, pointing to a photograph of Merview House in the window. 'It says price on application. Let's pretend we're potential buyers.'

'Why, Mam?'

'I just want to imagine it!' she said, spreading her hands wide and grinning like a naughty child.

Johnny Gallagher was a jovial ruddy-faced country man. They sat in his office as he chain-smoked Major cigarettes sitting behind a desk piled with papers, and told them all he knew about the Lavelle house.

'I believe it's been empty for decades,' he told them.

'Can you tell us anything about the family who lived there at the turn of the century?' Eoin asked. 'The Lavelle brothers? Ellen Lavelle?'

'Not too much,' he said. 'I believe the eldest brother, Alec, emigrated to America and the younger one, Rafe Lavelle, fought in the War of Independence. Never heard of Ellen Lavelle.'

'Who owns the house now?' asked Mairead.

'I'm afraid I can't tell you that,' Johnny Gallagher said, putting out his cigarette. 'But the seller is based in America, I believe.'

'Can you tell me if they're relatives of the Lavelles?' her mother pushed.

'I would imagine it's unlikely,' Johnny said. 'The house was bought by a local family, the Regans, in the fifties, but they never did it up and ended up selling to the current owners. The whole community was disappointed there were no renovations done in all these years...'

Johnny Gallagher paused to light another cigarette.

'But we're hopeful now. A few parties interested. What about yourselves? Can I take you out to look at it?'

'How much is the asking price?' her mother asked, acting as if she might be interested.

'Well, it's a lot of land. We're looking at around 1.5 million pounds.'

'That's a little over our budget,' her mother said, straight-faced. Mairead caught Eoin's eye. He looked like he was about to burst out laughing at her mother's audacity.

'Give me your business card, and we'll have a think,' her mother continued. 'And I wonder if you might be able to do me a favour, Mr Gallagher?'

'Certainly, if I can,' he said.

'I believe this house once belonged to my ancestors, the Lavelles. If anyone by the name Lavelle comes looking at the house, or anyone related to the Lavelles, can you give them my name and address. Tell them I would be very happy to hear from them.'

Her mother pulled out a small notepad from her bag and scribbled down her name and the address in Sligo. 'I'm not far away now. It would mean a lot to me.'

'No problem,' Johnny Gallagher said, taking her mother's note and placing it on one of his stacks of papers. 'Now do think about the property and let me know. It's a gem!'

As they drove back to Sligo, her mother fell asleep in the back seat, clearly exhausted from the exertions of the day.

'That was so interesting,' Eoin said as the car sped past the Iron Mountains, the afternoon shadowing into a golden evening.

'Thanks so much for bringing us,' Mairead said. 'It's so good of you to give up your Saturday.'

'Sure, I had no other plans,' he said, glancing over at her. His eyes were hazel again.

'Out at Merview House your eyes turned green like the lake,' she said.

'Did they?' he asked. 'It must have been the magic out there.'

'Did you feel it too?' she asked.

'Yeah, I mean I don't believe in fairies, but it was a strange place. Did you notice there were hardly any birds singing?'

'I heard a wood pigeon cooing.'

'Yeah, but that was all. No little birds or crows. Nothing.'

By the time they got back to her mother's house, the sun was setting. Her mother was completely out for the count in the back seat. Mairead tried to wake her up, but she was in a deep sleep. A little panic seized her, but as she put her ear to her mother's mouth she could hear her breathing in and out. She tried shaking her awake but her mam wasn't budging.

'I can carry her upstairs,' Eoin offered.

She watched him scooping her tiny mother up in a blanket and bringing her upstairs. The sight made Mairead want to cry. Her mother had never looked so vulnerable. She could see the pain pinched in her face even in sleep. Her mother must be in such agony, but she was keeping it all to herself. She didn't want to lose her mother, but she didn't want her to suffer either. After Eoin had gently laid her mother onto her bed, Mairead covered her with a blanket. Alfie lapped from his bowl of water in her mother's room and then jumped on the end of the bed. He yawned and looked at Mairead with a soft gaze. *I will keep her safe*, she imagined him saying to her if he could speak.

Eoin and Mairead went back downstairs. She turned on the

lamp in the kitchen and opened the fridge.

'Would you like something to eat?' she offered. 'A drink?'

'I should be getting back,' Eoin said.

'Why don't you stay over?' Mairead heard herself saying, surprised at her own boldness. 'You must be exhausted from all the driving,' she added by way of explanation.

She felt Eoin's eyes upon her and looked up at his face.

'OK,' he said. 'As long as I'm not in the way—'

'Of course not.'

She paused. Feeling a little awkward. Not knowing what to say. Eoin broke the silence.

'I've noticed something about your eyes too,' he said.

'Oh,' she said holding his gaze.

'They're the same shade of blue as the sea out west,' he said.

She felt herself blushing with the compliment. She hadn't felt such a strong attraction to a man for years. It was strange and uncomfortable but a little exciting and distracting too. It took her mind off her mother for once.

Eoin took a step towards her but before anything happened the telephone rang in the hall.

'Sorry,' she said, turning away and scurrying out the kitchen door.

It was a stranger's voice on the phone. A woman.

'Hello, sorry to bother you but I'm looking for Eoin,' she said.

Mairead gave a little start. Surprised that someone would know to ring for him at her mother's house.

'Oh right, hang on,' she said.

She went back into the kitchen feeling a little confused.

'It's for you,' she said.

Eoin looked surprised and hurried out the room.

She sat down at the kitchen table and toyed with the end of the tablecloth, pulling at the hem. He was only gone a few minutes but when he came back into the kitchen the atmosphere had changed.

'I'm so sorry,' Eoin said, looking uncomfortable. 'I have to go.'

'Is there something wrong?' she asked, concerned. Maybe i

was one of his four sisters? 'How did she have my number?'

'It's nothing serious, just annoying,' Eoin said, picking up his car keys. 'That was Aileen. She found your number in my address book. She knew I was coming here. She's locked out. I have to go back and let her in.'

'Oh!' Mairead felt the blood rushing to her face with mortification. She had got it all wrong.

'It's not what you think!' Eoin said, registering the look on her face. 'We just live together. It's temporary.'

'So is Aileen a friend?' she ventured.

'I wouldn't say that,' Eoin said. 'She's my ex.'

'Girlfriend?'

'Wife.'

Mairead tried to hide her disappointment. What a fool she was. Eoin was merely being kind to her because of her sick mother.

'Right, well, you'd better get going,' she said briskly, walking down the hallway and opening the front door for him.

'Mairead,' Eoin said. 'It's not like that. I've told Aileen about you—'

'What about me, Eoin?' Mairead's voice sounded so sharp to even her own ears. 'You're still living with your wife. I think you should go.'

He hesitated on the threshold.

'Please, Mairead, let me explain—'

'Just go,' she said resolutely.

As she soon as she heard his car driving off, the tears came. For her disappointment over Eoin, for the failure of her own marriage, but most of all for her mother. She sank to the floor of the hall and hugged her knees, pressing her face into the worn denim, smelling the boggy mud from the lake at Merview House.

ished she could find out what had happened to her for her mother's sake, but having drawn a blank at she had no idea where else to look.

CHAPTER ELEVEN

22 OCTOBER 1933

Ellen was on fire. Every part of her. The side of her face exposed to the harsh sunlight, her bare arms and legs and between her thighs. Deep inside of her. Her mind was telling her to get up but her heart didn't want to. Salty tears trailed down her cheeks, trickling onto her cracked lips. She didn't want to die but she was so tired, utterly beaten. She closed her eyes, imagining the sizzling Arizona sun searing the flesh off her bones. Months from now a wandering soul might find her white skeleton gradually fading to dust. She groaned, and with great effort rolled over onto her back. She had no idea how far she was from the road. She had to try to get up. She had to live. But instead, her body began instinctively to curl up, her head tucking in between her arms, her knees raised. Every single inch of her was in pain.

Something was crawling along her arm, but she didn't even have the energy to flick it off. The insect already believed her dead. Ellen was becoming as one of the rocks. Fossilised by all the dark things in her life. Sinking beneath the surface of the harsh desert. She began to say her confession. *Forgive me, Father, for I have sinned.* But then she stumbled in her mind. She wasn't ready to confess her sins yet.

A shadow fell upon her. She rolled back her head and opened her heavy eyelids. A figure was leaning over her. The face was hidden by a hat, but she could smell a woman's scent. The touch gentle and familiar. Her angel friend.

'Forget-me-not,' she whispered.

Bluebell.

Did she hear the woman speak the word back?

'I'm sorry,' Ellen whispered. 'Forgive me.'

The figure drew closer and was speaking to her, but it wasn't in English. Now she could see the face beneath the hat and it couldn't have been more different from her dear childhood friend.

'*Quédate despierta,*' the woman said. She had brown eyes, sun-creased at the corners. Her expression was deep with concern.

Where am I? Ellen thought as the woman's face blurred and she dropped away.

When Ellen came to again, she was no longer in the desert, although her skin was still on fire. Her surroundings were full of shadow. She was lying on her back on soft cotton blankets. She tried to move to see where she was but gave out a yelp of pain when she tried to sit up. Her skin was so tight and burned it felt like it would crack.

'*No, no, señorita.*' The same voice as before.

The angel from the desert appeared at her side. A real woman. She pressed a cool hand to Ellen's forehead and guided her to lie back down. Ellen whimpered in pain and the woman made some soothing noises. Ellen had never been mothered but she knew what it was to mother. She shifted to her not-so-burnt side as she watched the woman pick up the thick spiky stem of a plant. It looked like one of the cacti. She snapped it and juice dripped from its innards. She caught the juice in a clay bowl then began to drizzle it along the side of Ellen's face. It stung and she gave another whimper. A small hand grasped hers. She looked down to see a child with curly black hair and serious brown eyes. She stared into the little girl's eyes. The skin on her face began to calm while the woman covered all her exposed skin with the plant juice.

Another girl appeared with a small bowl of water and brought it to her lips. Ellen tried to drink but it hurt so much. The girl dipped a cloth in the water and squeezed it over Ellen's parched mouth. It felt like soft Irish rain as her lips softened and she was able to part them. Slowly, patiently, the girl dripped more water until she was able to bring the bowl to Ellen's lips and she could drink.

Ellen remembered doing the same thing for her own daughter, Brigid, two years ago when she'd been in bed with a fever. Her throat had been so sore and swollen, Brigid hadn't wanted to drink any water. But Ellen had known instinctively, as a mother, she must somehow get water into her to cool her down. She had taken a small teaspoon and dribbled the water on her daughter's dry lips, while at the same time laying cold wet cloths on her fevered brow. Eventually Brigid had been persuaded to drink some water before falling asleep. Ellen hadn't left her bedside for two nights, despite Giles telling her she needed to rest and in any case it was the nanny's job to watch over their sick child. Ellen had refused. Eventually, her child had recovered. She had wept with relief. Ellen had never been more afraid than those three days when her daughter was sick. Now she was far away from Brigid. Would never know if she was sick or would be looked after properly. The thought made her shake with grief. The woman looked at her in alarm. She put aside the rest of the plant juice. Placed a cool hand on Ellen's forehead, and hummed to her as if she was a fretful child.

Ellen closed her eyes. She was so heavy and tired. She could still see the red earth of the scorching desert. But now in the middle of it sprang an oasis of lush green trees and grasses. A waterfall of pure green water the same colour as her little girl's eyes. Butterflies were fluttering around her, and she was intoxicated by the scent of wildflowers from summers back home. She stepped into the pool of green and submerged herself in cool water.

When she awoke again the room was steeped in dark shadows. She shifted on the soft blankets and to her surprise she was no longer in agony. Whatever the woman had put on her skin had healed her. The doorway was open. She could see light from another room, hear voices and smell food, the scent of which she had never encountered before. Her stomach made a huge groan. She had no idea how long it had been since her frugal meal in the diner. Her whole body clenched at the memory of Frank and Vernon, and she placed her hand between her legs. This was where she was most sore. She had to forget about what had happened. She had been so stupid to trust strangers. But these people were strangers too. She didn't even speak their language.

The overriding hunger she felt drove her to get out of the bed she had been lying on. The floor was cool stone under her bare feet. She moved towards the light. The room felt like a little cave with thick walls and shuttered tiny windows. The perfect protection against the heat of the day outside. She put her hands upon the walls, realised they must be made out of some kind of clay mix. *How interesting Giles would find this building*, the random thought occurred to her. She bit her lip. Pushed thoughts of Giles out of her mind. He would not want her now anyway.

She walked through the doorway and entered a space glowing and golden. The wooden ceiling was low and from it hung a brass light fitting with two brass oil lamps on either side over a big wooden table in the centre of the room. By the window was a wooden dresser with an assortment of ceramic plates, cups and bowls on its shelves. It was dark outside and there were three candles lit on the dresser. In the far corner of the kitchen was a small white dome protruding from the wall. Ellen could see the flicker of flames within it and realised it must be an oven for cooking. By the side of the fire was a niche cut into the thick white walls with a large wooden cross, and a small statue of Our Lady. From beams above her were strung heart-shaped red and orange vegetables.

The whole family were sitting around the table eating bowls of food. The scent of it was different from any kind of food Ellen had smelled before. Aromatic, warming and herby. There was the smell of baking from the oven. An older boy and a man had joined the mother and two girls.

As soon as she walked into the room, they all looked at her, startled.

'Hello,' she said uncertainly.

The woman got up from the table and took her hand, led her to sit between the two girls. The little one looked up and gave her a shy smile. She must have been about the same age as Brigid. Her expression of open welcome brought a lump to Ellen's throat.

The woman pushed the bowl of food and a flat, soft round of bread towards her.

'Thank you,' she whispered. They were all staring at her as she took a small bite out of the bread.

It had to be the most delicious thing she had ever eaten in her entire life.

'Tortilla,' said the woman, giving her a broad smile and pointing at the bread Ellen held in her hand, and then at the oven.

Ellen picked up the spoon and scooped beans into her mouth. There was a fragrant red sauce on them.

'Oh my gosh!' She dropped the spoon with a clatter. Her mouth was on fire again.

The children laughed at her. The woman got up and picked up one of the small red heart-shaped vegetables which had been hanging from the rafters. Showed it to Ellen.

'*El chile*,' she said in Spanish.

'You can sure tell it's from the desert,' Ellen said, smiling back. The skin was still tight on her face. It was hot in her mouth, but she wanted to eat more, so she kept going though tears sprouted in her eyes from the effort.

Now she was with them, the family had stopped talking in Spanish, shy in her presence. Even so, it felt good to be sitting at their table sharing food. When she, Giles and Brigid had dined it had always been so formal with servants putting food on their plates and manners to observe. There had always been a sense of something missing.

After the meal, the man nodded at her, put on a hat and left the house. The woman offered her a chair by the oven. Ellen shivered and one of the girls got a cotton blanket and draped it around her shoulders. In the soft light she could see the blanket was covered by beautiful shapes, patterns and colours.

She watched the woman and her daughters gathering the food bowls. One of the girls went outside and returned with a pitcher of water. Her mother put some more wood on the fire, filled a big pot and hung it over the flames. When the water was warm the two girls cleaned the dishes. It was soothing to watch the women at their domestic tasks. Reminding her of the simplicity of her life at Merview House when she'd been still a girl. There was comfort in the daily domestic routines. As the two girls were placing the last of the crockery away, the door rattled open. The father and his boy returned. To her surprise, Ellen saw they had brought with them a priest.

'Good evening,' the priest said in English.

His white collar and black gown seemed out of place in the little rustic kitchen. Here was something just the same as home, even though everything else was completely different. Immediately she felt a little suspicious, remembering the priests back in Ireland. None of them could be trusted.

He took a chair from the table and drew it up alongside her, while the family settled down at the table and watched.

'My name is Father Joseph Jawlosky,' he said to her. 'And this is the Rodriguez family,' he indicated.

The priest's eyes were bright blue, full of youthful vigour, but his skin was sun-weathered and his hair bleached almost white by the sun. He had a neat beard of pale gold.

'Where am I?' she asked him.

'You're in the town of Scottsdale in the state of Arizona,' he told her. 'You're very lucky Señora Rodriguez likes to wander in the desert gathering plants for her potions!' He turned around and said something in Spanish to the family, and the father chuckled and patted his wife on the hand.

'She saved my life,' Ellen said.

'That she did.'

Emotion swelled up inside Ellen.

'Thank you,' she said in a small voice, turning to look at Señora Rodriguez. The Mexican woman held her gaze. It felt to Ellen as if her deep brown eyes could dig out her sorrow. Ellen looked away, ashamed of all she had done. Had she brought on what had happened to her? Those men said she had asked for it.

Detecting her distress, Father Joseph leaned forward. There was a scent of pine about him.

'What were you doing out in the desert?' he asked.

She shook her head. She never wanted to tell a soul what had happened to her.

'I was lost.'

Joseph held her with his gaze. 'But now you have been found. Your life begins again.'

He was different from the priests back home in Ireland. She could see sincerity in his blue eyes.

'But how?' Ellen said, overcome with a wave of emotion.

Her suffering rushed through her and her cracked heart split even wider. She felt like her breath was being snatched from her. When had her life of loss begun? On the very night she was born.

He did not quote the Bible at her. Instead, the young priest sat by her side and let her cry. Hot desperate tears. The family watched, the children wide-eyed to see her grief. But they were her witnesses, and she felt safe in the humble home. When she had no more tears to shed, she began to gulp in breath. All the while Father Joseph whispered, 'Take it easy, there now.' As if she were a spooked horse.

Señora Rodriguez got up from the table and placed a pot of water on the fire. Ellen couldn't see what she was putting in it but soon she smelt chocolate. She had never drunk chocolate until they had lived in New York. The scent brought her back to last Christmas with Brigid, but rather than shutting down the memory she let herself see it. Brigid with a chocolate mouth and grinning at her mother.

Oh, my love. She placed her hand on her breast, blinking as one last big tear rolled down her cheek.

The eldest daughter brought her a clay bowl of the steaming cacao, and one for Father Joseph.

'This will make you feel better,' he said to her, giving her a kind smile.

'Let us give thanks,' he said, and then some words in Spanish to the family. They cupped the bowls of cacao in their hands. The air in the house shifted around Ellen. The weight of her sorrow grew a little lighter. She took a sip of the cacao. It was like no other hot chocolate she had ever drunk in her life. Not sweet, but earthy, spicy, and rich. *Thank you.* The words surfaced in her mind, though what she had to be grateful for she had no idea. She took another sip.

'You see?' Joseph said, his expression of certainty calming her.

It was then she realised he hadn't asked her anything about who she was. Not even her name or about her accent. He had said, *Your life begins again.* As she sipped the rich chocolate, inhaling its compelling aroma, she decided to reinvent herself. She had done it before and now she must do it again. She let her tattered dream of Hollywood fame fade with each sip. It was time to retreat. Heal. For however long it might take.

CHAPTER TWELVE

5 AUGUST 1984

The day they went to Merview House together was the last time her mother got out of bed. It was as if the expedition had taken her last drop of strength.

The next morning, when Mairead had come in with her mother's morning tea, she had been hunched in the bed. Mairead couldn't help noticing her skin had turned yellowish.

'Can you get the doctor to come out?' her mother had asked her through clenched teeth. 'I need some pain relief.'

It was the first time her mother had asked for it. Mairead felt a wave of fear wash over her, but she tried to keep her voice calm.

'Of course, Mammy, I'll ring right away.'

After Doctor Keneally attended to her mother, he spoke to Mairead in the kitchen.

'I tried to persuade Brigid to go into hospital, Mairead, so she could be put on a morphine drip, but she refused,' he said. 'Do you think you can give her the morphine? She's in a lot of pain.'

Mairead nodded. It was happening. The end was coming, and she wasn't ready.

The doctor explained it was hard to tell how things might go.

Her mother might slip into a coma for a couple of weeks, or she could go at any time.

'It's clear the cancer has spread to her liver, now,' he said. 'All you can do is make her as comfortable as you can.'

'OK, thank you,' Mairead said, clasping her shaking hands.

'I'm so sorry, Mairead,' Doctor Keneally said. 'Please feel free to call me anytime.'

After the doctor left, Mairead tried getting hold of Stella but of course the phone rang out in her building in London. She chewed her fingernails, not knowing what to do. Stella's drama show was tonight. She didn't want to throw her daughter off, but at the same time, she had to get her to come home as soon as possible. She glanced at her watch. It was still the middle of the night in New York. She didn't want to wake her brother up either. It was agonising for him being stuck over in New York. She took out her address book. It fell open on Eoin's number. She glanced at his name, remembering how carefully she had written it in her book. Remembering those feelings of hope and possibility. She squashed them down. Eoin wasn't important right now. All that mattered was her mother. She flipped the pages. There was Niall's new phone number. The only way she could think of to reach Stella was through her ex-husband, who also lived in London.

'Niall, it's Mairead,' she said as soon as he answered the phone.

'Mairead! How are you?' Her ex-husband sounded flustered. Surprised by the sudden phone call. 'Stella told me about your mam. I'm so sorry—'

'Niall, I can't get hold of Stella,' Mairead interrupted. 'Mammy's not going to last much longer. She needs to come home.'

Her words felt so harsh and she heard the shock in Niall's voice at her brusqueness.

'Is there no hope?'

'No,' she gulped, a part of her wanting so much to reach out to Niall. He had been her closest friend for decades. It felt strange now to talk to him as if they had hardly known each other.

'Ah, Mairead, how awful,' he said gently. 'Of course, I'll find Stella right now.'

'Don't you have to go into work?'

'It's fine—' He paused. 'If I can't go, Lesley will get her.'

Mairead stiffened at the mention of Lesley's name.

'You can't tell her until after her play tonight, though,' Mairead said. 'She's got the main part. She has to do it. Mam wouldn't want her to miss out on the chance to be seen by an agent.'

'OK, so what should I do?'

'Are you going to see *A Doll's House*?'

'Of course we are,' Niall said.

Mairead tensed again. Niall and his boyfriend were going to be Stella's family representatives at her big moment. It hurt to know she was going to miss the play. But she had no choice.

'Can you tell her afterwards? Get her to book a ferry.'

'I'll buy her an airplane ticket,' he said.

'It's too expensive,' she argued. 'I don't have the money to pay you back.'

'Mairead, it's fine. I'll pay,' Niall said. 'Look, I can come with her if you need me—'

'No,' she cut him off, although part of her longed for his support in her hour of need. But it would only make things worse in the long run. He had left her and was never coming back.

Stella arrived two days later. Mairead drove up to Dublin airport to collect her. On the way back out west, she explained that her mother's cancer was terminal.

'Why didn't you tell me before?' Stella had been angry. 'I would have come sooner.'

'That's exactly why,' Mairead had said. 'Mam didn't want you to stop being Nora in *A Doll's House*.'

'That's not important compared to this,' Stella said.

'It is to Mam,' Mairead said. She paused, letting Stella take in the grim prognosis.

'Is there really no way she can get better?' she asked her mother again.

Mairead shook her head. 'No, love,' she said. 'Janice is with her right now, but I'm keen to get back.'

'Oh Mammy,' Stella said, reaching over and placing her hand on Mairead's knee as she drove. Mairead blinked back the tears. It felt so good to have her daughter with her but at the same time it made her mother's situation even more real.

'How did *A Doll's House* go?' she asked Stella.

'Really well,' she said. 'An agent talked to me afterwards. They want to meet me whenever I get back. I have to get a portfolio done.'

'That's fantastic, Stella,' Mairead enthused. 'You have to tell Mam.'

'It's been hard work this year,' Stella said. 'But I don't regret it.'

Mairead said nothing. She still felt Stella should have gone to university, but on the other hand, her daughter really was determined. Maybe she would actually make it as an actress.

As soon as they arrived back at Ballinakill Lodge, Stella had run upstairs to see her granny, while Mairead had let Alfie out for a run. When she came back in with the dog, Stella was in the kitchen looking shaken.

'Mammy, she's so different,' she said, her face pale, and her eyes loaded with tears. 'So sick!'

Mairead felt guilty. She had been with her mother every day and had forgotten how dramatic her deterioration had been. She should have warned Stella.

She opened her arms and Stella fell into them, sobbing into her chest. 'It's so awful, Mam,' she said. 'Poor Granny.'

But her daughter was strong, and after the first night, she

managed to gather herself up and put a cheerful face on for her granny.

They set up a vigil in her mother's bedroom. Every morning Stella gathered wildflowers and placed them in the window. They opened it wide so her mother could listen to the birdsong. Stella suggested they read to her. Childhood stories: *The Water Babies*; *The Lion, The Witch and The Wardrobe*; and her mother's favourites, *Alice's Adventures in Wonderland* and *Alice Through the Looking Glass*.

'My mother used to read these books to me,' Mairead's mother told her and Stella. She took another breath. Mairead knew it hurt her mother to talk but her eyes were bright with memory. 'I saw *Alice* on Broadway. It was spectacular!'

'That must have been wonderful!' Stella enthused.

The first night she'd arrived at Ballinakill Lodge, Mairead had told Stella about the hunt for Ellen Lavelle. How they had gone to Merview House hoping to learn more about her, though she made no mention of Eoin in the telling of the story. Her daughter had been fascinated to hear about her mysterious great-grandmother Ellen.

'You inherited your acting from my mother,' Mairead's mother said to Stella. She took another laboured breath. 'We made plays together. She could do different voices.'

This gave Stella an idea. She acted out different scenes in *Alice's Adventures in Wonderland* for her granny: the Mad Hatter's tea party, Alice meeting the Cheshire Cat in the woods, Alice playing croquet with the Queen of Hearts, and Alice meeting Tweedledum and Tweedledee. Stella even persuaded Mairead to take part, and they dressed up in bits and bobs to look the part, putting on silly accents. Their antics made her mother laugh, despite her pain.

Every afternoon they telephoned Mairead's brother, Darragh, in New York, and he spoke to his mother. When she could no longer talk back, her brother would play her music. He sang the Irish songs her mother loved. 'The Last Rose of Summer', again and again. The notes of his guitar warping on the distant telephone line to America.

At the end, she and Stella had sat on either side of her mother's bed holding her limp hands, still warm, and waiting. Alfie the dog curled up in a sorrowful heap at his mistress's feet.

'We can let her go now,' Stella had whispered to her mother, wise for her eighteen years. 'It's OK, Mammy.'

In the moment of losing her mother, she had never felt so close to her daughter.

It had been on the tip of her tongue: *She was never mine to let go*. But instead, Mairead had looked out the window at the big horse chestnut tree. It was the end of August and the leaves were turning, the tree's boughs rich with golds, reds and browns. She remembered climbing the branches of the tree when she'd been a little girl and getting stuck. Her mam had laughed at her.

'When you decide to come down, your tea's ready,' she had called over her shoulder as she sauntered away. 'I'll be in the workshop.'

Mairead had become even more frozen up in the branches of the tree. She had climbed it to rescue her cat, Polly. But of course, the cat had jumped out of the tree, no problem. In the end, they'd had to wait until her father came home from town and he'd shimmied up the trunk to get her down. She'd been shivering with the cold and still remembered how safe she'd felt as soon as he'd wrapped his big arms around her.

It was her daddy who had read her *Alice's Adventures in Wonderland* and tucked her in at night. Her daddy's family who they visited every Christmas. Now her mother was going, she missed her father even more. At thirty-seven years of age, she was an orphan.

Mairead had looked at her mother's face in dying. She appeared younger, as if all the frown lines of the decades had miraculously faded. Her skin almost as white as the pillowcase. There had always been this ethereal quality to her mother. Now, as the cancer took hold of her blood and flesh, her mother appeared even more fairy-like, her eyes glimmering sea green and immense in her pinched face.

As Mairead had watched her mother die, she believed she was ready to let go of the past and her grandmother's secrets. All that mattered now was this moment of passing. Her mother's last long exhale and then silence. Silence. Stella's sobs. Holding her mother's hand and feeling the warmth slowly ebb from her fingertips.

Wait! she wanted to shout out. *You never said I love you.*

She did not cry. Mairead sat quite still and felt her mother's presence depart from the shell of her body and all around her. She felt her hands upon her shoulders, the breath of her upon the nape of her neck. A sparrow landed on the window ledge, the bright beat of life as it looked at her. She saw her mother's love, brittle but honest, in its beady eyes.

Her mother had died on the last day of the school holidays. Those glorious weeks of summer when all her students would have been going on holidays with their parents, on camping trips, and stay-overs. During those long sweet days of summer which should have been full of no structure and no rules, Mairead had become a prisoner in her mother's house.

Now it was all over. The wake, the funeral. All the relatives had come and gone. Even Stella had gone back to London to meet the agent. Mairead sat on the end of her mother's empty bed with the green silk shirt she had washed and pressed for her mother on her last night folded upon her lap. It had taken over half an hour to get it slinky smooth, just how her mother liked to wear it in bed. Within the space of those thirty minutes, her mother had slipped into a coma. She never ended up wearing the shirt ever again.

Mairead got up off the bed and placed the green silk shirt in the bin liner full of all her mother's old clothes. Later she'd donate

them to the St Vincent de Paul shop. Stella had already picked out
a few items before she'd rushed back to London.

'Do you have to leave so soon?'

'I'm sorry, Mam, I don't want this agent to forget about me,' she
had said. 'But why don't you come over and stay with me as soon as
you can?'

'I've school starting up in a few days.'

'Mammy, you can't go back to work yet!'

'I want to get back to normal,' she had said. 'It's the busiest
time of year.'

Mairead needed to get back to work. The silence of her mother's house was getting to her. She wished so hard that she'd fulfilled
her promise and found her grandmother Ellen. But the last few
weeks of her mother's life had left no time for research. Eoin had
rung and left a couple of messages on the answerphone but she had
never called him back and he had stopped trying.

Mairead locked the door of Ballinakill Lodge. The *For Sale* sign
was already up outside the front gate. Stella had suggested her
mother might like to move into her childhood home in Sligo. It had
been in their father's family for generations.

'I'm not sure I can,' Mairead had said. 'There's so many
memories.'

'But, Mammy, it's so beautiful, with the views of the sea, and
the garden,' Stella said. 'It feels like home to me, more than our
house in Kells!'

'Well, do *you* want to live here?' she had asked her daughter.

'Course not, Mammy, I have to stay in London!' Stella had
said, running her hand through her wavy dark hair. She had
noticed it was the same texture as her mother's hair. Thick and
silken, different from Mairead's coarse curls.

What she hadn't told Stella was that she and Darragh would
have to sell her mother's house. She needed her cut to buy Niall
out of his half of their family home in Kells. Niall could, strictly

speaking, have thrown her out by now as the deeds and mortgage were in his name, but she reckoned his guilt stopped him from doing that. Even so, she couldn't forget the contents of the letter he'd sent her before her mother had got sick. He had been clear that he needed the money because he wanted to buy a flat in London. She gritted her teeth. His love nest with his boyfriend, Lesley. Her father's new relationship didn't bother Stella in the least; she just wanted everyone to get on. Mairead only wished her daughter could have been a little angry on her behalf.

Mairead walked over to the chestnut tree and placed her hand on its broad trunk. Felt the grooves of the bark in the flesh of her palm. She believed she would miss the tree and the garden more than the house. She stood on the rise of land by the tree. Already it was littered with the green prickly husks of horse chestnut shells, some of the nuts themselves gleaming like polished wood in the sunlight. Mairead looked out across the green fields to the table ledge of Ben Bulben and the glint of blue sea which always gave her a slight feeling of anticipation. This had been her view throughout her childhood. What she had looked at when she had dreamed of the future and of who she would become. This land was as much part of her as her parents' flesh and blood. She walked over to the *For Sale* sign and pulled on it. Began heaving it out of the soft earth. She was never giving up this house and land.

With the sign lying on the lawn, she turned to walk back to her car, where Alfie was waiting for her. Curled up on the back seat in a state of utter misery. The turquoise necklace swung around her neck, and she brought her hand up to steady the pendant.

It was time to go back to work, to dive into the enthusiasm of the new academic year with all those convent girls looking to her for guidance. But she knew nothing. The task of teaching them suddenly felt overwhelming. She sat in her car and stared up at the chestnut tree. The branches swaying and the leaves rustling, glinting gold and green. She saw herself as a little girl sitting up in the tree. Then she saw her mother as the little girl in the photograph album sitting on the branch next to her.

Mammy! Mammy!

Mairead tried to push the tears back in her eyes, but they kept falling in great heaving sobs. A torrent of all she'd bottled up during the wake and the funeral. She twisted around in the seat and tugged open the bin liner filled with her mother's clothes. Alfie looked up at her in concern. Mairead pulled out the green silk shirt. She tore her T-shirt off and buttoned up the shirt. It was a little small for her, a snug fit over her breasts but she didn't care. She smoothed the green silk shirt down over her front.

'OK, Mam,' she said into the car, as Alfie pricked up his ears. 'I'll find her.'

CHAPTER THIRTEEN

17 JULY 1937

Ellen walked the length of the church carrying the sprays of purple and violet periwinkles in her arms. Beneath the painting of Our Lady of Perpetual Help, she heaped the fragrant blooms. Their flowery scent wafted up and she remembered how they had called them flowers of death when she was a girl. There had been an old tradition to weave periwinkles into garlands when a child died. Their presence on the church altar felt foreboding but periwinkles were one of the few flowers which could survive the intense desert heat in July. Ellen needed to make her daily offering. She went down on her knees and prayed.

Every day for the past four years she had come to the church and prayed for her daughter Brigid. Religion was different in Arizona than it had been back home in Ireland, or even in the Irish community in New York. She had never forgiven the Irish parish priest, Father Peter, in Ballycastle for preaching against her family from the pulpit. She had only been a young girl, but still she had stood up and walked out the church. Feeling the blaze of her neighbours' eyes upon her. Most of them sympathetic, but still not willing to stand with her. The Irish priests had been traitors to their own people. It had made her uncomfortable with those she met in New York with her husband, Giles. Afraid of the Catholic church in New York's connections back home. The news from Ireland which they might acquire. But in Arizona, Father Joseph was nothing like any other priest she had ever known. He had never poked his nose into her affairs. Even in the confessional box. Not once in all the four years she had been living in Scottsdale, Arizona. Her faith was a personal matter. She found herself drawn to Our Lady more than God and Jesus, and to the different female saints Gabriella prayed to who were popular in Mexico. Today, as on most days in the past year, she was praying to Santa Muerte or Señora de las Sombras – Lady of the Shadows – for protection for Brigid from violence and for healing for herself. Santa Muerte was patron saint of all outcasts, which is what Ellen was.

She closed her eyes and squeezed her hands together. The overblown flowery scent of the periwinkles seemed almost inappropriate in the plain white adobe church, but then this was a different kind of church than the ones back home. Each fifty-pound adobe brick of clay, hay, soil and water had been made and carried by one of the local Mexican families, people like the Rodriguez family, who had been her saviours.

Four years ago, when she had first lived in Scottsdale, Ellen had worked side by side with Gabriella Rodriguez in the cotton fields, never asking for payment because Father Joseph provided her with a home and food. She had no longer wanted to go on to California. The shock of her rape had knocked all the confidence out of her. She wanted to stay in the tiny community which had taken her in. Here she could hide from the world.

After about six weeks, Father Joseph had shown her his small silversmithing workshop behind the priest's house.

'Before I became a priest, I studied architecture in New York,' he told her, sitting down at his workbench as Ellen gazed at all his tools in astonishment.

His revelation had shocked and unnerved her. Had he met Giles in New York? He must have known of his work. But she had never told him her married name – Ellen Rose. Since she had settled in Arizona, she had gone by the name Ellen Lavelle. Father Joseph liked to call her El. In time, everyone in Scottsdale knew her by this name.

'After the revolution in Mexico, I went to look at a little town called Taxco between Mexico City and Acapulco to study its baroque architecture,' he said. 'There I met other artists. Have you heard of the painter Diego Rivera or his wife Frida Kahlo? She is most remarkable,' he said, pausing as Ellen shook her head. 'I also met another American called William Spratling and he had opened up a silversmithing studio. He wanted to keep the silver mined in Mexico for the Mexicans.'

Ellen sat down on a stool next to Joseph.

'But what has this to do with being a priest?' she asked him.

'I will come to that later,' Joseph said to her, giving her a broad smile. 'I studied with Spratling, and his apprentice, Pineda, who to this day is the most skilled stone setter I have ever encountered. I learned a lot, but in my heart, I knew it was not my calling to make jewellery to be sent to galleries in New York for rich Americans.'

'How did you become a priest?'

To Mairead it seemed such a huge leap from silversmith to Catholic priest.

'When I returned to New York, my uncle, who was a priest, was visiting from Poland,' Joseph told her. 'I found I was more interested in spending time with him discussing theology than making jewellery. When I did go into the workshop, every time I made something it turned into a silver cross.' Joseph's eyes creased with amusement. 'In the end I finally took notice of the signs Our Lord was sending me. At last, I felt I had found my purpose.'

'And what is that?' she asked.

'Helping those in need,' he said simply.

Like you're helping me, she wanted to say, blushing and looking down at his elegant hands.

'I went to the seminary in New York, but I wanted to move out to the Southwest. I was keen to live among the Mexican people I had so grown to love. Because I speak Spanish, I was sent to Scotts-dale. As you've noticed, most of those who live here are originally from Mexico.'

Joseph spread his hands and smiled at her.

'It seems I have been fortunate enough to use my skills as a silversmith to create things of beauty which help generate an income for our small Catholic community in Scottsdale.'

Ellen had an overwhelming desire to see him make jewellery.

'Can I watch you work?'

'You can do more than watch,' he told her. 'I will teach you.'

'Why?' she asked him, quite astonished he would suggest such a thing. During the eight years of her marriage to Giles he had never once talked to her about his building designs apart from in a vague way. He would show off his achievements, pointing out from the Park Avenue apartment the slowly rising Empire State Build-ing. She had been so proud of him. But she remembered once she had asked him to explain exactly how a skyscraper could be so tall and not fall down. He had given her a patronising smile.

'You wouldn't understand, darling,' he had said.

He had made her feel so ignorant she had never asked him again.

'I think the task of making jewellery will help you,' Father Joseph had said to her. 'It requires focus to set a stone. You have to clear your head of everything else.'

Joseph had explained that during his time in Taxco, he had also travelled to the Sonoran Desert. There he had encountered the famed Sonoran turquoise, a rich sea-green and blue stone. Ellen had given a little jolt when he mentioned turquoise, remembering the beautiful necklace she had left behind for Brigid in the cabin of the boat less than six months before. Had it been one of the signs Father Joseph believed in?

Over the past four years, she had come across a great deal of turquoise. Most of the jewellery she had seen in Arizona was silver with either turquoise or coral. The intense blue of the turquoise in this region seemed to hold her captive. Once Joseph showed her how to set the stones, she was hooked on the quiet focused work. The Mexican designs Joseph worked on were more unusual than local work. He told her he was inspired by old Mexican designs – he called them Pre-Columbian and Mesopotamian – though they looked very modern to her eyes, reminding her of her husband's geometric forms in buildings, with angular corners, zigzags and diamonds. It was the Navajo jewellery which she had seen when some Navajo traders had passed through which she had loved most of all. They were different from the items she had seen sold in the shops for tourists on their weekly trips into downtown Phoenix. Joseph had told her why.

'The Navajo have been forced to create inferior silversmithing for the tourists and make things which don't belong in their culture,' he told her.

'Like the matchbook cover we saw,' she said.

'Yes, exactly,' he said.

The Navajo traders had stopped near to the white adobe church and laid out their wares for the local white and Mexican families to look at. Ellen had been drawn to a tiny ring with three little turquoise stones inset in a vertical row. She had traded the wristwatch Giles had given her for the little ring, as well as an uncut piece of turquoise. It had shocked her how easily she had taken the watch off her wrist as if it didn't belong there any more. By that time, she had been living in Scottsdale two years. Though she thought of Brigid every single day, her feelings for Giles had faded. When she thought about her daughter, the pain was still as sharp as ever in her heart. And when she thought about those she had lost in Ireland before she came to America, her sorrow still welled deep. But when she thought about her husband, Giles, she found she didn't miss him. She had been pretending to be someone else their whole marriage. The ideal wife. The woman he wanted her to be. But she had been such a young girl when she had met him on the boat to New York, and he had been over twice her age. With hindsight, she realised he had taken control of every single thought and decision in her life for all their time in New York. The one time she had asked him – no, begged him to do what she wanted, to stay in America, he had refused her point blank. As time passed, she found herself feeling a little angry at Giles, almost as if he had forced her to run away, which of course he hadn't. But the guilt at what she had done to him no longer weighed her down. She was sure he would have found a new wife in Ireland. A suitable mother for Brigid. She prayed the woman was kind to her daughter. She prayed Brigid was happy in her new life.

When she noticed Father Joseph looking at her empty wrist, he had made no comment apart from telling her he liked her new ring.

She showed him the turquoise stone on the palm of her hand.

'Will you help me make a necklace with this stone?' she asked him.

What had her relationship with Father Joseph been over the past four years? She had moved into his little adobe house the week she'd been rescued by Gabriella Rodriguez because there was nowhere else for her to go. She had learned to cook like a Mexican from Gabriella as, though a white man, Joseph favoured the spice and riches of Mexican fare. She had kept the house clean and washed his shirts by the river with all the other women. But of course she had not been his wife because he was a Catholic priest with a vow of celibacy. She was not even his official housekeeper. She had slept in her own little room on a small cot bed with a Navajo blanket Joseph had given her. In the evenings, they had gone into his little jewellery studio and he had taught her how to make her necklace. When he asked her to draw a design of what she wanted to make, she was astonished to find she remembered the necklace she had left Brigid in perfect detail. It wasn't even clear to her why she needed to make this necklace. All she knew was she had to. Then she would make her decision where to go to next. Her dreams of going to California were less substantial. The life of an actress which she had craved when she had been living in

Chicago and New York held little appeal for her now. The very idea of being back in a big city frightened her.

Ellen crossed herself, pressing her hand to her heart, and thanking Our Lady of Perpetual Help for giving her hope every day. Then she made her prayers to Santa Muerte again: *Protect my daughter, Mistress of the Night.*

She got up off her knees and walked over to the votive candle rack and lit one of the candles. Whispering to Our Lady and Santa Muerte again to send good fortune to Brigid wherever she was. The little ritual was so natural to her from years of lighting candles and praying in the village church back home in Ireland.

Outside the white adobe church, the light was fading. She gathered her shawl around her as she hurried back to Joseph's house to prepare supper. Last night she had finished the turquoise necklace. She was excited to put it on again and feel it upon her skin. It was almost a replica of the one she had given to her daughter. Apart from the diamonds and pearls, of course. In their stead, she had ringed the turquoise with tiny silver beads. It was lighter than the original necklace, which was made of gold. Still, when she put it on and looked in the cracked mirror in the washroom, it had seemed a perfect reflection of the necklace she had worn in her previous life of luxury. Everything else was different. Her red hair had grown long and wild. Her lily-white skin had gone from pink to honey brown in the desert climate. Her body had changed too. Not so soft, still lean but sinewy and strong from working in the cotton fields. She could also speak Spanish and listened dutifully to all the recipes Gabriella had taught her. Tonight, she was cooking fried chicken, corn tamales, with green salsa, beans and rice.

She heard men's voices as she approached Joseph's adobe house. Something made her pause on the threshold, and she was possessed by an unaccountable sense of foreboding. She shook it off and opened the door.

Two men sat at the table with their backs to her, while Joseph faced her. The room was billowing with cigarette smoke.

'Hello, El dear,' Joseph welcomed her. 'These two fellas are staying for dinner. Their car got a flat and I said they can camp out back.'

'It sure is decent of you, Father,' the man closest to her said. Ellen froze. That voice. She took another step forward as both men turned to look at her. She nearly screamed in horror, for sitting in her home were the two agents from the Bureau of Criminal Investigations: Frank and Vernon. They beamed at her, not a hint they knew who she was. Four years had passed since the night of her assault, but she had never forgotten them.

'Are you all right, dear?' Joseph asked.

Her shock must have registered clearly on her face. Frank was looking at her quizzically.

'Hey, you look kinda familiar?' he said, scratching his grizzled chin. 'Have we met?'

'No.' She emphasised the American accent she had adopted ever since she had settled in Arizona. If he caught her Irish accent, he might remember. She mustn't let that happen. Because what would they do to her, and Joseph, if they did? These men might work for the government, but they were violent and ruthless.

She turned her back on them and scurried into the kitchen. Her hands were shaking as she took a hold of the skillet. She couldn't make food for these men after what they had done to her. But she couldn't tell Joseph either. Because he was one small skinny priest, and they were two hefty brutes with guns. Icy cold anger swept through her. She didn't want anyone to ever know what those monsters had done to her. For all these years, she'd believed somehow it had been her fault. *Nothing's for nothing. What did you expect?* And now those two bastards were sitting in her home and smoking cigarettes. Being all friendly with a man of

God with not a drop of remorse. How many other girls had they treated the same as her? How many more would they hurt?

Ellen licked her lips. Out here in the Arizona desert she felt the righteous rage of her Irish self beginning to re-emerge. She was coming back to who she really was. A girl who knew what she believed in. All those privileged years in New York had been one play-act. The submissive wife. Now she felt the taste of violence in her mouth. The essence of malevolence within her which had driven her out of Ireland in the first place. She was no victim.

She placed the skillet on the fire and threw on the raw meat savagely.

She was going to cook her molesters the best meal of their lives – because it was going to be their last.

CHAPTER FOURTEEN

14 SEPTEMBER 1984

The yellow taxi hurtled through the traffic. Mairead felt dizzy from looking at all the lanes of weaving cars. All so shiny and clean compared the mud-spattered cars in rural Ireland. She clutched her hands in her lap. She couldn't believe she was actually in New York. For five years, she'd promised her brother Darragh that she, Niall and Stella would visit. But they never had. She had always been fearful of the long flight, and New York sounded so dangerous. She hadn't wanted to bring Stella – which had been ridiculous. Her daughter was now living in Hackney in London, which Mairead guessed could be just as dangerous for a young woman. But every time she had asked Stella if she was taking care, not travelling home on her own too late at night, her daughter had sighed, 'I'm grand.' Which had worried Mairead even more.

She placed her hand upon the turquoise necklace at her throat. The one thing she possessed which connected her to her mother and to her grandmother Ellen. In her handbag, she had a few of her mother's pieces to give to Darragh's wife, Josie. Before she had left this morning – which felt like a whole week ago – she had put on one of her mother's rings to replace the missing wedding band. It was silver with a tiny moonstone, the glimmer of which pleased Mairead. She put on another ring. A little cluster of garnets. Then a simple silver spiral on her middle finger. She ended up putting rings on all her fingers. The rings made her feel different. As if they gave her hands the ability to conjure a new kind of energy in her life.

It was strange to be travelling away from Ireland during the first week of term. She imagined all the girls in her history class confused when the substitute teacher walked in. Would she stick to the lesson plans Mairead had left her? She had called into school the week before to ask Sister Mary Stephen if she could extend her compassionate leave.

'I need to go to New York to see my brother,' she explained. 'He couldn't get home for the funeral.'

'How very unfortunate,' Sister Mary Stephen said, sitting at her desk, her expression emotionless. 'How long do you need?'

Mairead was quite stunned by the lack of empathy from her headmistress. She had been at the school for fifteen years and had never asked for a sick day or any out-of-holidays extensions. But Sister Mary Stephen hadn't offered her any extra time off. She had had to ask. All Sister Mary Stephen had done was send a condolences card.

'Two weeks.'

Sister Mary Stephen had raised her eyebrows.

'It's very late notice and right at the beginning of term,' she complained, then, seeing the look on Mairead's face, collected herself. 'Which of course you can't help.'

Mairead walked out of Sister Mary Stephen's office feeling a mixture of guilt and fury. Her mother had just died, and the nun appeared to lack any sympathy whatsoever. At the same time, she felt bad for abandoning her students at the start of the new school year.

As she stomped down the corridor, she turned a corner and ran smack into Eoin.

'Oh, I'm so sorry, are you OK?' Eoin asked her, catching her hands as she lost her balance.

'Yes, yes, thank you,' she said, righting herself, and snatching her hands away.

'How have you been?'

She looked at his face, his eyes filled with concern. He had no right to care about her. He had lied to her about his wife.

'I'm fine,' she said. 'Thanks for the card and the flowers.'

'I wanted to come to the funeral,' Eoin said, 'but after last time we saw each other, and you didn't return my calls and... well, I didn't know whether you wanted me there.'

She had missed him terribly, she wanted to tell him. But he had been right not to come. It would have been too much to cope with, seeing him on top of everything.

'I wouldn't have minded,' she heard herself say in a cool voice.

They stood in awkward silence, and she was about to move on when Eoin spoke again.

'I found something out for you. I was waiting until next week when we saw each other at work, but now you're here—'

He pulled his wallet out of his pocket and removed a folded square of paper.

'I met with my friend Sean for a drink last week. The one doing the research on immigration stories. He's been following the trail of Alec Lavelle, Ellen's father,' he said.

Mairead's heart lifted. She had got nowhere with her hunt for Ellen Lavelle since her mother died.

'Alec was involved in the steel industry. Made a lot of money and had a big house on the Gold Coast in Chicago. He died in 1960.'

'What about Ellen?' Mairead asked.

She was touched Eoin had gone to so much trouble, even after the bad ending to their day at Merview House.

'Sean can't find any mention of her in America, but that doesn't mean she wasn't in Chicago with her father. The lives of women, as you know, are less documented, especially if their names change through marriage.'

'That's a shame,' Mairead said, disappointed.

'However, Sean found a living descendant of Alec Lavelle in New York,' Eoin told her.

'This is so kind of your friend,' Mairead said. 'Why did he do all this for me? He doesn't even know me.'

'Well, once Sean gets hooked on a line of research he's a little like a bloodhound,' Eoin said, looking pleased. 'He also owes me a lot of favours!'

'Thank you, Eoin, you really didn't need to do all this,' Mairead said.

'I wanted to help you,' he said, looking awkward. 'I couldn't be at the funeral so it was the only way I could think how.'

She felt herself blushing.

'So, who is the descendant?' she asked, moving on to safer territory between them.

'It's his great-nephew.' Eoin took out the piece of paper as a shaft of light fell on him from the high convent windows, picking up red and gold in his dark curly hair and making his hazel eyes green like the time they'd gone to Merview House together. 'His name is Kyle Symes, and he lives in New York!'

'How did Sean find him?' Mairead asked.

'He's so clever!' Eoin said. 'It's also lucky he had been over at Columbia University in New York. One of the ways he finds descendants is by scanning the catalogues of auction houses in Manhattan to see if any articles from big estates are sold. He noticed a big sale a year ago of items belonging to the estate of Alec Lavelle in Chicago, the steel magnate. Among them was a painting by Picasso. He wrote to the auction house requesting they pass on his contact details to the seller in case it was a relative, but he's heard nothing back, so far.'

Eoin paused and began to spread out the paper on the windowsill. Mairead could see a family tree had been drawn on it in black ink.

'The university library has past editions of the *New York Times* on microfiche, so he looked for articles about the sale of the Picasso. There was a big write-up, complete with a picture of the great-nephew Kyle Symes in his swanky apartment in Manhattan.'

'Goodness, this is incredible!' Mairead said, scanning the family tree Eoin had drawn for her.

She could see clearly all the direct descendants of Alec Lavelle and the dates of their deaths – apart from Ellen, who was a mystery of course. She traced the line through his second wife and her brother, all the way down to Kyle.

'It's very unusual he's the only one left!'

'Apart from you and your brother, and your children, of course,' Eoin reminded her.

'Do you think it's Kyle who owns Merview House, and is selling it?' Mairead asked Eoin.

'Possibly, although didn't the estate agent tell us another family had owned it for years?' Eoin said.

'Oh yes, of course.' Mairead said. 'Thanks so much for doing all of this for me, Eoin. I really appreciate it.'

'But there's more,' Eoin said. 'Sean found Kyle Symes's address in New York. He lives in Manhattan.'

Eoin turned the piece of paper over.

His handwriting was big, full of curvy slants. He handed it to her.

'Thank you so much,' she said, clutching the piece of paper. 'This is incredible.'

'I just wanted to help you,' he said.

There was another awkward pause as they locked eyes. Eoin broke the silence first.

'Look, would you like to get a toasted sandwich in O'Flanagans, so we can talk? I just have to drop this into the computer room,' he said, waving a floppy disk.

A part of her wanted to say yes but she found herself shaking her head. Niall had hurt her so much by his lies. And Eoin had led her to believe he was single.

'I can't,' she said.

His face fell and he gave her searching look.

'I told you, I'm separated,' he whispered.

'You still live with your wife,' she hissed back.

He looked crestfallen. 'I really like you, Mairead.'

'Stop, please,' she said. 'I have to go.'

'OK, but let's talk about it. Maybe one night next week when we're back at school?'

'Maybe,' she mumbled.

He squeezed her hand. She felt the warmth of his fingers on hers before he slipped his hand away.

'Ring me any time, I mean it,' he said before he loped off down the corridor.

Too late she remembered she hadn't told him she wouldn't be in school next week. She'd be in America. She shoved Kyle Symes's address and the family tree into her handbag before walking out of the convent school. She could still see Eoin's smile. The warmth in his eyes when he looked at her. She pushed the images out of her mind. She needed to forget about him. He might say he was separated but he was living with his wife. She couldn't trust him, no matter how lovely he was.

The skyline of New York swung into view and Mairead's breath caught in her throat. It felt like she was in a movie. There was the iconic Empire State Building and the Chrysler Building. In the same district were buildings her grandfather had worked on. She felt a bloom of pride. As they got closer, she saw the Twin Towers, and the Statue of Liberty. The taxi came off the freeway. They drove past tall brownstone houses with broad steps and redbrick buildings with fire escapes which wound down floor to floor, just like the one Audrey Hepburn sat on in *Breakfast at Tiffany's*. She gave the taxi driver Darragh's address as the cab turned down a street which appeared to be right beneath the Brooklyn Bridge. In her whole life she had never seen such a big bridge, or one so beautiful. It took her breath away.

Although she hadn't seen her little brother since he'd left for America nearly ten years ago, he was as she remembered him. The same tousled chestnut brown hair, like their mam, with her green eyes too. But he had their father's mouth and chin. Darragh's personality had been as bubbly as Mairead's had been muted. He had been their mother's favourite, without a doubt, even though it had been Mairead who had excelled at school and gone to university. Darragh had dropped out of UCD after a year and gone off travelling.

'Mairead!' He swung her in the street. 'Welcome to Brooklyn Heights.'

She couldn't help laughing at his grand gesture.

'Oh Darragh, it's so good to see you,' she said, still giddy when he placed her on her feet.

He led her up some steps to a big door in one of those brownstone houses, pressing the buzzer and pushing it open.

They had to climb up to the top floor as there was no lift. Her brother's apartment was big and full of noise. As soon as she walked in the door, Darragh's wife, Josie, embraced her while her two little nieces, Casey and Holly, began jumping up and down in excitement.

'Aunty Mairead, Aunty Mairead!'

Mairead was shocked by how emotional she felt to see her nieces for the first time. Ever since Mam had died, tears had come so easily but she pushed them back and plastered a smile on her face. She didn't want to upset the little girls as they tugged on her to show her around the apartment.

After a noisy excited meal with present-giving, Darragh took Mairead to his bar. It was only two blocks away from the apartment. Everyone seemed to know her brother in this neighbourhood, giving him a wave or saying Hi, just like an Irish country village.

The bar was named Brady's Irish Pub. To see their father's surname above the door beside an Irish harp and a shamrock gave her heart a little lurch. Dad would have been so thrilled to see it.

Darragh showed her to a nook in the bar, and then went up and got them two pints of Guinness.

'Not as good as back home,' he said, taking a sip of his Guinness. 'But nearly.'

She drank from the silken black pint. She was beginning to feel tired. It was, after all, the middle of the night back home.

'Thanks for coming, Mairead,' Darragh said, looking serious.

She noticed her brother had picked up a slight American accent.

'Your family is just lovely,' she said. 'Josie's gorgeous, and the girls.'

Darragh beamed. 'Aren't they?' His face fell. 'I'm glad Mam got to see them last year, but I wish she could have got over again before—'

'It was so fast, Darragh,' Mairead said. 'Shocking fast.'

He nodded. 'I feel so bad I couldn't get over to say goodbye.'

'You said it on the phone.'

'Ah, it's not the same, Mairead.' His voice broke. 'But I couldn't risk it. You know... me and Josie are settled here with the kids, and the bar.'

'And Mam understood that, Darragh. You've a whole life here in America.'

They drank together, the atmosphere a little gloomy until Darragh shook himself and, leaning forward, gave his sister a smile.

'So, how's Stella's acting going in London? You must be very proud. She was around eight when I last saw her and now she must be what, eighteen? But you could tell she had star quality.'

Mairead rolled her eyes. 'I wanted her to get a degree first, go to university—'

'But she's very talented, sis.'

'Well, there's an agent interested in her already,' she admitted.

'See!' Darragh gave her a little friendly shove. 'And Niall?' he asked tentatively, looking down at his pint. 'How's he?'

Mairead shrugged. 'OK.'

'Did he come to the funeral?'

'I told him not to.'

'Ah, Mairead.' Darragh shook his head.

'"Ah, Mairead" what, Darragh? I couldn't have him there, not after what he's done to me,' she snapped.

'Come on, Mairead. Sure, everyone knew Niall was gay.'

Mairead stared at her brother in astonishment. Him too?

'What do you mean, "everyone"?'

'Mammy and me,' he said. 'Like, it was obvious after you had Stella. I never noticed before you married, but then I was only a kid.'

'Did Daddy know?'

'I don't know, Mairead. Does it matter now?'

Mairead felt heat gathering under her shirt. She opened another button, pushed back her hair. 'Of course it matters if my whole family believed my husband was gay and didn't tell me!'

'I didn't think it was my business. I assumed you had some sort of agreement,' Darragh said casually.

'Fuck's sake, Darragh!' Mairead exploded.

Darragh looked at her in shock.

'I don't think I've ever heard you swear before,' he said.

'It's just I wish I had known sooner,' she raged. 'All those years I wasted, thinking it was my fault.'

'Oh, Mairead.' Darragh looked doleful. 'I'm sorry. But at least you're both free now. Though Niall should be careful with AIDS in London. I've lost too many friends over here in the past few years.'

'He has a boyfriend, Lesley,' she said tightly. 'Anyway, what do I care if he gets AIDS?'

'Oh, come on, Mairead.' Darragh looked aghast. 'It's horrific.'

AIDS hadn't even been a thought on her radar until now. No

one talked about it in Ireland.

'And you too,' Darragh said, 'if you're going to make up for lost time. Always, always make sure the fella wears a condom.'

'Christ, Darragh, I'm still a married woman!'

'Well, I don't see a wedding band on you.' He laughed. 'By the way, loving all the rings. Are those Mam's?'

'Yes, is it a bit over the top?'

'Nah, it looks good. The new liberated Mairead!'

She sighed, feeling far from liberated. Already she was anxious about being away from her job and the other side of the world from Stella. What if her daughter needed her?

'So, what do you want to do tomorrow?' Darragh asked. 'I'm free in the daytime and minding the girls while Josie's at work. We could go to Central Park?'

'That sounds good.' She took another sip of Guinness. 'I've to go somewhere in the morning first.'

'Like where?' Darragh asked.

'I'm going to the Upper East Side.'

'Fancy! I can take you there the day after. We can go together?'

'I need to go on my own,' she said. 'For now.'

Darragh looked confused.

'Before she died, Mammy was obsessed with finding her birth mother, our grandmother.'

'I didn't know Mam was adopted!' Darragh said.

'She wasn't adopted. Her father – our grandfather Giles – was married to another woman in America before he came back to Ireland. Her name was Ellen. She travelled over on the same boat from Ireland in 1925. They must have met on the boat and they got married and lived in New York City for eight years. That was where Mammy was born,' Mairead told her brother.

'I knew Mam was born in America because I remember those books on the New York skyscrapers Grandpa worked on. Didn't he help build the Empire State Building? I'm always telling Josie and the girls that!'

'Yes, that's right,' Mairead said.

'I just assumed he met Grandma Olivia in New York,' he said. 'That's wild – he was married to someone else!'

'Uncle Leonard is a half-brother,' Mairead told him. 'He was born in Ireland. That's why he's so much younger than her.'

'I can't believe I didn't know Grandma Olivia wasn't her birth mother!' he exclaimed. 'I mean, she was dead before I was born, and Mam never talked about her parents to me.'

Mairead decided not to tell Darragh that she had always known, but she'd been told never to talk about it.

'When Mam was sick, she was calling out for her mammy,' Mairead told Darragh. 'She told me her mother had deserted her the night they were all due to sail home from New York to Ireland.'

'When was that?'

'I think around 1933. Mammy asked me to try to find her.' Mairead paused, emotion welling up within her. 'She really wanted closure before she was gone. To know why her mother had left her. But I didn't succeed.'

'It sounds like an impossible task, Mairead,' Darragh consoled her.

'I did find out there was a house which belonged to Ellen's father near Ballycastle in Mayo,' Mairead continued. 'I took Mammy there. That was something.'

'That's amazing, Mairead.'

Mairead told Darragh about Merview House, how grand it must once have been, before it was abandoned to decay.

'That's a real shame,' Darragh said.

'I've also discovered more about Ellen's father in America. His name was Alec Lavelle and he was a steel magnate in Chicago in the twenties and thirties.'

Mairead took another sip of her Guinness.

'He's dead now and the only living descendant of his I can find is his great-nephew, a man called Kyle Symes, who lives on the Upper East Side in New York.'

'So that's why you want to go there tomorrow morning?'

'It's a long shot, but maybe he knows what happened to Ellen?'

Darragh didn't say anything for a moment.

'But, Mairead, does it really matter, now that Mammy's gone,' he said gently.

'It matters to me,' Mairead said fiercely. 'I promised her.'

'Are you sure, Mairead?' Darragh shook his head. 'What's the point of going on a wild goose chase for a woman who is most likely dead too? And if not, well, Ellen had her whole life to come looking for Mam and never did. I guess she doesn't want to be found.'

Mairead gazed into her brother's concerned eyes. She knew he was only looking out for her. But he didn't understand. He had spent his whole life confident of their mother's love.

'You know how me and Mam never really got along?' Mairead said to him.

'Ah now, she loved you, Mairead,' Darragh defended their mother.

'Not as much as you.' Mairead held up her hand to stop her brother from interrupting. 'And that's fine because I was Daddy's favourite. But something happened between Mammy and me this summer. We got very close. In death, Mam really showed her vulnerability. I had never seen her so open.' Mairead paused, aware tears were trailing her cheeks, as she saw them glitter in her brother's eyes. 'She had never asked me to do something for her before and this was something she really wanted me to do: find her mother.'

She took out a tissue and handed it to her brother. He blew his nose noisily.

'Don't you think it would be interesting to find out our family's history?' she said, trying to lift the mood.

'Not really,' he said, shrugging. 'Most Irish families have a lot of sad emigration stories. What's the point of dredging over the past?'

'You've just negated my whole purpose as a history teacher!'

Darragh gave a small laugh and clapped her on the back.

'Sorry, sis, you go ahead on your heritage hunt then. But don't pull me into it.' He finished off his pint. 'Must say, showing up on some dude's doorstep claiming you're a long-lost cousin is not a very Mairead thing to do.'

Her brother was right. Her old self would have written letters. Been so careful and polite. But it felt like she didn't have time for all the niceties now. She just wanted to find out the truth. No matter how hard it might be.

CHAPTER FIFTEEN

17 JULY 1937

Ellen could see the distinctive outline of the castor bean plant against the moonlit sky. She flitted across the parched earth of the back yard, scissors in one hand, and a basket in the other. Joseph had had the castor bean tree planted because he believed it kept away gophers from their meagre crops of beet and potatoes. This had made Gabriella shake her head, and she told Ellen in Spanish it wasn't true at all. Moreover, it was not a good idea to have castor bean plants at all because they were highly poisonous.

'But we make them into castor oil?' Ellen had said to Gabriella in Spanish.

'That is for the big farmers. They have to be careful. It is poisonous when you crush the bean and grind the seed inside. It will kill you.'

Ellen could still hear Frank and Vernon's cruel laughter echoing inside her head as she snipped away at the plant, and let the beans fall into her basket. It was as if her head was filled with a red mist of rage. She had to have her revenge. No matter the cost.

Slipping back into the kitchen, she brewed the coffee.

. . .

Joseph had been surprised when she had not sat down with him and the other men to eat.

'Are you not joining us?' he had asked.

'No, I've work to do—'

He had frowned, clearly confused by her refusal. She had felt Frank's eyes upon her. Vernon was already shovelling food into his mouth.

'You sure do look familiar,' he said again.

She shrugged. 'I've never met you before,' she said with her back to him, before scurrying out of the room. She felt Frank's beady eyes burning into the back of her, as if branding her skin. Indeed, her skin had never fully recovered from the roasting it had got in the desert the day after her assault. The day she nearly died because of those monstrous men. She wanted to run in there screaming, stab him with the kitchen knife, or take the big hot skillet and slam it into his face. But that might not kill him, and she had to be sure.

Ellen ground the castor beans, careful not to get any of the powder on herself. She tipped it into the coffee pot along with the ground coffee beans and the hot water. Joseph never drank coffee this late in the evening. She carried the pot in with two tin mugs for their guests.

As she poured out the coffee, she forced herself to look at Frank and Vernon again to be sure they really were the two men she thought they were. There was no doubt it was them. Frank's thick meaty arms protruded from his rolled-up sleeves, and she would never forget Vernon's ice-cold blue eyes. She felt like vomiting when she thought of them touching her.

'Thank you kindly,' said Frank, looking up at her. It was in that little millisecond he caught her eye. Her heart stopped dead for a moment as he smiled at her. 'What a great little lady you have here, Father,' he said to Joseph. 'Where did she come from?'

Ellen felt her whole body turn cold. *He knows who I am. And he has no shame.*

'El's a great help with the church and community,' Joseph said, not answering Frank's question. 'Say, El, I'll have some coffee too. It smells real good.'

'I'll brew some fresh for you,' she said, panic plucking at her chest.

'Why, there's plenty here,' Joseph said, picking up the pot. He finished the water in his tin mug. 'No need to get me a fresh cup. Got one here.'

He poured himself a cup of the deadly liquid as Ellen watched on in horror. She had to act quickly. She darted over to the table to collect the dirty plates. As Joseph raised the mug to his lips, she knocked it clean out of his hand. It spattered onto the wooden floors, and he yelped as it splashed his shirt.

'I'm so sorry,' she gushed, relief flooding through her as she grabbed the pot. 'I'll make fresh.' She knelt down and picked up his mug. 'Clean up your mug too.'

She paused at the doorway to the kitchen. Glanced back and held her breath as she watched both Frank and Vernon drinking up their coffee. One after the other slamming the mugs down.

'Damn good coffee, Father,' Vernon said.

Gabriella had described to Ellen what happened if you ate the inside of a castor bean. She had warned Ellen about lots of the dangerous plants in the region, but she told her this was the worst.

'There is no cure,' she had emphasised, wagging her finger at Ellen. 'Nothing.'

Always she had been afraid of Ellen's less careful approach to foraging.

If you ate the inside of a castor bean, nothing happened for maybe ten hours. But after that the poison would make you vomit, then would come the bloody diarrhoea. This could go on for a whole day and night as you got weaker and weaker. Then everything in your body would stop functioning and you would die.

'Bad, bad death,' Gabriella said, shaking her head.

The next morning Frank and Vernon left at first light. She heard cursing, as one of them vomited out back.

'What the hell, Vernon,' she heard Frank say.

'I don't feel so good, Frank.'

'Come on, you just ain't used to the spicy Mexican food,' Frank barked. 'We got work to do.'

She heard the black Ford sputtering away. Lay in her bed quite still. Hands on her heart. What had she done? What if they survived and realised she had poisoned them? They were lawmen! Frank didn't sound sick in the least. She closed her eyes. She was bad deep down in her very essence. Because if those men died, it wouldn't be the first time she'd killed. There was the nightmare image again in her head: the entrance hall at Merview House with the sweeping staircase and the big chandelier. The ticking of the grandfather clock in the hallway. Looking up to the top of the stairs and seeing herself. *Don't come down. Don't come down.* The red mist descending as she ran down the stairs. Crimson blood pooling on the white marble floor. In one moment, her instinct to hit back had taken over.

After finishing her chores, Ellen hid in the workshop, focusing on setting coral into a silver bracelet. When it was done, Joseph would take it, along with all the other jewellery they had made, to sell in the tourist towns near the Grand Canyon to raise money for the church and its community. For now, she was on her own. Joseph had gone into Phoenix to buy some provisions.

Ellen stared at the tiny buds of red coral and took a deep breath as she deftly set it into the silver. She tried to shake out of her head the image of the two Bureau agents vomiting and collapsing on the side of the dusty road. But the picture just kept growing and growing. Blood spewing out of their mouths as their bodies shut down. She couldn't be sorry she had done what she did. No, she was more afraid that they wouldn't die. That they'd come back and hurt all the people she now loved. Father Joseph and Gabriella and the Rodriguez family. She would do anything for those she loved. It was to protect Giles and Brigid that she had run away in the first place. Her mind drifted to her abandoned husband and daughter. Usually when she was setting stones, she was able to banish these thoughts, just as Joseph had told her she would. The focus of her task kept her mind directly on the skill needed to place the stones in the settings. But she couldn't settle today. Where were Giles and Brigid now? She felt certain Giles would have remarried; after all, he was a wealthy, accomplished man. Did Brigid have siblings now? She paused in her work and saw her daughter in the garden at the big white house in Dublin. Little sailboats in the distance. Brigid playing croquet with her new family, and her new mother, like Alice in *Alice in Wonderland* with the Queen of Hearts. Brigid was laughing and running around, playing chase with a little brother. Ellen gritted her teeth. It hurt to imagine these things. Her daughter's life without her. But yes, she had done the right thing. Brigid's childhood was unblemished by the shame and heartache of discovering her mother was a murderer. Let alone witnessing the consequences if Ellen had returned to Ireland.

It was near dark by the time Joseph returned from Phoenix. Ellen was sitting out on the porch waiting for him wrapped up in a blanket and smoking a cigarette. She watched him turn off the old pickup and get out. His familiar gait as he glided towards the house.

He sat down next to her on the porch, as she blew out smoke.

'Strangest thing,' Joseph said. 'You know those two fellas that camped out back last night? Well, they got taken real sick on the road to Phoenix. Poisoned, I heard. One of them is dead.'

'Which one?'

Her voice came out a whisper, and Joseph turned to her. She could see the shock etched on his face despite the lack of light.

'El, what have you done?'

. . .

She made her confession. Putting out her cigarette, she pressed her hands together in her lap. She told Joseph how she had met Frank and Vernon. What they had done to her. When she told him this, she heard his horrified grunt.

'They're the reason I nearly died in the desert,' she said. 'When I saw them in my home it did something to me, Joseph.'

'Oh El.' He shook his head. 'Why didn't you tell me?'

'I'm telling you now,' she said.

'It's too late now,' Joseph breathed softly. 'Look what you've done.'

'They deserved it.'

Joseph said nothing for a moment.

'That was not up to you to decide. They would have had to face their sins in the next world all the same.'

She leapt up from her chair, the blanket falling. Her body charged with anger.

'Are you saying I should have done nothing?' she exclaimed. 'They brutalised me. They will go on hurting other girls, and yet they work for the government. They're FBI agents. I'm not sorry I did what I did, I'm not!'

'Oh El,' Joseph said again, his voice thick with disappointment.

'I'm not like you, Father, I can't turn the other cheek. I've never been able to.'

There was more she could tell him, but she knew she never would. This was bad enough. What would he think of her past in Ireland?

But also, his reaction hurt in a strange way. She wanted him to be outraged and wish those awful men dead because of what they had done to her. But he seemed more concerned about her actions than why she had done what she did.

She stormed past him and into her bedroom. She couldn't face seeing his expression.

. . .

The next morning Joseph was waiting for her at the kitchen table. As he picked up the coffee pot and poured them coffee, she remembered how coolly she had poisoned those two men. It was hard to believe she had done such a thing. She sat down and waited. She could tell he was getting ready to speak. He looked at her and his expression was grave.

'The man who died was named Vernon Willis. I don't know the fate of his companion, Frank Jackson.'

Ellen jolted. The idea of Frank surviving made her feel dizzy with dread.

'Did he recognise you?'

She nodded.

'You have to leave,' Joseph said. 'Because he will know it was you. We have castor plants in the back yard. It is a clear case of poisoning.'

'No,' Ellen gasped. She had done what she did so she could stay where she was. To protect her new life.

'You told me they're FBI agents. They have the law behind them.'

'But, Joseph, Frank might come for you...' She faltered.

'I will say I know nothing,' he said. 'That much is clear because I nearly drank the coffee.'

Ellen stared down at her mug of dark brown liquid in shame.

'Would you have let me die to enact your revenge, El?'

'No,' she gasped, tears welling in her eyes. 'No, Joseph, you are dear to me.'

He shook his head and stood up. 'I don't know who you are, but not the girl I thought you were.'

'Where will I go?' she sobbed.

'You need to get out of the State of Arizona. Out of America, in fact, because Frank is a federal agent,' Joseph said calmly.

She clutched her throat as if she were choking.

'But I don't want to go. Please, don't make me.'

'You made your choice when you put the castor beans in the

coffee,' he said sternly. 'They'll assume you'll head for the Mexican border because it's so close to Arizona. Therefore I think you should go to Canada.'

'But it's miles and miles to Canada!'

'I'll drive you to Los Angeles,' he offered. 'It's a long journey, but there's a way. Train to San Francisco and on to Seattle. Then the boat to Vancouver in Canada.'

'But where will I go in Canada?' she wailed. 'I've nowhere to go.'

Joseph looked at her with his clear blue eyes.

'I've a friend in Vancouver, a fellow priest; he will help you,' he said, pausing. 'And my uncle Jacob lives in the remote town of Tofino on the west coast of Vancouver Island. No one will find you there. I'll send him a telegram and he'll give you shelter until you find your feet.'

'But what then?' she said. 'Please, can't I hide out here?'

'If you stay here, you know they will find you.'

Ellen shook her head desperately.

'I believe you will prevail wherever you go. You survived the Arizona desert. But if I allow you to stay in America, you will be caught.' He sighed. 'And though what you did was wrong, I don't want to see you go to the electric chair for it.'

She gulped. The seriousness of the situation hitting her.

'Oh, Joseph, I'm frightened.' She ran over and clutched at his hands. 'I'm sorry, please forgive me.'

He took her in his arms, and she wept into his cotton shirt.

'It's not me who has to forgive you, child. You will find your way. The Good Lord will not abandon you,' he sighed, patting her head. 'Remember, all sins are forgiven on Judgement Day.'

But his words washed over her. She had stopped listening to the priests back home, and Joseph had never been God's representative to her. He had been her best friend. A guide out of the dark pain of her first years of loss. But now she was going to be thrust back out into the wilderness again. And it was of her own making.

Once again she had laid down her own desperate path of destitution.

'We will drive west this afternoon,' he said to her.

'Canada is very far away,' she whispered.

'Yes, it must be so. Leave behind all you have here, dear girl. And begin again.'

CHAPTER SIXTEEN

15 SEPTEMBER 1984

Mairead sat on the white leather couch feeling shabby in her jeans and T-shirt. She had never in her life been surrounded by such luxury. It was hard to believe this was the home of someone she was related to, even if somewhat distantly.

Kyle Symes must have been about ten years older than her, but he was in good shape. Thick brown hair and smooth tanned skin, with very white teeth. He sat opposite her on another huge leather couch, against the backdrop of a giant and colourful contemporary painting. To Mairead's left was a wall of glass with panoramic views of Central Park. Somewhere in the jungle of greenery her brother and nieces were playing where she had left them.

'Well, this is so neat.' Kyle beamed at Mairead. 'I thought I was the last living descendant of Great-Uncle Alec.'

Before Kyle, on his huge marble coffee table, Mairead had spread out the family tree Eoin had drawn for her.

'My grandmother's maiden name was Ellen Lavelle,' Mairead explained. 'She was Alec's daughter by his first wife, Dorothy. Have you heard of Ellen or my mother, Brigid?'

'Sorry.' Kyle shook his head. 'Never heard mention of

Dorothy, or Ellen or a daughter, Brigid. And I knew Great-Uncle Alec when I was a little boy. He was married to my grandfather's sister Julia. I guess she must have been his second wife, if you say he was married before in Ireland to a woman called Dorothy.'

'Dorothy died in 1910 when Ellen was only two,' Mairead told him. 'They lived on a big estate in the west of Ireland called Merview House. It's currently for sale. Do you own it now? The estate agent wouldn't tell us who it belongs to, but he did tell us the vendor is in America.'

Kyle knitted his brows.

'Nope, never heard of Merview House. Must have been sold on years ago. I don't think my great-uncle ever wanted to return to Ireland,' Kyle said. 'I remember Gramps telling me Great-Uncle Alec didn't have happy memories of the place.'

'And you're sure you've never heard of Ellen Lavelle?'

'Sorry, nope.' Kyle opened his arms in an expression of apology.

Mairead's heart sank. Kyle Symes was her only chance of a connection. If he didn't know anything about Ellen, then the trail stopped here in New York.

Kyle picked up the makeshift family tree. Stared at it hard.

'For an Irish family, there's not too many of us,' he commented. 'I mean, Alec had a brother, Rafe? But he didn't even marry! Can't believe you and me are all that's left. So, what are we to each other?'

'I think we're second cousins.'

Mairead was about to explain that Darragh and his girls and her daughter Stella were missing from the tree, but Kyle began speaking again.

'Say, are you OK? You look real pissed.'

His intimate tone surprised her. But she was frustrated, and clearly it showed on her face.

'I promised my mam I'd find her mother,' Mairead sighed. 'But I've failed. It was her dying wish.'

'Ah.' Kyle scratched his designer-stubbled chin. 'Dying wishes suck.'

The couch squeaked as Mairead got up. She picked the family tree up and tucked it back in her pocket.

'Well, thank you all the same, it was nice to meet you,' she said.

'Say, you can't just walk out,' Kyle exclaimed, raising his arms dramatically. 'It's real exciting to meet family from Ireland. Come have a drink with me?'

'Oh, it's not even lunchtime,' Mairead said. 'And don't you have plans?'

It was hard to believe this wealthy New Yorker didn't have a packed social itinerary. It was Saturday after all.

'We've time for a Martini!' Kyle said, grinning at her, and Mairead found herself accepting his offer.

She followed Kyle down his hallway of varnished wooden floors, past shelves of modern sculptures and artefacts from all around the world, into a kitchen gleaming with stainless steel implements. Everything was so clean and streamlined. He padded around the kitchen in his bare feet and Levi's jeans. It was hard to ignore how handsome he was. They were cousins and those kinds of thoughts were forbidden. Well, he was a second cousin... that wasn't so bad, she told herself.

Mairead found herself glancing at his backside in the jeans. The definition of his thighs through the denim. *Snap out of it, Mairead.* Her friendship with Eoin had awoken something within her which had been dormant for so many years. She had been fine when she hadn't thought about being with another man. With Niall she had given up, switched off. But now, as she slipped onto the high stool on the other side of Kyle's marble-topped breakfast bar, she couldn't help feeling a little stirring inside her. She realised she was frustrated. She and Eoin hadn't even kissed, but there had been sexual tension between them since the first time they met. Clearly, it was still there within her.

She watched Kyle make them two Martinis, all the time telling herself she really should leave. Then he came to sit next to her as they clinked glasses. The cocktail was very strong. Mairead felt the alcohol rushing to her head. She'd not eaten anything yet today. A small voice inside her head, sounding a lot like the sanctimonious tones of Sister Mary Stephen, whispered a warning. But Mairead took another sip. It tasted so good.

They drank two more Martinis, by which time Mairead was drunk. Kyle took her back into his vast lounge with views of Central Park to show her his vintage collection of jazz records from the twenties and thirties.

'If it wasn't for the speakeasies none of these greats would have found their way onto vinyl,' he told her, putting on a Bessie Smith record. 'This one was made in 1928. It's called "Empty Bed Blues",' he said, winking at her before offering her his hand. 'Want to dance?'

'Oh, I'm no good at dancing,' Mairead said, blushing deeply.

'Everyone can dance, if they just relax,' Kyle said, taking hold of her hand and pulling her up from the couch.

As Kyle drew her close, she felt the heat of his body against hers. She hadn't been this near to a man in years. She and Eoin had always been at arm's length. She felt a sudden surge of anger at Eoin. He had played games with her! Well, she didn't care about him any more. She was dancing with Kyle, and it felt so good. Part of her was terrified of what might happen next, wanted to pull away, but another part of her wanted to do the exact opposite. She felt his hips pressed against hers, his skin touching hers. She looked up into his eyes, and they glittered with suggestion. Before she could get her head straight, he bent down and kissed her on the lips. She had no feelings towards this distant cousin, and yet the fact he was a stranger made it easier to let go. Here in New York, in a place so different from where she lived, Mairead shed her schoolteacher persona. Of course, all the Martinis she had drunk helped, but she was conscious enough to be in control of her decisions. Suddenly she was swept away by a powerful need to let rip. She'd been sensible for her whole life, and what good had it done her? As if sensing her desire to set herself free,

Kyle kept kissing her. She pulled back once, breathless, and giddy.

'We shouldn't kiss, we're cousins,' she slurred.

'Precisely why it makes it all the more sexy,' he said, a mischievous glint in his eyes. 'The more forbidden the better.'

One minute they were dancing and the next he was leading her to his bedroom. She tugged off her T-shirt and kicked off her jeans. She was laughing. Big delicious belly laughs for the first time since her mother had died.

The next morning, they made love again as soon as they woke up. Kyle's bedroom was filled with light, and immense. It felt as if the bed itself was the same size as her whole bedroom back home. As he kissed her lips, her neck, her breasts, and all over her body she felt warmth seeping into every part of her. Each touch felt as if he was unlocking different parts of her body. Places she had shut away for years. There was a part of Mairead out of her body looking down at this woman hungry for sex in shock. Who was she? But deep inside was a part of her so buried, now Kyle had unearthed it, she had run amok. She had never been so present in her body. Never so free from hurting from the past or worrying about the future. All she wanted was this moment. Every time Kyle pulled her to him and their limbs entwined, she was able to let go of all the times Niall had turned his back on her. The nights her husband had made excuses and gone to sleep in the spare room. All those hours she had lain, staring up at the ceiling, believing she was so repulsive not even her husband could stand to make love to her.

But Kyle made her feel like a goddess. She could sense his admiration of her naked body. At first, she'd kept her eyes closed, a little shy. All their passion had been so immediate and spontaneous. They must have drunk at least four cocktails before he had taken her to see his bedroom.

At some point in the afternoon, she had rung her brother. Told him she was staying over with Kyle. They'd hit it off. Darragh being Darragh hadn't been bothered at all. If she remembered correctly his words were 'Way to go, sis, he's loaded.'

After they had made love for the first time, Kyle had insisted on taking her out for dinner. At first she had refused, but the effects of the Martinis had begun to wear off and she was very hungry. On the way to the restaurant, he had ordered his driver to stop the car outside the Gucci store on Fifth Avenue.

'Honey, you can't go for dinner where I'm taking you in jeans,' he had said, thrusting a bundle of dollar notes into her hand. 'Go pick a dress.'

She had squirmed with mortification.

'Oh no, I can just go back and get changed. Meet you later—'

'Indulge me,' Kyle said. 'Look, I'm excited to meet you! And believe me, I make a stack of money.'

'What do you do?'

'This and that,' he said. 'Mainly trading stocks on Wall Street.'

She had run into the store, grabbing the first item that caught her eye and she had enough money for. When she put it on in the changing rooms, she had been blown away by the sight of her own reflection. The sex had put a light in her eyes, and her skin was glowing. Her hair had fallen out of her uniform ponytail and was loose over her shoulders. Even her red lipstick looked more glamorous in this get-up.

The Gucci dress was now sprawled on the plush white carpet at the foot of the bed. She nearly squealed with delight to see it. A silvery slinky skin of exquisite couture.

After dinner, which she couldn't remember that much about as they had been drinking champagne rather than eating in the end, they had come back to the apartment for a nightcap.

As soon as they'd walked in, Kyle had started kissing her. They'd shed their clothes yet again. Flowed together in a sequence of melting passion. Rapture swept through her as they fell upon his bed. Kyle lifted her legs onto his shoulders and gently prised her apart with his tongue. She had never experienced anything like this in her whole life. As her body arched and she experienced her first orgasm with a man, release swept through her. This was so different from masturbation. This intimacy, the intuitive giving and taking of passion, and this connection. She felt a wave of anger at Niall and then deep utter sorrow. How could she blame him? If he had found this, well, it was intoxicating. After years in the desert, how can you turn down a glass of water?

Afterwards she and Kyle lay in each other's arms not speaking. She heard his breath deepen as he fell asleep, but the lovemaking had sobered her up a little and she felt wakeful. She lay on her side, his arms wrapped around her, gazing at the view from his bedroom window. It was a clear night, and the moon was full. Bathing the skyscrapers old and new in silvery light. The Chrysler Building glittered like a fantasy tower as the sky filled with so many stars. She stared at them all, thinking again about Ellen Lavelle.

What had made her abandon her little girl, Mairead's mother, Brigid? This damage had been passed down from her mother to her. What had broken them? Mairead had not thought well of Ellen. She had judged her for leaving her husband and child. But sometimes people did strange spontaneous things out of character. She felt she could understand Ellen's actions a little more now. Since she had walked into Kyle Lavelle's swanky Fifth Avenue apartment hours and hours ago, she hadn't thought once about her own daughter, Stella. Sometimes being a mother was limiting. But in this moment, Mairead was not a mother; she was limitless.

After they had started the day with sex, Kyle had brought her coffee in bed, and got back in to join her. In the morning light, she could see silvery grey streaking his dark brown hair. It made him even more attractive to her.

'Have you ever been married?' she asked him.

'Yeah,' he said, taking a sip of his coffee.

He shifted in the bed to put his arm around her. 'How about you?'

'I broke up with my husband last year.'

He was looking at her keenly and again she found herself not wanting to talk about Stella. Let him think she had no kids. It was simpler.

'Was it a bad break-up?' he pushed.

'Yes, very,' she said, not wanting to go into details.

Kyle picked up her hand in both of his and held it.

'Well, that's the wheel of life, honey,' he said. 'We've got to go through the bad times to get to the good.'

Kyle pulled her to him and then rolled her on the bed. 'And what a very good girl you are, Mairead.'

Later they ate on his balcony, looking out across Central Park. Hot buttered muffins, and more cups of coffee. The September morning was mild, and the sun softly graced her cheeks. To her surprise she looked up to see a golden hawk circling above the city in the unblemished sky. As she gazed up at the sweeping bird, Kyle spoke.

'I was thinking,' he said. 'I do remember mention of Ellen Lavelle now.'

Mairead looked over at him in surprise.

'Really?' she asked, hope surging through her. 'Do you know what happened to her?'

He had sunglasses on so she couldn't read his expression.

'Yes, she died,' he said, a pensive sound to his voice. 'I remember my grandfather telling me how sad it was that all of his brother-in-law's children had died before him. Remember the ones you have in the family tree?'

'Stephen and Georgia Lavelle? Alec and his second wife Julia's children?'

'Yes,' Kyle continued. 'Stephen died during the Second World War, and Georgia died of cancer in 1959 the year before her father. I think that might have been what killed him.'

'And Ellen?'

'If I remember rightly, my grandfather told me she went back to Ireland in the mid to late-thirties and died there. Not sure when.'

'Oh,' Mairead said, crestfallen with disappointment. 'What a wild goose chase!'

'Yeah, it's a bitch,' Kyle said, though he didn't sound bothered at all. 'But one good thing is your goose chase brought you to me.'

He leant over and kissed her on the lips, and Mairead felt herself stirring again. All thoughts of Ellen Lavelle faded away as her body thrummed with desire. This was all she needed right now.

CHAPTER SEVENTEEN

19 JULY 1937

They left at first light after a hasty goodbye with the Rodriguez family.

'El has to move on,' Joseph told them with no explanation.

Gabriella had looked at her with troubled eyes.

'But I thought you were happy here?' she said to her in Spanish.

Ellen bit her lip. She didn't know how to explain what had happened. To make Gabriella's sadness at her departure go away.

'We'd better get going,' Joseph said. 'I want to get further north and west before it gets real hot.' She knew what he was thinking. Before Frank came looking for her.

'I have something to give you,' Gabriella said to Ellen.

She disappeared into the other room and a few minutes later returned carrying a small beaded bag with long straps like a belt and a small figurine of La Santa Muerte.

'You tie the purse under your shirt, keep precious things like La Santa Muerte and money safe.'

'It's beautiful, thank you,' Ellen whispered, humbled by Gabriella's generosity. She had nothing to give her.

'I made it for you,' Gabriella said.

The bag was covered in tiny beads in many different colours. It was in a traditional Mexican pattern. The colours and shapes appeared as abstract pathways all connected to each other.

It was also the perfect size for Ellen's copy of the turquoise necklace she'd made. Still it hurt to think of Brigid and the day she might wear the original around her neck. Ellen would never see it on her. Not now she was on the run again. She felt a deep stab in her heart. She had to let her daughter go. There was no chance she would ever see her again. But the necklace she had created with such love and tenderness made her feel connected to Brigid somehow. She took it out of her purse, and gazed at the turquoise stone flecked with brown, and cracked with age. She slipped it into the beaded bag and under her blouse as Gabriella tied it around her waist like a belt. She could feel the weight of the necklace against her middle. It felt as if she was carrying the stone of her ancestors, despite the fact the turquoise had been from Arizona.

The morning she left Arizona, Joseph had driven in tense silence north out of Scottsdale for hours until eventually they hit Route 66.

'This will take us all the way to Los Angeles,' Joseph said as he joined the highway. Ahead of them was a truck piled with household belongings, with two boys sitting on its peak and staring back at them, their faces too miserable for ones so young.

'Poor creatures,' Joseph said, as they overtook the slow truck.

The cab was crammed with a whole family. Father driving, mother with a baby on her lap, and four children along with a grandparent all squeezed in. Their faces tight with desperation and hunger.

They were refugees from the states blighted by the dust storms, just as Gladys had told her.

'Where are they going?' she asked Joseph.

'I guess they're hoping to get work picking fruit in California,' he said. 'But I heard there's huge refugee camps and not enough work. These people are starving but no one is helping them.'

'That's terrible,' she said.

They drove west all afternoon, despite the heat. Ellen's dress though light was stuck to her with sweat but she didn't dare ask Joseph to stop because what if Frank had recovered and was already on their tail? What if he had a posse of other federal agents with him? As dark began to gather, they pulled off the road near a copse of pinyon pine trees. The air was a little cooler now, and she shivered in her damp dress. They made a fire and ate the tortilla and beans which Gabriella had forced on them that morning.

On the second day, they arrived in Los Angeles – the city which had been her original goal when she had got on the train in Chicago four years ago. Her dream of acting in movies seemed childish and stupid to her now.

They parked the old pickup, and Joseph walked with her towards the train station. She was to take a train to San Francisco, he told her. From there to Portland in Oregon, and the final part of the journey by train was to Seattle.

'Then you need to take a steamship to Vancouver in Canada,' he said. He took out a bundle of notes and gave them to her, as well as three letters with names and addresses. 'Here's a letter for Father Francis in Vancouver – he'll take care of you – and I've already sent a telegram to my uncle Jacob in Tofino. Just wire him when you know what boat you'll be on. But this is another letter with his address on it for you.'

'I can't take your money—'

'You have to. You'll need it for your tickets. The third letter confirms you're my sister, Ellie Jawlosky. Just in case any authorities stop you...'

His voice trailed off. Ellen looked at Joseph's earnest face. How had she dragged this good man into her wrongdoing?

'I'm worried you'll get in trouble when you go back. Won't you come with me?' she asked him.

'We built that church brick by brick,' Joseph said to her. 'I am never leaving it.'

'I'm sorry, Joseph.'

'It's done, El,' he said. 'But as long as you repent, God will grant you forgiveness.'

There was an awkward pause as she looked down at her coffee cup. The truth was she was sorry she had disappointed Joseph, but she was not sorry she had poisoned those evil men. In her heart she still wanted them dead for what they had done to her. What they would do to other lost and vulnerable girls just like her.

They sat at a cafe in the train station concourse, waiting for her train. There were so many women walking on their own like birds of paradise in their fashionable gowns, sunglasses and wide-brimmed raffia hats. She felt grimy after her day and night on the road, although she had bathed in a stream earlier that morning before they'd driven into Los Angeles.

The city was full of buzz because of the longshoreman strikes all down the west coast. There had been violent clashes with the police.

'All they want is decent wages and working hours.' Joseph shook his head as they looked at the image on the front of the newspaper he had bought at the station kiosk. It was of a policeman battering a striker in San Francisco. 'If the rich shared what they had, don't you think we wouldn't be in this Depression at all?' he asked. She wanted to tell him she didn't think it was that simple. There would always be strife between men over money, and land, and property. She knew that well, coming from Ireland. But Joseph's question was clearly rhetorical as he turned the page of the paper and continued to read. Then she saw him go very still and she looked over his shoulder at the headline.

WOMAN SOUGHT IN CONNECTION WITH
SUSPECTED POISONING

He raised his eyes and gave her a long look.

'Oh Joseph,' she whispered, clutching his hands.

'It's OK,' he said. 'There's no picture of you. You've just got to get over the border.'

She looked into Joseph's blue eyes, and it hurt so much to know she would never be comforted by them again. On their road trip when they had stopped for the night and slept by their campfire, curled up in their own blankets side by side, she had wanted so much to roll over towards him. She had imagined Joseph putting his arms around her and holding her. That was all she had wanted. Nothing more. But he was a priest. It was sinful of her to even consider he might want to hold her to him. He was no more than a very good Samaritan.

'I will pray for you,' he said softly, as he released her hands.

As she got on the train, Joseph leaned forward and tucked her hair beneath her hat. He handed her a packet of hair dye.

'If you get the chance, dye your hair,' he said. 'The red is very distinctive.'

She nodded, fighting back the tears.

'And send me a telegram when you get to Tofino,' he said. 'Make sure you use the name Ellie Jawlosky.'

'It's so far away.'

'Just keep going, El,' he said. 'You'll get there.'

She wasn't sure if he meant Tofino or to her destination in life.

Ellen leant over the side of the steamship *Princess Norah* and looked at the deep blue ocean as they chugged along the western coast of Vancouver Island in Canada. She had embarked in

Victoria at 11 p.m. and spent a restless night twisting and turning in her bunk. It was hard to let herself rest after weeks on the run. But it felt better to be moving again after days stuck in Victoria, waiting for the departure date for the boat. The hypnotic blue of the Pacific waters, the gentle sway of the boat, and the gulls circling above all helped to calm her. She hadn't realised just how much she had missed the sea until she had arrived in Seattle.

She had walked from Seattle train station with stiff legs all the way to the port to find out about the next boat. As soon as she had seen the first blue glint on the horizon, she had felt a wave of homesickness. Her thoughts returned to the west of Ireland all those years ago, and then to her daughter, Brigid, living by the sea in Dublin. She would be ten years old now.

It was in Seattle, in a run-down inn by the port, that she had bleached her red hair blond.

In Vancouver she had stayed with Father Francis, an old friend of Joseph's from his seminary days. When she had arrived by boat in Victoria, she had stayed in an inn run by the priest's sister, Magdalena. Ellen had had to wait a whole week for this final leg of the journey on the coastal steamer from Victoria to Tofino, winding through the inlets of Western Canada. The boat was full of well-to-do families on their holidays, dropping off at the stops on their way to stay in vacation houses or inns. She couldn't help remembering the desperate families she had seen in their trucks with their whole lives piled up in the back on Route 66. All they wanted was a home of their own. The idea of a holiday would have been like flying to the moon for them.

But soon Ellen let all the panic-filled images from her weeks on the run fade away. Nature was filling her with hope. She was captivated by the scenery. Leaning against the ship's rail on the deck for hours looking at the magnificence of the landscape, the big sky, and the giant ocean. It felt as if they were opening her inside out. The stretches of golden beaches, the thick rainforests fringing them. One day, she saw a brown bear and its cubs standing on rocks gazing at the boat as it chugged by. It blew her breath away. To see such animals in the wild, alone and strong, brought tears to her eyes. Another day dolphins swam alongside the boat, and she longed to join them in the water. And then there was the day she saw the big blue whale. An island of shimmering deep blue rising in a crest of clear water as its blowhole showered a fountain of water, then slowly it plunged back into the depths. She pressed her hands to her heart, watching as the great whale rose as if at one with the rhythm of the waves. She delighted in the fountain of water spouting out from its blowhole and the swell of the sea as it plunged back down to the depths. Ellen felt the echo of its presence long after it had swum away from the boat, on out into the vast Pacific Ocean. She closed her eyes, and she could see it still moving before her. It filled her with a sense of peace she had not felt in her whole life.

At the jetty in Tofino, Joseph's uncle Jacob was there to meet her. He was a jolly man, with a stronger New York accent than his nephew. Tofino was even smaller than Scottsdale. There appeared to be more boats in the harbour than houses in the town. Jacob owned and ran the only grocery and feed store, which was situated in the main street. Ellen was to work in the store alongside Jacob. He had arranged lodgings for her in the only inn in Tofino as Jacob explained it wouldn't be proper for her to live with him.

'Folk would talk since I'm not a priest like my nephew, oh certainly not!' he said, giving a hearty laugh as he clapped her on the back so hard she nearly fell over.

He was as jovial as Joseph had been serious but there was a similar look around his eyes which made Ellen like him immediately.

'There's a few visitors around because of the end of the summer season,' he said. 'But it gets real quiet in winter. Lots of rain and wind, boy are there storms,' he huffed. 'Miss the snow back east.'

'What brought you here?' Ellen asked him.

'Well, missy, I reckon I'm a little like you, on the run with secrets to keep.' He gave her a big wink. 'Not all the men in our family are as godly as my nephew.'

His words surprised Ellen, but she didn't pry. She understood the importance of keeping your own story closely locked inside. She had never told Joseph who she really was or where she had come from, and he had never asked.

Here in Tofino, she had a chance to be free from her tragic past, her heartbreak and her loss. She would strike a line through America, and another line through Ireland. She had thought she loved the desert of Arizona, but she felt totally different in this small settlement on the western coast of Canada. There were First Nation people here too, and Jacob taught her their name: *Tla-o-qui-aht*, which he said meant 'people from a different place'.

Ellen felt as if she were a different person who came from no place, while at the same time she could belong in any place. Here she was again, acting a part, this time as the storekeeper's niece from New York. There was not a hint of her Irish accent any more, which she had dropped while in Arizona. She remembered play-acting with Brigid. How her little girl had loved her mammy pretending to be characters from her storybooks. She had been manic and crazy as the March Hare, funny as the Mad Hatter, sleepy and dozy as the dormouse, bossy and scary as the Queen of Hearts, and her daughter's best friend as Alice. She had spoken in posh English accents, Irish brogue, and brash New York. Flitting in between. Just as she had done herself as a little girl when she used to play make-believe in Merview House. She had played the part of wife and mother, and she had played the part of the killer. They were all who she was, and yet none of them were who Ellen *really* was.

Her first week in Tofino, Ellen awoke every day expecting to come down to breakfast at the lodging house and encounter Frank Jackson sitting at the breakfast table, pointing his gun at her. She scanned the newspapers in Uncle Jacob's store, but they were Canadian newspapers, old ones too, and there was no mention of her or her crime within them.

· · ·

At the end of the first week, Uncle Jacob asked her if she could drive.

'Yes, kind of,' she said, remembering when she had learnt on the muddy, bumpy drive of Merview House.

'Well, OK then,' Uncle Jacob said, and sent her off in his pickup to deliver food to some of the outlying settlers and the logging camps. As she bumped along tracks through forests of huge monolithic trees, she felt humbled beyond anything she had experienced before.

At the end of her second week working for Jacob in the food store, Ellen had been walking back to her boarding house, shoulders sore from bagging grain, when she remembered she hadn't sent Joseph a telegram to tell him she had arrived safely. She immediately felt guilty for being so thoughtless. She was also anxious to hear from him. Had Frank turned up in Scottsdale looking for her? She turned around and walked back down the main street to the small telegraph house with the flagpole and the Canadian flag fluttering atop it.

As she approached, she saw two men sitting outside smoking pipes. One of them was First Nation, and the other man, wearing shirtsleeves, and a hat tipped over his forehead, must have been the telegraph agent.

As soon as she came closer, he knocked the hat back off his head and sat up.

'Hey there, are you Jacob Jawlosky's niece?' he asked.

She nodded. He was the youngest man she had seen in the settlement, apart from boys.

'Welcome to Tofino,' he said. 'This here is my friend Gregory Tom. My name's Jack Lanois, at your service.'

'Thank you,' she replied, blushing. His eyes were as dark as black coffee, his smile broad. His skin was tanned from the summer sun.

'We're just discussing the good news that the Canadian authorities have given this geographical area here its proper First Nation name.'

'Oh, what would that be?' she asked.

'Esowista Peninsula,' said Jack.

'Esowista means "captured by the clubbing of people who lived there to death",' added Gregory Tom, while Jack Lanois kept on smiling at her, with a challenging glint in his eyes.

If they were trying to shock her, she wasn't going to show it.

'Well, that sounds appropriate,' she said evenly. 'I don't know much about the history of Tofino, but it's the way it is everywhere where the original people are suppressed by their conquerors.'

'Sure is!' said Jack, getting up from his seat. 'And whereabouts are you from?'

It was on the tip of her tongue: Ireland. The longing to talk with these men and let them know she knew all about the suppression of a country's natives. But she held back.

'Nowhere,' she said, and Jack raised his eyebrows in amusement.

'Okay then Ellie Jawlosky from nowhere.' He held out his hand. 'I sure am glad to meet you. Nice to have some new folk coming to live in Tofino.'

She took his hand and looked into his eyes as she felt his warm grasp. She had a strange feeling, as if she'd met him before. His eyes widened as he looked at her and she sensed he was thinking the same thing.

She looked away, a little embarrassed by the connection between them.

'I'd like to send a telegram,' she told him.

'Sure thing, Miss Jawlosky,' he said. 'You're a miss, right?'

He looked at her from beneath his dark eyelashes.

She paused, rubbing the turquoise three-stone ring on the little finger of her left hand. The ring that had replaced the wristwatch Giles had given her. She had a sudden remembrance of her wedding band and diamond engagement ring, piled next to Giles's bed as he had slept in the cabin of the boat. Next to them was the glorious turquoise necklace she had left for Brigid. Though she saw this scene in her mind's eye, and knew in the eyes of God she was married, she had stepped into the shoes of the unmarried niece of her uncle Jacob from New York.

'Yes, I'm a miss. I want to send a telegraph to my brother in Arizona to let him know I arrived safely.'

'Right you are!' Jack said, looking pleased.

As the last few tourists left Tofino, and the rain swept in from the west, Ellen finally received a letter from Joseph. Her heart beating with anxiety, she tore it open.

Dear sister Ellie,

I hope this finds you well and you are settling into life in Tofino. I have never travelled to the islands of the west coast of Canada but in my visits to my friend in Vancouver I found the area quite beautiful. The nature filled with God's most magnificent creations.

I am writing to let you know of the news in America. First of all, I must tell you that not long after you left, I read of the death of FBI agent Frank Jackson. He had been suffering from sickness since his poisoning and never fully recovered. Two men dead from castor bean poisoning. You must take upon your shoulders the weight of the consequence of your actions and ask the Good Lord to look upon you with mercy. I pray for you every day.

The hunt for you was on the front page of the papers in Arizona for two weeks. FBI agents and the local sheriff visited us to ask questions about you. We told the truth. You had turned up out of nowhere four years ago and neither I nor the Rodriguez family had any idea where you came from. No one told them I had driven you to Los Angeles. The assumption was made that you had escaped to Mexico, but the cops who spoke to me had no idea

*why you did what you did. It seemed that Frank Jackson gave no
indication of your previous encounter before he died.*

*Furthermore, there was not one mention you might have gone
to Canada. However, as soon as you have read this letter, I suggest
you destroy it. I shan't be writing to you again. It is hard for me, as
a man of God, to come to terms with your actions and the lack of
remorse you displayed afterwards. I will pray for your soul every
day. I will never betray you. This I can promise. But you will not
hear from me again.*

Please give my regards to Uncle Jacob.

Your brother, Joseph

Ellen's hands were shaking as she came to the end of the letter.
She could almost hear the deep disappointment of Joseph's voice as
she read his words. Tears welled in her eyes. What would he think
of her if he knew her whole story? The terrible past she had left
behind in Ireland. Was she destined for hell, according to her
priest friend?

'Hey, hell is right here on earth, sister,' she remembered Gladys
telling her one day when Ellen had suggested they would pay for
their sins in the afterlife. 'It's the parched, baked-out land where I
grew up. That there is hell. I've been there and I ain't never going
back.'

She read the letter twice, and then she tore it into tiny pieces,
and threw it on the fire in her bedroom in the lodging house. She
stirred the fragments of paper with the poker, and watched until
every last trace of Father Joseph's words had been transformed into
blue flames. She sat in front of the fire hugging her knees and
remembering those cosy safe nights she had sat in front of the fire
in her grand apartment on Park Avenue in New York, with Brigid
curled up in her lap as she read to her from *Alice's Adventures in
Wonderland*. In her sepia-toned memory, all she saw was herself
and her daughter. Giles was gone from the picture. She had

released the mixed feelings she possessed for her husband from her heart. But her daughter would always remain locked inside her. She could never let her go.

CHAPTER EIGHTEEN

Money. Sex. Drugs. Mairead had lost her mind, and she had never felt so alive. When she looked in the huge mirror in Kyle's marble bathroom, she was a completely different woman. One by one, she'd shed her skins. Wife, daughter, even mother. She shook her head, smiling at herself, as her red hair cascaded down her back. Kyle wouldn't let her tie it up. He liked the hair on her head to be wild and untamed, though sent her to a salon to be waxed everywhere else. He lavished money on her. She had facials, eyebrow tinting and shaping, eyelashes dyed. It made her look different. At the make-up counter in Saks, the sales assistant had booked her in for a makeover and shown her how to apply make-up to accentuate the shape of her eyes. She had been doing her make-up wrong for years. She remembered Stella trying to persuade her to change her look, but she hadn't listened to her daughter and insisted on sticking with her thick blue eye shadow and bright pink lips. Now she wore red. Sultry, scarlet. She loved to see its imprint on Kyle's skin when she kissed him.

Every time the voice in her head asked her, *Why is Kyle Symes spending so much money on you?* she would silence it, because she didn't want to know, not yet. She was having too much fun. Before she came to New York she hadn't even realised how trapped she had been. But her life back home had been a prison. She might as well have been one of the nuns in the convent where she taught.

Two weeks ago, she'd missed her flight back home. She had gone out partying the night before with Kyle and some of his Wall Street friends. It had gone on all night. Having never so much as touched a joint her whole life, Mairead was snorting coke using rolled-up dollar notes. Afterwards she had wild sex. She felt as if she was on fire. When she woke up two hours after her flight had departed, Kyle promised he'd pay for another.

'You knew you weren't going yet, baby,' he said, as he rolled on top of her.

Later Mairead had telephoned Sister Mary Stephen from Kyle's apartment.

'I need to extend my compassionate leave,' she had told the headmistress.

Sister Mary Stephen had not sounded pleased.

'The girls are asking for you, Mrs Tully,' she said. 'When do you think you can come back?'

Mairead wanted to yell, *Stop calling me Mrs Tully*, but somehow she resisted the impulse.

'Not sure,' she said, distracted by Kyle coming into the lounge completely naked and carrying two Bloody Marys. 'Actually, I'd like to take a sabbatical for three months.'

'Excuse me?' Sister Mary Stephen said in shock. 'What did you just say?'

'I want to take a sabbatical,' she said. 'I've been a loyal employee for fifteen years and I need a break.'

'That's very unorthodox. I would need to go to the board – and we can't pay you.'

'Well, either give me a sabbatical or I'm leaving.' Mairead couldn't believe how assertive she was being.

'But your girls—'

'They're fine without me. I am sure the substitute is doing a grand job.'

Before Sister Mary Stephen could protest further, Mairead put the phone down. The idea of walking back into the stifling atmosphere of the convent school was inconceivable. She felt as if her wings were spreading. She had been confined by rules her whole life. But Kyle didn't follow any rules and he seemed much happier than she had ever been.

She was still officially staying with Darragh and his family in Brooklyn Heights, but she spent most of her time in Kyle's apartment. At first, when she'd told her brother she was taking a sabbatical from her job and staying on for a few weeks, he'd been pleased.

'You need a break,' he said, 'after the year you've been through.'

He was right; it had been an awful twelve months during which her marriage had broken up, her daughter had left home, and her mother had died.

'They say things come in threes,' Darragh said. 'So that's you done for a while.'

When she had told Darragh that Kyle had revealed their grandmother Ellen was dead, he hadn't seemed that bothered.

'We never knew her anyhow,' he said. 'Look, Mairead, you've spent your whole life trying to please Mam, and you're still doing it, even now that she's dead. You've got to let it go.'

So, she did. Forgot all about Ellen Lavelle and the mystery behind her disappearance. She stepped into the present moment with Kyle, maxing out her credit card, and letting go all of her inhibitions.

After a week, though, Darragh had expressed concern. She had popped over to pick up the rest of her stuff, telling Darragh she would be staying with Kyle for a while. He'd insisted they go out for a pizza. As they left his apartment for the restaurant, she was sure she saw Darragh and Josie exchange loaded looks.

'Are you OK, sis?' he had asked her over the pizza.

'I'm fine,' she said, nibbling on one slice. She wanted to be able fit into all the new clothes Kyle had bought her. She had already lost a lot of weight since she had got to New York, but she wanted to be thinner. Kyle said it brought out her cheekbones.

'It's just... me and Josie are a bit worried,' he said. 'You seem to be out partying a lot and taking substances you're not used to.'

Mairead cocked her head at Darragh. 'Come on, you guys smoke weed every night after the girls are in bed.'

'I know, I know, but we've always done that,' Darragh said. 'I'm worried you're going off the deep end.'

'I'm just having fun, Darragh,' she said. 'You forget how boring my life has been! I went to college, met Niall, got pregnant and had Stella when I was nineteen. I juggled college and having a baby and being a wife. I've been at the convent teaching for fifteen years. Paying my mortgage and bills. Being sensible.'

'Well, when you put it like that...' Darragh said, shrugging. 'I get it.'

He tucked into another slice of the giant pizza, while Mairead pulled the olive off hers and popped it in her mouth.

'I'm thirty-seven already! I want to have a bit of freedom while I still can.'

'Mam was always free-spirited,' Darragh said. 'It doesn't stop once you're forty.'

At what price? Mairead wanted to say. Her mother had been cold and distant. When she had finally opened up, she'd been dying and it was too late. That wasn't who Mairead was going to be.

'What about Stella?' Darragh asked. 'Does she know where you are?'

'Of course she does,' Mairead snapped. 'I sent her a postcard. She doesn't have a phone in her flat. It's the only way I can contact her.'

'You could call Niall. He's her father, and in London too.'

'Darragh, I am never talking to Niall again if I can help it.' Mairead tossed her hair. 'Look, Stella doesn't call me for weeks on end. Let her have a taste of her own medicine.'

She felt triumphant as she said it. She had felt so needy back home in Kells in her empty nest. When she had talked to Stella on the phone over the past year, she had sensed that her daughter felt sorry for her. She didn't want to be an object of pity. She wanted her daughter to admire her. See her as strong and independent. Stella was far from judgemental. She had a feeling she would approve of her letting her hair down. It felt good to detach from her role as a mother for the first time in her adult life.

'Well, OK then.' Darragh shrugged and grinned. 'Just be careful, sis.'

'I will.'

But she wasn't careful at all. She became nocturnal, staying out most of the night with Kyle and his friends. Dinners, clubbing, parties in big luxurious apartments. She drank more than she'd ever drunk in her life and took cocaine plus LSD. There had been six of them the night she dropped the acid. Three couples. And they'd all got naked while they were high. Mairead couldn't remember much of what had happened. At times, she blushed with the memory of it, but at other times she felt magnificent. Kyle said she was a goddess, and she adored his body as if he were a god.

Most days she slept in late and when she woke Kyle had gone to Wall Street to trade. She didn't know how he did it on so little sleep and hungover. Usually there was a stack of dollar bills on the table. The first day there'd been a note to go shopping and have some fun. After that he just left the money. It made her feel like a prostitute, which, if she was honest, turned her on. What would Sister Mary Stephen think of her now?

Once she'd dressed and shoved the dollar bills into her bag, she went out. Most days, no matter what she was wearing, she put on the turquoise, pearl and diamond necklace. Kyle was a great admirer of it.

'Wow, that's really something,' he said, the first time she'd worn it.

'It's an antique,' she said. 'Belonged to my mother.' She licked her lips. 'And to Ellen Lavelle. It's the only thing she left her when she abandoned her.'

Kyle's eyes flickered as he touched the giant turquoise. But he said no more.

Some days Kyle would call the apartment before she left and arrange to meet her for lunch. They'd snort coke and have sex in the washrooms in the restaurant. This was the most charged intense sex she had ever had in her life. Not that she had much to compare it with.

In the afternoon, she wandered around art galleries in SoHo or went to the Guggenheim Museum or the Metropolitan Museum of Art. In these hours alone, it felt like her imagination expanded. She felt a spectrum of emotions as she vibrated with the colours and forms on the canvas. Mostly she liked abstract art, but one day she went to an exhibition of black-and-white portrait photographs from the Depression era. She stood for hours looking at the haunted faces of men, women and children who had fled the dustbowl during the 1930s. This was the same time as her grandmother Ellen had disappeared in America. She found herself hunting the pictures. Could one of those women on the road have been her own relative? It seemed unlikely, but she couldn't help thinking it.

As Mairead left the show, she came across another exhibition of modern portraits. One of the images of a man with dark curly hair reminded her of Eoin. She had forced all thoughts of him from her mind but now, as she stared at the face of a stranger, she felt ashamed of how she'd treated him. Look what she was up to these days, and yet she had refused to have anything to do with him because he'd still been married. Well, it was too late now. She was all in with Kyle, wherever that might lead.

Mairead devoured the art of New York on these solitary afternoons. She remembered how much she had loved painting as a child. At what age had she put her paints away and decided to become sensible? But she had never been good enough, in her eyes – or was it her mother's?

One afternoon, on her way back to Kyle's apartment, she had gone into an art store and spent some of his dollars on canvases, paints, sketchbooks. She had gone crazy buying so many art materials she had to take a taxi back. By the time Kyle got home, she had painted one huge canvas with splashes of pink, purple, green and violet.

Kyle had loved the painting, and said she looked sexy spattered in paint.

'Let me wash it off you,' he said, leading her into the shower.

Indulge, indulge, these were the words Kyle lived by. There were times when he'd be encouraging her to take another line of coke, or pop another pill, and she'd see something in his eyes. Darkness. But then it was gone in a flash, and he'd be laughing.

One night she dreamed she woke up and found he had a knife to her throat. She couldn't work out why she'd dreamt such a horrible thing when he was her lover. It was only later, when she was soaking in the bath, that she felt a sting on the skin of her neck. She touched it with her finger, and there was a tiny dot of blood. When she dried off and looked in the big bathroom mirror, she saw a tiny cut on her throat. Clearly the weight of the necklace had nicked her skin. That's why she'd had the strange dream. But even so she didn't tell Kyle about it. He was mercurial, exciting, insatiable. She was quite sure Sister Mary Stephen would think him the Devil.

CHAPTER NINETEEN

As the seasons passed in Tofino, Ellen's fear ebbed away. Each day was a steady yet comforting repetition of the one before. Getting dressed, eating her toast and drinking coffee in the lodging house with her landlady, Lucy, and walking to Uncle Jacob's feed and grocery store. Helping fill the grain bags, and stock the shelves. Sometimes Jacob would send her out on deliveries to the logging camps, and other days she would be left in charge of the store while he went on one of his fishing trips. In the evenings she returned to the lodging house for her supper. The community was small and friendly. She never sent any more telegrams, but some-times Jack Lanois would come into the store. He might order some fishing tackle or buy coffee or other provisions for the small tele-graph office. They got to talking. He told her he was building his own cabin just past Cox Bay.

'It has the best views in the whole wide world!' he told her.

'And how do you know that?' she had teased him.

'Because I've been around,' he said, taking off his hat and pushing his hand through his thick curly hair. 'As have you, I guess, Miss Ellie Jawlosky from nowhere.'

'I've seen a few good views, all right,' she had told him.

'Well, when my house is built, I'll take you up there and show you,' he said to her. 'Would you like that?'

She had looked into his eyes, and she had felt no shyness at all when she had told him, yes, she would like it very much.

The routine of Ellen's days in Tofino might be the same, but the ever-changing tides of the ocean became the keystone of her life in this wild western region. Every night after supper, she would walk through town and down to one of the coves to watch the sun set over the waves as they crashed against the rocks. She would close her eyes and taste the salty spray on her lips. The sea transported her all the way back to Ireland. To her daughter across the sea. It gave her such solace.

The year turned. She witnessed battering storms during the winter, storms so fierce she couldn't take her walk to the ocean at night but had to make do with watching from her bedroom window in the lodging house while the walls shook. Gifts appeared from Jack Lanois, left on the threshold of her room. A beautiful white shell with tender pink innards. A piece of sea glass the same shade as her beloved turquoise. A round grey pebble perfectly smoothed by the sea. Bleached driftwood made into a small box inside which were a collection of tiny blue shells. Each gift he left was more beautiful than the one before. He never mentioned them when he saw her later in the store, even if it was the same day. But she knew they were from him, because always there would be a little scrap of paper and written on it was – *For Ellie from Nowhere.* A fact which amused Lucy, her landlady, immensely.

'I think Jack Lanois has his eye on you,' she would say to her as she passed her the pot of coffee over breakfast.

Rather than find his attentions annoying, as sometimes she had found her husband's, Ellen discovered she liked these little gifts from Jack Lanois. Her husband had bought her expensive jewels, but she'd sensed that his intention in giving them to her had been to show off his wealth to their so-called friends. She hadn't felt any attachment to those gifts. But the turquoise necklace had been different, because it hadn't come from him. It had been part of her time at Merview House. These things from Jack Lanois were different too. When she held the tiny shells in the palms of her hands, they appeared more precious to her than all the strings of pearls Giles Rose had bought for her during their eight-year marriage.

Spring blew in with an abundance of rain. She welcomed it. During her years in the dryness of Arizona, she had missed spring rains and rainbows. As the air warmed and the rainforests hummed with new life, Ellen was captivated by the vast scale of nature on this island off the western edge of Canada. It was as if everything she had loved about Ireland was here, only on a grander scale. The Atlantic had given way to the Pacific Ocean, the rock pools of Mayo to vast swathes of rugged coastland, the Irish chestnut trees to huge Canadian redwoods, the trout in the rivers to blue whales, and the kestrels swooping over Merview House to bald-headed eagles soaring above Tofino. And those bad-tempered black bulls in the fields of Ireland were nothing compared to the big brown bears.

By submerging herself in the miracle of all this nature, Ellen's heart was able to turn over, flipping like a pancake in the pan. How could she not feel hope blossoming inside her when she sat upon rocks at Cox Bay and watched sea otters playing in the sea. Life renewed. It was all around her. She remembered Father Joseph's words to her. She had to begin again.

Over a year had passed, and winter was upon them again. The wind whipped the Pacific into a hurl of surf and spray. One dark November afternoon, the rain already heavy and the winds beginning to strengthen, Jack Lanois turned up as Ellen was closing the store.

'I finished my cabin,' he told her proudly.

He stood before her, hands on his hips. 'Want to come see it?'

She peered out the small store window.

'Looks like there's a big storm coming in,' she said.

'Which is why I want to take you there right now,' Jack said. 'It's the best place to see the storms. Some folk like to hide away, batten down the hatches. But I like to stand outside in the storms. It's more exhilarating than any fairground ride!'

'Isn't that dangerous?' Ellen asked.

'Nope, you've just got to be careful not to stand too close to the ocean,' he said. 'There's nothing else can make you feel so alive!'

Ellen found herself agreeing. There was something about Jack Lanois she wanted more of. He always seemed to be smiling. It was hard to imagine him cross or sullen.

They put on big yellow sou'westers from the back of the store, and Ellen tugged on a pair of waterproof boots. Uncle Jacob waved them goodbye with a curious smile on his face.

The wind slapped into them as Jack took her hand and they walked together out of town towards Cox Cove. The sound of the wind made it impossible to talk, but she liked it that way. She held on to his hand, and it felt good. She trusted him to keep her safe. Up the rocks they clambered, stopping every now and again to admire the surf crashing dramatically against the coast. Their faces were gleaming with seawater, and Jack paused in the climb to tuck the wild straggles of her hair up into her hat again. The intimacy of his touch made her stomach flutter.

They stood facing the ocean together and held hands. She felt the wind almost lift her off her feet as it pushed into her. Jack was laughing and she found herself laughing too. It was scary but it was also exciting. The wind dropped for a second, and she relaxed her body.

'See,' Jack said. 'Isn't it the best feeling?'

She nodded, smiling back at him.

'Come on,' he said, leading her further along the coast.

They came to an overhang of rock, which offered them a little shelter. It was the perfect place to watch the storm. Ellen was awestruck at the power and fury of nature.

'Oh Jack!' she whispered.

He squeezed her hand as they watched the relentless surge of the ocean. It never gave up. It kept on coming. Again, and again, it beat against the land.

After a while, she realised she was shivering with the wet and cold.

'Come on, I've a fire lit in the cabin,' Jack said, sensing her discomfort.

He led her back out into the wind and helped her up the last bit of the climb. As she rounded a corner of the coast, she saw the little wooden cabin.

'You built this all on your own?'

'My friends helped me, Gregory Tom most of all.'

He opened the door and as she stepped inside the scent of wood and sea swept through her. A feeling came over her as if she was coming home, and yet she had never been in this cabin, nor even this part of Tofino before.

'Jack, I love it!' she enthused, taking in the cheerful fire as Jack threw more wood onto it. It reminded her of the interior of the Rodriguez home in Arizona. Simple, but filled with welcome.

'I sure am glad you do,' Jack said.

She turned to look at him, and for once he wasn't smiling.

'What is it, Jack?' she asked.

He came over and took up her wet hand in his. Brought it up to his warm lips and kissed it.

'Don't you know I'm in love with you?' he said.

'You are?' she said, looking into his earnest face. A tumult of emotions washed through her. Fear. Excitement. But also joy.

'Do you think you might consider one day...' He stumbled over his words, for once looking a little rattled. She had never seen Jack so nervous. 'Well, Ellie,' he said. 'Might you like to live in this cabin with me one day?'

For a minute she wasn't sure what he meant. Did he want her to cook and clean for him like she had for Father Joseph?

He pulled something from his pocket. It was a tiny ring of shell.

'This isn't much, and I'll buy you something bigger when I can, but I spent all I had on the cabin—'

'Is it a ring? Oh, Jack, did you make me this ring?'

'Well, no, I didn't make it, I found it on the beach. The ocean made it, Ellie.'

She looked at the tiny circle of shell and truly it was the prettiest ring she had ever seen. More beautiful than the diamond engagement ring Giles had given her, or the little Navajo ring she had bought herself or even the artistic creations Father Joseph had made. It was more beautiful because it had come straight from nature. Unadulterated.

'Miss Ellie from Nowhere, will you be my wife?' Jack asked, his voice shaking with emotion.

'Yes,' she said, holding out her hand so he could slide the ring onto her finger. It fit perfectly. 'And I'm not from nowhere any more, Jack. I'm from here.'

Ellen thought of her little girl Brigid, so far away. She knew that one day, though not now, she would tell Jack about her. He would help her go and get her. They would bring Brigid back to the cabin Jack had built for her in Canada. They would be a family. It was a wild dream. But in this moment of pure love, Ellen believed anything could come true.

Jack took her into his arms, and they kissed. The power of her love for him felt as immense as the crashing ocean outside the cabin. She had come home at last.

II

HOME

CHAPTER TWENTY

Ellen's home became these western reaches of Vancouver Island. Most mornings, she went out first thing, faced the ocean, and let it sweep through her. She would walk to the very edge of their land, arms open wide, even when the wind was so wild she felt like she could take flight. She let the sea open up her heart to feel the never-ending rawness of her loss and surrendered to it. She gave to the ocean what she couldn't give to her daughter.

Ellen had lived in Tofino for five decades with the love of her life, Jack. Their romance had been whirlwind and the marriage enduring. Even now, in their seventies, Ellen thought Jack the most handsome man in the world. They had had four children – all boys. Those boys had grown up, married, and had children. Ellen and Jack had twelve grandchildren all in all, and another one on the way. Ellen had a special place in her heart for all her boys, and all her grandchildren, but there was always a hole she never could seem to fill. There would be days when she would stare out at the ocean, thinking of her girl across the sea. But this wasn't even the right ocean. She was looking in the wrong direction, although if she looked far enough, she would come full circle. She might find her if she searched, though Ellen hadn't left Canada in all these years. She had never found the right moment to tell Jack and so the years had passed with her secret still locked inside her heart.

At the beginning of their marriage, she'd been so busy with their first child, Sam, and then Jack went to fight in the war. She had been terrified he might get killed or hurt, and she was ecstatic when he returned safely to her. In the following years, they had their hands full raising their family and making a living. When Uncle Jacob passed away, he left Ellen his store. With Jack's help, she'd turned it into an arts and crafts store for the tourists. They promoted and sold artwork by the local First Nation community without taking any profits off the top, and made their money by selling wholefoods and Jack's whaling tours for the tourists. Although there had been times Ellen had been tempted to make jewellery again, she never found the right time to tell Jack this was a skill she possessed. Because inevitably there would be questions. How come she could set stones in silver? Who had taught her how to do Mexican beadwork? Her artistic skills were part of her past and she couldn't go back, even in a small way. Besides, she decided she wasn't good enough. When she looked at the beautiful work from the local First Nation community, she was in awe.

When Jack returned from the war, he had got his old job back at the telegraph office, but after Ellen inherited the store, he gave it up to help her. His whale-watching tours had really taken off over the years. All the locals knew Jack had the knack for knowing where to take people to see pods of orca. Their eyes were always shining when they came back from the sight of orca in the wild, flying through the ocean, and bounding into the air, showering them with crystal drops of seawater.

When they did take holidays with the boys it was to go camping in the wilds. This had always frightened Ellen, because of the bears, but Jack was an experienced camper and in all their years they'd never had a scary incident although they'd seen plenty of brown bears.

When she was sixty, Jack had taken her to Toronto and

Niagara Falls. She had found the trip a little stressful, although she never told him so. Toronto was so big and noisy. The falls had been spectacular but the commercialism of the place had put her off. She had been happy to get back to Tofino.

Today was the first morning after their forty-fifth wedding anniversary celebration. The entire family had come for the party yesterday. Even Sam, who lived in London with his English wife, Rachel. They had flown over specially with their two children. It had been a wonderful day with her family gathered around her. She had felt so loved and adored, but even so there had been moments when she'd had to be on her own, to sit in her bedroom and clutch the turquoise and silver necklace around her neck. The copy of the one she had left Brigid all those decades ago. Jack knew to leave her be. He had long since stopped asking her what the matter was. Just as she never bothered him in his moments of silence, remembering the war. But since the summer, she had found herself getting more and more upset. Sitting staring out of the window, tortured by the loss of her daughter. It felt as keen as the day she had left her. She sensed something and it frightened her. This yawning grief within her, which washed over her in waves like a violent storm. Yes, it passed. But it always returned.

She lay on her side and looked at the alarm clock. It was six thirty in the morning, and she was wide awake. Jack was still asleep when she slipped out of bed, pulling a thick sweater over jeans. She would let him rest on. He was exhausted from all the grandchildren running around the house. She tiptoed down the stairs of their small house, currently heaving with sleeping bodies. It was a foggy morning, light beginning to change from night to white. The view of the sea was obscured by thick mist. She imagined the waters beyond the fog serene and still. The tide far, far out and the sand pristine and pale gold.

As she went into the kitchen to make her morning coffee, she came across Sam's eldest girl, Gemma. She was the only grandchild to have inherited Ellen's red hair. If she was honest, it was why Gemma was her favourite. The girl was sitting at the table, eating a bowl of Cheerios while reading a book, and swinging her legs.

'Good morning, honey,' Ellen said. 'What's that you're reading?'

'*Across the Barricades* by Joan Lingard, I'm in the advanced reading group in school,' Gemma told her. 'It's about a boy and a girl in Northern Ireland. They're from different sides, but they want to be friends.'

'Oh, that sounds like a good story,' Ellen said, surprised to hear Gemma's posh school had put such a political book on the curriculum.

Gemma set down the book. 'It is good, but the fighting upsets me,' Gemma said. 'It's so stupid. Why do the families have to be enemies?'

Gemma's words echoed through Ellen. Whispers from her past emerging like the fog outside. She would never be free from the yoke of it.

'It's complicated,' she said to Gemma. 'The conflict goes back generations.'

'They should just give it back to the Irish,' Gemma declared in her English accent. 'It's stupid!'

'If only it were that simple,' Ellen sighed.

'Good morning, ladies.' Jack appeared in the doorway in a thick red sweater, his grey hair ruffled.

'Good morning, Grandpa!' Gemma beamed.

'I thought you were out for the count, honey,' Ellen said.

'I dreamed I was sailing with the whales,' he laughed, 'and it woke me up. I feel this morning might be a good day to go out.'

'But the fog—'

'It's lifting, see.'

Ellen looked out the window. Sure enough, hazy shafts of sunlight were penetrating the swirling mist, revealing crisp winter-blue skies.

'Say, how about the three of us go on a secret adventure before the house wakes up,' Jack said, winking at Gemma.

Their granddaughter slapped down her book.

'Absolutely, Grandpa!'

Every fall, after all the tourists had gone, Jack and Ellen would go out in his boat most mornings. Far out to sea. Some days all they found was blue and emptiness, within which they shared the solitude and solace of a decades-deep love. But on other days the whales arrived. And this was one of those days.

It was always a thrill to see the still water ripple as a black fin passed through. As Ellen pointed it out to Gemma, her red-haired granddaughter clutched her hands in excitement.

All three of them delighted in these immense, strong and peaceful beings, performing for them in the waves.

Jack looked into Ellen's eyes and smiled at her. She held her granddaughter's hand as she sang to her whales. Bewitched by their glistening black skin, their eyes soft and kind, forgiving her. The same songs she had once sung for her baby girl. Old Irish ballads: 'The Wind That Shakes the Barley' and 'The Last Rose of Summer'. Each word brimming with meaning. Reaching out across the oceans. In nature, she hoped her daughter might have found her.

By the time they returned it was lunchtime. Everyone was up, making food, and the TV was blaring away in the living room. Ellen longed to turn it off, but the kids seemed transfixed by *Sesame Street* and she didn't want to overrule her daughters-in-law. Although they'd left a note to tell them they'd gone whale watching, Ellen could see that Gemma's mother, Rachel, was cross.

'You shouldn't have left out your sister,' she said to Gemma. But clearly her comment was directed at Jack and Ellen.

Ellen sat down on the sofa among all the children as her family talked at and over each other. She loved them all but at the same time she wanted them to go home. It was all very tiring and noisy.

Sam picked up the remote and flicked through the channels, setting off wails from the younger children.

'OK, OK, we'll go back to *Sesame Street* in a minute, I just want to see what's going on in the world.'

Ellen never watched the news. She had got in the habit of ignoring what was happening in other places because she had been so worried for years that, one day, she would be found. Carted off to stand trial for the murders of FBI agents Frank Jackson and Vernon Willis. On other days, it felt as if it wasn't something she had done at all. It had all been so long ago. There was nothing left of the woman who killed the two lawmen. She was no longer her.

'Oh boy, that's awful.' Sam whistled. He slid an arm around Rachel, who was sitting on the arm of his chair.

Ellen looked at the TV screen. She wasn't wearing her glasses, so what she was looking at was very hazy. There was a building ripped apart. Clearly a bombing.

'What happened?' she asked.

'A hotel hosting the Conservative Party Conference in England was bombed,' Sam told her. 'Thatcher's OK, but five people died.'

'The monsters,' Rachel said.

'Who are the monsters, Mummy?' Gemma asked.

'The IRA, they're evil terrorists,' her mother said vehemently.

'It's not as simple as that,' Ellen heard herself say.

'In what way is it not simple? It's terrorism, they're killing inno-cent people!' Rachel challenged her.

'People in the north of Ireland have been shot on their own streets and ignored for years. I think they wanted to bring the conflict to those in power – in England – to make them take notice.'

The whole room fell silent. Ellen's sons were all looking at her in astonishment. What did she know about the conflict in Ireland?

'They killed innocent people, and you're telling me that's OK?' Rachel said, her voice icy with fury.

'Of course not, it's never OK, but no one in the world makes much fuss when Catholic working-class civilians are shot on their own streets. Here we are, thousands of miles away in Canada, and this is big news because it's those in power.'

What was happening to her? She needed to shut up. And Rachel was right. It was a terrible atrocity. There was no way in the world you could justify terrorism. Yet she had been there right at the beginning. Ellen had seen the first injustices which had caused people to resort to violence.

'I think we need to change the channel, Sam,' Jack told his son. 'It's not suitable for the children.'

All the kids were staring up at the bomb-blasted scene. Sam quickly flicked back to Sesame Street, but a tense silence had descended upon the whole family. Ellen felt sick and dizzy. It was still going on. All these years later.

She got up and went upstairs. She needed to be alone.

'Sorry,' she said to Rachel. 'I didn't mean to be insensitive.'

Rachel still looked furious at her. She had just made her daughter-in-law dislike her even more.

In her bedroom, she opened her dressing table drawer and took out the necklace. Laid it on her palm. She thought about the original necklace and where it might be now. She stared at the greeny blue of the stone and the colour took her back to the lake at Merview House. She had forgotten about her childhood for so long, but the past year she had been having flashbacks. Little slivers of memory.

Forget-me-nots and bluebells. Running with her best friend through the woods. Making little boats out of long grasses and putting them on the still lake to watch them swirl on the green waters.

The door opened and Jack slipped into the bedroom.

'Are you OK, honey?' he asked, standing behind her, and looking at her reflection in the mirror. 'That was all a bit strange. Between you and Rachel.'

'Sorry, the bombing shocked me,' she said, looking back at his reflection.

'It sure is terrible,' he said. 'But it's the other side of the world. That sort of thing never happens here. It's got nothing to do with us.'

He put his hand on her shoulder. She twisted around on her stool and looked up at him. Her heart was thumping in her chest.

'But it does,' she said softly. 'Because I'm Irish, Jack.'

'Aw honey, I worked out your heritage years ago,' he said. 'Your red hair once you stopped dying it blond. Those beautiful songs you sing. They're all Irish. I mean, half of New York has Irish heritage and the other half is Italian.'

'No, I mean I was born in Ireland,' she interrupted.

Jack stopped talking. His eyes widening.

'I grew up in the west of Ireland,' she said.

'Why have you never told me that before?' he said, sitting down on the end of the bed in shock.

She swung around on her stool and looked into his face. For nearly fifty years, she had hidden all her secrets from him. She had not told him who she really was. It could continue that way to the end of her days. But now, she had an overpowering feeling she needed to share her story with him. Maybe as a result of spending so much time with Gemma in the boat, because the truth was her granddaughter reminded her of herself when she had been that age. How much she had loved to be on the water, with her dear friend. She needed to make her confession. She hadn't been ready before, but now she was.

'It's complicated, and it's a long story,' she said.

Jack nodded. 'I always knew you had secrets, and that's fine, Ellie. You don't have to tell me. I love you for you.' He put his hand on his heart. 'I know you without knowing your past.'

Her eyes welled with tears.

'I know, darling, but I want to tell you. I just don't know how.' She came to sit next to him on the end of the bed.

'How about you tell it like a story?' he said. 'Remember when I went to the therapist?'

She nodded. Twenty years ago, plagued by flashbacks to his wartime days and the horrors he'd seen, he'd sought professional help.

'I needed to offload so badly, but there was no way I could tell you the things I'd seen. I just couldn't.'

Ellen squeezed his hands. How fine they still were. The story of his life mapped within the pulsing blue veins and strong knuckles. His fingers curled around hers.

'The therapist got me to tell my story as if I wasn't in it. I talked about myself as Jack. Why don't you try that, honey?'

She nodded. 'I'll try.'

'But let's wait till everyone's gone, shall we? We'll have the place to ourselves. I'll make a fire and we'll sit together in front of it,' he said. 'Then you can tell me everything.'

'OK.'

Fear darted into Ellen's heart. Could she tell Jack all about her life in Ireland? She was terrified he would think differently about her once he knew. And there were things she would never be able to tell him, like what had happened in Arizona. Though, even now, she had no regrets about her actions. But Ireland was different. She felt deep remorse for what she'd done there. And all these years later, there was another girl, another voice in her head and she needed to speak for her. It wasn't her daughter. It was a love even older than the one she'd had for her first child. It was for a girl called Meg.

CHAPTER TWENTY-ONE

Kyle zipped in and out of the traffic in the rental car, which of course was a Ferrari. Mairead had never been in a sports car before, nor travelled at such speed. Her old self would have been frightened but Mairead was high on coke and loving every minute of it. As he drove with one hand on the wheel, Kyle had his other hand up Mairead's very short skirt. The speed and his touch were taking her right to the edge.

The weekend trip had been a last-minute thing. This morning in bed, Kyle had asked her if she wanted to join him and a work buddy for a golfing weekend in Scottsdale, Arizona.

'He's got a massive villa there with a pool, the works,' he said.

'I don't know how to play golf,' Mairead had said.

'Oh baby, you don't have to, you'll be hanging out with Ray's girlfriend, Tia,' Kyle told her.

Kyle and Mairead weren't the only ones Ray had invited to his weekend party; many of Kyle's trader friends and their girlfriends were in attendance. Mairead felt a little self-conscious in her bikini as she was both the palest and oldest woman there. The other women, including Tia, were all models or airline stewardesses. It struck her as odd that none of the men were married.

Still, the girlfriends were very friendly and kept telling her how beautiful and soft her Irish skin was.

'So natural and voluptuous,' Tia told her as they lounged by the pool drinking cocktails. Tia herself was blonde, tanned and toned, wearing a tiny thong bikini that left nothing to the imagination. 'I can see why Kyle likes you,' Tia praised her.

Mairead, feeling more relaxed now she'd shared a line of coke with Tia, confided: 'He makes me feel like a goddess.'

'You're so different from Gina,' Tia said.

Mairead lowered her sunglasses and stared at her.

'Who's Gina?' She hadn't meant to ask. She and Kyle had a rule: never talk about exes or the past; never talk about the future.

'His wife!' Tia exclaimed. 'Don't you know about her?'

'We don't talk about exes.'

Tia leaned forward and laid her hand on Mairead's bare knee. Mairead looked down at the scarlet-painted talons as Tia whispered, 'Oh honey, Gina isn't Kyle's ex.'

'So, he's separated. It's the same with me and my husband.'

'They're not separated!'

'But where is she? I'm living in the apartment. We hang out all the time—'

'She's back at the house with the kids. The apartment is for when Kyle's staying in Manhattan for work. He owns a big mansion on Long Island,' Tia explained, spreading her arms wide. 'They've all got wives. Ray's wife, Eve, knows all about me. This is a *girlfriends* weekend.'

Mairead looked at the nubile twenty-somethings lounging around the pool. Their ageing boyfriends had all gone off to play golf, but they would be back soon, pulling in their bellies, trying to act half their age. She didn't belong here at all. She might be a girlfriend, but she belonged with the wives.

'It's better being a girlfriend,' Tia sighed, leaning back on her sun lounger. 'I can move on when I want. I feel sorry for some of the wives. Imagine being stuck with these dicks, tied down with kids!'

'Well, if you think they're dicks, what are you doing here?' Mairead challenged.

'Ray's paying my tuition fees at college. Like, it's saving me literally thousands of dollars,' Tia replied, knocking back the dregs of her cocktail. 'Say, you want another, honey?'

Mairead didn't want another cocktail, but she nodded and watched as Tia slipped on her high-heeled mules and tottered off into the villa. A moment later a sick feeling came over her and, wrapping her kimono around herself, she made her way indoors.

She found Tia in the kitchen, slicing strawberries and popping them into their glasses.

'Do you want to go into town?' she asked. 'Kyle told me there are lots of art galleries in Scottsdale.'

'Oh no, I'm way too wasted,' Tia said. 'And you shouldn't drive either.'

'I was going to walk,' Mairead said, slipping the pair of linen trousers she'd left lying on the sofa over her bikini. She tied the kimono around her waist.

Tia arched her eyebrows. 'It's a bit of a hike,' she said. 'Let me call you a taxi. You don't want to ruin your skin walking in the sun.'

Mairead had been glad of the taxi, for her head was still foggy from the booze and coke, but it was a relief to get away from the party house. As she browsed in the art galleries in Scottsdale, she thought about Kyle. He had made no promises to her, but even so, to omit any mention of his wife and children... She felt deceived and annoyed, but it struck her that she wasn't in the least upset. Not like she had been when Eoin told her he was still living with his wife.

She entered a bookstore. It had been ages since she'd read a book that wasn't related to history and teaching. Even now, she found herself scanning the history shelves. She was interested in the history of this popular tourist resort. What it might have been like to live here before it became a party resort for the wealthy. By the looks of some of the titles, it had been a pioneering town. She found some interesting volumes on the Navajo people who were the first inhabitants of this part of Arizona, then drifted into the true-crime section, remembering how Eoin had teased her about her guilty pleasure. A book entitled *Killers of Arizona* caught her eye, and she picked it up. She flicked through the accounts of murders and unsolved mysteries dating back to the nineteenth century, and was about to put it back on the display when a page fell open on the story of two FBI agents who had been poisoned with coffee dosed with castor beans in 1937. Before he died, one of the agents, Frank Jackson, claimed his attacker had been a woman working as a housekeeper for a priest in Scottsdale. The motive for her attack was unknown. The woman had never been caught and was never seen nor heard of again. Her name was Ellen Lavelle.

Mairead gave a little yelp. She read the story again. It couldn't possibly be the same Ellen Lavelle! Surely not? It was way too much of a coincidence. Kyle had told her that her grandmother had died in the mid to late thirties in Ireland, so it couldn't be the same woman. Unless he had lied.

She bought the book, then went into a cafe and ordered an Americana coffee with double shots to sober up while she read through the story again. It seemed Ellen Lavelle had been a house-keeper for the Catholic priest at the old adobe mission church Our Lady of Perpetual Help in Scottsdale. It was a ridiculous long shot, but since she was here in the very place where it had happened, she might as well go and investigate. It was possible the priest, Father Joseph Jawlosky, might still be alive.

Back out on the street she asked a passer-by for directions to the old adobe mission church. As she walked briskly down the street she took in the implications of her discovery. If this Ellen

Lavelle was her grandmother, then she might be related to a murderer. Did she even want to find her now?

The white adobe church gleamed in the afternoon light. Mairead opened the door and walked into the cool interior. Her eyes were immediately drawn to an ornate statue of Our Lady lit up by rows of votive candles. The wantonness of the past weeks slipped off her shoulders and the familiar guilt began to nag at her. The cloying scent of lilies, wafting from vases at the base of the Virgin Mary statue, brought her back to her mother's funeral. And her mother's dying wish for Mairead to find Ellen. She had allowed the excesses of the last few weeks to get in the way of her quest. Even if she wanted to turn around, leave the church and run all the way back to the party house to get wasted with Kyle, she knew she mustn't. She'd made a promise and she had to try to keep it. Besides, what she had read was too intriguing.

There was a little information kiosk at the back of the church, selling candles and prayer books. Behind it sat a Mexican woman with grey hair, threading beads.

'Hello, I wonder if you could help me,' she asked, not quite knowing where to begin.

The woman nodded.

'Yes, hello.' Her English was heavily accented.

'I wonder, do you know anything about Ellen Lavelle?' She showed the woman the book she'd bought in the store.

The woman flinched when she saw the cover of the book, and its title.

'Lies,' she hissed. 'El never killed no one.'

'You knew her?' she asked, her heart beginning to race. But the woman had clammed up; she merely shook her head in response.

'Do you know where she is now?' Again, the woman shook her head, and bent down to her beading again.

'It's just... well, I think she might be my grandmother,' Mairead said desperately. She pulled open her kimono and showed the woman her mother's turquoise necklace. 'She left my mother this necklace.'

The Mexican woman looked up and as soon as she saw the necklace, she gave a little cry and dropped her beading.

'What is it? Please, tell me, I've come a long way,' Mairead pleaded.

The woman stood up and came out from the kiosk. She was very small, the top of her head level with Mairead's shoulder. She reached out and touched the necklace.

'El,' she whispered, her eyes misting as she gazed at Mairead's face. 'You look like her.'

'Do you know if she's alive still? Where she is?' Mairead asked, her heart beginning to race.

The woman looked at her as if trying to work out whether she could trust her.

'I don't know if she's alive,' she said. 'For many years I didn't even know where she went to. But she was a good woman, not like they say in the book.'

'Did you know her well?'

For the first time the Mexican woman's face broke out in a smile.

'Oh yes,' she said. 'My name is Gabriella.' She became pensive, staring at the necklace.

Mairead took it off. 'You can look at it more closely, if you like.'

Gabriella held it in her hand.

'El made one like this, with turquoise from the Navajo, and with silver,' she said. 'No pearls or diamonds. She took it with her.'

'Where did she go?' Mairead tried again.

'I asked Father Joseph many times, but he never told me.' Gabriella sighed. 'He is with God now. Only He knows the truth about what happened, but I don't believe El murdered those men on purpose. If she killed someone, it was a mistake.'

Mairead was confused but resisted the urge to interrupt. The

Mexican woman continued to speak: 'A few years after Father Joseph died, I got a postcard from El. It was a big surprise. The postcard was of a big blue whale and on the back, she wrote how the whale was her guardian angel now. The postmark was a place called Tofino in Canada. I have no idea where it is.'

Mairead's head was in a whirl. Not only was Ellen Lavelle alive, she was in Canada.

'When did you get the postcard?'

'It was a long time ago,' Gabriella said. 'Maybe twenty years ago.'

Mairead's heart sank.

'I never heard from her since,' Gabriella said.

Mairead sat down on one of the church pews.

'You are an image of her,' Gabriella said, pointing at Mairead's red hair. 'I see her in you.'

Mairead looked at Gabriella. The older woman's eyes were misted with nostalgia.

'If you find her,' she said to Mairead. 'Tell her I have been praying for her all these years. Yes?'

'I'm not sure if I'll go all that way. I don't even know where Tofino is,' Mairead said.

'You've come this far,' Gabriella told her. 'Don't give up now. There was a reason we met, don't you see?'

She took a little medal of Our Lady from her pocket and placed it in Mairead's hand.

'Our Lady of Perpetual Help – she will guide you,' Gabriella told her. 'She will never give up on you.'

When Mairead got back to the villa, the men had returned from golfing and the party was kicking off. Most of the girls had gone topless and were prancing around in the pool, high on coke.

Mairead had never felt so out of place in her life. She ignored Tia's calls for her to come and join in, and slipped upstairs to the bedroom she shared with Kyle. She wanted to leave now. She'd throw her few fancy things in the new Gucci bag Kyle had bought her and get a taxi to the airport. She had no desire to see Kyle. She knew it was rude, but reasoned he deserved it for keeping quiet about his wife and kids and the big mansion on Long Island.

However, when she went into the room, she could hear the shower running in the en suite. She had hoped he would be downstairs with the others.

Mairead tried to be as quiet as possible as she stuffed her things into the bag, but before she was done she heard the shower turn off. She froze, bag in hand, as Kyle came out of the bathroom, a white towel tied around his waist, his six-pack tanned and glistening with drops of water.

'Hey, baby, there you are. Where you been?'

'I got bored,' she said. 'I went into Scottsdale to look at the art galleries.'

'That's cool,' he said. He looked at the bag in her hand. 'Are you going somewhere?'

'Yeah,' she said. 'I want to go back to New York.'

'Right now?' he asked, incredulous.

'Why didn't you tell me you're married with children, and you've got a big house on Long Island?'

'Because it's got nothing to do with what we have,' he said, walking towards her. He was incredibly sexy, half naked, and a part of her was turned on, but when she looked at his face his teeth appeared too white, and the smile in his eyes wasn't sincere.

'Come on, we're going to have so much fun tonight,' he said, taking the bag from her hand, and kissing her. His hands began to trail over her body as he let his towel fall down.

'But what do you see in me?' she asked. 'I'm so much older than the others—'

'You're so much hotter too, Mairead,' he said, rubbing his naked body against her so she could feel his erection hard and keen against her belly.

She knew he must be lying. He had been lying all along. She wanted to ask him why he had told her Ellen Lavelle was dead, but instead she found herself kissing him back. Letting him slide her kimono off and undo her linen trousers. His fingers slipped into her bikini bottoms and pressed against her clitoris. Her breath deepened. A voice inside her was warning her to stop but he was so persuasive, and her body wanted this.

He got a condom from the locker and put it on his cock while she watched. She had never really looked at a penis so closely before. Not even Niall's. She felt herself wet just imagining the sensation of him inside her. He pulled off her bikini bottoms and lifted her up against the wall. He pushed up into her and they fucked against the wall. It was hot, hard and fast. She wanted him to go deeper and deeper. She wanted him to turn her inside out. They came together, both breathless. She slid down the wall as he pulled out.

'That's why I like you,' he said. 'Those girls don't fuck like you. Women your age are so much better at sex.'

She nearly asked him how he knew this fact but didn't bother. She got up, and without a word went into the shower room. She washed him off her. All the while, her heart was thumping in her chest, warning her to get away from Kyle Lavelle.

When she came back into the bedroom he had dressed. He was wearing designer jeans and a pale pink shirt. He was holding up a skimpy sky-blue backless dress for her to wear.

'This will look great with your necklace,' he said. 'Don't wear any panties.'

She took the dress in her hands. It was tiny. Honestly, she'd be horrified if Stella ever wore such an item. But even so she slipped it on over her damp body.

'Kyle, I need to ask you something,' she said, as he helped zip up the side of the dress.

'Sure, baby.'

'Why did you tell me Ellen Lavelle died in Ireland...' She paused to lick her lips, which were suddenly dry. '...when she didn't?'

She felt him go still beside her.

'I didn't tell you that,' he said, stepping away from her.

'Yes, you did,' she insisted. 'How did you know?'

'Well, how do you know she didn't?' he countered, his eyes suddenly hard.

It was on the tip of her tongue to tell him about the book, *Arizona Killers*, and the Mexican woman in the Catholic church. The fact she had just been told Ellen Lavelle had been alive and living in Canada twenty years ago. But something about the look on Kyle's face told her not to. He wasn't smiling at her any more.

'Baby, you're getting real obsessed with this long-gone grandmother,' he said. 'I mean, your mom's dead now anyway. What's the point?'

His words stung.

'I promised I'd find her,' she said.

Kyle shrugged. 'I break promises all the time,' he said. 'It's how I survive.'

Mairead was really beginning to dislike Kyle Symes. She felt ashamed she'd just had sex with the man.

'I want to leave, Kyle,' she said in a quiet voice. 'Right now.'

'Are you fucking serious?' he snapped, irritated. 'It's a big party night!'

'I don't want to party any more,' she said. 'You lied to me. I'm going to call a taxi.'

She went towards the door, but he stood in her way.

'How do you know I lied, eh? Come on,' he challenged her. 'We're leaving tomorrow anyway, what's the big rush?'

'I just don't want to hang out with you,' she said.

His expression changed. He looked furious.

'Do you know how much fucking money I've spent on you? Thousands! Have you any idea how much debt I'm in? Up to my fucking balls! But I've got to get out there and show these guys I'm on top,' he said, pressing a finger into her chest, right between her ribs, so hard it hurt. 'So no way is my old has-been girlfriend walking out on me.'

'There's plenty of young women by the pool for you to fuck!' she hit back, hurt by his words.

He pushed his finger into her flesh even more. Poking her to emphasise each word. 'You. Aren't. Going. Nowhere.'

She shook her head. 'I don't want to—'

Suddenly he laughed, removing his finger, all the tension gone from his face.

'Honey, there's no flights back to New York tonight. You'd be sleeping on the stinking carpet in Sky Harbor Airport. Just hang out one more night.'

She was still smarting at being called a 'has-been', but she supposed he had a point.

'OK,' she gave in. 'But when I get back to New York, I'm moving on.'

'If you want,' he said lightly. 'But where to?'

She nearly told him about going to Canada, but again something stopped her.

'Back home, Ireland,' she lied, adding, 'I'm going to try to find out who's selling Merview House.'

'Is that so?' Kyle's voice had gone up an octave. 'Let me know if you find anything out.'

She had no intention of ever communicating with Kyle Symes once they parted ways, but she didn't say that, of course. Something felt off and she couldn't wait to get away from him. But for now, she let him lead her downstairs and pour her a glass of chilled white wine. They joined the others outside, who were already high. She saw Tia sitting on top of Ray, having sex with him right by the pool.

'Hey, we got something special for us tonight,' Kyle said picking up a fist-sized plastic bag of white powder from one of the pool tables. 'Want to try it with me?'

'Is it coke?' she asked him.

'No, I believe it's called Adam,' he said. 'It's fucking wild, and totally legal!'

Well, if it was legal, Mairead thought, it couldn't be that strong.

If she was going to get through this night of hedonism she might as well let loose one last time.

Mairead sat with her back against the wall, her knees drawn up, and hugged herself. She was frozen, she was roasting. Her heart felt like it was going so fast she was about to explode. *Breathe,* said a voice deep down inside. *Stay calm.*

But panic was welling up in her and she began to hyperventilate. Sweat trickled down her face.

Why was this drug affecting her more than anyone else? The others were all dancing around her, the room a swirl of light, smoke, and pulsing bodies. Kyle was grinding his body against one of the young girls. She didn't even know her name. It was like everybody loved everybody and they couldn't get enough of each other. She had felt that way too at the beginning of the night. Joined in with all the cavorting. But then something had happened to her.

She got on all fours and starting panting. Her heart was squeezing tight, and she wanted to vomit but she couldn't.

'Hey, honey, are you OK?' Tia's face loomed in front of her, her pupils dilated.

Mairead tried to speak, but no words would come out, only drool. She heard Tia calling to Kyle.

'Hey, Kyle, there's something wrong with Mairead.'

'Get her to be sick,' he said, not even coming over.

Tia dragged her into the bathroom. She was clearly out of her depth.

'Just throw up, sweetie,' she said, closing the door behind her.

Mairead was alone. It felt like she was dying. She clung to the loo seat, retching and trying to be sick.

The bathroom door opened again. Relief washed through her, thinking it was Tia come back to help her. But instead, Kyle crouched down by her side. He removed her hands from the sides of the toilet seat and closed it.

She tried to push him away, so she could puke. Her whole body was heaving, retching, but he clamped her hands over her own mouth.

His eyes were like razors as they cut into her.

'No one dumps me,' he hissed. 'You dumb bitch.'

What had he done to her? She writhed as she felt vomit pressing against her fingers and sliding back down her throat. She had to get whatever was in her out.

'I think I might have given you rather a lot of Adam,' he said, giving her a nasty wink.

She writhed again and kicked out with her legs. He lost his balance and fell backwards, releasing her hands. She doubled over and vomited all over the white tiles.

'Oh, for fuck's sake,' he said, getting up. 'You're disgusting.'

But she didn't care. She wanted this toxic stuff out of her.

After hours of vomiting, and drinking water from the tap, she began to feel a little better. She sat by the side of the bath, her heart still hammering away. Her head was a mess. What had just happened? Had Kyle tried to kill her with recreational drugs?

Eventually she fell asleep, lying on the bathroom floor in her own vomit.

She awoke in the shower, gasping for air. Kyle was in it with her, and she immediately backed away in terror. Was he going to drown her now? But his brown eyes were filled with concern as he gently washed her down. Cleaning all the sick off her. When he was done, he carried her out of the bathroom wrapped in a big towel and tucked her up in bed.

'Poor baby,' he said, kissing her forehead. Then he slid in next to her and fell asleep.

She wanted to get out of the bed and out of the house, but she couldn't move. Her eyes closed and she was gone again.

. . .

In the morning there was no mention of what had happened the night before. When they came downstairs with their things, a crew of cleaners was working hard to clear up their disgusting mess. All the women were Mexican and Mairead thought of Gabriella. She felt very ashamed as they made their way out of the house and got into Kyle's Ferrari.

'How are you feeling?' Kyle asked, patting her knee.

'Fragile.' Her voice was a hoarse whisper, her throat so sore from vomiting it hurt to speak.

It was a short drive to the airport. They gave back the rental car, and checked in. Kyle bought them two coffees and they sat side by side in silence, waiting for their flight. Mairead's head was throbbing; it was all she could do to think, let alone speak.

'I'm sorry I lied to you about my wife,' Kyle said eventually. 'Sometimes I tell lies and I don't even know why. It would be easier to tell the truth, but my default is to lie.'

'I get why you lied about your wife,' Mairead croaked. 'But why did you lie about Ellen being dead?'

'I wanted to help you and it seemed to me you'd never find out what happened to her,' he said.

'How do you know?' Again, she was tempted to tell him about Gabriella and what she'd found out.

'Well, how do *you* know she isn't dead?' he challenged.

'Because…' She faltered. 'Because of this.' She pulled the book *Arizona Killers* out of her bag and threw it at Kyle.

He flicked through the book, pausing when he came to the page on Ellen Lavelle.

'Holy shit!' he exclaimed, and then burst out laughing. 'Looks like she really was the black sheep of the family.'

'It might not be her,' Mairead heard herself saying defensively.

'Did they ever find her?' Kyle asked, his eyes narrowed. 'She could still be a wanted woman?' Her instincts told her not to share what Gabriella had told her.

She shook her head. 'I'm sure the statute of limitations must have passed – it was almost fifty years ago.'

Kyle looked thoughtful as he read through the story again. 'I wonder where she is now.'

His fascination was making her feel a little on edge. She put her hand to her sore head.

'What happened last night?' Mairead whispered. 'What did you try to do to me?'

'Yeah,' he said, closing the *Killers of Arizona* book but not giving it back to her. 'That was bad. I kind of lost it. You made me mad, Mairead,' he continued, but there was no hint of apology. 'I'm under a lot of pressure – you've no idea. And things haven't been going too well lately. I've run up a lot of debt.'

'But you own a mansion on Long Island, the apartment on Fifth Avenue—'

'It's all for show.' He talked over her, giving her a short laugh. 'A sham. Actually, I'm broke.'

She stared at him, incredulous.

'But not for long,' he added. 'Got some promising deals happening right now. It's tough, though,' he said. 'Dog eat dog out there on Wall Street.'

'It's not a world I care for,' Mairead said under her breath, so that Kyle didn't hear. His erratic mood swings unnerved her.

It was the last proper conversation she had with Kyle. On the plane she slept and once they landed in New York, she insisted on taking a taxi straight to her brother's place in Brooklyn.

'Don't you want all the designer stuff I bought you?' he said.

'Give them to your wife,' she said.

'God, you're an ungrateful bitch,' he said, a hint of admiration in his tone.

She was getting in her taxi when he called out his parting words.

'If Ellen's anything like you, she's probably still going strong.

The amount of stuff you had last night would have taken down a horse.'

She whipped around but he was already getting into his cab, showing her the finger as he got in. The yellow taxi sped off into the surging New York traffic and he was swallowed up. She hoped she would never have to cross paths with him again.

CHAPTER TWENTY-TWO

Jack handed Ellen the mug of cocoa and sat down next to her on the couch. They had the house back to themselves. Of course, she loved seeing all her children and grandchildren but today Ellen was relieved when they had all finally driven off. Sam and family were going to stay with her youngest, Lucas, in Victoria for a few days before heading back to London. Gemma had given her a tremendous hug before she left.

'Love you, Grandma,' she said.

'Love you too, sweetheart,' she had said fondly, placing her hand on the little girl's head. She prayed Gemma would be well and happy. Not see or experience the things she had done when she was the same age.

Ellen sipped her cocoa and curled up on the couch next to Jack. The fire was crackling in the fireplace and the drapes were closed. She imagined the inky sea rolling under the waning full moon along the rugged coastline of her beloved island. She closed her eyes for a second to listen to the distant sound of the waves and remembered another rolling sea on the western edge of Ireland. It felt as if no time had passed whatsoever, although the whole of her life had happened in between. Ellen opened her eyes and looked at Jack.

'Shall I begin?' she asked him.

'Only when you're ready,' he said. 'No rush, Ellie, honey.'

'I'm ready,' she said, cradling her cocoa. She would step off the cliff and show her husband the truth at last.

19 MAY 1915

Ellen laid the table in her nursery with her china doll's tea set. There were three places set at the table and she had four cups, and saucers, and one little teapot, so there was one left over. Today was her seventh birthday and she was going to have a Mad Hatter's tea party just like in her favourite storybook, *Alice's Adventures in Wonderland*. She was going to be Alice. She had already put on her blue dress and a white apron, as well as getting Mrs Murphy, the cook, to tie a blue ribbon with a bow in her hair.

She looked out the window of the nursery. The view was over the front lawn, the green lake and the front drive. She didn't like to look at the lake because that was where her mother had drowned. She had only been two years old when it happened. She didn't remember her mother at all. Even when she looked at the portrait of her at the top of the staircase, nothing about the willowy lady in the painting was familiar to her. Her mother, Dorothy Lavelle, had been a great beauty, and a catch. Her daddy had brought her over from England to live here in Merview House the year before Ellen was born. Sometimes Ellen would stand in front of the painting of her mother and stare and stare with all her might. But the only impression it left on her was the necklace around her neck with the blue star surrounded by tiny white orbs and diamonds and the white roses attached to the bodice of her mother's black gown. They were like the roses in the gardens at Merview House in late summer. Overblown and prickly.

When she was six, Ellen had asked her daddy what had happened to her mother. Where was she? This was when he had told her about the lake. He had put on a very serious face, and he had said sometimes in life tragic accidents happened. This was what had happened to her mother: she had fallen into the lake and drowned.

Ellen stared past the still green lake waters and caught sight of her tea party guests coming up the drive. There was Meg, running ahead of her brother Finnian. Bringing up the rear was their aunt Norah, who looked after them. Ellen waved from her nursery window and Meg looked up and waved back at her. Meg was her best friend. Truth was, apart from her china doll and her teddy bear, Meg and Finnian were her only friends. Ellen liked to pretend Meg and Finnian were her real sister and brother. She wished it were so. Finnian was ten, three years older than her, and Meg was five, two years younger than her. Ellen was nearly as tall as Finnian, but Meg was tiny. Sometimes she called her little wren, because she was like the bright tiny bird with the big song. It was Meg's birthday in two days' time, but no one liked to celebrate it because not only was it the day before Ellen's mother had drowned in the lake but it was on this day Meg's mother had died, while she was birthing Meg. Ellen thought this must be even worse than your mother drowning in a lake, because Meg was the reason her mother was dead – although no one ever said that to her.

Ellen had known Meg and Finnian all her life because their daddy looked after her daddy's horses, and he was best friends with her uncle Rafe. Ellen loved the little lodge Meg and Finnian lived in because it was always so warm and cosy. Aunty Norah lived with them, and she always seemed to be baking fresh bread, which she brought to the big house too. Ellen's father had hired Norah to be Ellen's nursemaid after her last nanny had left last year. This made Ellen very happy because she spent nearly every day with Finnian and Meg. Her project was to turn Meg into a little lady just like her, which was why she was teaching her to read. Finnian was attending the village school and could read already, but Ellen believed they didn't teach the girls so well and this made her cross.

Sometimes Ellen would overhear Finnian and Meg talking to each other in Irish. She'd ask them what they were saying, but Finnian would order Meg not to tell. Afterwards, Meg would always tell her and it would be something boring like, *I don't want to play with girls*. But in Irish.

They weren't allowed to speak Irish in the village school so it wasn't often Ellen heard Finnian and Meg speak in Gaelic, but it felt like a secret she was excluded from. She wanted to go to the village school with them, but her father said she was to have her own governess and do her lessons at home.

Ellen heard Meg as she came charging up the staircase and tore into her nursery.

'Happy birthday!' she sang at the top of her voice.

Being around Meg felt like dancing in the wind. Ellen was told all the time to be a young lady and watch her manners, but Meg was free to be whoever she wanted to be.

'Let's have the tea party outside!' Meg declared, her little hands on her hips. Already her smock was mucky from running through the woods.

'Daddy said it's going to rain,' said Ellen.

Meg shook her head vigorously. 'The garden,' she insisted, stamping her foot.

Ellen always obeyed Meg. She might be two years younger than her, and poorer than her too, but it was always Meg in charge.

Meg carried the tablecloth all folded up and pressed to her chest so it wouldn't trail, while Finnian, Norah and Ellen carried the tea things out. The day was chilly and the grass was damp, but they set up on the front lawn all the same.

'Dress up!' Meg demanded, pointing at Ellen's *Alice in Wonderland* dress.

'Yes of course,' Ellen said. 'Come on, Finnian.'

'I don't want to dress up,' he complained. 'Sure, it's bad enough being at this stupid tea party.'

Even so he followed Ellen up to her nursery.

'I think you have to be the Mad Hatter, Finnian,' Ellen said, putting a top hat of her father's on his head.

'No! No! I want to be the Mad Hatter,' Meg protested, grabbing the hat and putting it on her own head. It was so big on her that it fell down over her eyes. Finnan and Ellen laughed at her, and Meg started laughing too.

'Am I going mad?' she asked, marching around the room, arms outstretched as if they were playing blind man's bluff. Meg was so good at remembering lines from *Alice in Wonderland*. She even put on the Mad Hatter's voice.

'Yes, you're mad, bonkers, off the top of your head, but I'll tell you a secret...' Ellen replied as Alice, tapping Meg on the back as she spun around.

'All the best people are!' Finnian chimed in, whipping the hat off Meg's head.

The three of them fell about laughing. They laughed until their tummies ached, and they hadn't even had any birthday cake yet.

After the tea party, having scoffed most of the sandwiches and cake, Finnian lost interest and went to look for his father in the stable yard. But Meg stayed.

'Time for a bluebell hunt,' she announced, getting to her feet and shaking crumbs off her smock. Ellen wasn't brave enough to go into the woods without Meg. Sometimes when she looked at them from the window of the nursery, she imagined she saw shadows flitting through the trees. She was scared they had something to do with why her mother drowned. She didn't want them to get her too. But Meg wasn't afraid of any shadows in the woods. She rampaged through the trees as if every part of the woods was her domain, leading the way to the beds of bluebells, hazy and fragrant.

'Ah!' sighed Meg, falling down among the flowers.

Ellen lay down next to her, and together they held hands.

'Promise we'll be friends forever,' Ellen said to Meg.

'Always,' Meg said back.

After a while, hearing their names being called, the two girls ran back to the house. The light was fading, and it must have been very late. It was Meg's aunt Norah calling for them. When they came around the back of the house, she was waiting for them along with Meg's father, Mr O'Hanley, and her brother, Finnian. Ellen was shy of Meg's father. He was tall and tanned from working outside, and he had a special way with the horses. Ellen was a little afraid of horses. Sometimes she would see her father and Uncle Rafe out riding with Meg's father early in the morning. The three men looked so gallant as they galloped through the fields and disappeared from view.

Meg ran ahead of her, and her father scooped her up and put her on his shoulders, much to Meg's delight. Ellen's father had never put her on his shoulders. She looked on with envy as her friend leaned over and pressed her cheek next to Mr O'Hanley's, wishing her own father would allow her that close.

'Run along indoors, Miss Ellen,' Norah said to her. 'Your father wants to see you in the library. Mrs Murphy and I have put away the tea things.'

'Thank you, Norah,' she said, climbing the steps into the back kitchen. She stopped on the threshold and turned to watch Meg and her family heading back to their lodge, the four of them in unity. She felt such a longing to be with them, to sit with them by their cosy turf fire and listen to Aunt Norah singing them songs. To be tucked up in bed with Meg rather than having to climb into her own empty bed.

. . .

Ellen knocked on the door of the library and waited for her father's command to enter. Her father was standing in front of the blazing fire smoking a cigarette and her uncle Rafe was sitting in an armchair with his red setter Roxy at his feet. In her uncle's hand was his usual glass of whisky, glinting gold in the firelight. Ellen stared at her father in surprise because he wasn't dressed in his country jacket and riding breeches. He was dressed like a soldier, and so was Uncle Rafe.

'Ellen, I hope you had a happy birthday,' her father said, putting out his cigarette.

'Yes, Father, I did,' she replied demurely.

'I am glad to hear it,' he said. 'Finnian tells me your tea party was a great success.'

The two men guffawed and Ellen reddened. It felt as if her father and uncle were mocking her. Tears sprouted in her eyes.

'What's wrong, child?' her father asked, noticing instantly.

She didn't want to admit it, but she didn't like to see her father dressed as a soldier.

'Father, are you and Uncle Rafe playing dress-up?'

Her father frowned.

'No, my child,' he said in a serious voice. 'It's not a game. Your uncle Rafe and I are leaving tomorrow to fight in the war.'

'The war!' she said in fright. 'Has it come to Ireland?'

'Not yet,' she heard Uncle Rafe say in a quiet voice.

'We have joined the cavalry,' her father told her. 'We are leaving for France tomorrow to fight the Hun.'

'But why is it just you and Uncle Rafe? Why isn't Mr O'Hanley going too?'

'He is staying in Ireland to look after the horses, and all of you,' Uncle Rafe said.

Ellen saw her father look at Uncle Rafe in a strange way. A tightening of his eyes and mouth. It was something to with Meg and Finnian's father, but she didn't know what.

'Please don't go, Father,' Ellen said, clasping her hands as tears began to spill from her eyes.

Her father bent down and took her hands in his. How she wished he would pick her up or give her a handkerchief to wipe her tears.

'You must be a brave girl and be good while we are away,' her father said. But there was a distant look in his eyes, as if he had already left. Although, when Ellen thought about it, her father always had that look in his eyes, as if he was never really there. She had thought about this in church when she was on her knees praying: 'Dear God, please look after my mother in heaven, and Meg's mother too.'

The priest had talked about the body and the soul. Could her father's body be in one place and his soul in another? Maybe it was with her mother, at the bottom of the green lake at Merview House. Had it jumped in after her mother when she'd fallen in?

9 JANUARY 1919

Her father was leaving again but this time it was for America.

'Please, Daddy, don't go,' eleven-year-old Ellen had begged him yet again.

Her father had looked at her with his pale grey eyes. His expression so calm. Since he had returned from fighting the war, he was even more aloof towards her than he had been before.

'I will send for you,' he reassured Ellen. 'But I need to establish myself first. I will find a house for us to live in and a new mother to look after you.'

Ellen almost gasped in shock. 'A new mother?'

'Yes, and one day there'll be brothers and sisters too.'

Ellen frowned. These plans of her father's were troubling. She didn't want a new mother, and she certainly didn't want any brothers and sisters taking away what little attention her father paid her. Besides, she already had Meg and Finnian.

'If it doesn't work out, will you come back?' she asked.

Her father looked very serious.

'I believe I am never coming back to Ireland, Ellen,' he said.

'Your uncle Rafe will accompany you to America as soon as I have everything set up.'

Ellen turned to look at her uncle Rafe. He was standing by the front door, looking away from his brother and leaning on his walking stick. He had come back from the fighting in France with a bad leg, but it didn't stop him from going out riding every morning with Meg and Finnian's father.

'Alec, I told you, I'm not leaving Cillian and the others – and you shouldn't either. I've pledged my loyalty to Michael Collins and a free Ireland,' Rafe said, turning to look at his brother. His expression was fierce. 'If you must go, then bring your daughter with you.'

'I have no one to mind her in Chicago,' Alec said. 'It will be rough for a while, until I get set up.'

There was an awkward silence between her father and his brother. As if they were both caught up in their own inner thoughts and had forgotten she was right there, standing between them.

'Do you not remember that our great-great-grandfather fought for the rights of Catholic people in Ireland?' Rafe challenged her father. 'What's happened to your patriotism, Alec? Now's the time to fight for independence!'

'I saw enough fighting on the fields of France and Belgium, enough suffering in the trenches,' Alec said emphatically. 'I want no more of warring.'

'You're a coward,' Rafe hissed. 'But of course I will look after little Ellen. Just make sure you send for her soon.' With that her uncle limped out of the entrance hall, Roxy, his dog, trotting after him.

Her father waited until he was gone, then knelt down beside her and drew a beautiful necklace out of the inside pocket of his coat.

'I was going to bring this with me, but I think you must have it now, Ellen,' he said. 'It belonged to your mother and is a family heirloom.'

'She's wearing it in her painting,' Ellen said, staring at the necklace. She reached out to touch the star-shaped pendant bejewelled with turquoise, pearls and diamonds, but Alec gently stopped her.

'It's not a plaything, Ellen. Keep it somewhere safe. When you join me in America, you may bring it with you.'

Her father held up the necklace as the diamonds and pearls ringing the turquoise stone sparkled in the pale wintry light.

'This keepsake is to remind you that I look forward to the day I can see you wearing it for me.'

Ellen took the necklace into the palms of her small hands. It was still warm from her father's touch. She held it tightly as she watched him ride away on his horse, with Mr O'Hanley and the stable boy, Jimmy, for company. Her uncle Rafe didn't accompany him, nor did he come out of the library all night.

Ellen waited for her father to send the ticket for her passage to America. She waited the whole spring, but it didn't come. Instead, a great many strangers came to Merview House. Most of them men. But sometimes women too. They all had guns, even the women, but they weren't in army uniforms. They piled into the big dining room for hours and had heated discussions. Ellen would listen at the door until Mrs Murphy whisked her away with a worried look on her face. One night, after all the people had left, Ellen overheard Uncle Rafe and Mr O'Hanley arguing about Finnian. It had been a long time since she'd seen Finnian. He'd long stopped wanting to play games with her and Meg.

'Your boy is too young to get mixed up in the fighting,' Rafe had warned Mr O'Hanley.

But Finnian's father was adamant: 'This is my boy's struggle too. He's the future of Ireland.'

Apart from the mystery of the secret meetings, Ellen and Meg had little interest in the struggle for Mother Ireland. Their world was one of fairy folk and magic in the thick woods at the back of the estate. Over the years, Ellen had overcome her fear of being in the woods and would happily spend hours with her best friend building fairy houses or dams in the stream, and talking to the little people they believed were there all the time watching them.

'I think the fey folk took our mammies,' Meg told Ellen one day. 'If we keep looking, they could be here in the woods. Maybe we can find the way into their land.'

'I don't know if we should go there,' Ellen said. 'We might not get back.'

Always the girls stayed out longer than they should and got smacked with a wooden spoon by Aunty Norah when they finally showed up muddy and messy from their day in the woods.

'It's not safe for two young girls to run amok,' she admonished them. 'What if you'd got caught by the Black and Tans?'

The girls learned to equate the Black and Tans with the bogeyman, only worse because there were lots of them and, according to Mr O'Hanley, they were British thugs who'd been sent to beat up Irish patriots.

18 FEBRUARY 1922

The girls' long dreamy days together came to an end when Meg was sent to the village school while Ellen got yet another governess. Ellen's father had been gone three years and she was fourteen. Surely, she was now old enough to travel to America? But she had stopped asking her uncle Rafe because he had become so busy with the fight for an Irish Republic. Besides, in her heart, she knew she loved Meg more than her father. She could never leave her behind.

By this time, Aunty Norah had married and moved into her own cottage. At the age of twelve, Meg was left to keep house in the estate cottage for her father and brother.

At the village school the boys teased Meg and pinched her, and the girls said she was uppity because she played with the Brit Ellen Lavelle at Merview House.

'She's not British, she's Irish like us!' Meg defended her friend.

But sometimes Meg did wonder why it was Ellen lived in such a big grand house with no shortage of food, when all the other villagers lived in cottages with tiny windows. Some of them all sleeping in one room.

Meg hated school not just because of the other children but also because the teacher hit her with a stick, telling her she mustn't speak Irish. Her brother Finnian never went to school any more because he refused to give up speaking Irish. He had become a wild feral boy. Days on end Meg was left on her own in the estate cottage while her father and brother disappeared.

Every day after school Meg ran through the woods to Ellen's house and they would play make-believe games, dressing up in her mother's old dresses.

One afternoon, Ellen showed Meg the necklace. She had hidden it under her mattress.

'It belonged to my mother,' Ellen told Meg. 'That stone is called turquoise.'

Meg had never seen such a beautiful thing in her entire life. She kept staring at the blue stone and it felt like it was something magic. As if it could cast spells.

Ellen let her put the necklace on and Meg paraded around the bedroom feeling very grand.

One afternoon the girls were disturbed in their game of dress-up by a commotion downstairs. Ellen took the necklace off Meg and hastily shoved it under her mattress. They could hear men's voices raised in argument.

'Uncle Rafe,' Ellen said to Meg. 'He always shouts when he's had his medicinal whisky.'

'That's Daddy shouting back,' Meg whispered.

The girls looked at each other in shock. Rafe and Cillian were best friends, just like them. Why would they be yelling at each other in such rage?

They crept over to the top of the staircase and looked down at the men. Rafe was red in the face while Meg had never seen her father so enraged. The sight made her shiver. Her daddy had been away for weeks and he looked so very different from the daddy who tucked her into bed at night and sang 'The Wind That Shakes the Barley'. His hair was wild and matted, and his clothes filthy with bog muck. He had a rifle slung over his shoulder.

'We can't back down,' Cillian said to Rafe.

'They'll butcher us if we don't compromise,' Rafe replied. 'It's a good deal. There'll be no more killing.'

'But they're still in charge!' Cillian yelled. 'Irish Free State? It's a trick to get us to submit!'

'We've a chance for peace,' Rafe insisted.

'At what price?' Cillian countered.

The men glowered at each other.

'I can't be involved any more,' Rafe said.

'Because you're scared,' Cillian hissed.

'How dare you!' Rafe exploded. 'I fought in the Great War, and I've seen enough young boys dead to haunt me for the rest of my days. Do you want Finnian's life cut short?'

'I don't want him ashamed of his father for not sticking to his beliefs.'

'For God's sake, man,' Rafe shouted, 'if you continue with your struggle, they will send the full might of the British military. They'll crush us. But if we accept the treaty, inch by inch we can claw back autonomy.'

'I don't have time for inch by inch,' Cillian said, and catching sight of Meg at the top of the stairs, he beckoned to her. 'Come on, Meg, we're going home. Getting out of this traitor's house.'

'Don't think you can stay in the estate cottage if you continue, Cillian. You'll have to find another home.'

'I wouldn't want to stay,' Cillian said in an icy voice. 'I resign!'

Meg looked at Ellen with tears in her eyes.

'No, I don't want to leave, Daddy,' she said.

'Come here at once.'

But the two girls clung to each other until Meg's father came up the stairs to pull them apart. Meanwhile Rafe had gone into his library and banged the door shut.

'Don't leave me with him,' Ellen begged Meg's father. 'When he drinks the whisky, he shouts a lot. It's scary.'

But Mr O'Hanley ignored her, and prised Meg from her arms.

The girls sobbed as they were parted. It felt like their hearts had been cut out.

1 MAY 1922

The woods were filled with bluebells. Meg had trudged all the way there from Aunt Norah's cottage, where she now lived with her aunt and her husband Michael, another IRA man. Meg's father and Finnian were away in the Iron Mountains, hiding out with the republicans.

Her aunt's cottage was always so noisy. Within the space of three years Norah had had three babies and it was Meg's job to help her. She hadn't been back to school in weeks. Every day was taken up with washing nappies and feeding babies.

But this afternoon, all three babies – even the three-year-old – had fallen asleep on the bed with their mother. It had been Meg's chance to escape. She knew precisely where she wanted to go. She hadn't seen her dear friend Ellen for so long, and she missed her. The last time she'd seen her was when Ellen had turned up at their cottage door, but her father had been there and sent her away, despite the girl's tears.

'Please, Mr O'Hanley,' Ellen begged. 'Uncle Rafe is so angry all the time. He shouts at me.'

But Meg's father ignored her.

'It's not my business, child. He chose his side.'

Meg climbed over the stone wall and entered the lands of Merview House. On this side the thickets of bluebells were even more dense, spread before her in a purple haze. The scent filled her with longing for the days when she'd play here every day with Ellen. Eventually she reached the far side of the woods and the view opened out so she could see the lake and gardens of the big house. To her surprise right by the lake, there was Ellen with her uncle Rafe. He was swinging a sack in the air, and she was pulling at his arms.

'Please, Uncle, they're just two little kittens, and I'll look after them,' she begged him.

'We've too many cats,' he said, hurling the sack into the lake as Ellen screamed. Uncle Rafe turned his back on his distressed niece and limped back to the big house.

Ellen began wading into the lake, but Meg knew her friend couldn't swim. Without thinking of the consequences, she tore out of the woods and across the gardens in her bare feet. Running and then jumping into the lake. Swimming past Ellen. She saw the sack bobbing and heard the mewling of the kittens. She grabbed the sack and swam back to shore. Untying the bag with shaking cold hands, she freed the two terrified kittens. One was black, and one was ginger.

'Meg, Meg!' Ellen cried out. 'Oh Meg!'

The two girls laughed and cried. They didn't care if Ellen's uncle Rafe saw them from the windows of the big house.

'He's so drunk he won't remember,' Ellen assured her. 'Tomorrow, he'll ask me where the kittens are and forget he tried to drown them!'

'What shall we call them?' Meg asked.

Ellen looked around her. By the lake were little clumps of bright blue forget-me-nots. They were the same colour as Meg's eyes.

'This one is called Forget-me-not,' she said, picking up the ginger one.

'And this one is Bluebell,' Meg said, the image of the bluebells rising in her mind.

'Forget-me-not and Bluebell,' Ellen said, smiling. 'I've missed you so much.'

'Me too.'

The girls embraced. Made their secret silent pact. They would never let others separate them again. They would meet every night in the woods.

'I have a plan,' Ellen whispered to Meg.

Meg's eyes widened. 'What is it?'

'Let's run away to America together,' she said.' Get away from all the angry people. I hate it,' Ellen said. 'We can go and live with my father.'

'But he might not want me,' Meg said.

'Of course he will. He won't turn you back!'

The idea excited Meg. She was so bored in Ireland. On the days she escaped her life in the cottage, she didn't go to school any more. Instead, she ran down the windy boreens and lanes all the way to the edge of the land. She stood atop the craggy cliffs and watched the waves pounding and frothing against the land. She looked far out to sea and dreamed of going beyond the horizon to far-off lands. Places filled with adventures and new beginnings. Places where she could become someone else. Where make-believe was real.

'I want to come with you more than anything,' she said to Ellen, clutching her hands. 'But how will we pay for the tickets?'

'I have some money hidden away,' Ellen said. 'I took the bus to Dublin and sold some of my mother's jewellery in a pawn shop on O'Connell Street.'

Meg was hugely impressed by her friend's audacity, but then a thought occurred to her: 'You didn't sell the necklace?'

'Oh no, I'm going to wear the necklace when I see my father next.' She smiled at Meg, though her eyes flickered with anxiety. 'That way he'll know it's me.'

'Of course he'll know it's you, with or without the necklace!' Meg declared.

'At the moment, I don't have enough money for both of us.' Ellen frowned. 'But I'll think of a way.'

'You could go on your own,' Meg suggested reluctantly.

Though she would be bitterly disappointed if she was left behind, she wanted her friend to escape the drunken rages of her uncle Rafe more.

'I am not going without you, Meg,' Ellen promised. 'We will get the money for the ticket. I will hunt for more treasures in the house. Besides, we need to be patient. We can't abandon Bluebell and Forget-me-not until they're a little older!'

'Where will we hide them?' Meg asked Ellen.

'Don't worry, Jimmy the stable boy will help,' Ellen said. Her friend had become more audacious since Meg had last seen her, and more confident. 'He's sweet on me. He'll hide the kittens in the stables.'

When Meg got home her aunt Norah was so angry with her for leaving her alone with her crying babies that she picked up the wooden spoon and gave her a battering. But Meg didn't care. She and Ellen were reunited. And they were going to America together.

CHAPTER TWENTY-THREE

20 OCTOBER 1984

Mairead had never seen a forest like this in her life. She slowed her steps right down as she walked across the forest floor, enjoying the sensation of the thick moss bouncing under the soles of her shoes.

There was so much space between the trees yet looking up she couldn't see the treetops, they were so thin as they disappeared into the sky. She imagined being right at the top of one, looking down at herself so small, and insignificant. Pockets of blue sky peeked at her. It was a sunny afternoon, but Mairead didn't want to go out into the light, not yet. The air was cool and damp under the constant shade of the trees, a place to retreat and think. This lush rainforest was so quiet it felt as sacred as a church. It reminded her of the passage of time. The trees were here long before her grandmother Ellen had arrived in this part of Canada. Long before the first of her ancestors had ever drawn breath.

Mairead stopped walking. Placed her hands on her heart, sensed its panicked fluttering. She felt the heat rising to her chest, her cheeks. Anxiety pressing in on her temples. Ever since she'd taken those drugs in Scottsdale, any time she felt slightly stressed, she began to feel sick and close to hyperventilating. She hoped these feelings would gradually go away. But though she still felt a little fragile and raw, she was not giving up now. Mairead was looking for answers of her own in the story of her ancestor. If she figured out the puzzles of the past, understood where she came from, it might help her work out where to go.

Here in this rainforest it didn't seem to matter so much that nothing would ever be the same again. It made her feel better, walking in solitude through the ancient trees, absorbing their woody scent, the cool sanctuary of forest soothing her. Her mother would have loved the rainforest.

Mairead left Cathedral Grove and got back into her rental car and set off again on her way to the town of Tofino right on the western edge of Vancouver Island. As she drove, she imagined Ellen Lavelle's journey west. If she had come here back in the thirties, how would she have travelled? Most likely by boat rather than by land. But as Mairead followed the road through the towering trees, she understood why this was the perfect place to run away to. Remote, steeped in shadows, sheltered by old-growth forests. As she drove into Tofino town, she detected the comforting blink of blue on the horizon. As always, the ocean seemed to offer the opportunity for escape: freedom to sail anywhere in the world.

Mairead got a room at the first motel she came upon. She asked the owner of the motel, a young, bearded man, whether he knew of a woman called Ellen Lavelle, but he'd told her no. She sat on the balcony of her room, wrapped up in a blanket against the October chill, and drank a cup of tea as she gazed at the intense blue of the Pacific Ocean. It was different from the Atlantic, bigger and more placid – the father ocean, whereas the Atlantic was the mother ocean, choppier and more capricious.

The shadows were lengthening, and the sun was sinking as she walked down Tofino's main street. All along its length were signs for spa treatments, surfing and yoga studios interspersed with art galleries, craft stores, trendy cafes and restaurants. She had no idea how she was going to find her grandmother in this place. She guessed she just had to keep asking.

One sign in the window of an arts and crafts store piqued her interest.

Tarot Readings
Tamara de la Luna

The sign was decorated with tiny stars and moons. Mairead had never had her cards done, always dismissed it as a load of rubbish. Her mother had decks of them back at the house in Sligo. She had got Stella into it as a teenager, which had annoyed Mairead immensely. But now she was intrigued. If she could do all the things she'd done with Kyle, then a tarot reading wasn't that way out.

'OK, Mam, let's see what Tamara de la Luna has to say, shall we? Maybe she'll find Ellen Lavelle for me.'

Tamara de la Luna was a young woman not much over twenty with a nose piercing and a tiny blue tattoo of a hummingbird on the inside of her forearm.

As Tamara shuffled the cards, she spoke in a low voice.

'My readings are awakenings tapping into your subconscious,' she explained. 'So, everything I tell you is what you already know deep down.'

Mairead wanted to say something smart like *What's the point then?* But as she looked into Tamara's eyes – a thousand shades of brown, flecked with green, even amber – she found herself wondering if the girl could read her mind.

'What if you see something bad? Will you tell me?'

Mairead didn't want to know if something terrible was going to happen, especially if it was about Stella.

Tamara smiled at her benignly. Clearly, she'd been asked this question many times.

'The tarot tell you what you need to know. Remember, you

always have free will. So, they are like a blueprint of your life as it is now and in the coming three months.'

Tamara deftly laid out Mairead's spread: cross in the centre, circle of cards around it and a line down the side.

'Depending on the cards, they can either be affirmative or guidance, maybe even a warning, but you can change the direction you're taking. Always,' Tamara said firmly.

Mairead looked down at the tarot cards spread upon the table. The first thing she saw was the colour yellow. So much of it filling up so many of the cards. Big golden coins, cups of blue water, wooden wands sprouting tiny green leaves, and sharp silver swords.

Tamara's words began to resonate. When Mairead looked at a card and thought something, Tamara spoke it. It was all laid out before her: her marriage break-up, her estrangement from her daughter, her mother's death. Even Kyle came up as the Devil. Tamara gave her a piercing look as she placed her hand on the card.

'This is in the recent past,' she said. 'A figure trying to manipulate you through sex and money.'

'But it's over now?'

'Yes,' Tamara told her. 'There's a Queen of Swords crossing your present situation. All of what is happening right now connects to her.'

'What's a Queen of Swords?' Mairead asked.

'A feminine energy of airy quality, possibly an Aquarius, Gemini or Libra.'

'My mother was a Gemini,' she told Tamara.

'I don't think it's your mother, because this woman is on a quest now. She's speaking her truth, and she lies in your pathway,' Tamara said.

Mairead had no idea what zodiac sign Ellen Lavelle was. Could she be the Queen of Swords?

'Does that mean I'm going to meet her?' Mairead asked, feeling a little excited. Maybe it really was Ellen? *Calm down*, she told herself. *Remember you think tarot cards are hocus-pocus.* But Tamara had been spot on so far. How could she know all these things about her?

'She's why you're here in this room with me!' Tamara exclaimed, opening her hands wide, the rings on her fingers glinting in the evening light.

'What can you tell me about her?' Mairead asked, her heart beginning to beat faster with anticipation.

'All is not what it seems.' Tamara picked up another card in the spread. 'She holds the sword of truth, but she is yet to speak it. She crosses a Queen of Pentacles – an earthy woman. Is that you?'

'Yes, I'm Taurus. But I haven't met her. I'm looking for her.'

Tamara was so easy to talk to. Mairead opened up more about her mother's death. How it had been her dying wish for Mairead to find her grandmother Ellen, who had abandoned her as a little girl.

'I've been told she came to live in Tofino in the thirties,' Mairead said. 'Her name is Ellen Lavelle. Have you heard of her?'

'I'm sorry, no,' Tamara told her.

Mairead's heart plummeted. 'Can the cards tell you if she's dead?'

'No, I'm sorry, I can't tell you that,' Tamara said. 'Oh but look, you have the Knight of Cups turning up in the future.' Tamara's voice brightened. 'That means a lover!'

Mairead had no intention of ever contacting Kyle Symes again.

'That's the past,' she said, shaking her head. 'I'm done with all of that.'

After Mairead paid Tamara, she asked if she could recommend a place to eat.

'Why don't you join me and my friends?' Tamara suggested. 'We're meeting up at the Wickinnish Inn later. There'll be music too.'

'Oh, I couldn't intrude—'

'You're very welcome!' Tamara said. She gave her directions on how to get there. 'We'll be there in about an hour or so.'

'OK,' Mairead said. 'Why not?'

. . .

Mairead went back to her motel. She had a shower, changed her shirt and put on the necklace, then a sweater over it to keep warm. The night was chilly as she made her way to the Wickinnish Inn. Tamara waved her over to join her and her friends in an enclave with big glass windows. Although it was dark outside, Mairead could hear the sea's constant rhythm. It felt so comforting, she began to wonder how she had lived without its sound for most of her life.

Tamara and her friends were at least ten years younger than her, but they didn't seem to care so why should she? A guy called Josh was playing the guitar and singing Johnny Cash's 'I Walk the Line'.

When Stella was a baby, she had danced with her in her arms to Niall's Johnny Cash album. Her heart ached to think of the loss of the child her daughter had been; Stella had needed her when she was little, but now it was Mairead who needed Stella.

'Hey, I love your accent,' Tamara said to her. 'Where are you from?'

'Ireland,' Mairead said.

'Ireland! Why, that's where Ellie and Jack have gone today!' Tamara told her.

'Who are Ellie and Jack?' Mairead asked her, something niggling at the back of her mind. Ellie... Ellen, was it a coincidence?

'They own the store where I read tarot cards,' she said. 'You were in it today. I'm looking after the store for them while they're away.

'It was all a bit sudden,' she added. 'But apparently Ellie is Irish too! I never knew it. Always thought she was from New York.'

'How old is Ellie?' Mairead asked.

Tamara put down her drink and gave Mairead a long look before answering.

'Why are you asking?'

'I think Ellie might be my Queen of Swords,' Mairead whispered.

Tamara's eyes widened. 'That's crazy...' She paused, thought for a second. 'Well, they celebrated their forty-fifth wedding anniversary a few days ago, so I guess she must be in her seventies?'

Mairead's chest constricted, and her heart began to beat faster. Had she really found her grandmother at last? This Ellie could be her! The heat was rising up her neck, and she felt so hot all of a sudden. She pulled off her sweater and as she did so, Tamara clutched her arm.

'Where did you get that necklace?' she gasped.

'It was my mother's,' Mairead said. 'But it was Ellen's once. She left it for her the night they were separated all those years ago.'

'Oh my!' Tamara exclaimed. 'Ellie has one very similar. I mean, it looks more crafty, and there are no diamonds. But it's the same style, and the star shape with the big turquoise is almost identical.'

Mairead couldn't speak she was so blown away. Up until this very minute, she had doubted she would ever find her grandmother. In all the vastness of America and Canada, after decade upon decade.

'This is incredible!' Tamara gushed. 'You've come all the way here looking for her, and meanwhile they've gone to Ireland. I thought it was a vacation. But maybe they've gone to find you?'

Mairead placed her hands on her pounding heart. The sea hushed outside the window, and she took deep breaths in time with its pull in and out. The distance was not so vast. They were across the sea, but they were getting closer. In her grandmother's story was a place Mairead could begin again. But then she remembered the book Kyle had taken from her: *Arizona's Killers*. Although the Mexican woman Gabriella had sworn Ellen was innocent, and Tamara painted a picture of a sweet old lady in Tofino, there was never smoke without a fire. What kind of woman was Ellen Lavelle, really? Mairead began to doubt her mission. The truth was she had used the search for her grandmother as an excuse to run away from her real life. But now she had to go home and put her life back together again. She had no idea who she was any more.

CHAPTER TWENTY-FOUR

13 OCTOBER 1984

Jack had brought out the whisky and poured them both a small glass. It was getting late, and Ellen was tired, but she couldn't stop her story now. If she did, she might never have the courage to tell her husband everything.

'I know a little about the Irish War of Independence,' Jack said as he handed her the glass of warming amber. 'But I've never heard of the Civil War.'

'It was far worse,' Ellen said. 'Neighbour against neighbour, rifts in families. One brother a free stater, the other a republican.'

She took a sip of the whisky and felt its burn in the back of her throat. She closed her eyes for a second and went back to a terrible dark time. When she opened her eyes again, Jack was waiting. She took a deep breath, and she began.

21 SEPTEMBER 1922

Meg and Ellen kept their promise and met in the woods nearly every evening. It was dangerous in those days. Sometimes they might come across a random republican irregular running for his life. Since Michael Collins had been killed in Cork in the August of 1922, the Free State army had become more violent. The girls had heard of terrible things. IRA boys who had surrendered being shot down with no compunction. Meg was afraid for her father and brother. She only saw them now and again when they came to Norah's cottage late at night and gobbled down plates of stew. Norah's husband Michael had dropped out of the IRA because of his family and the way things were going. He tried to encourage Cillian to do the same. But her father was vehement he would never give up. Meg could see the same passion shining in the eyes of her brother, Finnian.

'Cillian, have you no sense?' Aunt Norah had given out. 'You'll be executed. Finnian's just a lad. Is that what you want?'

'They sold us out!' Cillian said. 'We fought for a republic, not a treaty which expects our leaders to make an oath to the English king!'

'But the majority of people have voted for it,' Norah continued. 'They want an end to the death and fighting. Too many mothers have lost their boys.'

But there was no convincing Meg's father. Sometimes if it was a very dark night and it was safe for them to stay awhile, he and Finnian would sleep on Aunt Norah and Michael's bed, top to toe. Meg sat in the corner of the tiny room and watched them sleeping. On guard, in case she heard the march of Free State army boots on the lane outside. Her father and brother were like two peas in a pod, as her aunt Norah would say. Meg almost felt envy for their closeness, which was stupid because she had no desire to be hiding out in boggy fields and mountains, running into skirmishes with Free State troops. Every time they stayed, she memorised their faces in case it was the last time she would ever see them. Her father's narrow nose and chiselled cheeks. His eyelashes unusually long for a man. The sandy hair thinning and the lines on his face. She thought about her mother, whom she had never known, and wondered if he still missed her. When she looked at her brother, Finnian, she felt an even deeper twist of love. He was only seventeen, and yet his face had hardened into a man's. When he opened his eyes the look of them was haunting. But Meg realised they had always been so, ever since he was a little boy.

In December 1922, none were feeling much cheer for Christmas. The wind and rain swept in from the Atlantic. Everything was damp, cold and soggy; even the peat fires sputtered pathetically in the cottage. Meg was helping her aunt Norah with the baking when her uncle Michael burst through the door back from the pub.

'They shot some of the irregulars,' he said, shaking off his wet coat.

'Who? Michael, is it Cillian? Finnian?'

'I don't know yet,' he said, his face grim. 'But they chased them like rabbits across the fields. They didn't get them all. Some got away.'

Norah crossed herself. 'Please God they're all right,' she said. 'Oh, Michael, where will it end?'

'There's more,' Michael said. 'They were on land belonging to the Lavelle estate. They're saying Rafe Lavelle gave them away.'

Meg felt herself going very still.

'Sure, Rafe and Cillian were childhood friends, he'd never—'

'Brothers have turned on their own brothers, Norah. This war has split our country, and made men do terrible things to each other.'

The next day they found out the names of the men killed by the Free State army. Cillian and Finnian were not among them. But Meg couldn't help thinking about her father and brother. As the rain lashed against the cottage windows, she thought of them struggling to find shelter and survive in the winter landscape. She hated being stuck in the cottage worrying about them.

Every evening she buttoned her coat tight, pulled a hat over her head, and battered through the rain and wind to meet Ellen in the woods. Here it was dry, and the two girls sat together on tree stumps, and fantasised about their new life in America.

'We'll go to the movies together in the big picture houses,' Meg enthused. 'And the theatres on Broadway!'

'And take a streetcar in New York,' Ellen joined in.

They listed all the things they would do, which they had no hope of ever experiencing in the west of Ireland.

'We'll go dancing, Meg!' Ellen said, clapping her hands. 'Handsome young men will be flocking to be our beaus!'

'I can't dance!' Meg moaned.

'I can teach you.'

The two girls waltzed through the trees as the rain pattered on the leaves above.

One evening as Meg was walking home, jumping over puddles, and dreaming of summer nights in New York City, she heard shouting coming from outside her aunt and uncle's cottage. She climbed over a stone wall and ran across the field in case there was trouble. To her surprise, it was Rafe Lavelle, drunk and raving on their doorstep.

'Where is he?' he snarled at her uncle Michael, who stood in the doorway.

'We've no idea,' Michael said tautly. 'You'd best be getting home now, Mr Lavelle.'

'They killed my horse!' Rafe screeched. 'An innocent animal! They shot a perfectly healthy creature stone dead.'

Meg felt her hands going cold, her fingers icy. Surely her father would never do such a terrible thing?

'I know it was Cillian because only he knew how much I loved Duke,' Rafe said, pointing his finger at Michael. 'He's asked for it now.'

'Leave me out of it,' Michael said, slamming the door.

'You forget, Cillian's hiding places were mine too!' Rafe shouted at the shut door. 'I'll find him.'

As he turned around, Meg ducked behind the wall. She watched as Rafe limped down the lane into the downpour, his tall humped figure fading into the gloom. *Poor Ellen*, Meg thought, hating the idea of her friend being in that house alone when her drunk and angry uncle came home. She only hoped he would not take his rage out on her friend.

Meg never knew if Rafe Lavelle was responsible or not, but two days later her father Cillian O'Hanley was found hiding in the blowholes at St Patrick's Head. He was executed on the spot by two Free State soldiers from Dublin. Finnian was not found, and no one knew where her brother was.

When she heard the news, Meg realised she had been expecting it. All those vigils she had spent keeping watch over her sleeping father had been a preparation for his wake. She sat beside his dead body staring at the hole in his jacket from the bullet wound as Aunty Norah sobbed beside her. But Meg was tearless. She looked at her father's face and thought, *He's only sleeping. Wake up, Daddy. Sing me another song.*

It was only later, in the woods, that Meg let herself cry while Ellen held her in her arms.

'I promise I'll get us out of here,' Ellen whispered, stroking her friend's hair.

Meg never told Ellen about her uncle Rafe's drunken threats. Even if he had given her father away, what could Ellen do about it?

And where was Finnian? She prayed for her brother. Terrified he would be found and shot too. He was just a boy, but there was no mercy in the Civil War, on either side.

CHAPTER TWENTY-FIVE

1 NOVEMBER 1984

Mairead turned the key in the door and stepped into her old house in Kells. She put down her suitcase. The place looked so different. Smaller and yet more empty than when she had left it. She heard a sound from upstairs and footsteps running across the landing. She recognised them, of course. Stella! What was she doing home in Ireland?

Her daughter came thundering down the staircase and threw her arms around Mairead, taking her breath away.

'Mammy!' she yelled. 'You're back!'

Mairead hugged her daughter in return. It wasn't until she was in her arms that she realised how much she had missed her darling Stella.

'You were gone so long,' Stella said, pulling back. 'I was getting worried you were going to stay in America forever.'

'Well, I did think about it,' Mairead teased, looking around her old home and already feeling a little stifled.

'For God's sake, Mam, don't say such things,' Stella said, giving her a playful slap. 'It's not funny.'

Her daughter thought she was joking but Mairead knew for

certain she couldn't stay living in her old house. It was filled with memories of her marriage – years and years when she and Niall had been in denial. She didn't regret it – of course not. How could she, when it had given her Stella. But she had no desire to be faced with those memories every day. She needed a fresh start.

Mairead started by taking the wedding photograph of her and Niall down from the hall wall, ignoring the stack of post Stella had dumped on the table. She walked down the hall into the kitchen, Stella following her. She opened a drawer and put the photograph in it.

'Well, I am definitely going to move out of this house anyway,' Mairead said.

Stella took a seat at the breakfast counter and looked at her uncertainly. 'Are you sure? You love this house.'

Everything was so sterile, Mairead thought. The pictures on the wall were just awful. Generic watercolour landscapes of Ireland and pictures of boats. How had she become so bland?

'I do not,' Mairead said firmly.

Stella raised her eyebrows in surprise.

'Well, you do want you want, Mam,' she said.

'What are you doing here anyway, Stella?' she asked. 'What about drama school?'

'We've a few days off,' she said. 'I rang Uncle Darragh and he said you were coming home, so I took the Slattery's boat and bus to surprise you.' Stella beamed at her.

Mairead was moved by how much trouble Stella had gone to. Ringing America must have cost her a fortune. Never mind the boat from Holyhead.

'Well, it's great to see you,' Mairead said.

'I've missed you, Mam.' Stella put her head on one side and scrutinised her mother. 'You look different,' she said. 'Your hair, and your clothes.'

'I decided to have a makeover,' Mairead said, pulling her hair out of its ponytail and shaking it.

'Well, you look great,' Stella said, clearly impressed. 'So, tell me all about America! Darragh said you met someone.'

Trust her brother to blab.

'Oh, that's over,' Mairead said quickly, hoping never to set eyes on Kyle Symes again.

'Are you OK?' Stella asked.

'Yes, yes, totally,' Mairead assured her. 'How about you?'

Stella sighed, her eyes filling with tears. 'Well, things have been a bit difficult, Mam.'

For the next hour, over several cups of tea, Stella told her mam about her disastrous love life, and the pressures of drama college. While she hated the thought of her daughter being unhappy, it felt wonderful that at last Stella was confiding in her.

'And how's your father?' she asked, noticing Stella had carefully left him and Lesley out of her stories of her life in London.

'They're good,' she said. 'I like Lesley, he's very kind.'

Mairead nodded. To her surprise, she found this didn't bother her in the least. In fact, she was glad for Niall.

'I'm going to sell the house,' she told Stella. 'So, your dad can have half the money. It'll help him get set up in London. Are you OK with that?'

'Of course I am,' Stella said, looking surprised.

'I'm going to move west, into my mam's house. I've decided not to sell it.'

'Oh Mammy, it's such a beautiful house, that's a great idea.' But then Stella frowned. 'What about your job, though?'

Mairead gave a short laugh. 'I'm giving it up.'

Stella looked shocked. 'But what are you going to do? I thought teaching was your life.' She bit her lip. 'I mean, I was always so jealous of your star students. I thought you liked them more than me.'

Mairead looked at Stella in astonishment. 'Oh Stella, there's no comparison to how much I love you. It's true I cared a lot about the girls but I need a break from teaching, maybe forever.'

'To do what?' Stella asked, clearly intrigued.

'Well, I'm not quite sure, but I'll work it out.'

Stella was laughing at her mother. 'I can't believe it: the woman who's always had everything planned down to the last detail, stepping away from it all to just go with the flow. What happened to you in America?'

'It's a long story,' Mairead said, enjoying the intimacy between them. It had been so many years since they'd sat and talked like this. 'Let's go out for dinner and I'll tell you all about it over a bottle of wine.'

Of course, she didn't tell Stella everything. In fact she left out most of what had happened in America. The wild sex with Kyle Symes, snorting coke and partying all night, and what had happened at the party in Scottsdale. It all felt like it had happened to someone else anyway. But she did tell her about her hunt for Ellen Lavelle. How it had brought her from Arizona to Canada.

'I found her, only to discover she had gone on vacation with her husband to Ireland!'

Stella was blown away by the story. 'Maybe she's here looking for you, Mammy?'

'I don't know, it's been so many years; she could have come a long time ago if she was going to do that.'

'But it's too much of a coincidence,' Stella insisted.

Mairead took another sip of her wine. It was late and she was exhausted from her journey.

'Let's go,' she said, leaving a generous tip for the waitress.

'Mammy,' Stella said, her eyes glittering from too much wine. 'We have to go and find the house where Ellen Lavelle was from.'

Mairead felt an ache in her heart remembering the afternoon she'd spent with her mother and Eoin at Merview House. It seemed so very long ago now.

'I already found it. I brought your granny to see it,' she said. 'It's empty. All boarded up.'

'You never told me!' Stella accused her.

'There was a lot going on with Mammy. I'm sorry, love.'

'No, I'm sorry, Mam.' Stella reached out and squeezed her hand. 'Can we go there tomorrow? We can stay in Granny's house overnight, if you're up to it.'

'I don't know. I'm very tired.'

'Please, Mam, I have to go back to London on Sunday, and I really want to see the house. It's part of my heritage! Besides, we might find out something else about Ellen Lavelle.'

'OK,' Mairead heard herself agreeing.

Despite having been so tired, Mairead woke up in the middle of the night on American time. She tossed and turned in the bed, but she couldn't go back to sleep. In the end she gave up and went downstairs to get a cup of herbal tea. As she walked down the hall, she saw the stack of post. She picked it up and brought it with her into the kitchen. Most of it was circulars or bank statements, along with a few condolence cards. But at the bottom of the pile was a cream envelope with slanted script. She recognised the hand-writing immediately from the note Eoin had given her all those months ago. Her heart beating a little faster, she opened the letter.

It was dated one month ago.

Dear Mairead,

I heard from Sister Mary Stephen you've taken sabbatical and are spending some time with your family in America. I'm glad to hear you've taken this time out and I hope you're doing well. You're very missed in work. (I've no one else to do the cryptic crossword with at lunchtime!)

I'm very sorry how things turned out between us. I didn't mean to lie to you about Aileen; the two of us have been separated for years. We married very young and knew quite soon after we weren't for each other. Since neither of us could afford our own place, we've lived together as friends for years. I suppose we got lazy and neither of us bothered to formalise our separation or move on. It was never an issue until I met you. I know it's too late, but I want to let you know that I've moved out of the house I shared with Aileen and I'm now renting a flat in Dublin. (The address is at the top of this letter.) I've no phone yet, but please do drop me a line if you'd be interested in meeting up sometime.

I'm also writing to let you know a piece of information about your family home which I thought you might not be aware of. I was reading the Irish Times *the other day, looking at the property section for places to buy, when I saw an article about Merview House. It told how the property had lain empty for years because of absentee owners in America but that now it was up for sale – which of course we knew when we went to see it. However, the article gives the name of the owner: Kyle Symes. If you remember, on the family tree I gave you he's the great-nephew of Ellen's father, Alec Lavelle. Apparently, the property has hundreds of acres and extensive woodland as well as a fresh fishing lake. The price has now gone up to two million Irish pounds. I'm not sure if you can prove a claim on the property through your mother's birth certificate, but I would imagine you might need to investigate his entitlement to the estate. I hope you don't think I'm interfering, but I thought it important you should know this.*

Wishing you all the best,

Eoin

Ellen sat staring at the letter in shock. Everything started to fall into place. She felt a sudden wave of nausea and just made it to the downstairs toilet before she vomited. Shakily she made her way back into the kitchen and had a big glass of water before she picked up the letter and read it again. Kyle Symes was selling Merview House for two million Irish pounds. He had lied to her about that too. It had stayed in her family all these years. And of course he wanted to conceal the information from her.

'Oh my God,' she whispered.

He hadn't been into her at all. He had merely been trying to delay her return to Ireland so that he could sell the property before she got back. But then, when she tried to end things with him, what had been his intention when he had given her all those drugs? With shaking hands, she clutched the letter, clarity dawning on her. He had told her he was up to his neck in debt and would have to sell his mansion on Long Island, lose his wife and kids, his whole excessive lifestyle. There were people who would do terrible things to protect their lies. Would Kyle Symes have gone as far as murder? Her eyes dry and tight with horror, she recalled those dreams of him with a knife to her throat. Had they really been imaginary? When she thought about him, she could still see those hard eyes. She brought a hand to her throat. He had *hated* her.

Mairead slowly read the letter again with a pounding heart.

Eoin had reached out to her, but was it too late? She had so much to be grateful to him for, especially this revelation. She folded the letter neatly on the breakfast counter, her mind made up. She was going to look into Kyle Symes's claim on the house.

History was a process of investigation. As a history teacher, she knew she had the skills to track down the last will and testament of Alec Lavelle, Ellen's father. Then she could find out whether the house in fact belonged to her family, not Kyle.

The next morning, her eyes grainy from lack of sleep, Mairead drove Stella west to her mother's house. On the way, she collected Alfie from the kennels. He was overjoyed to see her, leaping and bounding all over her. As Mairead let him lick her face, she realised how much she had missed the poor animal. He had been with her right at the end of her mother's life, just like Stella.

As soon as they pulled into the drive of her mother's house, Alfie got excited and began barking in the back of the car, his tail wagging like crazy. She and Stella looked at each other.

'Poor Alfie,' Stella said.

They let Alfie out of the back, and he ran to the front door, panting with anticipation. Mairead's mouth was dry as she pushed the key into the lock. This was a mistake. She wasn't ready to come back. As if reading her thoughts, Stella put her hand on her shoulder.

'It's OK, Mam,' she said.

Alfie tore through the house looking for his mistress, and when he couldn't find her, he started scratching her closed bedroom door and whining.

As she followed the dog from room to room, it struck Mairead that while her own family home had been bland and empty, her mother's house was full of colour, crammed with artwork from artist friends and things she'd picked up on her travels around the world. There were so many stories in her mother's house. So many sides to the woman she had been, and yet her own daughter had never really known her. Mairead felt waves of loss wash over her. She mustn't let that happen to her and Stella.

'Let's get out of here for a bit,' she said.

'But we only just arrived,' Stella said.

'I know, but Alfie's upset. Let's take him for a walk,' Mairead suggested. 'We could go on to Merview House right now.'

'If you've the energy, Mam.' Stella looked at her, concerned. 'I can see you're really tired.'

'I'm grand,' she said.

Mairead needed time to come to terms with living in her mother's house. It was filled with emotion, but it was also filled with a sense of belonging she had never felt before. She wished her mother could have lived long enough to see how much she had changed.

The front gate of Merview House was still chained, but as before, they squeezed through the gap in the wall. Alfie ran ahead of them, happy to be free and with his family again, even if his mistress was missing.

The crisp November day was softening to a misty evening. A full moon was rising in the sky as the sun sank away. The woods seemed to whisper as they walked through them, and Mairead was glad she wasn't on her own.

'It'll be dark soon,' she said. 'We should be quick.'

'It's this way,' called Stella, running ahead, a slight shadow in the fading light. Mairead ran after her and soon they emerged from the trees onto the overgrown front lawn. Merview House stood before them: the collapsed roof, the big stone portico and boarded-up windows. This time she noticed a *No Entry – trespassers will be prosecuted* sign on the door which hadn't been there before.

Stella was already walking around the back of the house. She tried the back door, but it was now locked. As she rattled it, a murder of crows took off from the roof where they had been sitting watching them. Mairead turned to face the jungle of a garden, which looked even more overgrown than when she'd visited with Eoin. The lake glinted at the end of it.

'It's so beautiful, Mam,' Stella said. 'Imagine if this actually belonged to us!'

Her eyes gleamed with excitement.

'Well, most likely not,' Mairead said, not wanting to mention Kyle Symes or Eoin's letter.

'Oh look, there's a little chapel, and a graveyard.'

Mairead hadn't noticed the tiny church and cemetery the first time she had come with her mother and Eoin. It was tucked behind the house, partly concealed by a stone wall. Stella ran over to the graveyard and began walking through the tombstones as Mairead followed her. Alfie at her heels.

'I love reading gravestones,' Stella told her. 'I know it's a bit creepy, but I like to imagine the stories of all the people buried beneath them. It's nice to know how much they were loved.'

Mairead couldn't relate. She disliked graveyards and always felt as if someone was watching her when she went into one.

Particularly now, at twilight, with the rooks and crows screeching around them.

'Sometimes I go to Highgate Cemetery in London – did you know that Karl Marx is buried there?'

'Yes, of course. Come on,' Mairead said, feeling suddenly very anxious. 'Let's go.'

'Oh Mam, are you scared?' Stella teased gleefully.

'We need to be able to see to get back through the woods; I don't have a torch with me.'

'There's a full moon, and...' Stella paused. 'Mam, look at this!'

'What is it?' Mairead said. She was shivering, suddenly very cold. Something about this graveyard unnerved her.

'Mam! Come here!' Stella called her over.

Mairead huffed over to where Stella was standing looking at a small grey gravestone.

'Look!'

Mairead read the gravestone:

> Ellen Lavelle
> Beloved Daughter of Alec Lavelle
> Born 19 May 1908 ~ Died 25 August 1925
> *I have spread my dreams under your feet;*
> *Tread softly because you tread on my dreams.*

She recognised the quote. It was from a poem by W.B. Yeats, 'Aedh Wishes for the Cloths of Heaven'; Mairead had studied it at school and had always loved it. She shook her head sadly. So Ellen Lavelle was dead. She had been chasing a wild dream all this time. If only they had seen the graveyard the first time they'd visited Merview House, her mother would have found the closure she had so desperately wanted before she died.

'That can't be right,' said Stella. 'Look at the dates, Mam!'

Mairead read the inscription again: *Born 19 May 1908 ~ Died 25 August 1925*. It didn't make sense. According to this tombstone, Ellen Lavelle died at the age of seventeen. In Ireland. So who was the Ellen Lavelle that Mairead had been chasing across America for the past few weeks? Who was Ellie Lanois of Tofino in Canada? And who was the woman who had given birth to her mother in 1927 and abandoned her on the boat back to Ireland in 1933?

One thing was for certain: she wasn't Ellen Lavelle.

CHAPTER TWENTY-SIX

13 OCTOBER 1984

'Darling, you don't have to go on,' Jack said to her, as he handed her a tissue.

Ellen dabbed her eyes. Her cheeks were wet with tears.

'No, I need to tell you the whole story, Jack,' she said, taking another sip of her whisky. She felt it fortifying her. She was getting to the hardest part of the story, and she was terrified of her husband's reaction. But she couldn't pass through this life without telling the man she loved most in the world what had happened to her in Ireland. Why she had run away.

'OK, honey,' he said, pouring a little more whisky into her glass. 'I'm listening.'

MAY 1923

The Civil War had ended, and the anti-treaty republicans had lost. But the violence was far from over. People were bitter and hurt. Damage had been done between families that would take generations to heal; in some cases it would never be laid to rest. For months, Meg waited for her brother, Finnian, to return but he never did. After a while, she realised he was never coming back.

Meg continued to live with her aunt and uncle, who now had four children. She had to share a bed with the three eldest children, while new baby Siobhan slept with her parents. Uncle Michael worked as a labourer on local farms and his pay was meagre. There was never enough food to go around, and Aunt Norah was getting very thin. Meg didn't need to be told. She had just turned thirteen, and she needed to find work.

She shared her concerns with Ellen as they celebrated their birthdays among the bluebells. Ellen had brought the cats – Bluebell and Forget-me-not – in a basket, along with some bread and cheese she'd taken from the kitchen.

'But why don't you come and live with me!' Ellen exclaimed, putting down the maths primer she was helping Meg work through.

'I don't think your uncle Rafe would allow it,' Meg said, remembering the rift between her father and Rafe Lavelle.

'Mrs Murphy said she's looking for a new housemaid,' Ellen said. 'You could take the position. Uncle Rafe won't remember who you are! Just don't tell him your second name.'

Meg should have been grateful, but she couldn't help feeling a little aggrieved at the prospect of being Ellen's servant. She had always thought they were friends and equals.

Even so, she hugged Ellen and thanked her. It would help her aunt and uncle, who had been so good to take her in for all these years.

However, to Meg's surprise, her uncle Michael wasn't keen on the plan.

'Are you sure you want to go and live in Merview House with that bastard?' he said.

'Michael! Mind yourself!' Aunt Norah gave her husband a slap on the arm.

'It's an opportunity,' Meg told them. 'And I can bring you food from the kitchen.'

Aunt Norah was delighted at the thought of Meg employed and able to provide food for her hungry children. Having so many mouths to feed had left her exhausted.

'You're a great girl to sort yourself out,' she said, patting Meg on the back.

Working as a maid at Merview House wasn't easy. Although she was living in the same house as her best friend, Ellen, Meg saw less of her than before. There was no time for their nightly strolls in the woods, which meant Ellen could no longer pass on what she'd learned from her governess. Meg sorely missed her 'lessons'; she had loved learning.

And if Meg thought she had worked hard for her aunt, it was nothing compared to the amount of chores she had to do in her new position. She was up at five every morning cleaning out the grates and laying fires. Then it was time to help Mrs Murphy prepare breakfast, collecting the eggs from the hen house and learning how to cook them exactly the way Rafe Lavelle liked them. As soon as that was done she had to wash the dishes in the big sink, which she could only reach by standing on a stool; collect vegetables from the kitchen gardens, since the gardener's boy had run off to join the IRA; prepare the vegetables for dinner; lay the table and serve dinner, then wash the dishes again. And on top of that there was the polishing of silver, dusting of furniture, floor cleaning and bed making. Every night she fell into her own attic bed exhausted, only to be awoken a few hours later by the cockerel at the break of day.

Ellen was disappointed too. She had imagined wistful days with her best friend, Meg, sitting in her parlour, drinking tea and painting pictures of their future together in America. She wasn't sure if Meg was cross with her, because every time she saw her Meg was frowning and huffing. If Ellen tried to help her in her tasks, she was told not to get in her way, which hurt her feelings

and left her feeling lonelier than she had in the days before her
best friend came to live in the same house.

It was only very rarely, on nights when Uncle Rafe went out,
or was so drunk he'd fall asleep at the dinner table, that the two of
them could be together. On those occasions Ellen would go into
the living room and play modern music on the piano, hoping that
Meg would creep away from her chores and join her, singing
along as she played. Meg had the sweetest voice and sang all the
Irish ballads her father had taught her with tears shining in her
eyes.

MAY 1925

Two years had passed, with Ellen and Meg saving every penny
they could for the boat to America. Ellen was shocked by how
pitiful Meg's wages were. At this rate they were never going to get
away. In the end she took the bus to Dublin and sold some of her
mother's pearls and some china ornaments from the back parlour,
which was always shut off. No one ever went in there, so she was
confident Uncle Rafe wouldn't miss the items.

In June 1925, Ellen, almost an adult now, learned to drive in
her uncle's old Bentley. As soon as she got behind the wheel, she
loved it. When no one was watching, she'd take Meg for a spin
down the bumpy lane, showing her best friend how to manoeuvre
the vehicle. As they drove, the two girls would scream with excitement: 'Watch out, America! Here we come!'

It was on one of these days they decided to take the boat
leaving Galway harbour for New York and Boston on 25 August.
They didn't dare leave it any longer: Ellen's uncle had told her he
was going to send her to a finishing school in England.

'He might as well send me to prison,' she told Meg. 'He says I
need to have manners put on me. But it's not my fault all my
governesses know less than me!'

Meg smiled at her friend. She had seen her in action, mocking
one of her governesses because the woman didn't know the Vikings

had founded Dublin. The governess had handed in her notice the next day. At the last count, Ellen had seen off ten governesses.

'Uncle Rafe says there are no more governesses left in the west of Ireland!' Ellen exclaimed, turning off the car engine. 'So, I've bought my ticket for the boat.'

'You have?' Meg asked her in surprise.

'Yes! I drove to Galway and bought it as soon as Uncle Rafe announced my forthcoming internment. But I didn't have enough to buy a ticket for you as well, so I'll have to drive into Galway tomorrow and sell the carriage clock in my bedroom. With that and the money I got in Dublin back in May, we should have enough.'

'I feel like we're stealing from your uncle.'

'Not at all! My father is the eldest son, and this house is his. So if I was a man, I would inherit the house and all the stuff in it.'

Meg clutched her hands, her heart tight in her chest. Were they really going to go? She could hardly believe it.

'The boat leaves Galway harbour at six in the evening, so we'll have to set off in the morning. I can drive us there.'

'Won't your uncle miss the car?'

'He'll still be in his morning stupor. You know he doesn't get up until noon. I'll get Jimmy the stable boy to come with us, so he can drive it back.'

'Won't Jimmy get into trouble?' Meg ventured.

'Why? He can say I ordered him to do it. I'm seventeen now. My uncle can't control my life any more, Meg.'

Ellen leant forward and clasped Meg's hands.

'I am so excited, Meg,' she gushed. 'Our lives are about to begin.'

Meg tried to feel the same excitement, but she felt a nagging dread in her stomach. In her experience, things never went the way you hoped they would.

On the evening of 24 August, Ellen was lit up with excitement. Even her uncle Rafe noticed at dinner time.

'What's up with you?' he slurred, as he poured more claret into his glass.

'Nothing at all, Uncle,' Ellen said sweetly, winking at Meg as she leant over to serve the potatoes. 'I am looking forward to fine weather tomorrow.'

'Ah yes, we should go riding,' he said. It was something he often said when he was drunk, but he and his niece had never been out riding.

The girls had arranged to meet in Ellen's bedroom at first light. When Meg pushed the door open of Ellen's room, she was sitting on her bed, fully dressed, her green Louis Vuitton suitcase beside her.

'I couldn't sleep a wink,' she whispered.

'Nor could I,' Meg said.

The two girls did a little jig in Ellen's bedroom. At last, the day they had waited for so long had come.

'Have you written to your father?' Meg asked as they gathered their things together.

'No, but he'll be so pleased to see me!' Ellen declared.

'I thought he knew we were coming—'

'Stop worrying, Meg,' Ellen said. 'It will be totally grand.'

'Do you even know where he lives?'

'Of course I do! I have his address written on the back of my boat ticket. He lives in Chicago.'

Meg wasn't so sure Alec Lavelle would be happy to see them. It had been over six years since he had left Ireland and his promise to send for his daughter had gone unfulfilled. But whether Alec Lavelle welcomed them or not, Meg had nothing to lose. Ireland was filled with loss. Her mother, her father, and most likely Finnian too. She had no reason to stay here.

As they made their way across the landing, they heard someone banging on the door downstairs.

They crept to the top of the stairs and looked over the banisters. As they did so, the front door swung open. Meg let out a gasp. There in the big hall at Merview House was her brother, Finnian. Or was it him? He looked so different. It had been two years and yet the boy had turned into a man, his black hair unkempt, his face unshaven, and his eyes blazing. He was wearing tattered trousers and a big coat. In his hand was a revolver.

'Rafe Lavelle!' he was yelling. 'Come out, you bastard!'

'Oh no,' Ellen whispered.

As she spoke, Rafe Lavelle emerged from his library. He was still dressed – had probably never gone to bed. Meg could almost smell the whisky seeping through his pores. Yet he wasn't falling-over drunk. It was as if he'd drunk himself sober. Like Finnian, he was clutching a revolver.

'Who the hell are you?' he bellowed, clearly not recognising Finnian, just as he had never recognised Meg as the daughter of his childhood friend. The man he had betrayed.

'I'm Cillian O'Hanley's son and I've come to have my justice,' he told Rafe.

Finnian raised his gun, but Rafe held out his hand.

'Calm down, boy,' he said. 'You've got it all wrong. I never told them where Cillian was hiding out—'

'You're a liar,' Finnian said, his voice raw. The gun wavered in his hands.

'Stop, Finnian, don't do it! My uncle never let on about your father, I promise.' Ellen was tearing down the stairs, still holding on to her case. Meg followed close upon her heels.

Finnian glanced at Ellen and then at Meg.

'What are you doing—' he began, but before he could finish the sentence a shot rang out and he stumbled backwards, dropping his revolver on the hall floor. Blood was oozing from his shoulder.

'No!' Meg screamed, tearing towards her brother. Fury fuelled her small body as a red mist filled her head. She didn't hear Uncle Rafe telling Ellen, 'He's fine, I only injured the boy, he'll be grand.' All she felt was pure rage at the man who had betrayed her father. No one else had known the hiding place in the blowholes on St

Patrick's Head – it was there that Cillian and Rafe had hidden during the fight for independence, declaring themselves blood brothers. Rafe had broken their bond. He had betrayed his friend. He'd as good as shot her father himself. She hated him more than any living being. She hated him for hitting Ellen. She hated him for not knowing who she was. She hated him for his lack of remorse. Meg picked up Finnian's revolver and fired it wildly in the direction of Uncle Rafe. She missed. He laughed at her and then his voice turned cold as ice.

'For that I'll finish the little Fenian bastard off.'

'No, Uncle, no, it's Finnian,' Ellen cried out, pulling on her uncle's arm, but he slapped her away and took aim.

'No, Meg, don't – please, Uncle Rafe, don't,' Ellen screamed. But her friend's words washed over Meg. She fired again. So did Uncle Rafe.

Meg never knew whose bullet killed Ellen because she stepped between them, her arms spread wide like a bird. And then she fell, and lay still on the hall floor. Meg dropped her gun and ran over to Ellen. She was so shocked she didn't even scream. Her friend had a gaping wound in her chest, and there was blood seeping from her back.

'Ellen, no!' Meg gasped.

Another gunshot and Meg braced herself for the impact. But she felt nothing, and when she looked up, she saw Uncle Rafe toppling like a felled tree, a gunshot wound in the centre of his forehead. She twisted to look behind her. There was her brother, Finnian, holding the gun in one hand, his shoulder still pumping blood.

'He was going to kill you, Meg,' he said. He took a step closer. 'Is Ellen dead?'

'No, no, no,' Meg cried, rocking to and fro, cradling her friend in her arms.

Ellen's eyelids fluttered, and she could hear her gasps for breath, but she was so deathly pale, as if the life was ebbing from her with every second.

'Take the ticket,' Ellen whispered. 'The money. Both of you. Run.'

'No, I won't leave you,' Meg said fiercely.

'Now,' she whispered. 'The servants. Go. Drive.'

Ellen closed her eyes. 'Forget-me-not,' she whispered.

'Bluebell,' Meg whispered back, choking on the word. She felt Ellen, so light in her arms, and then heavy. She was gone.

'Come on!' Finnian was tugging on Meg's sleeve. 'She's right, we've got to go.'

Meg laid Ellen back down on the white marble floor. She was covered in blood, but she didn't care. She grabbed the suitcase and Ellen's purse, then followed Finnian outside. It was a glorious morning. The air was filled with birdsong, and the sky was a pale duck-egg blue as mist rose from the gardens.

She ran away from Merview House and never looked back, although the image of that morning would remain with her for the rest of her life. She could still feel the dew-laden grass under her feet, smell the wild scent of the rhododendron bushes and the trees as the August sun burned away the mist.

'This way,' she told Finnian, running towards the stable block and the garages.

'Where are you going?'

They had no chance on foot. She knew that much. She supposed her brother had never expected to walk away from the confrontation.

Meg slid open the garage door and took the keys of the Bentley from the hook on the wall.

'Get in,' she said, opening the door of the car and throwing Ellen's case in the back.

'You know how to drive?' Finnian asked incredulously.

'Ellen taught me,' she said in a hoarse voice. Dear sweet, lovely Ellen. Her one and only true friend who was lying dead on the floor of Merview House, all because of her. She had killed her. She suppressed a sob. Ellen had told them to run. She would do what Ellen had told her.

Finnian squeezed in beside her, wincing as his injured arm hit the side of the car.

Meg started up the engine, and it fired up first time. She looked at the pedals and tried to remember which one to press with her foot. Take the brake off – she remembered that. They stuttered forward, and she pressed harder. The car took off out of the garage and down the drive of Merview House.

Meg followed the road along the coast to Galway. The boat was due to depart in three hours. They'd get there just in time.

'I've a ticket for the boat to America,' she told her brother. 'I've enough money for you too.'

'We've got to get someone to fix up my arm,' he said.

'Is it still bleeding?'

'I've bound it with my shirtsleeve, but the bullet needs to come out.'

'We'll find a doctor in Galway.'

'No, Meg. It's too risky. I've got to go to people I know.'

'But Finnian, you'll be found and shot if you don't leave with me today.'

He reached out with his good hand and placed it on her knee.

'I can't go with you, Meg,' he said. 'Even if we find someone to fix my arm, I have to stay here.'

'No, Finnian, you'll die if you stay in Ireland.'

There was a long pause and Finnian sighed.

'I'll not leave my comrades,' he said. 'I'll not give up the fight for a republican Ireland.'

'Oh Finnian, why?' Meg sighed. 'Daddy's dead.'

'And that is why, Meg. I've got to stay for Daddy's sake; it's what he would have wanted.'

Meg was broken into pieces. She was losing everyone she had ever loved. On such a beautiful day. The sky flawless blue, and the green fields lush with long swaying grass as she drove by.

'You can drop me in the next village,' he said. 'I know someone there.'

'Are you sure?' she whispered.

'Yes, Meg.'

It was so early, there was still no one about, just a black cat wandering across the road. *Not for luck*, Meg thought desperately as she parked outside a stone cottage with a green door.

'I'll be seeing you, Meg,' he said.

She shook her head. 'I doubt it.'

'We will see each other again one day,' her brother said. 'I feel it.'

'Wait,' Meg said, opening Ellen's purse. She handed him the money Ellen had saved for her ticket. She didn't need it now; she had Ellen's own ticket.

'Don't you need it?'

'Take it – use it to help with the fight for a republican Ireland,' she said.

Her brother leant forward, took the money, and kissed her forehead.

'I am so sorry about Ellen,' he whispered.

'Stop,' Meg said, her eyes filling with tears again. 'Else I can't drive on.'

'Go, Meg, like she told you to. Go to America and be free of all this.'

Meg looked behind her as she drove off, the car bouncing along the bumpy village road. She saw Finnian standing at the roadside, clutching his injured arm and staring after her. He didn't move at all. Tall, thin and proud.

· · ·

She cried all the way to Galway. On the outskirts of the city, she pulled in by the River Corrib and washed the blood off her hands and face, then changed into one of Ellen's pretty dresses. She felt awful to be wearing her friend's clothes. She threw her own blood-soaked serge dress and bag of things into the river. Hopefully folk would think she'd drowned.

When she got to Galway harbour, she parked the car and left the key in it. There was no one left to drive it now anyway, she thought bitterly.

'Name?' the man asked her as she went to board the boat.

She nearly said Meg O'Hanley, but then she took another breath. Pulled Ellen's first-class ticket from her purse.

'Ellen Lavelle.'

The man trailed his finger down the passenger list.

'Here you are, Miss Ellen Lavelle. Are you travelling on your own?'

'Yes,' Meg said, clutching Ellen's purse with one hand and holding her case with the other. Any minute now he would see right through her. Call the guards on her. But instead he smiled and waved a hand for her to proceed to the waiting room, instructing her to take a seat there. When it was time to board, a steward would escort her to her cabin.

Meg sat down among the other travellers as her legs turned to jelly. A cabin of her own – first class! Ellen had planned for them to travel in style to America.

Ellen.

Meg closed her eyes, trying to erase the image of her beautiful friend lying in a pool of blood on the floor of Merview House. By now the guards would surely be hunting for her and Finnian. She said a little prayer for her brother, clutching at the cross around her neck.

She was rigid with tension, jumping at the sound of every new passenger entering the departures area. At last, they were invited to embark. She climbed up the gangway, her spine taut, her legs stiff. The steward showed her into her first-class cabin. The luxury was breathtaking: silver lamps on the table and nightstand, a bed twice the size of the one in her attic room at Merview House. A closet for her clothing, and her own private bathroom. In Ellen's dress she found herself moving differently and speaking in another voice: dropping an octave and adopting an English accent, the way her friend had done when imitating her many governesses.

After the steward left, she sat on the bed and opened Ellen's suitcase. She'd glimpsed the small jewellery case when she pulled out the dress, but she'd forgotten about it until now. She took it out and opened it. There on its bed of velvet was Ellen's mother's turquoise and diamond necklace. It glittered at her. She put it on, feeling like the imposter, the thief she was. She looked in the mirror and placed her hand on the necklace. It must be worth hundreds of pounds. It was then she remembered she had given all the money in Ellen's purse to Finnian. All she had was her ticket, Ellen's clothes, and the necklace. She fingered the jewels. Already it felt like hers, though the idea of someone like her ever owning such an item was beyond her dreams. Soon she would have to sell it to survive. Meg stared at herself and saw Ellen reflected back.

Find another way, her friend whispered to her. *It's my keep-sake. It's how to remember me. Always.*

CHAPTER TWENTY-SEVEN

15 NOVEMBER 1984

How quickly Mairead managed to dismantle her old life. She shed years of carefully constructed security within one week. She began with a telephone call to Niall in London. She had thought it would be awkward talking to him. Almost a year had passed since they had broken up and she had only spoken to him once in all that time.

'It's so good to hear from you,' Niall had said, sounding nervous on the phone.

'How are you?' she asked.

'I'm doing well,' Niall said. 'I've changed careers. Don't laugh, but I'm going to become a maths teacher.'

It was as if a piece of the puzzle about Niall had suddenly slotted into place.

'Oh Niall, I know you'll be a brilliant teacher,' she said with conviction.

'That means a lot to me,' he said, 'coming from you.'

'I mean it.'

'And how are you? I'm sorry about your mam. I would have come to the funeral but—'

'I know, I'm sorry I didn't let you. I was in a bit of mess and... well, I was still angry with you.'

'And you're not now?' Niall asked tentatively.

'No,' she said. 'In fact, I'm sorry.'

'What have you to be sorry for, Mairead?' Niall said, sounding surprised.

'Because I knew how unhappy you were for a long time, and I just put my head in the sand,' she said. 'I manipulated you to feel bad, so you'd stay.'

'That's a bit harsh on yourself, Mairead,' Niall said. 'I was very confused for a long time.'

She sighed. 'Well, at least we did a great job with Stella.'

Niall's voice warmed. 'She's great, isn't she. Lesley loves her—' He broke off. 'Sorry.'

'No, it's fine, I'm glad Stella gets on with Lesley. I'm happy you've found someone.'

'Oh Mairead, thank you.' Niall sounded like he was going to cry. Mairead hurriedly changed the subject.

'I'm ringing to let you know that, if you're OK with it, I want to sell the house.'

'Are you sure?' he said.

'It's only fair. We bought it together. You should have your half.' She paused. 'Besides, I want to move out.'

'I thought you loved that house,' Niall said.

Why did her husband and daughter think she loved this unremarkable estate house? Was that who she had been? Unremarkable and suburban?

'I'm moving out west,' she said. 'I'm moving into Mam's and I've given up my job. Don't laugh, but I've enrolled on an art course at Sligo College.'

'Mairead, that's amazing!' Niall enthused. 'I always loved your paintings.'

'When did you ever see me paint?'

'Don't you remember? After Stella was born, for about a year, you used to paint whenever she was sleeping. It was as if having a baby unleashed all this creativity inside of you.'

'Oh yes, I do remember.'

Mairead had a vague memory of a series of paintings of flowers. She had been given so many flowers when Stella was born, she had pressed some of the more splendid ones. Over the first months of Stella's life, whenever her baby girl took a nap, if she wasn't too exhausted herself, she'd paint one of the flowers. The painting gave her energy, made her feel even more connected to her baby.

'I wonder where those pictures are now,' she mused.

'You tried to throw them out, a few years later.' Niall paused. 'You were having a bad day.'

Mairead tried not to remember her bad days. She used to get so angry. Slam things around and shout at Niall. Now she realised she was just frightened to face the truth. They hadn't belonged together and she had felt trapped.

'But I kept them,' he said. 'Some of them are in the attic, and your mam took some.'

'My mam!' Mairead exclaimed in shock.

'Yes, she thought they were really good,' Niall said.

'Why didn't you ever tell me that—'

'Well, you thought you'd got rid of them. Sorry,' Niall said.

Mairead felt a wave of loss and longing sweep through her. She wanted so much to talk to her mother. Ask her why she had never told her she liked her paintings.

'She believed in you, always,' Niall said gently.

She found herself breaking down sobbing on the phone. It was so good to talk to Niall after all this time. He was, after all, her oldest friend.

'It's OK, Mairead, let it out,' he kept saying. 'I'm here for you.'

After they said their goodbyes, she ran herself a bath, filling it with bubbles like a child. She got into the hot soapy water and lay back, letting the warm water buoy her. She submerged herself for a few seconds before coming back up for air. Warm water streamed down her body and her eyes stung. Her mother was gone. Her grandmother – whoever she might be – was gone. She had to stop running away into the past. The present could be anything she wanted it to be. As for the future, she had to stop worrying.

The next day, Mairead went into St Bernard's to give in her notice. She was expecting to feel guilty as she walked down the familiar corridor to Sister Mary Stephen's office. But she didn't at all. There was a bit of nostalgia, but mostly she felt free. These girls, their grades and their futures were no longer her responsibility.

Sister Mary Stephen wasn't as surprised as Mairead thought she would be.

'I guessed something was up, Mairead,' she said coldly. 'Seeing as you've been away so long.'

'I'm sorry at the short notice, Sister,' Mairead said.

'Not at all,' the nun said to her. 'The substitute, Miss White, is grand.'

If she was trying to bother Mairead or make her jealous, it wasn't working.

'I wish you all the best for the future, Mairead,' she said curtly, although she didn't sound like she meant it.

'Thank you, Sister.'

Mairead wandered down to the staff room, half hoping she'd bump into Eoin. Was it coincidence or had she planned to give her notice on the day he usually came in to teach computers? But he was nowhere to be seen. When she peeked through the window in the door to the computer lab, she saw a different teacher. In the staff room she presented her old colleagues with a box of Black Magic chocolates. They told her that Eoin had given in his notice a few weeks ago.

'It wasn't worth his while coming down from Dublin for just the day,' said Diana, the physics teacher. 'His business is going really well, so it's not as if he needed to work here.'

. . .

Out in the car park, Mairead sat staring out the windscreen and trying to suppress her disappointment. But she just couldn't. She hadn't realised until this moment how much she'd been hoping to see Eoin again. She took out the letter he had sent her, which she'd put in her handbag, and read it again. He wanted to see her. He had written it down! What was she waiting for? She glanced at her watch. It was five o'clock already.

Follow your heart. It was as if she could hear her mam speaking to her. That had been her mother's mantra and she had always let it guide her. Even if it had upset her daughter. Her mam had never compromised her feelings for anyone else in her life.

She had no schedule to live by any more. No school assignments to mark, no time she needed to be up in the morning. She didn't want to live as chaotically as she had done in New York, but she wanted to keep a sense of flow in her life. She turned the ignition and set off in the direction of Dublin.

Two hours later, having got lost several times even after consulting her book of roadmaps, Mairead pulled in on a quiet residential street in Drumcondra. The streetlights were lit and an orange halo surrounded each one as she got out of her car and locked the door. Now she was here, she was beginning to feel nervous. She took a deep breath, listened to her intuition, and after a second strode up to the front door of the building. There was a row of doorbells outside. She found Flat 3. Rang the bell. She waited for what seemed like ages. Then a window opened above her, and there was Eoin, his dark curly hair longer than she remembered.

'Mairead!' he said, looking shocked. 'Is that you?'

'Hi,' she called up.

'Wait there, I'm coming down.'

A few minutes later, the door opened. She felt her throat go dry with nerves, and her heart was thumping in her chest. Despite all the drugs she'd done with Kyle, he had never made her feel like this. And neither had her husband of nineteen years.

'I got your letter,' she said to Eoin. He towered over her. She had forgotten how tall he was.

'Come in,' he said. 'It's freezing outside.'

He took her hands and led her into the house. She followed him up the staircase as he opened the door into a tiny flat.

'Sorry,' he said, looking embarrassed. 'It's a bit of a mess. I've not long moved in.'

There were boxes all over the place, and hardly any furniture. Just a few big floor cushions and a low coffee table.

'Do you want a tea or a coffee?' he said. 'Something to eat—'

'I came because I wanted to apologise for what I said to you,' she interrupted. 'It was narrow-minded, and I don't know why I was so... so...' She struggled to find the right word. '... so *stupid*.'

Eoin gave her a big smile, and she found herself smiling back with relief.

'Mairead, you're not stupid,' he said. 'You were upset about your mam, and I should have told you about Aileen. It's just I liked you so much and I didn't want to scare you off.'

He put his hands in his pockets and looked sheepish. 'But that backfired on me!'

'You liked me?' Mairead asked him, taking a step towards him.

'Yes. I mean, I still do.'

'You do?' she said, taking another step towards him.

'I think you're fucking gorgeous,' he declared, his cheeks turning scarlet.

'Well, that's good to hear,' she said, taking one final step so she was just a hair's breadth from him. 'Because I feel the same way about you.'

Eoin leant down and kissed her on the lips. It felt as if the kiss lasted forever, and yet was over in one second. He cupped her head in his hands, and she felt herself melting into his touch as he kissed her again. Mairead put her hands around his waist and he pulled her towards him.

'I've been in love with you for months,' he whispered over her head.

His words were like honey to her. Opening her up to desire in such a sweet, natural way. So far removed from the drug-fuelled lust with Kyle, or the sexless hugs with Niall. She kissed him again, with her eyes open, and as she looked over his shoulder, she saw it was snowing outside. Soft spinning feathers of ice fluttering past the window.

'I think I'd better stay the night,' she whispered. 'It's snowing.'

'Oh yes, too dangerous to drive,' Eoin said, kissing her again before taking her by the hand and leading her into the bedroom.

The next morning, as Mairead lay within the crook of Eoin's arm, the two of them looked out of his bedroom window at a completely white world. It rarely snowed in Ireland, and when it did, everything tended to grind to a halt. It looked so magical and pure. Mairead knew she would never forget this moment of utter peace.

'I might get snowed in with you for a few days,' she whispered.

'That's not going to be a problem with me!' Eoin said, kissing her again. She nestled into him.

'Tell me, what happened with your hunt for your grandmother,' Eoin asked her. 'Did you find her?'

Her mind flicked to Kyle Symes. She didn't want to tell Eoin about any of what she had done in New York. Although maybe one day she might. Instead, she told him about her search for Ellen Lavelle and how it had brought her to the graveyard of the big house only to discover she had died at the age of seventeen.

'So my grandmother wasn't Ellen Lavelle,' she said. 'I've no idea who she was!'

'That's crazy,' Eoin said.

'I've decided to let the whole thing go,' Mairead said. 'What's the point anyway? It's all ancient history.'

She said these words to Eoin, but it still needled her that she would never solve the mystery of her grandmother. Merview

House was not hers to fight for if Ellen Lavelle wasn't her grandmother. The letter from Alec Lavelle's estate had arrived with a
copy of the will as she'd requested, but she hadn't even bothered to
open it. She'd just flung it into her bag along with the rest of her
clobber.

'So what are you going to do now?' Eoin asked.

'Well,' she said, tracing his face with her finger, 'I am going to
start living, Eoin – like never before!'

CHAPTER TWENTY-EIGHT

Jack dropped his empty whisky glass on the rug. Ellen watched it roll over to knock against the coffee table leg. She couldn't look at his face, but she could hear the shock in his voice.

'I don't understand,' he said. 'How can Ellen be dead?' He paused. 'You're Ellie, you're Ellen.'

'I am now,' Ellen said. 'And I have been for many, many years. But my real name is Meg O'Hanley.'

Slowly she raised her head to look at her husband. He was staring at her, wide-eyed.

'So the story you just told me about Ellen and Meg – you're Meg, the younger one. The girl who became the maid in the big house...' He trailed off.

'Yes, I'm the girl who fired the gun and killed her best friend.'

'It was an accident.'

Ellen shook her head. 'I wanted to kill Rafe Lavelle. I was consumed with rage. I still remember how much I wanted to hurt him.'

'He had just shot your brother! You believed him responsible for the death of your father.'

Ellen gave a tiny smile.

'Are you actually defending me?' she asked Jack.

He looked pensive. 'I have seen some things during my time in the army I never believed possible. Extremes of humanity and inhumanity. No one can tell what they are capable of.'

'Oh Jack.' Her voice broke. 'I've been so frightened to tell you.'

Jack leant forward and took her hands in his. 'You didn't mean to kill your friend. You were only a child, Ellie. Just fifteen years old!'

Her heart ached with love for her husband. How could he be so understanding?

'But what happened next?' he asked her. 'Tell me everything.'

'OK,' she said, though she knew she would never reveal her secrets from Arizona. They would be buried with her. But Ireland was home. And she wanted to go back.

25 AUGUST 1925

As the RMS *Athena* departed from Galway harbour, Meg hid in her cabin. Every footfall outside her door made her freeze in terror until it passed on. It was only when she looked out her porthole and saw they were out at sea that she braved opening the door. The ship rolled gently, and it was the strangest feeling as she made her way down the narrow corridor and climbed the steps up to the deck.

Outside, the sun was beginning to sink in the sky, and the sea was washed with golden light. She gripped the rails and looked back at Ireland. A tiny bolt of green on the dark blue line of the horizon. Regret ripped through her. How could she have run away and left Ellen to bleed to death? But another voice, Ellen's, spoke to her inside her head.

You know I was gone, Meg. You had no choice but to run.

She was completely alone. The big adventure in America now seemed daunting to Meg. She had no one to go to. She couldn't even consider turning up at Ellen's father's house in Chicago. Alec

Lavelle would hear of the tragic loss of his daughter and send her right back to face the authorities.

Meg gripped on to the rail and looked down at the churning water. Tears rained down her face and dripped off her chin. She hunted for a handkerchief, but there were none in the pockets of Ellen's summer coat. The sea beckoned to her with its deep hypnotic blue. Wouldn't it be easier to climb over the rails and jump into the water? She couldn't survive in America on her own.

'Can I be of any assistance, miss?'

She hadn't been aware that anyone else was on this deck. But now there was a figure at her side. She turned to look up at a tall man with thick brown hair and a big moustache. He was holding the white square of a linen handkerchief.

'It's clean,' he said, offering it to her.

Meg was red with mortification. She had never been talked to with such consideration by a man such as this. A gentleman. Sometimes Rafe Lavelle had had male friends visit for hunting and drunken dinners afterwards. She tried to avoid them as much as possible because if their eyes lit on her they were likely to bother her with pinches and leering comments. But this man was looking at her with respect as if she were a lady.

'Thank you,' she mumbled, aware of her rough hands from all the housework she'd done over the years as she wiped her eyes and cheeks. She offered the handkerchief back, and he waved his hand.

'Keep it, please.'

She looked at the square of pure white linen and read the initials G.R. embroidered on it.

'Giles Rose, at your service,' he said, tipping his hat at her.

Meg was possessed by the desire to laugh out loud. A part of her was tempted to tell him, in her strongest Irish brogue, that her name was Meg O'Hanley from the back of beyond, but she stopped herself. She knew what she had to do. Become Ellen.

'Miss Ellen Lavelle,' she said, her cheeks blushing with the lie.

'It's an absolute pleasure to meet you,' he said. He paused, and she wasn't sure what she should say in response. She wished he'd leave her alone.

'Are you sad to be leaving Ireland?' he asked her.

She nodded. 'Those I love, more than Ireland.'

'Ah yes,' he said. 'I shall miss my family too. But Miss Lavelle, the future awaits us in America. We are fortunate to have this opportunity.'

He was right, of course. How lucky was she to have this chance to start anew. But all she wanted was to run home and hide in the bogs. She was terrified of the future.

'Are you travelling alone, Miss Lavelle?' he asked her.

'Yes, I am,' she said.

'I am too,' he said. 'It's very courageous of you.'

'I've dreamed of going to America for years,' she said in a small voice. But had she? This had been Ellen's dream and she had just gone along with it because she wanted to be with Ellen.

'Me too,' Giles enthused. 'I'm an architect. So, you can imagine my excitement when I got a position at an architecture firm building skyscrapers in New York.'

She looked up at Giles Rose. He was older than her. Possibly even the same age that her father would have been, although his eyes were bright and youthful. She had seen some pictures of New York in the magazines Ellen had shown her. The tall needle-like buildings. The size of the city. She couldn't believe that in a few days she would be walking among them.

'May I invite you for a stroll around the deck, Miss Lavelle? You might like to take my arm if the ship begins to roll.'

Meg hooked her arm through Giles's as he guided her around the deck. His presence already made her feel safer.

'Did you know they have a fabulous orchestra which plays while we dine?' he asked.

She shook her head. Afraid to tell Giles she had never in her entire life even seen an orchestra.

'I hope you don't think it presumptuous, but would you like to dine with me this evening?'

Meg said yes because she didn't know how to say no.

Later she dressed for dinner in one of Ellen's silk gowns. It was too big for her. Ellen had been broader and taller than Meg. But the style was loose and the fabric was so exquisite Meg felt she got away with it. She looked at the turquoise necklace. Stared at it for a long time. Then she took it out of the case and put it on. It made her feel different. As she looked in the little cabin mirror, the necklace gleamed at her. It was like her protective shield. When she wore it this evening, she would become Ellen. She would draw on all those lessons Ellen had taught her in the woods back home and become an educated young lady of class. She would let Meg go as if she really had jumped overboard and was now all the way back across the sea in Ireland.

Giles Rose spent every minute he could with Ellen on the four-day journey to New York. Every morning after breakfast he insisted that they took a stroll either on the lower sheltered promenade deck if it was chilly, or on the upper decks if it was fine. He was a great believer in fresh air and keeping busy. Ellen was never sure whether this was always his way or whether he detected her low mood. Every meal they ate together, and over the course of the journey, she learned he was a widower. His wife had died during the Spanish Flu epidemic in Dublin in 1918. They had had no children. Ellen didn't ask him his position on the War of Independence. She didn't want to know any more about politics and allegiances because it had destroyed so much in Ireland. It was evident that Giles had no interest in politics, and this pleased her. He was from a wealthy family in Blackrock, County Dublin, and owned a big house by the sea with a conservatory. Leaving his ageing parents behind, he was off to America to seek his fortune as an architect.

'This is the forefront of innovation,' he said. 'I got bored designing the same kind of buildings in Dublin. I wanted to be challenged.'

Ellen admired Giles for his passion. Unlike her father and brother's passion, which ripped apart people and sought to destroy, Giles wanted to build things. Create a way forward. *But only because he has the privilege to do so*, another voice at the back of her mind needled her.

After luncheon, Giles invited her to join in some of the games provided for the entertainment of passengers. On the deck they would play quoits, throwing hoops over sticks, and shuffleboard, pushing discs with a cue. Her favourite game was bull board. Giles was very impressed with her ability to throw the small pieces of lead and have them land on the numbered squares. She never landed on one of the squares painted with bull heads. When she focused on throwing the lead, it reminded her of skimming stones with her best friend on the lake back at Merview House. It helped her remember happy times, not the dark moments of her departure.

After tea, often taken on deck, drunk from fine china cups and with little triangles of cucumber sandwiches – which she used to make for the Lavelles but had never been allowed to eat – Ellen retired to her cabin to read. It felt incredibly indulgent to lie on her bed and read books. Giles had recommended Charles Dickens from the ship's library. For the first time she experienced how it might have been to live the life of her friend. Her belly full, all the time in the world to brush her hair, read books, and make herself look pretty.

Each night she took care getting ready for dinner. Worried she might give herself away, she studied pictures in *The Lady* magazine, which she had obtained from the ship's steward. She had often helped her best friend with her hair, so by the second night she had mastered the art of pinning her own hair into an elegant coif. With her needle and thread, she was able to take up the hems of the dresses. They were still too big, but at least they didn't drag on the floor.

She could barely eat dinner because she was so bewitched by the music the orchestra played and still full from tea in any case. Afterwards, Giles retired to the gentlemen's lounge to smoke a cigar and play cards, while she joined some of the other ladies and played dominos. She listened attentively to how they spoke and the things of which they spoke, and did her best to emulate them. Who would have known she was such a good actress?

On the fourth day, there was great excitement as land was sighted. America. She had made it to the other side of the sea, and she could never go back.

Giles stood by her side and took her hand in his. It was the first time he had touched her so intimately. It felt very comforting to feel his big hand wrapped around hers.

'Dearest Ellen, I know we've only known each other a few days,' he said, 'but I am quite certain of my feelings.'

She turned to look at him. He looked down at her, his eyes brimming with devotion, and she felt humbled by it. No man had looked at her that way in her entire life.

'Would you do me the honour of being my wife?'

She gawped at him, open-mouthed. This talented, wealthy and respected gentleman wanted her to be his wife!

'Please, my dear, do give me an answer,' he said, frowning and looking a little worried.

'Oh,' she gasped. 'It's just I am so overwhelmed, but yes, yes, yes!'

She hadn't even thought about it. Giles had shown her such kindness and attention. What would she have done without him? Of course she should agree to be his wife. She was so lucky to be saved by this man! What would her fate have been if she had not met him?

Giles beamed at her, and took her in his arms, kissing her on the lips. She felt the whiskers of his moustache tickling her skin, and the softness of his lips on hers. He tasted of tobacco smoke.

She had to stand on her tippy toes to reach him, but he lifted her up, so her feet left the ground and she started to laugh. She had never thought she could laugh again. But here she was; less than a week had passed since she had left behind tragedy, and she was laughing. This was when she knew there was something bad in her. This little seed of evil which had killed her mother in childbirth. Which had made her steal her friend's life. She pushed the dark thought out of her head as she kissed Giles more deeply. Her best friend would have wanted this for her.

The day after they arrived in New York, Giles bought Ellen a diamond ring at a big jewellery store called Tiffany and Co. He had taken rooms at the Plaza Hotel with views of Central Park on one side and on the other of all the new skyscrapers slowly being stacked higher and higher by men on scaffolds. If she wasn't gazing at her diamond ring in astonishment, Ellen would watch the men working on the skyscrapers in awe as they swung from the scaffolds like lithe monkeys. The ease with their bodies, their youth and lack of fear reminded her of Finnian. If he had come with her, he could have got a job building a skyscraper. The thought brought a tear to her eye, and she chastised herself.

You're not Meg any more, she whispered to herself. *You're Ellen.*

They were married within a month of arriving in New York and she walked out of St Patrick's Cathedral Mrs Ellen Rose. Giles had rented a huge apartment on Park Avenue in the Upper East Side. He was so busy with his work he had employed a housekeeper and maid to assist Ellen in furnishing the apartment. What fun she had choosing the most modern furniture. There was so much space! Her aunt and uncle's whole cottage would have fit into the lounge with its breathtaking views of Central Park.

Every morning when she awoke with a heavy heart, and tears

drying on her cheeks from the memory of her dear lost friend, Ellen forced herself to paint a smile on her face. She had to make the most of all this good fortune, otherwise everything, all the pain and suffering, would have been in vain. But it was hard. There were times she was lonely when Giles was gone for hours. She would drink a glass of claret on her own, then another, looking out at the heave and hum of this growing city beneath her and feeling apart from it all.

About a year after they had settled in New York, as Ellen drank her claret one evening and waited for Giles to come home, she experienced a sudden wave of nausea. She raced to the bathroom to vomit the wine and her luncheon. She felt ghastly. Sitting back on her heels, she counted the weeks since she had last bled. She gave a little gasp of surprise. Placed her hands on her belly. She was pregnant! She should have been frightened, but she wasn't. She was small and so young. Only sixteen – although Giles thought she was eighteen. How could she carry a baby? But hope washed over her, and she couldn't stop the feeling of euphoria. She was going to have a baby. She would love her child with all her heart, and she would never feel lonely again. If the baby was a boy, she would name him Cillian after her father (although Giles might have an opinion on it, she knew how to persuade him). But her baby was a girl, and she called her Brigid, after the patron saint of Ireland.

13 OCTOBER 1984

The bulb went in the lamp and the room fell into sudden darkness. *Brigid.* Ellen said her name again in her head, as Jack got up and fumbled around for a torch in the drawer of the sideboard. As he switched it on, the beam of light hit her face. She blinked.

'Sorry,' he said, his voice hoarse. 'I'll go get a bulb.' He found his way to the light switch and turned it on and the room was blasted with light. She felt exposed. The soft ambient cocoon of her storytelling shattered.

'Turn it off, please, Jack,' she said. 'Just get the bulb or light a candle.'

She felt Jack looking at her. His silence was loaded. 'OK,' he said, flicking it off and leaving the room to find a bulb. She sat in the darkness.

'Brigid,' she whispered.

For years she had tried to stop herself from thinking of her daughter. She had had four big healthy boys and they had taken up all her time and energy for decades. But at the back of her heart, always there was Brigid. Her baby girl. So small and delicate when she was born. With a curl of dark hair upon her forehead, and those Irish green eyes. When Brigid had been born, Giles had cried. Poor Giles. She had been wicked to deceive him, but she had been a girl herself. Half his age. When she thought about it, if one of her sons had married a teenage girl, she would have been disgusted with him. Maybe Giles Rose wasn't such a victim after all.

But Brigid... She laid her hands on her lap, palms up, and imagined she could feel her baby girl's weight upon them again. Hear her newborn mewling cry. The smell of her as she suckled at her breast. Her heart was opening out into a chasm. Where was Brigid now? A pain struck her suddenly, so fierce in her heart she thought at first she was having a heart attack. She gasped, slowed down her breathing, took another breath. She realised that from the moment Brigid was born she had felt a thread between her and her daughter, but now it wasn't there any more. Panic fluttered inside her. What had she been waiting for all these years? Why had she never gone to look for Brigid?

The lamp came back on, and Jack had also lit a candle.

She raised her eyes to him, and he was very still in his seat.

'Ellie, is it true?' he whispered. 'Are you married to someone else? Do you have a daughter?'

'Yes, Jack.'

She could see now this revelation was far worse than her story of murder. He was able to understand how a desperate girl might run away from an accidental killing, even take on her friend's identity and never tell him. But not that she had been married before, and had a child.

Jack continued to look at her. His face stern. She squirmed under his scrutiny.

'Giles could be dead,' she said. 'I mean, if he's still alive he would be over ninety years old.'

There was a pause.

'That's not the point,' Jack said. 'You never told me.'

'I'm sorry,' she said in a small voice.

'Where's your daughter?' he asked her. 'What happened to Brigid?'

It hurt to hear Jack say her daughter's name. Out in the open. Brigid was real. In her head, she was still a little girl in her arms, pointing at the stars. But Brigid would be in her late fifties now. She would have her own family. She would possess her own story, beginning with the abandonment of her mother. Thinking this hurt.

'She's in Ireland, I believe,' Ellen told Jack in a shaky voice. 'Giles took her back to Ireland when she was six. I couldn't go with them.'

'Because of what had happened?' Jack asked her.

'Yes, Giles thought I was Ellen Lavelle. I couldn't risk being discovered. I was wanted for murder, Jack—'

'But why didn't you keep Brigid with you—'

'I had no money, no power, Jack! I was young. Scared. I nearly went with them, but then at the last minute I panicked.' She gave a low sob. 'I ran away.' She put her hands over her eyes as tears leaked through her fingers. 'I abandoned Brigid.'

Jack watched her in silence. He didn't move to comfort her. She could feel his deep shock. This was not the woman he had thought he had married. She could see he was struggling to come to terms with the fact she had deserted her own child.

'So much time has passed,' he said. 'Why did you never tell me before? I'm sure the statute of limitations would apply, so you wouldn't have to worry about a murder charge. It's been over half a century, Ellie.'

'I don't know,' she wept. 'I thought it was better just to leave it be.'

'Oh Ellie,' Jack said, getting up from his seat and sitting next to her. She lowered her wet hands and looked at him.

'I've never forgiven myself,' she whispered.

'Then it's time you did, my love,' he said at last.

Relief swept through her. She had been so frightened he would hate her for her lies.

'I think we need to go to Ireland.'

'What!' She looked at him, wide-eyed.

'Yes, I'm taking you back home.'

'My home is here.'

'That may be, Ellie – or should I call you Meg now?' He gave her a gentle smile. As always, he had the ability to lift her out of her darkness. 'But we need to go to Ireland. I want to see where you grew up. I want to know all about you.'

She stared into his earnest face. She knew the questions would come eventually. Where had she gone after she abandoned her baby? And she would tell him some of it. But not the whole tale. He must never know how deep into darkness she had let herself fall when she lived in Arizona. Under the roof of a man of God, she had murdered two bad men. And still, she had no remorse.

'Let's go to Ireland and find Brigid.'

'I'm not sure if I can go back,' she said, her eyes still swimming with tears. Brigid echoed inside her in the same way as the name Ellen. Such distance between them. It felt like forever.

'We can start with a tour of Europe, ease into it,' he said. 'You've always wanted to go to Rome, remember? I can show you some of the places I remember from the war.'

He had never suggested they go back to revisit the places he'd been during the war, and Ellen knew how huge this was for him.

'OK,' she said. 'Let's do it.'

'Tell me the rest of the story,' Jack said, putting his arms around her. She rested her head on his shoulder and closed her eyes. She was a young mother again in New York in 1927 and it was wonderful!

CHAPTER TWENTY-NINE

1927

After what she had left behind in Ireland, one would think it impossible for Ellen ever to be happy, but those first years in New York had times of intense joy. Though she wasn't in love with him, Giles was a kind husband. A man who provided for his family, working hard to establish himself in New York as an architect, and attentive to the well-being of his wife and child. But it was being a mother that changed her world and filled the yawning void left by the loss of her best friend. Brigid was a balm to the deep guilt she felt. If she could be a good mother, might God forgive her for what she'd done? It had been a mistake, but murder was murder, was it not? Worse still, she'd assumed the identity of her dead friend.

She remembered her wardrobe as Ellen Rose in those early years in New York. Giles loved her to dress in shades of blue. Said it looked well with her red hair and pale skin. She had a French seamstress who made dresses in the Parisian style, while her maid was skilled in the latest hair styles. They were quite a picture, Ellen and baby Brigid, as she paraded through Central Park with her new perambulator. Even if she always had one eye over her shoulder for a Lavelle relative hell-bent on revenge.

Giles had hired a nurse. She had hated to leave Brigid with her, but it was her duty as his wife to accompany him to all the city engagements he had to attend as part of his tenure.

Every time he'd ask her, 'Why don't you wear your mother's turquoise necklace? It complements your eyes and your blue silks.' She refused. Pretended it reminded her of her mother too much, which was a lie. She had always been a motherless girl. It was her friend she was thinking of when she picked up the necklace. She had worn it on the boat as a talisman, but now it became a weight around her neck. The guilt gouged away at her heart, along with fear that the truth would follow her to New York.

Ellen remembered glorious fall mornings as a young mother. Sunlight dappling the windowpanes, the trees laden with golden leaves as she nursed Brigid in the big bed, four feather pillows propping her up, her head sore from a night of dinners and clandestine drinking while being waited on hand and foot. She had become a lady! Sometimes she laughed out loud at the notion of it. Brigid would look up at her with her penetrating baby stare.

No one would believe it! How things have turned out, she would whisper to her babe, tickling her tummy until she giggled in response. In these moments, she reasoned she'd had to act as she did else Brigid would never have existed.

But no matter how much she tried to hold on to fleeting moments of bliss in her life as a new mother, they were edged in shadow. How Ellen loathed the formal events with Giles in New York. What if they came across someone who knew the real Ellen Lavelle? What if Ellen's father Alec turned up from Chicago, having heard his daughter was in New York? Her past would be exposed, and she would be carted off. Returned to Ireland a criminal. This privileged existence and her baby would be taken from her in one fell swoop. Her life would be over!

Ellen lived in fear of revealing her origins every time they went out to dine. Stuck between two high society men, she'd be terrified to eat a morsel in case she picked up the fork or spoon the wrong way. Instead, she would drink, careful to watch how the other ladies held their champagne coupes. She'd drowned her fears in intoxicating bubbles. After a few glasses, she would be seized with the urge to go out into the city and dance at one of the speakeasy jazz clubs. Often Giles had to chaperone her home before she made a spectacle of herself in front of his peers.

'You're behaving very badly, Ellen,' he would hiss angrily. 'You're letting me down.'

How she wanted to scream at him: *My name is Meg, not Ellen.* But instead, she would laugh at him, call him vain and shallow, tell him he had no idea what it was like for real men who had beliefs they would die for! She would laugh hysterically until he slapped her silent and she flopped on the floor of their bedroom.

Afterwards, Giles would be all contrition, rocking Ellen by the dying fire in their bedroom. It was in these moments, when he tucked the hair behind her ears and told her he was sorry, that she'd be tempted to spit out the truth. But no matter how drunk she was, she never did. Instead, she placated him. Told him she was out of control and deserved it.

'I shouldn't have married you,' he said. 'You're too young for me.'

'No, Giles,' she reassured him, stroking his face. 'I've never been happier.'

As he made love to her, she would close her eyes and pray for another baby. One more innocent who would love her just like Brigid.

This was the house of cards Ellen had built in New York in 1927. It was only a matter of time before it would fall apart, and her past would chase her across the whole of America from east to west. Until she found herself in a small town on an island on the edge of Western Canada. Here she would come home at last, the furthest away from Ireland she had ever been. But her trail had been bloody and desperate. The girl she had once been, the girl across the sea, Meg, was silenced forever. She became Ellen, and El, and then Ellie. She forgot altogether who she really was.

CHAPTER THIRTY

Mairead and Eoin dragged the Christmas tree down the hall of her mother's house, spraying the floor with pine needles while Alfie barked excitedly at the commotion.

'I think it might be a little too big,' she said to Eoin through the spiky branches.

'Not at all,' Eoin said with confidence. He kicked open the living room door and they brought it in on its side. As they levered it upright, its top touched the ceiling.

'There, it's perfect,' he said, putting his arm around her waist.

'But what about the angel that goes on the top!' she protested. 'There's no room for it.'

'Good point,' he said. 'We'll have to chop a little off the top.'

'I told you it was too big.' She was laughing at him.

'I know, I know,' he said, grinning, 'but it's going to look great once we're done with all the decorations.'

It was the first Christmas Mairead had looked forward to since Stella was little. She should have been dreading it because her mam would be missing. But somehow, being in her house, making it her and Eoin's home now, she felt close to her mam. Stella was coming over from London, and Mairead had made the brave decision to invite Niall and Lesley. They would all be together on Christmas Day.

In previous years, Mairead had always gone into a frenzy of pre-Christmas baking, but this year she and Eoin were keeping things simple. Stella had got them all to agree to a vegan Christmas on condition she would cook the nut roast. She had already appointed Lesley as her assistant. All Mairead and Eoin had to do was supply the wine.

They had nearly finished decorating the tree when the doorbell rang. Alfie began barking as he ran to the door.

'It must be the postman with another package,' Mairead said, dropping some tinsel onto Eoin's hair.

But it wasn't the postman. She opened the door to an elderly couple. They were bundled up in big down jackets and looked very cold.

'Hello, can I help you?' she asked. The woman was staring at her intently, but it was the old man who spoke first.

'Ellie, she's you,' he said in a Canadian accent, gazing wide-eyed at Mairead. 'She looks just like you when we met.'

Mairead's heart skipped a beat.

She saw now that there was something familiar about the woman, who was still gawping at Mairead, unable to speak. Again it was the man who spoke:

'My name is Jack Lanois and this is my wife, Ellie. Well, her real name is Meg O'Hanley, but she used the name Ellen Lavelle too...' He trailed off, clearly not knowing what to say next.

'Are you Brigid's girl?' whispered the woman, her eyes glistening with tears.

'Yes,' Mairead said, comprehension dawning on her. 'I'm Mairead.' She paused. Her throat suddenly dry. So, it had been true. This was the couple from Tofino on Vancouver Island whom she had missed meeting in October. 'And are you... my grandmother?'

The woman nodded. She was shaking uncontrollably.

'Please, come in, you look frozen.'

She took their coats. As Ellie handed her coat to her, she saw a glint of silver on her neck. She was wearing a V-neck sweater in pale blue, and there upon her chest was a copy of her mother's silver and turquoise necklace. There were no diamonds, but the design was the same. It was all the confirmation Mairead needed.

'How did you find me?' Mairead asked.

'We telephoned the agency selling Merview House and asked if anyone had been looking for Ellen Lavelle,' Jack Lanois told her.

'My mother left this address with the estate agent,' Mairead said, remembering their visit in the summer.

'Yes, he gave it to us,' Jack confirmed.

She led them down the hall into the living room, Alfie trotting behind them. Eoin had just turned on the fairy lights and the tree was sparkling. He'd also thrown more peat on the fire, and it was crackling away. The room was filled with festive cheer, cosy and inviting.

'Your house sure is nice,' said Jack, looking very awkward as he stamped his cold feet.

'This is Eoin, my boyfriend,' Mairead said, as Eoin looked at her questioningly. 'This is Jack and Ellie Lanois. Please do take a seat.'

They both perched on the couch.

She licked her lips. 'Your necklace,' she asked Ellie. 'Where did you get it from?'

Ellie looked into her eyes. It was shocking to realise they were the same as hers. Dark navy blue like the sea on a stormy day.

'I made it,' she said.

Her husband turned to Ellie in astonishment. 'I never knew you made it, honey,' he said.

'Yes, I did many years ago. An old friend taught me how to silversmith when I was in Arizona.'

'Was that Father Joseph, you told me about?'

'Yes,' Ellie told her husband. 'I made the necklace so that if I ever found Brigid she'd know I was her mother.'

Eoin was looking at the old couple with a confused expression.

'Ellie is my grandmother, Eoin,' Mairead explained.

Eoin couldn't contain his excitement.

'Oh my God, Mairead has been looking for you,' he said. 'So, you're the mysterious Ellen Lavelle!'

'Well, that's the thing.' Jack spoke up. 'She's not really Ellen Lavelle,' he said. 'It's a long story, but there's a very good reason why she pretended to be Ellen, why she ran away—'

'And abandoned my mother as a little girl?' Mairead interrupted.

She couldn't help herself. She felt angry on behalf of her mother. But also for herself. The memory of being abandoned by the woman sitting before her now was the reason her mother had never let herself get close to her own daughter. The real sea Ellie had put between herself and her daughter Brigid had turned into a vast sea of emotional distance between Mairead and her mother. They had only crossed it right at the end of her mother's life and it had been too late.

'Where is Brigid?' Ellie asked her.

'We've come a long way,' Jack told them. 'She wants to explain. Make amends.'

'Where is she?' Ellie asked again, her tone a little panicked.

Eoin and Mairead looked at each other.

Eoin put his hand on her back, and only then did she realise she was shaking.

'I'm sorry,' she whispered, looking into Ellie's frightened face. 'My mother passed away in August.'

'Oh no, no,' Ellie wailed, burying her face in her hands, and then turning to her husband.

He took her in his arms as she wept big, racking sobs. They

were strangers to her and yet Mairead felt overcome with sorrow and guilt for having been angry with her. There was no doubt that the woman's anguish was genuine. Still shaking, her teeth chattering with shock, she felt Eoin put his arm around her and looked up at him, tears pricking her eyes.

'I've lost her again,' Ellie sobbed. 'Oh Jack, my heart. I can't bear it.'

'No, no, you haven't lost her,' Mairead said, pushing back her own tears and steadying her voice. 'She's here all around us, see. This was my mother's house and she loved it.'

'She's right, Ellie,' Jack said gently.

'I can show you everything,' Mairead offered. 'I've boxes of photographs. And look—' She took down one of the framed photographs on the mantlepiece and showed it to them.

'This is my mam, with my daughter Stella when she was six,' she said. 'You've a great-granddaughter too.'

Ellie stopped weeping and took the photograph in her hands. She stared down at her daughter.

'She's beautiful,' she whispered.

'Yes, she was. And she was very talented. She made jewellery, like you. She won awards. Became famous in Ireland.'

Ellie's face brightened a little. 'She was happy? Had a good marriage.'

'Yes,' Mairead said. 'My father adored her. He passed away seven years ago.'

'She was a good mother?'

'Yes,' Mairead lied. 'My mother was very loving. I've a brother too: Darragh. He was very close to Mam.'

Ellie looked relieved. She visibly sagged in her seat.

'Let me get you a cup of tea, or something stronger,' Eoin offered. 'Whisky? You've both had a big shock.'

'Thank you, young man,' Jack said. 'Whisky would be great.'

. . .

While Eoin served their guests whisky, Mairead went and got boxes of photograph albums, catalogues from her mother's exhibitions, and of course the original necklace.

When she saw the necklace, Ellie gave a wry smile.

'I stole that necklace,' she said, and Mairead saw a little spark of mischief that reminded her of the gleam that used to come into her mam's eyes.

'I think it was the reason why my mam got into making jewellery. I think she made so many beautiful things because it was the only way she could connect with you.'

'Oh,' Ellie said, looking emotional again.

It was huge, this task of showing her mother's life to Ellie and Jack. Soon they were all getting very tired. After an hour or so, Jack got up and said they should leave. They were staying in a B&B in the village. But would it be possible for them to visit again and look at more photographs?

'Do you have any Christmas plans?' Mairead asked as she handed them their coats.

'No,' Jack said. 'We thought we'd be home by now. But it took us a lot of hunting to find out where your mother lived. So I guess we'll be spending Christmas in Ireland.'

'Join us. Then you can meet my daughter, and my family,' she said. 'I know Stella would love to meet you.'

'You can tell us your story,' Eoin added.

'It's quite some tale,' said Jack.

Mairead liked him a lot. She hoped she would be with someone like Jack when she was Ellie's age. Maybe it would be Eoin, even. They watched from the doorstep as the elderly couple drove off.

'Well, that was quite extraordinary,' Eoin said as he closed the front door.

'I can't quite believe it,' Mairead said.

'How does it feel?' he asked, pulling her towards him. She breathed in his scent and longing curled through her body.

'It makes me feel whole,' she said. 'As if a tiny part of me was always missing and now it's complete.'

'Four generations of women. Ellie, your mother, you and Stella. Your stories waning and waxing, interweaving throughout time,' Eoin said to her.

'Like the tides,' Mairead added. 'Like the sea. Like a mother's love.'

Eoin brought her hands to his lips and kissed them. *Always there.*

Mairead felt her mother at her shoulder. The surge of love all around her.

She came back for you, Mam, she whispered inside her head. *Your mammy came back.*

CHAPTER THIRTY-ONE

30 DECEMBER 1984

Meg had the dream again. She was running through New York City, the wind buffeting her as she held on to her cloche hat with one hand and the green Louis Vuitton suitcase with the other. She ran through the shadows of the skyscrapers as they rose above her in the pre-dawn light and it felt as if she were running through the trees back home.

'Mammy,' she heard Brigid calling to her.

'I'm coming,' she called back.

At last, she was at the harbour, and there was the boat. Relief washed over her. They hadn't departed yet. She ran up the gangway just before it was removed, hurried across the deck. The sun was rising in the east. Flooding the boat with glorious light. She clambered down the steps to the lower decks and all the way to their cabin. There was Brigid waiting for her in her rosebud nightie. Clutching Annie, her doll.

'Mammy,' she hiccupped, her face wet with tears.

'I'm here now, darling,' she said, dropping her case and folding her child into her arms.

'Don't leave me, Mammy,' Brigid whispered.

'Never,' Meg said.

She woke up. It had been a dream. It wasn't real. Meg sank into her grief. Regret and despair dragging her down. She had left Brigid, and now her little girl was gone forever.

She felt Jack stirring in the bed beside her. It was still dark, and she didn't want to disturb him. She slipped out from under the covers and wrapped her cardigan around her. The room was freezing. She hunted for her thick woollen socks in her suitcase and pulled them on. She sat in the chair by the window and tweaked back the curtains a little. The moon was at its first quarter. She could see the shadow of its whole orb behind the illuminated half. Their view from the window in the B&B was of the sea. It was calm tonight. A pathway of silver upon its still surface. They had been back in Ireland nearly two weeks and already she felt different. She had become Meg again.

Jack had noticed immediately how her voice had changed. As soon as she started speaking to her countrymen and women, the west coast lilt returned and her longing for home intensified. Her hair softened from the damp air into springy curls. She'd felt this island in every cell of her body each time they stopped the rental car to take a walk in nature. It wasn't that she didn't love Tofino – the wide skies, vast ocean, and her big beautiful blue whales – but the west of Ireland was a landscape etched upon her soul. The fields framed by crumbling drystone walls slipping all the way down to the turquoise sea. The drumlins, hillocks and ancient stones appearing out of nowhere. They drove the twists and turns of the narrow roads, through bogs wild as moonscape, and past the dark tight woods. Everything packed much closer together than in Canada. As if the Irish landscape possessed more secrets, locked within the shadows of these woods, hills and loughs. This was the land of her people.

When she and Jack arrived at the west coast the Atlantic Ocean roared before her, hammering against the battered cliffs, frothing white, spouting through blowholes on the edge of the land. The temptation to let herself go and fall into its depths was always in her, but she resisted, instead filling herself with the sea's raw essence. Recognising Meg again in its fury.

Tomorrow was New Year's Eve, and it would be the last full day she and Jack would spend with Mairead and her family. Over the past week, as each day had gone by, she had felt the loss of Brigid less keenly because of Mairead and her daughter Stella. Mairead had been so warm and welcoming, as had her boyfriend Eoin, but it was Stella who Meg fell in love with. She was so feisty, and passionate. A girl true to herself and believing in her dream of becoming an actress. She reminded Meg of her own youthful ambition.

Meg had told Mairead and her family the whole story of Ellen and why she had left Ireland, explaining that this was why she had abandoned Brigid. Mairead had listened attentively, along with Eoin and Stella, her ex-husband Niall and his boyfriend Lesley. Meg had seen no judgement in their eyes. She was impressed by this modern family and sensed they were a little more open-minded than her own boys, though she loved them dearly. When they returned to Canada, she would tell her sons all about their Irish niece and great-niece. How they had had a sister called Brigid, who had been a famous silversmith in Ireland. Already, she was nervous about how they might react. But she owed it to them to tell them who their mother really was.

Mairead had given her some of Brigid's jewellery, which had moved Meg intensely. She was wearing a beautiful silver bracelet with spiralling patterns and set with tiny garnets like drops of blood upon the silver. She held it up now and let the silver shimmer in the moonlight shafting into their room through the gap in the curtains. Meg adored the bracelet. It occurred to her that she and her daughter had shared the same talent. Her daughter had pursued a career Meg had given up on, just as Stella was pursuing her dream of being an actress. Next year, Meg would turn seventy-five, but all the same, it wasn't too late to start creating again.

Stella had proposed a trip to Meg's old village, Ballycastle, to see where she grew up. Jack had been asking her the same question every day they had been in the west, but Meg had not been sure she could face her old townland.

'We can go to Merview House too,' Stella suggested, her eyes bright. 'As far as I know, it's still up for sale, so we can slip in through the wall. Me and Mam did it.'

'If you're ready,' Mairead had joined in. 'We can show you Ellen's grave.'

'It's your last chance, honey,' Jack had added. 'We're leaving the next day.'

It had been decided that Mairead, Meg and Stella would drive to Ballycastle, together with Alfie the dog, while the men took Jack to a real Irish pub for a pint of Guinness and a session. Apparently, Niall was a great fiddle player, and Eoin was just about OK on the tin whistle. Meg was nervous to go without Jack, but she could see how tired her husband was. He needed to relax before they made the long journey back to Canada. He'd also wanted to experience an Irish session the whole time they'd been in Ireland and hadn't yet managed it. Besides, this was a trip she wanted to take without him. It was so very private, even from the man she had spent the last five decades with.

It was a windy wet day as Mairead drove them along the coast. The Iron Mountains loomed above her. As they entered County Mayo and drove along the peninsula towards Ballycastle, she remembered that last drive she'd taken with her long-lost brother, Finnian. The day Ellen had died.

As they drew closer to Ballycastle, Meg was stunned by how little the landscape had changed. It was as if only yesterday she had travelled down the same laneways and boreens, with the empty wide beaches and the foaming sea by her side. The rain lashed against the car but the sound of the windscreen wipers was comforting. The blades seemed to be moving to the same rhythm as her heartbeat. *Steady, Meg. Nice and easy, let yourself go back.*

They drove past St Patrick's Head and Meg thought of her father, Cillian, hiding down the craters of the blowholes and being dragged out by the Free State army, then shot dead as he stood on the edge of the cliff with his arms up. Seagulls screeching all around him in alarm as the sound rang out.

The rain eased as Mairead drove them into the village of Bally-castle. Stella reached forward from the back seat and squeezed her hand.

'We're here, Granny Meg,' she said.

All her other grandchildren called her Granny Ellie. She wasn't even Stella's granny but her great-grandmother. It was going to be very confusing if all the families ever got together. The thought of such a gathering filled Meg with eager anticipation. Yes, next summer, she would organise something. Pay for her Irish girls to come over to Tofino if they couldn't afford it.

Meg got out of the car, her legs and hips stiff. She stood on the pavement and looked down the main street of Ballycastle. Very little had changed. She walked slowly, looking at the houses on either side. Past Healy's where her uncle Michael and her father used to drink. On she walked through the village, wondering if any of Michael and Norah's children, her cousins, were still alive. She made her way towards their cottage. Mairead and Stella walked by her side.

'I'm going to show you Aunty Norah's house,' she said to them. 'I lived here with her for a few years when I was a girl.'

They walked all the way down the main street of Ballycastle and out the other side. On towards the sea, as the road steepened, and they climbed up a little hill. Over the crest, Meg saw the little cottage in the distance. It was still there. The sight filled her with relief. It had been painted white, with a cheerful red door, a new roof and a modern extension was attached to its side. They reached the gate to the cottage, and she paused at the entrance, uncertain what to do.

'Shall we knock and see if there's anyone in?' Mairead suggested.

'I'm not sure,' Meg said. 'Last my cousins heard of me, I was on the run for murder.'

'Granny Meg! You didn't murder anyone, it was an accident,' Stella exclaimed.

'They might not be there,' Meg said in a weak voice, panic fluttering inside her.

As they dithered at the gate, the door of the cottage opened. They must have been seen from the cottage windows loitering around the gate. A tall thin elderly man emerged from the cottage wearing a big coat. He stood in the doorway and stared over at them. Meg held her breath.

The old man began to walk towards her.

'Is that you, Meg?' he called out in a shaky voice. 'Am I dreaming?'

In the old man, Meg saw the young man her brother once was. Her heart cracked open with emotion.

'Finnian!' she cried, rushing towards him. 'Oh, Finnian, it's me.'

The old man tottered towards them, his arms open wide.

'Come here to me,' he called to her as she fell into his arms.

The joy at their reunion was so great that neither of them could speak. Mairead and Stella bustled around them making cups of tea in her brother's kitchen while Meg and Finnian held hands. She gripped him so tightly she thought she might break his thin bony hands, but she didn't care. She had never in all her years expected her brother to still be alive.

'Ah, Meg,' he kept saying, tears trickling down his cheeks. He pulled a big handkerchief from his pocket and wiped his eyes with his free hand. 'I thought I'd lost you for good.'

Once everyone had had several cups of hot sweet tea, the siblings began to share their stories while Mairead and Stella listened in fascinated silence.

'I came after you,' Finnian said. 'I followed you to America.'

Meg was so stunned by her brother's revelation she couldn't speak.

'Once my arm had healed, I realised you were right, Meg,' Finnian told her. 'I was on the run, and it was only a matter of time before there'd be a gun pointed at my head.'

The old man sighed. 'It had all gone so wrong,' he said, shaking his head. 'Brother against brother. I wanted the violence to end.

'I still had the money you'd given me, so I bought a ticket on steerage and took a boat a few months after you left. When I got to New York, I looked for you,' he said. 'I just assumed I'd find you, but no one among the Irish I met in New York had heard of Meg O'Hanley.'

'Oh Finnian,' Meg said, pressing her hand to her heart. 'You came looking for me!'

'Of course I did,' he said. 'I didn't want you all alone and fending for yourself.'

'I changed my name,' she said. 'And I married.'

'Ah God,' Finnian said. 'Of course you did! But I kept trying to find you. I got a job as a construction worker on the Empire State Building.'

'You helped build the Empire State Building?' Mairead asked.

'I sure did.'

'But my grandfather worked on it as an architect,' Mairead said, suddenly stalling as she realised who she was talking about.

'My first husband, Giles Rose,' Meg intervened.

'You're not serious?' Finnian said. 'We were that close to each other?'

'But we could have been miles away, Finnian, because I was in a different world from you by then,' she said. 'I was so lonely, living among the wealthy and the privileged, and you were with folk like us.'

'It was a grand time,' Finnian said. 'Until the Depression fully hit New York. Then I headed west.'

Finnian told them how he had settled in California and worked on a fruit farm before taking it over. He had got married and had three children: a boy and two girls. Twenty years ago, his wife had died of cancer, and with his children all grown up he had returned to Ireland. He thought it was for a visit, but when he saw that Norah and Michael's old cottage was up for sale, he had bought it.

'It was like as soon as I came back, I couldn't leave again,' he explained.

Meg knew how he felt. Her longing for home was overwhelming. Every inch of this place was a part of who she was. When she was away from it, she hankered for it. No matter how much time had passed.

'Aren't you lonely, with your family in California?'

'One of my girls has moved to Ireland too,' he said. 'She lives in Dublin with her family, and visits all the time. I've plenty of friends. Go down to Healy's most nights for a pint and game of cards with the fellas. That's all I need.

'I had to come home,' Finnian added. 'This is the ground I want to be buried in when I go.'

'Do you ever think about that day?' Meg asked her brother. 'About what happened to Ellen?'

'Of course I do,' Finnian said. 'We were young and foolish. But it was an accident, Meg.'

'I've been afraid to come back for so long,' she said.

Finnian looked pensive for a moment.

'You should go visit Merview House,' he said. 'It's going to be sold soon, but at the moment it's deserted. You can walk around it.' He paused. 'I often visit Ellen's grave and put flowers on it for you.'

'Oh Finnian,' Meg said, touched beyond words.

'There's something you never knew, Meg, and I feel I should tell you,' Finnian said hesitantly. 'It's about our mother...'

Meg looked at Finnian in surprise. She had never known her

mother. Maggie O'Hanley had died giving birth to her. She had always felt guilty about it as a child and had trained herself not to think about it too much. But Finnian was five years older than her. He had known their mother.

'I was there the day you were born.' Finnian paused. 'And the day our mother died. I remember I ran through the woods to get help, but the only person at the Lavelle house was Ellen's mother, Dorothy Lavelle. She came with me, and I believe she did save your life, but not Mam.'

Meg knew the story. She and Ellen had talked about it sometimes in the woods together. The bond they shared because their mothers had died within the same twenty-four hours.

Finnian frowned. 'Maybe it's too late to tell you now, but I think it's only right you know...'

'What is it, Finnian?'

'I have shadowy memories of our mother. But I remember one time looking for my mam, and finding her in the woods with Ellen's father, Alec Lavelle. And when Mam was in agony giving birth, she wasn't calling out for our dad, she was calling for Alec.' He sighed. 'That's why I ran to the big house.'

Meg's head began to spin. What was Finnian trying to tell her?

'While Dorothy was trying to help our mam give birth, shouting out to me to get hot water and cloths, I heard Mammy make a confession to her. I know I was only five, but I'll never forget what she said:

'"Forgive me, Dorothy," Mam told her, "but this child is Alec's. We love each other. Please forgive me."'

'Dorothy Lavelle near dropped the scalding water on our mam, she was so shocked. That was when she stopped helping her. Mam was screaming and writhing in agony, but Dorothy Lavelle just stood there and watched. I was begging her, tugging on her arms, but the woman might as well have been made of stone.

'Then Mam gave such an almighty scream that Dorothy seemed to come to. She tried to help her then, but it was too late for Mammy. She could only save you.'

Finnian gave a shaky sigh. 'When Alec Lavelle turned up, he fell on his knees and sobbed to see our mother dead. Right in front of his wife, too. I will never forget the sight.'

'What are you telling me, Finnian?' Meg said in a whisper.

'What I'm saying is, we have the same mam, but your father was Alec Lavelle.'

'Oh my goodness,' Meg gasped. 'But that means—'

'Yes, Ellen was your sister.'

Of course. The bond between them had always been more than friendship. An intuitive understanding of each other. A deep recognition. She remembered when they had all been so little. Her, Finnian and Ellen, playing together in the woods. Running among the bluebells. The scent of those summer days returned to her. Their innocence. The sense of belonging. It had been no coincidence their mothers had died with just one night between them. Dorothy Lavelle hadn't fallen into the lake by accident. Meg remembered hearing the whispered rumours her whole childhood. Ellen's mother had taken her own life the morning after Meg's mother had died in childbirth. Now she understood why.

'Why didn't you tell me Ellen was my sister, Finnian?' Meg asked.

'I didn't want Daddy to find out. I was afraid it would destroy him.' He sighed and shook his head. 'The day Ellen died, I thought about telling you, but I knew it would only make it worse, like.'

Meg took all the information in. She had been Alec Lavelle's daughter too. She remembered the day she had stood outside his house in Chicago decades ago. What an imposter she had felt, watching him with his wife and boy. But in fact, she had been his child too. Would he have acknowledged her? It seemed unlikely, given that he had never sent for Ellen.

'I just realised something.' Mairead suddenly spoke up.

Meg had almost forgotten she and Stella were still there, sitting quietly at the kitchen table and refilling the pot of tea from time to time.

'Merview House,' she said. 'It's being sold by Alec Lavelle's great-nephew Kyle Symes for millions.'

'Oh yes, I know,' Finnian said. 'Apparently, there's an interested buyer who wants to turn it into a luxury hotel for tourists.'

'Let me just check something,' Mairead said, pulling her bag onto her lap, and rifling through it.

'What's up, Mam?' Stella asked.

'Well, I'll explain in more detail another time, but when I went looking for you, Meg, I found Kyle Symes,' she said.

Mairead pulled a letter from her handbag.

'Here it is,' she said. 'So, when I thought I was the granddaughter of Ellen Lavelle, I wrote to the estate of Alec Lavelle asking to see the will.'

'You did what, Mam!' Stella exclaimed.

Mairead blushed. 'Kyle Symes is a horrible man and, well, I just thought I'd check that Alec Lavelle had left the house and lands in Ireland to him.'

'And did he?' Finnian spoke up, his eyes pricked with interest.

Meg was beyond surprised by all this information. She hadn't really understood until now how hard Mairead had tried to find her after her mother died. It was very touching.

'I never opened it, because once I found Ellen's grave, I thought, what's the point?' Mairead took a breath. 'But Meg, since you're Alec Lavelle's daughter—'

'Oh, I don't think he would have acknowledged me in his will,' Meg said with confidence.

'Let's see, shall we?' Mairead said, ripping open the envelope. She scanned the pages.

'For God's sake, Mam, what does it say?' Stella exclaimed.

Mairead jumped up, waving the paper at Meg.

'He did leave it to you! All his American property went to his wife and their descendants in the States, but Merview House is in trust. It states right here: *I hereby leave in trust all my properties in Ireland to my daughters, Ellen Lavelle and Meg O'Hanley. In the event of either of their deaths, it will be solely inherited by the other.*

This property will be in trust for them to claim for twenty-five years following my death. After which time it will revert to my wife and her descendants.'

'Mammy, does it say when he died?' Stella's voice was high with excitement.

Mairead read another sheet of paper attached to the will.

'Yes – he died on the fifth of March 1960.'

'Oh my God!' Stella said. 'You've got three months to make your claim.'

Meg felt dizzy and confused with all the information. Her father had not been her father. Alec Lavelle was her father. Ellen had been her sister. And together, they had inherited the big house. The same place where she had worked as a maid, scrubbing the floors, emptying out grates, and cleaning chamber pots. She owned all of it!

'Oh, my Lord,' she said, her heart skipping a beat.

'Steady on, girls,' Finnian cautioned Mairead and Stella, who were whooping around the kitchen. 'You're going to give my sister a heart attack.'

He reached forward and took Meg's hands. 'Isn't that a fine thing, Meggie. Who would have thought?'

She nodded and looked into her brother's eyes. She had just discovered she had inherited a house worth millions, but that meant nowhere near as much to her as finding her brother again.

After they left Finnian's cottage, Mairead drove them to Merview House. Meg's house. They had been so long with her brother, the sky was already losing light.

'Oh my,' she said to her excited granddaughter and great-granddaughter. 'What will Jack say?'

'We have to get on to the lawyer in America immediately,' Mairead insisted. 'Stop that bastard Kyle getting away with it.'

'Mam! I never heard you call anyone a bastard before,' Stella said.

'Believe me, he's a real bastard!' her mam said again.

Mairead pulled up outside the chained gates, and Meg got out of the car slowly. She stood in front of the gates. In her mind's eye she saw Rafe Lavelle's old Bentley bumping down the long drive as she and Finnian made their escape.

Stella showed her the gap in the wall, and Mairead helped her through. They walked between the trees and Meg imagined she could hear children's laughter. Her eyes were misty with the emotion of her memories, and she thought she saw two girls running ahead of them. One with red hair and one with brown hair. One small and one tall. Weaving in and out of the trees. Singing songs together. Collecting bluebells and forget-me-nots. At this time of year, the woods were sparse, although where the trees were denser the forest floor was covered in soft wet moss.

There was the big house. The overgrown drive sweeping in front of it. They approached the front door, but of course it was locked. They peered through the boarded-up windows and walked around the majestic Georgian house. Meg put her hand on the old stone. This house was hers!

Past the little chapel, and into the small graveyard. There was Rafe Lavelle's grave. She was surprised by her feelings of compassion for him. He had been a broken soul like so many men of that period. Would he really have shot her dead? She would never know because Finnian took his life before he had the chance.

Stella took one of her hands, and Mairead the other as they approached the small gravestone. She read the name: *Ellen Lavelle*. And the lines from the poem.

> I have spread my dreams under your feet;
> Tread softly because you tread on my dreams.

The lines from Yeats' poem brought back a memory of Ellen reading it to her down by the lake on a summer's day. Bees buzzing around them as she had laid her head on her friend's lap and listened, the words resonating in her. How did the line before go...?

> But I, being poor, have only my dreams;
> I have spread my dreams under your feet;
> Tread softly because you tread on my dreams.

Ellen had made her feel rich with her dreams of the future. The poem had seemed new to her then, but now it was an old poem. An expression of Meg's history. It felt as if a part of her was buried here in the Irish earth. The identity she had assumed for over half her life. Now she was Meg again. But Ellen had been her sister and they had never known it.

Around the edges of the gravestones, Meg saw the first snow-drops pushing through the heavy earth. Tiny delicate petals of pure white innocence. She let go of Mairead and Stella's hands and took a step forward. She felt she should say a prayer, but her mind was empty of words. She pushed her hands into her coat pockets and the fingers of her left hand closed over a stone she had picked up on the beach near Mairead's house where they had gone walking the day before. In her right-hand pocket, she felt the outline of a tiny shell she'd collected on Long Beach in Tofino when she had gone walking last fall. She took both items and placed them on the grave. The shell and the stone. Fragile and enduring. Ellen and Meg.

Meg closed her eyes and listened to the rustle of the bare branches in the wintry wind. She felt the raindrops falling onto her cheeks. She smelt the Irish land where her roots were buried so deep. The citrus pine, and the earthy forest floor. She heard the motherly coo of the wood pigeon and the whispers of her and Ellen as young girls from all those years ago.

'Forgive me, Ellen,' Meg whispered.

Forgive yourself, Ellen whispered back.

Meg opened her eyes and spread her arms wide. She gathered her granddaughter and her great-granddaughter to her. Her heart was lighter than it had been in all her life.

A LETTER FROM NOELLE

I want to say a huge thank you for choosing to read *The Girl Across the Sea*. If you did enjoy it, and want to keep up to date with all my latest releases, just sign up at the following link. Your email address will never be shared and you can unsubscribe at any time.

www.bookouture.com/noelle-harrison

The Girl Across the Sea is written from my heart. It is a story which reaches back generations inspired by Irish family histories of emigration, including my own family. This is the story of two women – Ellen and Mairead – spanning decades from the Irish Civil War in the 1920s to the Great Depression in the 1930s, and to the emergence of modern Ireland in the 1980s. With Ellen and Mairead we travel from the woods, boreens and bogs of western Ireland across the Atlantic to New York and Chicago, and across the breadth of America to Arizona and on to Western Canada. Grandmother and granddaughter, they are unknown to each other and on different journeys, yet connected by the thread of their ancestry and the urge to find a sense of belonging. To understand that home is a feeling rather than a place.

Always the sea separates loved ones, while at the same time the ocean's constant movement is a source of hope and new beginnings. A mother loses a daughter, a daughter loses a mother, two best friends are separated, a broken heart cracks a woman's sense of self.

Who am I? This is the question at the core of *The Girl Across the Sea*. As Ellen follows her broken trail from mobster Chicago to the red deserts of Arizona to the vast stormy skies of Western Canada, she carries her Irish past with her always. It is the key to her authentic self. And as Mairead learns, by opening our own hearts to the struggle of our ancestors, we can release feelings of loss, heartache, and loneliness while gathering in a sense of connection and presence in our own lives.

I hope you loved *The Girl Across the Sea*, and if you did, I would be very grateful if you could write a review. I'd love to hear what you think, and it makes such a difference helping new readers to discover one of my books for the first time.

I love hearing from my readers – you can get in touch on my Facebook page, through Instagram, Twitter, Goodreads or my website.

Thanks,

Noelle Harrison

www.noelleharrison.com

 facebook.com/NoelleCBHarrison

 twitter.com/NoelleHarrison

 instagram.com/noelle.harrison5

ACKNOWLEDGEMENTS

Thank you to my agent, Marianne Gunn O'Connor, for always believing in me, and to my editor, Lydia Vassar-Smith, for all her insight and patience. Thank you to all at Bookouture publishers for all their hard work and dedication.

I am so grateful for the love and support of my friends and family. Thank you all! In particular, thanks to Kate Bootle, Becky Sweeney, Lizzie McGhee, Laura Lam and Thalia Vazquez for their support while writing this book. Thank you to all friends in Scotland especially Skye Kleman, Hailey O'Hara, Bex Hunt and Sandra Ireland. To my son, Corey Ansley, and my daughter, Helena Goode.

Thank you to my brother, Fintan Blake Kelly, and sister-in-law, Eimear. To my aunty Joyce, my sister Jane, my brother Paul, and to all my family, wherever they are in the world. Thank you to my friends Monica McInerney and Sinead Moriarty. Thank you, friends from Norway: Tracey Ann Skjæråsen, Ila Moldenhauer, Nina Rolland, Elisa Bjersand, Sidsel Humberset, Joan Mikkelsen, Marianne Rosvold Mølholm and Ann Seach. Thank you to all my family and friends in Ireland especially Barry Ansley, Mary Ansley, Donna Ansley and Bernie McGrath. Thank you to everyone who attends my writing courses, yoga classes and retreats, in particular our *Write from the Heart* weekly group.

Finally, dear reader, I so appreciate you stepping into my fictional worlds. You bring meaning to my words. From my heart to yours, thank you.

Manufactured by Amazon.ca
Bolton, ON